penguin books

danger and beauty

Born and raised in the Philippines, Jessica Hagedorn is well known as a performance artist, poet, and playwright. She is the author of the novel *Dogeaters* (available from Penguin), which was nominated for the National Book Award. For many years the leader and lyricist for the Gangster Choir band, she is presently at work on a screenplay and on a second novel.

DANGER AND BEAUTY

JESSICA HAGEDORN

penguin books

PENGUIN BOOKS
Published by the Penguin Group
Penguin Books USA Inc., 375 Hudson Street,
New York, New York 10014, U.S.A.
Penguin Books Ltd, 27 Wrights Lane, London W8 5TZ, England
Penguin Books Australia Ltd, Ringwood, Victoria, Australia
Penguin Books Canada Ltd, 10 Alcorn Avenue,
Toronto, Ontario, Canada M4V 3B2
Penguin Books (N.Z.) Ltd, 182–190 Wairau Road,
Auckland 10, New Zealand

Penguin Books Ltd, Registered Offices:
Harmondsworth, Middlesex, England

First published in Penguin Books, 1993

10 9 8 7 6 5 4 3 2 1

PUBLISHER'S NOTE
These are works of fiction. Names, characters, places, and incidents are the product of the author's
imagination or are used fictitiously, and any resemblance to actual persons, living or dead, events,
or locales is entirely coincidental.

Some of the poems and stories in this book first appeared in *Four Young Women: Poems*, edited by
Kenneth Rexroth (McGraw-Hill, 1973); *The Third Woman: Minority Women Writers of the United
States*, edited by Dexter Fisher (Houghton Mifflin, 1980); *Early Ripening: American Women's
Poetry Now*, edited by Marge Piercy (Pandora Press, 1987); *The Forbidden Stitch: An Asian-
American Women's Anthology*, edited by Shirley Geok-lin Lim, Mayumi Tsutakawa, and
Margarita Donnelly (Calyx Books, 1989); *Home to Stay: Asian-American Women's Fiction*, edited
by Sylvia Watanabe and Carol Bruchac (The Greenfield Review Press, 1990); *Out From Under:
Texts by Women Performance Artists*, edited by Lenora Champagne (TCG Press, 1990); *Colors of a
New Day: Writing for South Africa*, edited by Sarah Lefanu and Stephen Hayward (Pantheon
Books, 1990); *Out of This World: An Anthology*, edited by Anne Waldman (Crown, 1991); *Two
Stories by Jessica Hagedorn* (Coffee House Press, 1992); and in *Open Places, IKON, Sonora
Review, River Styx*, and *City Lights Review*.

LIBRARY OF CONGRESS CATALOGING IN PUBLICATION DATA
Hagedorn, Jessica Tarahata, 1949–
   Danger and beauty / Jessica Hagedorn.
      p.   cm.
   ISBN 0 14 01.7340 4
   I. Title.
PS3558.A3228D57   1993
   811'.54—dc20   92–23245

Printed in the United States of America
Set in Electra
Designed by Cheryl L. Cipriani

In memory
of Kenneth Rexroth,
1905–1982

CONTENTS

INTRODUCTION

PAPOLOGIA

Let's see. You got the colonial door . . .
then the postcolonial
then the hybrid state . . .
What does it mean
if you have to get down on your knees
just to get through?

It is 1992 in New York City. Identity has been discussed, refuted, celebrated, collapsed, reconstructed, and deconstructed. I am reminded of previous forays into that same jungle within. Who are we? People of color? Artists of color? Gay or straight? Political or careerist? Decadent or boring? Or just plain artists? It is 1973 and I am living in San Francisco. It is a glorious and heady time, this shaky transition out of the burned out sixties. Things are uncertain and therefore exciting. Jimi Hendrix and George Jackson are dead, but Angela Davis has finally been released from prison.

Defiant, naive, and passionate, we are sprouting up all over the Bay Area—artists of color who write, perform, and collaborate with each other, borders be damned. We are *muralistas*, filmmakers, musicians, dancers, painters, printmakers, small press publishers, playwrights, poets, and more poets. . . . San Francisco seems to be more a city of poets and musicians than anything else. Rock 'n' roll, R&B, the funk mystique of Oakland, the abstract seduction of jazz, and the glorious rants and chants of *loup garous*, gypsies, sympathetic cowboys, and water buffalo shamans: Al Robles, Ishmael Reed, Norman Jayo, Ntozake Shange, Victor Hernandez Cruz, Janice Miri-kitani, Thulani Davis, David Henderson, Alejandro Murguia, Ed Dorn, Alta, Serafin and Lou Syquia, Kitty Tsui, and on and on. . . . They are my teachers and peers, kindred spirits, borders be damned. A movement is afoot to assert ourselves as artists and thinkers, to celebrate our individual histories, our rich and complicated ethnicities. And there are the hangouts and venues, both funky and informal, for our presentations and performances: The Intersection, The Blue Unicorn, City Lights Books in North Beach, Minnie's Can-Do Club in the Haight-Ashbury district, La Peña in Berkeley, and the Kearny Street Asian American Writers Workshop on the border where Chinatown, North Beach, and the financial district intersect. The

I-Hotel (for International). The Galeria De La Raza in the Mission District. Project Artaud, on Potrero Hill, Mapenzi, where you might catch the Art Ensemble of Chicago. Or The Keystone Korner (kitty corner to a police station, which is always dangerous) for Cecil Taylor, Weather Report, or Airto and Flora. The Both/And Club on Divisadero Street, for Bobby Hutcherson or Archie Shepp. Some of these places last only a few years, some barely. Some still flourish. City Lights Bookstore, opened by poet Lawrence Ferlinghetti in 1953 is finally designated a National Literary Landmark on Friday, June 26, 1992—according to a clipping an old friend sends me from *The San Mateo Times*. Kenneth Rexroth, who is responsible for having my poems first published, takes me there when I am a teenager. We shop for books and talk to real poets and one or two glamorous poseurs. Kenneth seems to know them all. His flat on Scott Street is the ultimate boho heaven for me. Poetry is respected. Writing is life. I am awed by his library of ten thousand books in all sorts of languages; a kitchen stocked with Japanese goodies; Cubist paintings on the walls; and a living room where you might chance upon James Baldwin, Gary Snyder, or Amiri Baraka (then known as Leroi Jones)—in town for a hot minute. I am grateful even then for my esoteric and streetwise literary education.

Five of these early poems from the Rexroth-edited anthology *Four Young Women* (McGraw-Hill, 1973), have been included in the first part of this collection, "The Death of Anna May Wong." The year 1973 is when I begin discovering myself as a Filipino-American writer. What does this newfound identity mean? The longing for what was precious and left behind in the Philippines begins to creep in and take over my work.

I meet the poet Stephen Vincent at a reading I give in Berkeley around 1974. My work by then is becoming more rhythmic and musically influenced, meant to be "performed" before an audience. I dream about putting a band together. A dance band around words. Other poets understand the need for this. I am encouraged to dream more dreams. It is 1974 in the Bay Area and anything is possible. Stephen is interested in editing a collection for his new press, which he calls Momo's Press. The first book of poems and prose is called *Dangerous Music*, published in 1975—the same year I form my band, The West Coast Gangster Choir. I am consumed by music. How to fit rock 'n' roll into such dark words? I also return to the Philippines after an absence of many years. My first journey back and my musical experimentation are profound sources of inspiration for much of the material in this particular book, which did well and went into three printings. Selections from *Dangerous Music* constitute the second section.

My satin sisters, Thulani Davis and Ntozake Shange, are most of the reason I move to New York in 1978. I miss my band, but I'm not worried —I know we will eventually regroup in this scary place. Thulani, Ntozake, and I perform our poems to music in "Where the Mississippi Meets the Amazon" at Joseph Papp's Public Theater. Oz Scott directs, and David Murray conducts an all-star, "sizzling orchestra." It is an intense collaboration among volatile poets and musicians, and I fall in love with New York. I continue writing, well aware that my voice has hardened, become more dissonant and fierce. It is time for another book—and in 1981, *Pet Food & Tropical Apparitions* is published by Momo's Press. Containing a novella, poems, and prose pieces, it constitutes the third section of this book.

"New York Peep Show" covers the years 1982–1992. It contains new and unpublished writings—poems, prose pieces, cultural commentary, performance text. During this period I also write a novel, *Dogeaters*, which I later describe as "a love letter to my motherland: a fact and a fiction borne of rage, shame, pride . . ." and most certainly, desire. It is a book I thoroughly enjoy creating, something I set out to write on my own terms and in the English I reclaim as a postcolonial Filipino. I like to think that these ongoing personal and artistic explorations and discoveries, both playful and deadly serious, are also reflected in this final section of *Danger and Beauty*. It will never end, I hope—whatever "it" is. The gift, the quest, the visions, the dreams in secret languages. The songs and the storytelling.

It will never end; it is still writing itself.

the death of Anna May Wong: poems

1968-1972

AUTOBIOGRAPHY PART ONE:

MANILA TO SAN FRANCISCO

The pistol, yes.
Sheets of paper horizontally folded.
Men carry clocks
Into the room.
The pistol.
A letter to my father
Forgotten.
Voices from open windows
Do not break rules.
Two lips kiss.
The sun rises
On the other side of the continent.
Every morning . . .
A plate and spoon beside the pistol.
Raised to the temple,
Its body is not quite round,
Sleek gray stone in my hand . . . a cup
Of milk spills.
The pistol is pressed to the skull—
Open mouth
Like butterfly wings
Murmuring supplications
Instead
Another kiss

Voices repeat the rules
From open windows.
Each clock
Strikes a different time
In Spain
A gypsy servant named
Candles of the Sun

Dances
On your birthday
And you will never forget
Her smell
And her dwarf-lover
Who followed you
Into the mountains . . . asking you
To wear his shoes

That Gabriel
He's so polite
My dead brother who is buried. (My mother's
Hemorrhage is a lump in the grave)
That Gabriel
My brother; my uncle;
My father;
The dwarf:
Who carries a pistol
And wears rubber shoes

Your ankles
Are too frail
For these mountains
But you persist
In climbing them anyway
So you can say:

"I've seen the ruins
Of Guernica; in my hometown
There's even a nightclub named
Guernica."
Candles of the Sun
My sandalwood gypsy . . .

The pistol, the pistol,
Yes!

I live on the street
Of police ghosts and pimps . . .
The rebels who avenge them
Ask for money
And threaten to blow
My brains out.

The pistol, the black revolver
The nightmare
The swollen eye
The gun!
I will gun you down,
I will shoot you
I will kill you.
I will molest you
I will assault you
I will kiss your cunt
I will blow you up.
I will shoot! I will
Gun you down!
But not . . . but not . . . forever . . .
Not yet.

In Hong Kong
A girl
Her coarse hair flies
In the afternoon wind
She is a genuine colony concubine
Who drinks tea
At exactly four-fifteen at the
Peninsula hotel (Oh yes, baby, in

a silk shantung-slit yellow-legged
fantasy)
An all Chinese
orchestra
Plays Mantovani
and Monteverdi and George Gershwin

There is a border
One cannot cross
Although the guards are not visible.
George Gershwin
Mantovani and Monteverdi
Have not ceased
Being British
In Kowloon
But across territory lines
The guards remain
Invisible.

Two magazines
A cigarette-filled abalone shell.
The invisible weapon.
Down the street
Sleeps the wife
Of a revolutionary.
Avenge them all,
On behalf of Chrysler-Pontiacs!
There are twenty-four tactics
According to the pamphlet.
The inevitable result
Is the inevitable electronic solution.
Oh, lies! Lies! Lies!
I am neither or either.
Perpetrator, traitor, user of soap!
Lies! So thin

So metallic, so invisible!
Police shadows
On ghost motorcycles
Patrol the streets. It is too late—
I am up before dusk
Watching the sunset . . . It is too soon—

In Asia
One dies slowly
Fanning off the heat
With a stiff palm leaf.
I love you, Garcia Villa
You are not the only one
Who is going to die
In the city
Wearing velvet slippers
And a patched red shirt

You are a man
In between airplanes
Semi-retired, a not so notorious
Professor of the word

A torpid university dream.

In Asia
One dies too slowly
Without weapons . . .

In America
The smell of death pervades
Among its women
In department stores . . .
They linger, tubercular sparrows
With bony throats and sooty lashes

Peering elegantly
From behind diamond-clear counters.

My country of old women!

My sweet nicotine-tooth
Prostitute . . .

Give me a receipt
For your time.

1968

AUTOBIOGRAPHY PART TWO:

ROCK AND ROLL

We boogied when I was eight
I had just learned to dance
Carl Perkins sang "Matchbox"
And I hated him

But anything was better
Than Bill Haley or Frankie Laine
Until Elvis and Little Richard;

I wanted them so much
I would've known how to fuck them then
In joyous appreciation

When I was ten
It was Etta James
I didn't know what she looked like,
If she was male or female

I worried about my odor
When I did the slowdrag
And the guys had their
Sideways erections
To Etta James

And then
Chubby Checker and Joey Dee
Red shirts stained with sweat

Tight white toreador pants
American tennis shoes—

In 1960 Elvis was a drag
Harry Belafonte gave a concert
At the Coliseum
The older chicks dug him.
(He wore a beautiful tangerine
Shirt open at the throat)

Fabian was doing his tiger
We posed for a photograph
Together
Cost me three pesos
And an autographed lace
Handkerchief

1962 and Philadelphia Italians
Fabian Frankie Avalon Dion and the Belmonts
With poufed blond hair

I was in Hong Kong
Buying Bobby Vee records
And then Tokyo
Buying Paul Anka
"Live at the Copacabana"

San Francisco
Was a gray dream
A gray meat market harbor

I thought it was Chicago

My mother cried
A lot then
Her face was gray

The Four Seasons were very big
For some reason
I hated them.

My first weeks in
San Francisco and I was
Surrounded by faggots;
Lovely gilt-frame
Antique queers:
My uncles my mothers
My dubious friends—

Bill Haley was dead
Bobby Vee was dead
Little Richard in some church

Yes, yes Little Anthony
Was very big then . . .

I will never forget him.

March 1969
Dedicated to the poet
Victor Hernandez Cruz

THE DEATH OF ANNA MAY WONG

My mother is very beautiful
And not yet old.
A Twin,
Color of two continents:

I stroll through Irish tenderloin
Nightmare doors—drunks spill out
Saloon alleys falling asleep
At my feet . . .

My mother wears a beaded
Mandarin coat:
In the dryness
Of San Diego's mediterranean parody
I see your ghost, Belen
As you clean up
After your sweet señora's

mierda

Jazz,
Don't do me like that.
Mambo,
Don't do me like that.
Samba, calypso, funk and
Boogie
Don't cut me up like that

Move my gut so high up
Inside my throat
I can only strangle you
To keep from crying . . .

My mother serves crêpes suzettes
With a smile

And a puma
Slithers down
            19th street and Valencia
Gabriel o.d.'s on reds
As we dance together

Dorothy Lamour undrapes
Her sarong
And Bing Crosby ignores
The mierda.

My mother's lavender lips
Stretch in a slow smile.
And beneath
The night's cartoon sky
Cold with rain
            Alice Coltrane
Kills the pain
And I know
I can't go home again.

1971

FILIPINO BOOGIE

Under a ceiling-high Christmas tree
I pose
      in my Japanese kimono
My mother hands me
                    a Dale Evans cowgirl skirt
and
   baby cowgirl boots

Mommy and daddy split
No one else is home

I take some rusty scissors
                  and cut the skirt up
    in
      little pieces

(don't give me no bullshit fringe,
Mama)

Mommy and daddy split
No one else is home

   I take my baby cowgirl boots
               and flush them
                      down
                the
                  toilet
(don't hand me no bullshit fringe,
Papa)

I seen the Indian Fighter
Too many times

        dug on Sitting Bull
              before Donald Duck
In my infant dream

These warriors weaved a magic spell

14

more blessed than Tinker Bell

(Kirk Douglas rubs his chin
and slays Minnehaha by the campfire)

Mommy and daddy split
There ain't no one else home

                    I climb a mango tree
                            and wait for Mohawk drums
(Mama—World War II
 is over . . . why you cryin'?)

Is this San Francisco?
Is this San Francisco?
Is this Amerika?

buy me Nestle's Crunch
            buy me Pepsi in a can

Ladies' Home Journal
                and *Bonanza*

I seen Little Joe in Tokyo
I seen Little Joe in Manila
I seen Laramie in Hong Kong
I seen Yul Brynner in San Diego
and the bloated ghost
                    of Desi Arnaz
dancing
        in Tijuana

Rip-off synthetic ivory
                    to send
                        the natives
        back home

and
        North Beach boredom

        escapes
        the barber shops

on Kearny street
                where
                        they spit out
                                red tobacco

                                patiently

            waiting
                    in 1930s suits

and in another dream

                        I climb a mango tree
and Saturday
                afternoon
                        Jack Palance
                                bazookas

                        the krauts
                and
                    the YELLOW PERIL
                            bombs
                                    Pearl Harbor

1971

CANTO DE NADA

her name is nada
daughter of ainu and t'boli
igorot and sioux
sister to inca and zulu

born from the mouth of a tree
the lullaby of joe loco
and mongo
turquoise eye
the lullaby of pattie labelle
and the bluebells
flowers of her smile
the strut   the style

she is the punk
the dancing girl
the brand new bag
purple and red
the brand new bag
the sweetness
the lullaby of herself
the riff of a biwa
the daughter of a sorceress
the gong
the dragon lady's baby

she is the punk
the dancing girl
la cucaracha   who can even
get up from her own o.d.

every night the color
of her hair
she is the song
soul sister number one

the brand new bag
her jewels are as loud
as her love

her name is nada
mother to rashid
koumiko   carmen miranda
ylang-ylang   ruby delicious
she is the cocaine princess
with the hundred dollar nose
gettin higher because she got
to aim for the stars

she is the star
she is the city
flaunting sequins
and butterflies
she is peru   mindanao
shanghai

the divine virgin
waitin for a trick
on the borderline
between emeryville
and oakland

at noon on sunday
at noon on monday
at noon   hail mary
full of grace

she is nada   all music
she is nothing   all music
she is the punk   all music
the dancing girl   all music

she is nada   nothing
she is the real thing

and in her womb
one could sleep
         for
           days

February 1972

dangerous
music:

1975

SORCERY

there are some people i know
whose beauty
is a crime.
who make you so crazy
you don't know
whether to throw yourself
at them
or kill them.
which makes
for permanent madness.
which could be
bad for you.
·you better be on the lookout
for such circumstances.

stay away
from the night.
they most likely lurk
in corners of the room
where they think
they being inconspicuous
but they so beautiful
an aura
gives them away.

stay away
from the day.
they most likely
be walking
down the street
when you least
expect it
trying to look
ordinary
but they so fine

they break your heart
by making you dream
of other possibilities.

stay away
from crazy music.
they most likely
be creating it.
cuz when you're that beautiful
you can't help
putting it out there.
everyone knows
how dangerous
that can get.

stay away
from magic shows.
especially those
involving words.
words are very
tricky things.
everyone knows
words
the most common
instruments of
illusion.

they most likely
be saying them,
breathing poems
so rhythmic
you can't help
but dance.

and once
you start dancing
to words
you might never
stop.

SOUVENIRS

when you don't have it
or worse yet
when you got it
n the silent woman
bathes you n feeds you
n kisses you
on behalf of yr mama n papa
n you get sent off
to the convent
for some french culture

life is cheap

in manila
where the sun is scarlet
like a beautiful slut
waiting for yr eyes
to meet hers
in the darkness;
like an indian mango
that are her lips

in manila
the women wearing veils
of black lace
on sundays
veils that smell
of sandalwood n the virgin mary

sanctity n piety
are their names
n do you remember
that pink-faced
spanish missionary
who raped my great-grandmother

when she was fourteen years old?
(i asked him if he was god)

in manila
my grandmother's eye
turned blue
before dying
n her secret was revealed
like a giggle
like a slow smile
from behind handpainted
pink ivory fans
scented with jasmine
n the virgin mary
sanctity n piety
are their names
n perez prado
has a number one hit
with "patricia"
on the radio

life is cheap

igorots on horseback
n the old women
chewing betel nut
in the palengke
selling kangkong leaves
the memory of war

it's so sweet sometimes

in manila
the nuns with headdresses
like the wings of doves

piety n sanctity
are their names
n their sweat
stale n musky
in the woolen robes they wear
in the heat of a tropical day
hiding breasts n cunts
n beating you
into holy submission
with tales of purgatory
n the black saint of lima
martin de porres
n lapu lapu
was just another pagan
who cut off some spaniard's head
n magellan's statue looms instead
like a nightmare in manila
where you dream colors
of the first donald duck movie
you've ever seen
underneath a mosquito net

it's so sweet sometimes

n tito puente has a hit
n it's latin night
at the coliseum
n you don't know
these musicians
come from someplace
called new york
it's just another major event
to you
a ten year old child
twitching her ass

n doing the cha-cha in her seat
at the coliseum

it's so sad sometimes

yr mama looking so young
n beautiful
n you can't understand
what she is
or who you are

in manila
the president's wife
dictates martial law
with her thighs
sanctity n piety
is her name
as she sips tea
in madrid

life is very cheap

PEARL

when pearl was young she wanted to be a dancer / rouge on her cheeks
n ruffled skirts billowing as she twirled in her dreams on patios overlooking
pre-war manila bay / she said so / n auntie mary n uncle domingo were silent
in the religious aura of the dining room in pearl's house / n pearl's mother
beat her with a bamboo cane at least twenty times after auntie mary n uncle
domingo went to bed /

when pearl was nineteen years old / still without rouge on her cheeks /
she married a young man named alfonso who was one of the best dancers
in town / everyone said so / sometimes comparing him to valentino or errol
flynn / after they were married pearl had all the time in the world to go to
movies / alfonso encouraged her to rouge her cheeks n marcel her hair /
finally / finally / pearl's dreams materialized in the mirror / right there in front
of her / she could see herself / tango n rhumba like a naughty lady / like they
all did in pre-war manila sleaziness / n when alfonso was in a particularly
good mood / he would buy her satin dresses with rhinestone straps so that
even her shoulders sparkled /

sometimes pearl thought she was happy / especially when alfonso took
her to the queen bee cabaret / n she knew / she just knew / everyone was
watching them dance with some envy / she could pretend she was ginger
rogers n he was fred astaire in *swingtime* / alfonso always looked right for the
part / with his pencil-thin black moustache / n his Tres Flores brand pomaded
hair /

by the time pearl was twenty-one / she still hadn't given birth to a
child / her mother refused to speak to her / thinking she was bewitched /
alfonso / bored with dancing / bored with the movies / bored with the heat /
bored with the emptiness of pretty young matrons who gossiped / played
mahjong / n attended mass on sundays with the same obscene intensity /
alfonso / bored with all this / took a mistress who was older than pearl / some
said actually close to thirty /

her name was blanca / blanca luna / she was a hostess at the queen bee
cabaret / n she couldn't really dance / but o / she had eyes like japanese
almonds / n a voice so throaty it made you shiver /

now pearl had entire days n nights to herself / she embroidered incredible
needlepoint designs that became so fantastic n elaborate the women would
visit her just so they could marvel at her work / pagodas n clouds on satin /

colonial figures on brocade wearing rainbow dresses / mandrills making love to gypsy virgins / pearl's dreams n titillations were transformed on cloth / women began bringing her their blouses n plain evening gowns which they wanted ornately monogrammed with their initials / after leaving her house they giggled behind her back /

pearl was still going to movies / mostly by herself / sometimes / when there wasn't much sewing to be done / she would dance in the stillness of her living room / fabrics scattered on the floor around her feet / flies buzzing in the stuffiness of the afternoon / n sometimes / when pearl was feeling really lonely / she would sing to herself / lover man / where / can you be / she began to resemble dorothy lamour / n wore hibiscus in her hair / even when she was alone / in the great / big / empty / house

CRISTINA

1.

auburn is a chic color
not too much red
if you overdo it
you look like a whore

wheat is the new shade
in clothing
wheat suede coats
wheat silk shirts
wheat gabardine pants
with matching luggage
and matching south american
tycoons
with cigars stuck in their mouths
to chauffeur you around
in mercedes-benz sedans

2.

older men make better lovers
they know how to treat you good
at all times
offering arabian stallions
and private helicopters
as homage
to your timelessness

this is the life
the movie is based on
where rita hayworth
changes her name
and loses twenty pounds

3.

never admitting her love
my mother's anger
is her real strength
like an aging tigress
still beautiful
in the afternoon light

i could never tell her
how much i want to touch her
sometimes

fear runs deep
in her eyes
i can see it mingle
with her rage
the paranoia there
what could doctors tell me
that i haven't already guessed

the paranoia
that raised me
and cristina
with her wonderful breasts
stunning the world
in her saks fifth avenue
brassiere

4.

i've lost my appetite
for love
many times
but it's my mother

i still think of
as all women
a common occurrence
but still frightening
when i'm alone

     5.

my mother plays rita hayworth
in my dreams
and she dyes her hair
auburn

leaping
on cafe tables
and tempting men
with her fiery flamenco

in hollywood
some kind of ethnic mix-up
between mexico
and spain

those latin lovers
they all sigh

but not true
not true

only the dagger
in her thigh
does not lie

SONG FOR MY FATHER

i arrive
in the unbearable heat
the sun's stillness
stretching across
the land's silence
people staring out
from airport cages
thousands of miles
later
and i have not yet understood
my obsession to return

and twelve years
is fast
inside my brain
exploding like tears

i could show you
but you already know.

you greet me
and i see
it is you
you all the time
pulling me back
towards this space

letters are the memory
i carry with me
the unspoken name
of you,
my father

in new york
they ask me if i'm puerto rican
and do i live in queens?

i listen to pop stations
chant to iemaja
convinced i'm really brazilian
and you a riverboat gambler
shooting dice in macao
during the war

roaches fly around us
like bats in twilight
and barry white grunts
in fashionable discotheques
setting the pace
for guerrillas to grind

the president's wife
has a fondness for concert pianists
and gossip is integral
to conversation

if you eat enough papaya
your sex drive diminishes
lorenza paints my nails blue
and we giggle at the dinner table
aunts and whores
brothers and homosexuals
a contessa with chinese eyes
and an uncle cranky with loneliness
he carries an american passport
like me

and here we are,
cathedrals in our thighs
banana trees for breasts
and history all mixed up
saxophones in our voices
when we scream
the love of rhythms
inherent
when we dance

they can latin here
and shoot you
for the wrong glance
eyes that kill
eyes that kill

dope dealers are executed
in public
and senators go mad
in prison camps
the nightclubs are burning
with indifference
curfew drawing near
soldiers lurk in jeeps
of dawn warzones
as the president's daughter
boogies nostalgically
under the gaze
of sixteen smooth bodyguards
and decay is forever
even in the rage
of humorless revolutionaries

in hotel lobbies
we drink rum

testing each other's wit
snakes sometimes crawl
in our beds
but what can you do
in the heat
the laziness makes you love
so easily

you smile like buddha
from madrid
urging me to swim with you
the water is clear
with corpses
of dragonflies and
mosquitoes
i'm writing different poems now
my dreams have become reptilian
and green

everything green, green
and hot

eyes that kill
eyes that kill

women slither
in and out of barroom doorways
their tongues massage
the terror from your nightmares
the lizard hissing nervously
as he watches
you breathe

i am trapped
by overripe mangoes

i am trapped
by the beautiful sadness of women
i am trapped
by priests and nuns
whispering my name
in confession boxes
i am trapped
by antiques and the music
of the future

and leaving you
again and again
for america,
the loneliest of countries

my words change . . .
sometimes
i even forget english.

THE BLOSSOMING OF BONGBONG

Antonio Gargazulio-Duarte, also fondly known as Bongbong to family and friends, had been in America for less than two years and was going mad. He didn't know it, of course, having left the country of his birth, the Philippines, for the very reason that his sanity was at stake. As he often told his friend, the painter Frisquito, "I can no longer tolerate contradiction. This country is full of contradiction. I have to leave before I go crazy."

His friend Frisquito would only laugh. His laugh was eerie because it was soundless. When he laughed, his body would shake—and his face, which was already grotesque, would distort—but no sound would emit from him.

People were afraid of Frisquito. They bought his paintings, but they stayed away from him. Especially when he was high. Frisquito loved to get high. He had taken acid more than fifty times, and he was only twenty-six years old. He had once lived in New York, where people were used to his grotesque face, and ignored him. Frisquito had a face that resembled a retarded child: eyes slanted, huge forehead, droopy mouth, and pale, luminous skin. Bongbong once said to him, "You have skin like the surface of the moon." Frisquito's skull was also unusually large, which put people off, especially women. Frisquito soon learned to do without women or men. "My paintings are masturbatory," he once said to the wife of the president of the Philippines. She never blinked an eye, later commissioning three obscene murals. She was often referred to as a "trendsetter."

Frisquito told Bongbong, "There's nothing wrong with being crazy. The thing to do is to get comfortable with it."

Not only had Frisquito taken acid more than fifty times, he had also taken peyote and cocaine and heroin at a rate that doctors often said would normally kill a man. "But I'm like a bull," he would say. "Nothing can really hurt me, except the creator of the universe."

At which point he would smile.

Bongbong finally left Manila on a plane for San Francisco. He was deathly afraid. He wore an olive-green velvet jacket, and dark velvet pants, with a long scarf thrown casually around his scrawny neck. Frisquito saw him off to the airport. "You look like a faggot," he said to Bongbong, who was once named best-dressed young VIP in Manila. Bongbong felt ridiculously out of place and took two downers so he could sleep during the long ride to America. He arrived, constipated and haggard, and was met by his sister and brother-in-law, Carmen and Pochoy Guevara. "You look terrible," his sister said. She was embarrassed to be seen with him. Secretly she feared he was homosexual, especially since he was such good friends with Frisquito.

Bongbong had moved in with his sister and brother-in-law, who lived in a plush apartment on Twin Peaks. His brother-in-law Pochoy, who had graduated as a computer programmer from Heald's Business College, worked for the Bank of America. His sister Carmen, who was rather beautiful in a bland, colorless kind of way, had enrolled in an Elizabeth Arden beauty course, and had hopes of being a fashion model.

"Or maybe I could go into merchandising," she would say, in the afternoons when she wouldn't go to class. She would sit in her stainless-steel, carpeted electric kitchen. She drank cup after cup of instant Yuban coffee, and changed her nail polish every three days.

"You should wear navy blue on your nails," Bongbong said to her one of those afternoons, when she was removing her polish with Cutex lemon-scented polish remover. "It would look wonderful with your sallow complexion." "Sallow" was a word Bongbong had learned from Frisquito.

"Sallow? What does that mean?" Carmen never knew if her brother was insulting or complimenting her.

"It means pale and unhealthy," Bongbong said. "Anyway, it's in style now. I've seen lots of girls wearing it."

He wrote Frisquito a letter:

Dear Frisquito,

Everyone is a liar. My sister is the biggest one of them all. I am a liar. I lie to myself every second of the day. I look in the mirror and I don't know what's there. My sister hates me. I hate her. She is inhuman. But then, she doesn't know how to be human. She thinks I'm inhuman. I am surrounded by androids. Do you know what that is? I'm glad I never took acid.

I wish I was a movie star.

Love,
Bongbong

The apartment had two bedrooms. Pochoy had bought a leather couch and a Magnavox record player on credit. He owned the largest and most complete collection of Johnny Mathis records. At night Bongbong would lie awake and listen to their silent fucking in the next room, and wonder if Carmen was enjoying herself. Sometimes they would fuck to "Misty."

Carmen didn't cook too often, and Pochoy had a gluttonous appetite. Since he didn't believe in men cooking, they would often order Chinese food or pizzas to be delivered. Once in a while Bongbong would try to fix a meal, but he was never talented in that direction. Frisquito had taught him how to cook two dishes: fried chicken & spaghetti.

Dear Frisquito,

I can't seem to find a job. I have no skills, and no college degree. Carmen thinks I should apply at Heald's Business College and go into computer programming. The idea makes me sick. I am twenty-six years old and no good at anything. Yesterday I considered getting a job as a busboy in a restaurant, but Carmen was horrified. She was certain everyone in Manila would hear about it (which they will), and she swears she'll kill herself out of shame. Not a bad idea, but I am not a murderer. If I went back to Manila I could be a movie star.

Love,
Bongbong

Bongbong stood in the middle of a Market Street intersection, slowly going mad. He imagined streetcars melting and running him over, grinding his flesh and bones into one hideous, bloody mess. He saw the scurrying Chinese women, no more than four feet tall, run amok and beat him to death with their shopping bags, which were filled to the brim with slippery, silver-scaled fish.

He watched a lot of television. His eyes became bloodshot. He began to read—anything from best-sellers to plays to political science to poetry. A lot of it he didn't quite understand, but the names and events fascinated him. He would often visit bookshops just to get out of the apartment. He chose books at random, sometimes for their titles or the color of their book jackets. His favorite before he went crazy was *Vibration Cooking* by Verta Mae Grosvenor. He even tried out some of Verta Mae's recipes, when he was in better moods on the days when Carmen and Pochoy were away. He had found Verta Mae's book for seventy-five cents in a used-book store he frequented.

"What is this?" Carmen asked, staring at the book cover, which featured Verta Mae in her colorful African motif outfit.

"That, my dear, is a cookbook," Bongbong answered, snatching the book out of her hands, now decorated in Max Factor's "Regency Red."

On the bus going home there was a young girl sitting behind Bongbong wearing a Catholic school uniform and carrying several books in her pale, luminous arms, which reminded him of the surface of the moon. When the bus came to a stop, she walked quietly to the front and before getting off she turned, very slowly and deliberately, and stared deeply into Bongbong's eyes. "You will get what you deserve," she said.

One time when Bongbong was feeling particularly lonely, he went to a bar on Union Street where young men and women stand around and drink weak Irish coffees. The bar was sometimes jokingly known as a "meat factory." The young men were usually executives, or trying to look like executives. They wore their hair slightly long, with rather tacky muttonchop whiskers, and they all smoked dope. The women were usually chic or terribly hip. Either way they eyed each other coolly and all wore platform shoes.

A drink was sent to Bongbong from the other end of the bar by a twenty-eight-year-old sometime actress and boutique salesgirl named Charmaine.

She was from Nicaragua, and quite stunning, with frizzy brown hair and the biggest ass Bongbong had ever seen.

"What're you having?" she asked, grinning. Her lips were moist and glossy, and the Fertile Crescent was tattooed in miniature on her left cheek.

Bongbong, needless to say, was silent for a moment. Ladies like Charmaine were uncommon in Manila. "Gimlet," he murmured, embarrassed because he disliked the idea of being hustled.

Charmaine had a habit of tossing her head back, so that her frizzy curls bounced, as if she were always secretly dancing. "Awright," she said, turning to the bartender, "bring the gentleman a gimlet." She giggled, turning to look fully at Bongbong. "I'm Charmaine. Wha's your name?"

Bongbong blushed. "Antonio," he said, "But I go by my nickname." He dreaded her next question, but braced himself for it, feeling the familiar nausea rising within him. Once Frisquito had told him that witches and other types of human beings only had power over you if they knew your name. Since that time Bongbong always hesitated when anyone asked him for his name, especially women. "Women are more prone to occult powers than men," Frisquito warned. "It comes natural to them."

Charmaine was smiling now. "Oh yeah? Whatisit?"

"Bongbong."

The bartender handed him the gimlet, and Charmaine shrugged. "Tha's a funky name, man. You Chicano?"

Bongbong was offended. He wanted to say No, I'm Ethiopian, or Moroccan, or Nepalese, what the fuck do you care . . . Silently he drank his gimlet. Then he decided, the nausea subsiding, that Charmaine wasn't malicious, and left the bar with her shortly after.

Charmaine showed him the boutique where she worked, which was next door to the bar. Bongbong stared at the platform shoes in the display window as if he were seeing them for the first time. Their glittering colors and whimsical designs intrigued him. Charmaine watched his face curiously as he stood with his face pressed against the glass like a small child; then she took his arm and led him to her VW.

She lived in a large flat in the Fillmore district with another sometime actress and boutique salesgirl named Colelia. They had six cats, and the place smelled like a combination of cat piss and incense.

Colelia thought she was from Honey Patch, South Carolina, but she wasn't sure. "I'm all mixed up," she said. Sometimes she thought she was a geechee. She was the only person Bongbong knew who had ever read *Vibration Cooking*. She had even met Verta Mae at a party in New York.

Bongbong spent the night in Charmaine's bed, but he couldn't bring himself to even touch her. She was amused, and asked him if he was gay. At first he didn't understand the term. English sometimes escaped him, and certain colloquialisms, like "gay," never made sense. He finally shook his head and mumbled no. Charmaine told him she didn't really mind. Then she asked him to go down on her.

Dear Frisquito:

I enrolled at Heald's College today so that Carmen would shut up. I plan on leaving the house every morning and pretending I'm going to school. That way no one will bother me.

I think I may come back to Manila soon, but somehow I feel I'm being trapped into staying here. I don't understand anything. Everyone is an artist, but I don't see them doing anything. Which is what I don't understand . . . but one good thing is I am becoming a good cook.

Enclosed is a copy of *Vibration Cooking* by Verta Mae.

Love,
B.

Sometimes Bongbong would open the refrigerator door and oranges would fly out at him. He was fascinated by eggs, and would often say to his sister, "We're eating the sunset," or "We're eating embryos." Or he would frown and say, "I never did like chickens."

He began riding streetcars and buses from one end of the city to the other, often going into trances and reliving the nightmare of the streetcar melting and running him over. Always the Chinese women would appear, beating him to death with silver-scaled fish, or eggs.

Bongbong saw Charmaine almost every day for a month. His parents sent him an allowance, thinking he was in school. This allowance he spent lavishly on her. He bought her all the dazzling platform shoes her heart desired. He took her to fancy nightclubs so she could dance and wiggle her magnificent ass to his delight. She loved Sly Stone and Willie Colon, so he bought her all their records. They ate curry and spice cake every night of the week (sometimes alternating with yogurt pie and gumbo) and Charmaine put on ten pounds.

He never fucked her. Sometimes he went down on her, which she liked even better. She had replaced books and television in his life. He thought he was saved.

One afternoon while he was waiting for Charmaine in the bar where they had met, Bongbong had a vision. A young woman entered the bar, wearing a turban on her head made of torn rags. Her hair was braided and stood out from her scalp like branches on a young tree. Her skin was so black she was almost blue.

Around her extremely firm breasts she wore an old yellow crocheted doily, tied loosely. Her long black skirt was slit up the front all the way to her crotch, and underneath she wore torn black lace tights, and shocking-pink suede boots, laced all the way up to her knees. She carried a small basket as a handbag, and she was smoking Eve cigarettes elegantly, as if she were a dowager empress.

She sat next to Bongbong and gazed at him coolly and deliberately. People in the bar turned their heads and stared at her, some of them laughing. She asked Bongbong for a match. He lit her cigarette. His hands were trembling. She smiled, and he saw that some of her teeth were missing. After she smoked her cigarette, she left the bar.

Another day while Bongbong was walking in the Tenderloin, he had another vision. A young woman offered to fuck him for a mere twenty-five dollars. He hesitated, looking at her. She had shoulder-length, greasy blond hair. She had several teeth missing too, and what other teeth she had left were rotten. Her eyes, which were a dull brown, were heavily painted with midnight-blue mascara. She wore a short red skirt, a tight little sweater, and her black sheer tights had runs and snags all over them. Bongbong noticed that she had on expensive silver platform shoes that were sold in Charmaine's boutique.

He asked her name.

Her voice was as dull as her eyes. "Sandra," she replied.

He suddenly felt bold in her presence. "How old are you?"

"Nineteen. How old are you, honey?" She leered at him, then saw the blank look on his face, and all the contempt washed out of her. He took her to a restaurant where they served watery hamburgers and watery coffee. He asked her if she had a pimp.

"Yup. And I been busted ten times. I been a hooker since I was thirteen, and my parents are more dead than alive. Anything else you wanna know?"

Her full name was Sandra Broussard. He told her she was beautiful. She laughed. She said her pimp would kill her if she ever left the business. She showed him her scars. "He cut my face once, with a razor," she said.

He felt useless. He went back to the apartment and Carmen was waiting for him. "We've decided you should move out of this place as soon as possible," she said. "I'm pregnant, and I want to redecorate your room for the baby. I'm going to paint your room pink."

He went into the bathroom and stared at the bottles of perfume near the sink, the underarm deodorant, the foot deodorant, the cinnamon-flavored mouthwash, and the vaginal spray. They used Colgate brand toothpaste. Dove soap. Zee toilet paper. A Snoopy poster hung behind the toilet. It filled him with despair.

Bongbong moved into Charmaine's flat shortly after. He brought his velvet suit and his books. Colelia reacted strangely at first. She had been Charmaine's lover for some time, and felt Bongbong would be an intrusion. But all he did was read his books and watch television. He slept on a mattress in the living room. He hardly even spoke to Charmaine anymore. Sometimes they would come home from work in the evenings and find Bongbong in the kitchen, preparing Verta Mae's Kalalou Noisy Le Sec or her Codfish with Green Sauce for all of them. Colelia realized he wasn't a threat to her love life at all. Life became peaceful for her and Charmaine.

During the long afternoons when Colelia and Charmaine were gone and the cats were gone and the smell of piss from the catbox lingered in the chilly air, Bongbong would put on his velvet suit and take long walks in the Tenderloin, trying to find Sandra Broussard. He thought he saw her once, inside a bar, but when he went in, he found it was a mistake. The woman turned out to be much older, and when she turned to smile at him, he noticed she wore the hand of Fatima on a silver chain around her neck.

When he really thought about it, in his more lucid moments, he realized he didn't even remember what Sandra looked like anymore. Dullness was all he could conjure of her presence. Her fatigue and resignation.

Charmaine, on the other hand, was bright, beautiful, and selfish. She was queen of the house, and most activity revolved around her. Colelia always came home from work with a gift for Charmaine, which they both referred to as "prizes." Sometimes they were valuable, like jade rings or amethyst stones for Charmaine's pierced nose, or silly—like an old Walt Disney cup with Donald Duck painted on it.

Bongbong found the two women charming and often said so when he was in a talkative mood. "You are full of charm and your lives will be full of success," he would say to them, as they sat in their antique Chinese robes, painting each other's faces.

"You sound like a fortune cookie," Charmaine would say, glaring at him.

He would be silent at her outbursts, which naturally made her more furious. "I wish you'd tell me how much you want me," she would demand, ignoring her female lover's presence in the room.

Sometimes Charmaine would watch Bongbong as he read his books, and she would get evil with him out of boredom. She was easily distracted and therefore easily bored, especially when she wasn't the center of attention. This was often the case when Colelia was at work and it was Charmaine's day off.

Bongbong said to her, "Once you were a witch, but you misused your powers. Now you resent me because I remind you of those past days."

Charmaine circled Bongbong as he sat in the living room immersed in *Green Mansions* by W. H. Hudson. He had found the hardback novel for one dollar in another secondhand-book shop, called Memory Lane.

"I'm going to take my clothes off, Bongbong," Charmaine would tease. "What're you going to do about it?" Bongbong would look up at her, puzzled. Then she would put her hands on her enormous hips. "Men like me most of all because of my ass, Bongbong . . . but they can't really get next to me. Most of them have no style . . . but you have a sort of style—" By this time she often removed her skirt. "I don't wear panties," she said, "so whenever I want, Colelia can feel me up." Bongbong tried to ignore her. He was getting skilled in self-hypnosis, and whenever external disturbances would occur, he would stare off into the distance and block them slowly from his mind.

The more skilled he became in his powers, the more furious Charmaine would get with him. One time she actually wrenched the book from his hands and threw it out the window. Then she lay on the couch in front of him and spread her legs. "You know what I've got, Bongbong? Uterina Furor . . . That's what my mother used to say . . . Nuns get it all the time. Like a fire in the womb."

To make her smile, Bongbong would kiss her between the legs, and then Colelia would come home and pay more attention to Charmaine and Bongbong would cook more of Verta Mae's recipes, such as Stuffed Heart Honky Style (one of Charmaine's favorites), and everything would be all right.

Charmaine's destructive moods focused on Bongbong twice a month, and got worse when the moon was full. "You're in a time of perennial menstruation," Bongbong told her solemnly after one of her fits.

One morning while they were having breakfast together, Colelia accused Charmaine of being in love with Bongbong. "Why, I don't know—" Colelia said. "He's so funny-looking and weird. You're just into such an ego trip you want what you can't have."

Charmaine giggled. "Forever analyzing me! Don't I love you enough?"

"It's not that."

"Well, then—why bring him up? You never understood him from the very beginning," Charmaine said. "Or why I even brought him here in the first place. I must confess—I don't quite know why I brought him home myself. Somehow, I knew he wasn't going to fuck me . . . I really didn't want a fuck though. It was more like I wanted him around to teach me something about myself . . . Something like that, anyway."

Colelia looked away. "That's vague enough."

"Are you really jealous of him?" Charmaine asked.

Colelia finally shook her head. "Not in that way . . . but maybe because I don't understand him, or the two of you together—I am jealous. I guess because I feel left out of his mystique."

Charmaine embraced her, and the two of them wept.

Bongbong's visions and revelations were becoming more frequent. A Chinese woman with a blond wig and a map of the world on her legs. A black man with three breasts. A cat turning doorknobs. A tortoise crawling out of a sewer on the sidewalk, and junkies making soup out of him. Frisquito assassinating the president of the Philippines who happens to be his wife in drag who happens to be a concert pianist's mother . . . The visions were endless, circular, and always moving.

Dear Frisquito:

Yesterday a friend of Charmaine's named Ra brought a record over by a man named John Coltrane. Ra tells me that Mr. Coltrane died not too long ago, I believe when we were just out of high school. Ra decided that I could keep the record, which is called "Meditations." I believe it is the title of one of your paintings.

Every morning I plan on waking up to this man's music. It keeps my face from disintegrating. You once said your whole being had disintegrated long ago, and that you had the power to pick up the pieces from time to time, when it was necessary—such as the time you gave an exhibit of your works, for the benefit of the First Lady. I think there may be some hope left for me.

Yesterday I cooked Verta Mae's Uptight Ragout in your honor.

Love,
B.

Bongbong now referred to himself as "B." He could not stand to speak in long sentences, and tried to live and speak as minimally as possible. Charmaine worried about him, especially when he would go on one of his rampages and cook delicious gumbo dinners for herself and Colelia, and not eat with them.
"But B," she protested, "I never see you eat anymore."
One time he said, "Maybe I eat a saxophone."
He loved the word "saxophone."

His parents stopped sending money, since Carmen wrote them that he had never attended one day of school at Heald's Business College. His father wrote him and warned him never to set foot in the Philippines again, or he would have him executed for the crime of deception and subversion to one's parents, a new law put into practice in the current dictator's regime.

Bongbong decided to visit Carmen. She was almost six months pregnant, and very ugly. Her face had broken out in rashes and pimples, and her whole body was swollen. Her once shimmering black hair was now dry and brittle, and she had cut it short. Her nails were painted a pale pink, like the bedroom that had once been his. He stared at her for a long time as they sat in the kitchen in silence. She finally suggested that he see the baby's room.

She had decorated the room with more Snoopy posters, and mobiles with wooden angels hung from the ceiling. A pink baby bed stood in the center of the room, which was heavily scented with floral spray.

"It's awful," Bongbong said.

"Oh, you're always insulting everything!" his sister screamed, shoving him out the door. She shut the door behind her, as if guarding a sacred temple, and looked at him, shaking with rage. "You make everything evil. Are you on drugs? I think you're insane," she said. "Leave this house before I call the police." She hated him because he made her feel ashamed in his presence, but she couldn't understand why.

Frisquito, who never answered any of his letters, sent him a check for a considerable amount of money. A postcard later arrived with "Don't Worry" scratched across it, and Frisquito's signature below the message. Bongbong, who now wore his velvet suit every day, went to a pawnshop and bought a soprano saxophone.

In the mornings he would study with Ra, who taught him circular breathing. He never did understand chords and scales, but he could hear what Ra was trying to teach him and he surprised everyone in the house with the eerie sounds he was making out of his new instrument. Charmaine told Colelia that she thought Bongbong was going to be all right, because Bongbong had at last found his "thing."

Which was wrong, because Bongbong's music only increased his natural visionary powers. He confessed to Ra that he could actually see the notes in the air, much as he could see the wind. Ra would smile, not saying anything.

Bongbong watched Charmaine at the kitchen table eating breakfast, and when she looked up at him, she would suddenly turn into his mother, with Minnie Mouse ears and long, exaggerated Minnie Mouse eyelashes, which glittered and threw off sparks when she blinked. This frightened him some-times because he would forget who Charmaine was. As long as he could remember who everyone was, he felt a surge of relief. But these moments were becoming more and more confusing, and it was getting harder and harder for him to remember everyone's name, including his own.

Colelia decided that Bongbong was a "paranoid schizophrenic" and that she and Charmaine should move out, for their own safety. "One of these days we'll come home from work and find all our kitty cats with their throats slit," she said. She refused to eat any more of Bongbong's cooking, for fear he would poison her. "He doesn't like women basically. That's the root of his problem" she told Charmaine. "I mean, the guy doesn't even jack off! How unnatural can he be? Remember Emil Kemper!"

"Remember Emil Kemper" became the motto of the household. Emil Kemper was a young madman in Santa Cruz, California, who murdered his grandmother when he was something like thirteen years old, murdered his mother later on after he was released from the looney bin—cut her head off—and murdered about a million other female hitchhikers.

Charmaine sympathized with Bongbong, but she wasn't sure about him either. Only Ra vouched for his sanity. "Sure the cat is crazy," he said, "but he'll never hurt any of you."

Bongbong practiced the saxophone every day, and seemed to survive on a diet of water and air. Charmaine came home from the boutique one night and brought him two pairs of jeans and two T-shirts. One T-shirt had glittery blue and silver thread woven into it, and Bongbong saw the shirt become a cloud floating above his narrow bed. "Well," Charmaine said, trying to sound casual as she watched Bongbong drift off dreamily, "aren't you going to try it on? Do you like it? I seriously think you should have your velvet suit dry-cleaned, before it falls apart."

Bongbong touched the cloud. "Oh, how beautiful," he said.

He never wore the shirt. He hung it above his bed like a canopy, where he could study it at night. His ceiling became a galaxy. To appease Charmaine (he was very sensitive to her feelings, and loved her in his own way), he wore the other shirt and sent his velvet suit to the cleaners.

Frisquito sent him more money the next month, and Bongbong bought a telescope.

Dear Frisquito,

Do you know I am only five feet and two inches tall? Without my platform shoes, of course. Why do people like to look like cripples? Yesterday I saw a fat young woman wearing platform shoes that made her feet look like boats. Her dress was too short on her fat body and you could see her cellulite wobbling in her forest-green pantyhose. Cellulite is the new fad in America. Some Frenchwoman discovered it and is urging everyone to feel for it in their skin. It's sort of like crepe-paper tissue that happens when you put on too much weight. I told the fat young woman she was beautiful, and she told me to fuck off. She was very angry, and I realized there are a lot of angry people around me. Except in the house I live in, which is why I've stayed so long.

The Coltrane record is warped from having been left in the sun. I am writing a song about it in my head.

> With my telescope I can see everyone, and they don't have to see me.

Love,
B.

Bongbong often brought the telescope up to the roof of their building and watched the people on the streets below. Then at night he would watch the stars in the sky and try and figure out different constellations. Charmaine took him to the planetarium for his birthday, and they watched a show on Chinese astronomy called "The Emperor of the Heavens," narrated by a man called Alvin. Bongbong was moved to tears. "I love you," he told Charmaine, as they lay back in their seats and watched the heavens.

But he had forgotten that she was Charmaine Lopez, and that she lived with him. He thought she was Sandra Broussard, or the blue lady with the rag turban on her head. When the show was over, he asked her to marry him.

He didn't say another word until they reached the flat. He cooked Verta Mae's Jamaican Curried Goat for birthday dinner and Colelia baked him a cake decorated with a sugar-coated model airplane. Bongbong removed the airplane and hung it next to the canopy above his bed.

After dinner he asked Charmaine if she would sleep with him. She didn't have the heart to refuse, and kissing Colelia on her forehead, followed Bongbong into his room. The next morning Charmaine told Colelia they should both move out.

"Was he a freak? I mean, did he hurt you?" Colelia asked.

Charmaine shook her head. "No. But I don't want to live around him anymore. It may be best if we left today."

They packed their clothes and rounded up their cats and drove away in Charmaine's VW, leaving Bongbong with a note on the kitchen table: "We will send for the rest of our things. Forgive us. C & C."

Bongbong awoke from a beautiful dream, in which he had learned how to fly. Everything in the dream had an airy quality. He floated and glided through the atmosphere, and went swimming in the clouds, which turned out to be his glittery blue sweater. Charmaine Lopez and her dancing girls did the rhumba in the heavens, which were guarded by smiling Chinese deities. Alvin from the planetarium sang "Stardust" for him as he flew by. He was happy. He could play his saxophone forever. Then he saw Frisquito flying far away, waving to him. He tried and tried, but he couldn't get any closer to him. Frisquito became smaller and smaller, then vanished, and when Bongbong opened his eyes, he found Charmaine gone.

He decided to stay in the flat, and left the other rooms just as they were. Even Ra stopped coming to visit, so Bongbong had to teach himself about the saxophone. There were brief moments when he found that the powers of levitation were within him, so while he practiced the saxophone he would also practice levitating.

Frisquito,

Just two things. The power of flight has been in me all along. All I needed was to want it bad enough.

Another is something someone once said to me. Never is forever, she said.

Love

He didn't sign his name or his initial, because he had finally forgotten who he was.

EASTER SUNDAY

if i wrote a poem a day
i think i'd be okay
not worry so much
about bein' crazy
n not doing enough
i mean   when you're crazy
it seems like you should sing about it
all the time!   but
sometimes i lose my voice
i get a sore throat
i get laryngitis of the soul
n nothing happens

who can stay crazy
under all this pressure?
it makes you wanna
wear a short dress
n hang it up

maybe even get married
to a hip dentist
who drives an XKE
n has access
to a lotta cocaine

i could serve it
in an arty dish
n get my spoons custom-made
by a superhip oriental jeweler
n everybody could talk
about what an outside person
i really am

if i played my bass
all day

i think i'd be okay
i could be like the wind
n hum
like ten thousand locusts
i mean when you're crazy
it seems like you owe it
to yourself
to sing all the time!

but sometimes
things get in the way
i hear rumors about myself
i spread rumors about myself
i lie
sit on my fat ass
n listen to distractions
other than myself
or fall in love
which isn't too bad sometimes

but it makes you wanna
wear a lotta hats n eat mushrooms
get into a strange sportscar
instead of your usual spaceship
go to parties
and bore yourself
to death
involve yourself
in impersonal passions
talk too much
n get spiteful

let us stay crazy
under pressure
let us stay crazy

under pressure
let us stay crazy
under pressure

(i gotta sing
  about it
  all the time)

LISTEN

I am a thief
    your guardian angel
      who watches you

      watch out

This is the music of thieves
    dancing in the night

      chasing away murderers
        who haunt bedrooms
          and threaten my love

      watch out

I am a thief who smiles
    and invents words
      to sing with animals

I wear the hat of a thief
    and my wings are invisible

I am your guardian angel
    your most secret lie

I conjure up whistles and tears
    for your children

      trust me

I twist lyrics into melodies
    as gifts for my friends

      remember my smell
      in the streets
        of your cities

and listen

    always listen

        to the silent air

SOLEA

there are rapists
out there

some of them
don't like asian women
they stab them
and run off to lake tahoe
in search of more pussy
in casino parking lots

thelonious monk
reminds me of you
and i forget
about this place
it's nice

but then
i have to put in
an appearance
at family dinners
and listen to other voices
my blood
in the warm gravy
and the kiss i reserve
only for little children

i can't play
those records
all the time
thelonious monk
is only joyful
in a hurting kind
of way

there are sad men
out there
some of them
don't like me
they like to talk
about corpses and dirt
and how life used to be
so good
when they were young
in the war

i like to kiss you
like i do
little children
it tastes good
but i have to leave
the room sometimes
is deep
wanting to be crazy
and painting my toenails
gold
and seeing universes
in my colors

there are killers
out there
some of them
smile at me
they dream
about snipers on the freeway
aiming machine guns
and conga drums
at innocent drivers
in their volvos

and mustangs
and dodge darts

new york
reminds me of you
so do the locks
on my door
and the way i look
sometimes
when i feel
schizophrenic

there is real beauty
in my eyes
when i lose my mind

i understand you better
this way
and it doesn't hurt
so much

anymore

SEEING YOU AGAIN
MAKES ME WANNA WASH THE DISHES

go into other rooms
collect myself
compose melodies
on my face
scrub the feelings
down
so i can smile

make comments
about the dirt
on my kitchen
floor

the walls
that sometimes
close in
on me

i don't know
who it was
we made ourselves
into

i don't know why
love is a word
that gets thrown
around
so casually

i guess
i'm easily excited
why
the myths ever start
or why dreams

are our only
bearable source

remain part
of the questions
you chose
never to answer

pieces of paper
and tarnished jewels
line my bed

the songs
i'll never finish
the titles
our names
the lyrics
our history
and lies

enough to fill the silence

martha & the vandellas
crooning

come
        and get

        these

                memories

JUSTIFIABLE HOMICIDE

television dictates amorphous lies
to my unborn children
telling me that

murderers have mobilized
into the suburbs

and are wiping out americans

in their grocery stores
and living rooms

my unborn children listen
with seashell ears

to these pale ecclesiastic litanies
and poets die
with tumors in their eyes
and the islands are bleeding

outside america's doors

outside america's freezers

and eager-eyed cornsilk women dance
a bellydance

for hornplayers in velvet jackets

and three sequin-lipped teenyboppers
writhe
in los angeles motelrooms

for you
for you
for you   o my children

and carmencita the mermaid
what's she gonna do about it
except get more food stamps

and richie
he went and shot somebody else
and pedro
he went back
to outerspace
he wants to shower blessings
and stop the cursing
in his heart
but somehow
it's so hard

and jaime
he got caught
raping a movie star

he may have already died
in the electric chair
they still got them   where i come from

americans go to sleep
in their apartments and freeways
and bungalows and ranches
and condominiums
and waterbeds

and get hipper by the day
copping anthropological myths
and musical secrets
to solo with
in symphony orchestras

o my children
my unborn children
i take you from my womb
and photograph your smiles
with love

violence is so simple
                    the knifeblade
                              and daddy's home

junior n tito's names
          scrawled proudly on a bus
                              dolores loves sonny forever
                                        on the greyhound depot toilet wall

          the heart sleeping

                    sleeping

                         sleeping

NATURAL DEATH

la lupe on the dick cavett show
refuses to discuss fidel and the cuba
she once knew
o the grandeur of it
all gone now

she's come to america
to live in her dream
gold lamé jumpsuits
and rhinestone cloaks
you can't judge a man
by the length of his

o the grandeur of it

young girls paint moustaches
on their faces
young men wear yellow satin dresses
eating star-spangled sandwiches
in the saturday night parade

and bodies are buried
in saran wrap on the beach
fragile blossoms wither on beds
in southern california heat

the toilet paper heiress is kidnapped
by mysterious forces
her mother prays in a cathedral
in the darkness of her riviera sunglasses
calling out to god
when her daughter is revealed
as robin hood

o the grandeur of it

mysterious forces
and telephone calls
from anxious mothers
in the milky way
warning all daughters to beware

beware of nightclubs
and cuban mamas
beware of the street
beware of doorbells and abortions
beware of pregnancy
beware of public transportation
beware of frozen meat
and strange men
and rabid animals
beware of strange colors
strange smells
strange sounds
strange feelings
beware of loneliness
and the rhythm
of your heartbeat

LATIN MUSIC IN NEW YORK

made me dance with you
tito   eddie   n ray
somewhere with plumjam eyelids
i danced with you
in a roomful of mirrors
in miss harlow's house

the white girl's in town
and i smell death
the poet dying in a bar
body shaking in time
to lady day's song
          he's dying in a nod
          in a lullaby
          of ambulance haze
          and chloral hydrate
          they burned his brain

somewhere
i saw the white girl smiling
la cucaracha was up all night
hiding her spoons   her mirrors her revolutions
in the morning
          the trace of vampires
          still there
          in the blood   even after a bath

you can't wash it away
you can't hide it
again and again
i looked under my bed
      inside a perfume box
          in the argentinian dagger
             the baby wolf gave me

                    in your eyes
                        in a furtive smile
                        in a good fuck
                            in the boogaloo i do
there's no escaping it
    somewhere   with plumjam eyelids

i danced the tasty freeze shuffle with you
the reds   the blues   the tango con tu madre
it's there
in town for the night
a guest appearance   a quick solo
death gets hyped
and i'm in love again

latin music in new york
made me dance with you
azúcar y chocolaté
the alligator dream
of a tropical night

death makes a quick run
to las vegas
trying to take the poet
with him

latin music in new york
made me dance with you
tito   eddie   n ray

revolutions are creeping out
from under my bed!

and i sing a song for you
        and you
              and
                  you

CANTO NEGRO

dancing
the spirit shaking everyone
your faces are flowers of darkness
eyes closed
in dancing ecstasy
the spirit shaking everyone
shake
shake
children of the jungle
calling me to sing
forget my nightmares
mangoes staining my lips

what is the spirit
that moves us
when we sing
in a thousand backrooms
funky with dopesmells
and pretty men and women
the spirit shaking everyone

we feel so beautiful
a whirlpool of silver eyes
and silver sweat
the spirit moving us
like holiness
in the sway of our bodies
the joy in our voices
humming the dance
the trance
of one night's voodoo
celebration

the moon is almost full
and there's danger

in the air
your faces are flowers of fire
burning
the toucans are flying
macaws are shrieking
and it's forever
in the moment we stop
and start again

what is the spirit
that moves us
unspoken magic
weaving dangerous colors

it's our birthday
and we sing a baptism
for our souls
our godliness

(higher and higher
we dance
out into the street

you ask me
if i
want to die

and i say
no
not yet
not tonight

it's too beautiful

and i want
to love you.)

SOMETHING ABOUT YOU

this is for ntozake
 of the painted sacred monkeys
  on the beaches of the caribbean
  the chinese ladies weep
   into their ivory fans
    as she dances the bomba

and this is for pedro
 in brooklyn and puerto rico
  and the beautiful blueness
   of the water of my voices
   the music will save you
    from madness
     if you listen

and this is for rose who is dead

and thulani with the moon in her hair

this is for the cartoon lady ifa
 of the planet venus with the green eyes
  and the darkness of her
   that all new orleans weeps
    as she dances for lena horne
     and dorothy dandridge
      who is dead

and this is for the wizard
 who swallows his tears
  like diamonds
   lost in the caves
    of his gentle throat
     the music will consume your sadness
      if you keep singing

this is for the one whose aura was silver

and this is for the man
  who chases butterflies and alcoholics
    in latin nightclub dreams
      and kisses me with zoom lenses
        on the beaches of the hollywood freeway
        all the hibiscus bloom
          as you devour iguanas

and this is for the men who loved me

and the one i love

and the child who is a mirror

this is for the one who bears light
  who is the color of egypt
    the cuban drummers are joyous
      when nashira moves across the floor
        of crying laughter

something about you
  all of us
  with songs inside
    knifing the air of sorrow
      with our dance
        a carnival of spirits
          shredded blossoms
            in the water

pet food &
tropical apparitions:

1981

MOTOWN / SMOKEY ROBINSON

hey girl, how long you been here?
did you come with yr daddy in 1959 on a second-class boat
cryin' all the while cuz you didn't want to leave the barrio
the girls back there who wore their hair loose
lotsa orange lipstick and movies on sundays
quiapo market in the morning, yr grandma chewin' red tobacco
roast pig? . . . yeah, and it tasted good . . .
hey girl, did you haveta live in stockton with yr daddy
and talk to old farmers who emigrated in 1941?
did yr daddy promise you to a fifty-eight-year-old bachelor
who stank of cigars . . . and did you
run away to san francisco / go to poly high / rat your hair /
hang around woolworth's / chinatown at three in the morning
go to the cow palace and catch SMOKEY ROBINSON
cry and scream at his gold jacket
Dance every friday night in the mission / go steady with ruben?
(yr daddy can't stand it cuz he's a spik)
and the sailors you dreamed of in manila with yellow hair
did they take you to the beach to ride the ferris wheel?
Life's never been so fine!
you and carmen harmonize "be my baby" by the ronettes
and 1965 you get laid at a party / carmen's house
and you get pregnant and ruben marries you
and you give up harmonizing . . .
hey girl, you sleep without dreams
and remember the barrios and how it's all the same:
manila / the mission / chinatown / east l.a. / harlem / fillmore st.
and you're gettin' kinda fat and smokey robinson's gettin' old

ooh baby baby baby
ooh baby baby
ooh . . .

but he still looks good!!!

i love you
i need you
i need you
i want you
ooh ooh
baby baby
ooh

THE LEOPARD

once undressed
your markings
are displayed
with elegance
the languid dance
before you execute
your prey

as if
i didn't know
i was the kill.
your tongue
camouflaging growls
with a kiss.

in costume
you casually join
the crowd
gaping at museum walls
oohing and aahing
with the best of them.

you slip a hand
into my dress
tenderly fondling
each breast
as if
i didn't know
about those claws
pulled back
inside the fur.

PET FOOD

In the distance I could hear the Four Tops singing
Standing in the shadows of love . . .

"**My candelabra are missing!!!**" Auntie Greta's Mario Lanza shriek pierced the tense silence in the living room of our tiny, overfurnished apartment.

My mother Consuelo rolled her eyes at the familiar sound of Auntie Greta's high-pitched voice. "There he goes again," she muttered to herself, annoyed. She was not speaking to me.

I studied my beautiful mother's face, wanting to touch it. Even in anger she seemed so vulnerable. I liked to think she was vulnerable to me, ever since my entomologist father had run off with the nubile Princess Taratara to the rain forests of Mindanao. They claimed to be on an expedition hunting for prehistoric dragonflies.

We were sitting across from each other in the cluttered living room: my mother Consuelo on the Empress Josephine couch, her frail body lost in the busyness around her. A leopard-skin rug hung on the wall above her head. The rug was one of her prize possessions—a gift from my father when they were still together. I was seated on the ornately carved Spanish colonial chair we had brought on the ship with us when we came from the islands. My mother and I had been sitting like this for more than an hour, and my ass was killing me. I had been trying to explain why it was important for me to move out of her house.

"Dios mío!" she kept moaning. "You'll be the death of me yet!" Her eyes hardened, and her voice suddenly changed from weepy martyr to righteous district attorney. "I know who's responsible for this. It's that so-called friend of yours, Boogie. I warned you about him, but of course, you never listen. You're always defending those smelly friends of yours."

"Boogie doesn't *smell*," I retorted. "He wears tangerine oil."

"That boy smells like a fruit, all right," my mother said smugly. "He's no good—a drug addict with too many crazy ideas. DON'T SMIRK!" she snapped at me. "I wasn't born yesterday, you know. It's all in the eyes, George. I can see the *end* in his eyes. That boy's always hopped up. Pretends he plays the piano. Pretends he plays the guitar. A DISGRACE TO THE RACE, that's what he is. Oh, well." She sighed again. "Wasn't he born here anyway?"

"Yeah," I said. "In Stockton. His family covers their couches and lampshades in plastic."

My mother was triumphant. "**I knew it!** That boy's an American-born Pinoy with no class. He's going to drag you down with him."

"That's not true," I said. "Boogie's one of the gentlest, most sensitive people I know. He looks out for me."

"Looks out for you??? You think I don't know about your little adventures with that low-life fairy? Always running off to so-called concerts with him, coming home at three in the morning and watching television until seven? He smiles up in my face and says, 'Good evening, Mrs. Sand. Thank you so much for letting George go out with me.' Meanwhile, you come home late and can't sleep at all! *DRUGS!* Drugs and sex—that's all you kids think about! You were all right before you met him," she whined.

We went around in circles, crying and hurling accusations at each other, until Auntie Greta stormed into the apartment, his Chihuahua Revenge on a rhinestone-studded leash. Revenge was quivering and shaking and yapping at everything in sight.

My mother pressed a carefully manicured hand to her forehead. "GRETA, PLEASE—that dog of yours should be put to sleep. *She stinks.* Every time you drag her in here I have to get down on my hands and knees and shampoo the rug! And her goddam yelping gives me a headache."

I smiled. "Hello, Auntie Greta," I said, pretending my mother wasn't there. "How's your day been?"

Auntie Greta gave my mother a deadly look. "Thank you, dear—it's been perfectly dreadful. My antique Barcelona candelabra are missing."

"One of your boys must've stolen them," my mother suggested sweetly.

Auntie Greta plopped down on a pink brocade Louis Quinze chair and placed the shivering Chihuahua on his lap. "My boys? My dear, how could you say such a thing?"

Auntie Greta, my dear uncle and aunt all in one, was a distant relative on my mother's side of the family. He had been in America for twenty years and worked in San Francisco as a semi-fashionable hairdresser in a stuffy salon that still believed in pincurls. His clients were a small but loyal group of wealthy matrons who liked their hair set, teased, and dyed silver blue. When my mother left my father and took me to America, leaving behind all the *tropicalisme* in our lives, she had no choice but to look up Auntie Greta, the only person she knew in San Francisco. Auntie Greta helped raise me by acting as a handy and enthusiastic chaperon, especially when my mother didn't want to be bothered. I was very fond of Auntie Greta— he loved the movies as much as I did and tried unsuccessfully to sneak me into the gay bars he frequented so I could have my first drink with him, "just like a grown-up." He looked at me with some embarrassment while my mother lit a cigarette and ignored me.

"Greta dear, you know exactly what I'm talking about," she said coolly. "I'm referring to those boys on the street you pick up and bring home—the ones you feed and clothe, who are always beating you up and burglarizing your apartment."

Martha and The Vandellas' *Your Love Is Like a Heat Wave* was churning in my head as I looked away, avoiding Auntie Greta's pained expression. I had to agree—my mother was right. In fact, that was the very reason she had asked Auntie Greta to move out of our apartment—he kept bringing these surly and suspicious youths home, making my mother more paranoid than ever. He finally moved to a studio on the floor directly above us, and except for the times when he was involved in a "hot romance," we saw him every day at dinnertime.

Auntie Greta's eyes widened in horror. "Oh my God, Consuelo! You don't think that sweet boy Alex could've done it, do you? Not Alex! He's not capable of such an act."

My mother sailed off into the kitchen to make a pot of coffee. "Oh no?" she called out cheerfully from the kitchen. "Your boy Alex is certainly capable of anything, darling. It's all in his eyes. *I can tell.* Plus he's got a weak chin—that's why he's trying to grow that mangy beard. Who does he think he's kidding? As I was just telling my daughter George—who never listens to her mother, of course—all these young people are after the same thing these days—drugs and sex, drugs and sex—and they want it all for *free.*"

I sat there quietly, listening to my mother putter around the kitchen and trying not to lose my temper. I turned to Auntie Greta. "I'm leaving."

"Leaving? But you haven't had dinner yet," he said, looking concerned.

I shook my head. "I'm leaving *home*—and the sooner the better. That's why she's pissed at me."

"I wondered why she was pretending you were invisible," Auntie Greta said, "but then I've always thought Consuelo was into high drama. I never know what to expect when I come downstairs. She's so moody."

"Well, I'm packed and ready to go."

"Do you have any money?" Auntie Greta asked.

I shrugged. "A little bit I saved from the birthday check Dad sent."

He stared at me with some amazement. "But that's not enough! Where are you going to go? You don't even have a job! Where are you going to live? This is all too sudden, even for me—" Auntie Greta said, getting more upset by the minute. "Dear girl, why don't you stay here a while longer, get yourself a job, then move out? That's the sensible way to do things."

I grinned. "Oh, Auntie Greta. I'll be all right. I have friends. They'll look out for me."

"Look out for you? Who's going to look out for you the way your mother and I look out for you? Consuelo may be temperamental, but she's a tigress who loves you *fiercely*."

I grimaced, but Auntie Greta ranted on. "It gets in the way sometimes, but she cares, she really does!"

"I can't take it," I said, "she's too *intolerant*. And she hates Boogie so much."

Auntie Greta sighed. "She just doesn't understand the American way of life. It's too fast for her. Everything's changing, including you." He paused, studying me carefully. "You're not in trouble, are you?"

I shook my head, still grinning. I was going to miss Auntie Greta very much.

"What about drugs?" he asked. "Consuelo informed me that she found a joint in your bookbag once. I had to give her some of my Valiums to calm her down. Was that true?"

I nodded, remembering how Consuelo had burst into my room the morning after she found it, as I was on my way to school. "Everyone experiments," was all I had said to her, which sent her further into her rage.

"Dear George," Auntie Greta pleaded, "you must be careful about the company you keep. Who am I to tell you this, you're probably thinking . . . but I *know*. Aren't you going to college? Don't you have any plans?" Auntie Greta's desperate tone made me nervous.

"Not really," I replied. "I just want to live on my own for a while. Maybe write a little bit. See what happens."

"See what happens? My dear, you're much too vague—no wonder Consuelo's so upset!" Auntie Greta groaned.

I stared off into space.

He got up from the chair and reached into the pocket of his elegantly tailored gabardine pants. "Here. It isn't much, but it should help," he said, handing me a roll of bills.

I tried to give it back to him, but he ignored my outstretched hand. "Take it, for godsake—I know you'll need it," Auntie Greta said, in a firm tone of voice that was new to me. "Let us know as soon as you get settled. And please—please be careful."

I felt like a son being sent off to an unpopular war as I stood uncertainly in the dim foyer, waiting for my mother to come out of the kitchen so I could say goodbye. She never did.

Maybe she heard everything that was said between Auntie Greta and me and, angry as she was, that was enough for her. She often said that walls have ears.

Telling myself over and over again that I had done the right thing, I sang this as I walked down the street:

> *Little Richard*
> *Tutti-Frutti*
> *Fats Domino*
> *I'm walkin' . . .*
> *are you ready for a brand-new beat?*
> *Summer's here*
> *the time is right*
> *for dancin' in the street . . .*
> *Sal Mineo*
> *James Dean*
> *Marlon Brando*

Rat-hole
Rabbit-hole

*and **Goodbye, Feets!***

The sign dangled from the fire escape in front of the shabby building.

STUDIO APT. FOR RENT

I entered the lobby of the dimly lit building, one of those Victorian San Francisco dwellings that must've been grand in the early 1900s. Times had certainly changed—the neighborhood had quietly deteriorated and the building had decayed right along with it. It still had marvelous dark wood panelings and daffodil-shaped art nouveau lamps along the walls, but the carpets were stained and faded, and you could smell grease emanating from the apartments. Another faded sign in the lobby read:

STANLEY GENDZEL—MANAGER—APT. 1
COLLECTOR OF ANTIQUES—PARROT MAN EXTRAORDINAIRE

I hesitated before knocking on his door. Bells tinkled faintly, and someone came toward me down the dark, dank hallway. I put my suitcase down and whirled around to face the young man who stood there staring at me. Could this be Stanley Gendzel? I wondered.

Barefoot, the young man held a large orange cat in his arms. The cat gazed at me with the same dispassionate curiosity.

The young man and the cat bore a striking similarity—the young man with copper-colored skin, slender and beautiful, with his ominous lion's-mane hair, the color of brown fading into reddish gold, much like the extraordinary cat's thick fur. After a few moments, the young man put the cat down, and we both watched it scurry away into the darkness.

"I'm looking for the manager," I said.

The young man smiled. "Manager?"

Oh no, I thought, this couldn't be Stanley Gendzel!

"I'm looking for a place to live," I said, as firmly as I could. Looking for an apartment of my own was one of the momentous decisions of my life, and I was determined to act as adult and businesslike as possible.

"Oh," the young man said, still being playful with me. "A *place*. You need a place."

"I certainly do."

"Then you need to see Stanley."

There was a moment of silence, and we looked each other over like two animals sniffing each other out.

Suddenly he said, "Let me show you my guitar."

I shook my head. "No."

"Let me show you my cello."

"No." Where was Stanley Gendzel?

"Let me show you my saxophone."

"No!"

"Let me show you my soprano saxophone."

"Hmmmm . . ." I was getting curious.

"Let me show you my bass saxophone."

"Oooh . . ."

He was relentless. "Let me show you my bass clarinet."

"Oh dear," I sighed, slowly wearing down.

"Let me show you my bass."

My favorite instrument. I looked him dead in the eye. "Upright or electric?"

He grinned. "Both."

It had been a long day. I decided I must be falling in love, and to hell with Stanley Gendzel. "Well," I said, "maybe . . ."

His grin widened, and suddenly—like magic—the dank and forbidding hallway seemed less gloomy. "My berimbau? Caxixi? Sansa?"

He was so enthusiastic and radiant I had to give in.

"OKAY!" I responded, smiling back at him and taking his hand.

I followed him up the first flight of stairs, and he pulled out a gleaming gold key and unlocked the door to an apartment. The living room was littered with every kind of musical instrument imaginable, and an orchestra of children was playing. Their faces were painted like ornate African and Balinese masks. Bells hung from the ceiling. We began to dance in slow motion, lost in some kind of sensuous waltz.

My first and only lover so far had been Junior Burgess, who could sing as compellingly as Smokey Robinson, seducing me sweetly with his voice while telling me stories of all my favorite Motown groups. But this young man who held me in his arms was different. He made me so nervous I blurted out "I love you" in the middle of our dance.

His face was devoid of expression, like the cat who sat purring in the room, so sure of its regal beauty. "I know," he said, not unkindly.

"My name is George Sand."

"I know," the young man said.

"Your name is Rover."

"Exactly," he replied, twirling me around the room. I don't know how much time we spent in that room, the children's orchestra continuously serenading us with their dissonant circus music, the purring orange cat never once taking his amber eyes off our dancing bodies. And I didn't care.

I floated out of Rover's apartment in a daze, starting back down the stairs in my second attempt to locate the mysterious Stanley Gendzel, manager of this illustrious building. I dragged my battered suitcase behind me, unsure of what had just happened. All I remembered was that late afternoon softly changed into night, and the children's orchestra stopped playing, and Rover and I stopped dancing, unwinding slowly like two figures twirling on top of a music box. The big orange cat rubbed against our legs, and Rover picked him up and carried him in his arms, stroking his fur gently. He kissed me on my lips, then once—very tenderly—on each of my eyelids. "I will see you again," was all he said.

A darkly beautiful Sephardic Jewish woman came bounding up the stairs as I was on my way back down to Stanley Gendzel's apartment. She seemed to be in her early twenties, dressed in interesting layers of clothing my friend Boogie would've called "flea market glamour." Crocheted doilies had been sewn together into a lacy shirt worn over red satin pajamas. The pajamas were stuffed into embroidered Nepalese boots. She was carrying a blender in one hand and a large portfolio in the other.

"Hey," she called out in a friendly way. "You new in the building? Silver Daddy's new piece of cheese, perhaps?"

"Uh, no."

She peered at me from under the thick fringe of her black eyelashes. "My name is Momma Magenta," she finally said.

"Hi. I'm George."

She never flinched. "You're very much his type, you know. Are you Indian or something? Mexican? Italian, somewhat?"

"No, not any of those," I said wryly.

"What about Japanese? That's Silver Daddy's new trip. THE JAPANESE . . . He's busy editing an anthology of esoteric Japanese poets. 'O Momma Magenta,' he's always telling me, 'you've got all the right ingredients. Long black hair, black eyes, big tits, a small waist, and a big ass . . . but you aren't JAPANESE!' I'm always showing him my portfolio, you know," she chattered confidentially. "After all, Silver Daddy's one of America's oldest living legends, with plenty of connections in the art world. But all he ever wants to do around me is talk about pussy."

"Oh. You're an artist?"

Momma Magenta was obviously pleased that I had asked this question. "Yeah, that's right. I do rock 'n' roll posters. Wanna see my portfolio?"

"No thanks. I don't have time. I'm looking for a place to rent."

"Well, you've come to the right place. Silver Daddy owns this building, see. He's what you might call a bona fide *artiste* and slum landlord all rolled into one. He lives on the top floor, in his fashionable ghetto penthouse. You're in luck. Silver Daddy just ordered Stanley Gendzel to kick one of the tenants out. He was a poet from New York named Paolo. Trouble was, he was a smack freak, and broke all the time. HEY—wanna buy a used blender?"

I started down the stairs. "No thanks, really. I think I should go see about renting this apartment," I said, waving goodbye to her.

"Good luck with Stanley." She waved back. "Don't let *him* chew your ears off. And don't be surprised when Silver Daddy invites you up for one of his famous dinner parties."

———

Something that resembled a shriveled-up spider with bushy eyebrows for antennae opened the door. "Whadda ya want?" he croaked, looking me up and down.

"I'm interested in renting the apartment," I said. "Are you Mr. Gendzel?"

"Yup. I'm Stanley Gendzel. Come in, come in." He stepped aside to let me through the door. I pretended not to notice that all he had on were faded, yellow boxer shorts. A large green parrot was perched on his shoulder.

He ushered me into his grimy kitchen and pulled out a chair for me. For a long while no one said a word. I watched Stanley scratch the bird's head, cooing softly to the creature. Then he pulled out a box of birdseed and nonchalantly placed some seeds on the tip of his tongue. The parrot pecked the food off Stanley's outstretched tongue while the old man stared at me suspiciously.

"Are you a college student?" he asked suddenly, when the parrot had finished his dinner.

"No, I'm a poet," I blurted out, wondering if I'd said the wrong thing.

Stanley was visibly upset. "A poet! Not another one!"

It had been such a long, grueling day that between my mother's and Auntie Greta's hysterics and Momma Magenta's aggressiveness, I decided I just couldn't accept Stanley's disapproval. I had to convince this strange man that I had to have the apartment this very evening. Besides, it was getting late and I was hungry.

"Yes," I said, as calmly and politely as possible. "I'm a very responsible person, in spite of what you might think. How much is the rent?"

"Well," Stanley said, scratching the parrot's head once again, "it's one of the worst studios in the building. That heroin addict never cleaned up after himself. Always sipping grape soda and munching Twinkies! It's a wonder he's still alive. Left behind reams and reams of paper—some with writing on it, some without. I didn't have the heart to destroy his work, even though Silver Daddy didn't think too highly of it. He ordered me to go in there and disinfect everything and burn all the boy's manuscripts. Imagine! I just couldn't do it," Stanley repeated, shaking his head slowly.

"I'm glad you didn't. I'm sure Paolo would appreciate it," I said.

"Humph!" Stanley snorted. "Paolo didn't appreciate anything—that's why he was so self-destructive. Anyway, I haven't cleaned the place at all, so you can have it for eighty dollars a month, no cleaning deposit necessary. The toilet works. If you wanna paint it, Silver Daddy will insist on raising the rent, so I wouldn't advise it. Just leave well enough alone."

I got up to go. "Thanks very much, Mr. Gendzel."

"What'd you say your name was again?" he asked.

"I didn't. My name is George Sand."

"Interesting name for a young girl. You look very interesting, by the way. You wouldn't happen to be Japanese, would you?"

"No, I'm from the Philippines, actually. My mother brought me here when I was very young," I replied.

He seemed totally disinterested. "Oh. *The Philippines.* All I remember is that big fuss about MacArthur. Well, it doesn't really matter. I'm sure Silver Daddy will invite you to dinner as soon as you move in. It's part of the rituals around here, his own way of getting to know each tenant. The only one he never invited was Paolo. . . ."

"Perhaps I'll show him some of my poems."

Stanley Gendzel arched one of his extravagant eyebrows. "He'd be utterly delighted, *I'm sure.* That's the right attitude to take with that old lecher! He's working on some Japanese translations right now, y'know. Had some Japanese nobility up there helping him out. Flew her all the way from Tokyo. Called her Camembert for short. She called him Daddybear."

The only thing I had when I moved in was a sorry-ass little suitcase crammed with notebooks and journals, a pair of jeans or two, and a memory of my mother Consuelo's face when I went out the door of her house. When I finally telephoned to say I was all right, Auntie Greta picked up the phone and answered in a solemn voice, "Good evening . . . the Sand residence."

"Hello? Auntie Greta?" My own voice seemed unusually high to me.

"My dear George—are you all right?"

"Yes. I got a place—my own apartment. Is Mom there?"

"Your mother can't come to the phone, dear. She's not feeling well," Auntie Greta said.

"You mean she won't talk to me."

He cleared his throat. "Let's just say your mother is under sedation—high blood pressure, you know. She couldn't handle your leaving us too well."

"Well, tell her I'm all right. I'm living on Webster Street," I said.

"Webster Street??? Webster Street and what???"

"Oh, you know—near the freeway," I replied. I knew what was coming.

"Dios mío! You're living in *that* part of town?" Even Auntie Greta couldn't bring himself to say it: the ghetto. Bodies bleeding on the front steps of my building, virile young things with guns as erect as their dicks, leaping in and out of Chinese grocery stores. My mother's darkest fears.

I sighed. "Don't worry, Auntie Greta. There's a famous person living in this building. His name is Silver Daddy. He's my landlord."

"I've never heard of him," Auntie Greta said.

"Of course not," I retorted, exasperated. "You don't read the papers, except for movie listings. Mom doesn't read the papers, either. Well, if you did, you might know about his column in the Sunday arts section. He writes on all the new stuff going on in the art world."

"Well, I don't know about that, young lady. I do read the paper from time to time! I know you've always thought yourself above us." Auntie Greta was obviously offended.

"Oh Jesus, there you go sounding like my mother," I said.

"You know what they say—association makes for assimilation. Listen, George, do you have enough locks on your doors and windows?"

"Yes."

"I'll break the news to your mother gently. And please, dear, keep in touch. Are you getting a phone?"

"No. But there's a pay phone in the lobby," I said.

"A *pay* phone! In the *lobby*! OH MY GOD!"

I figured it was better if I hung up first.

Family matters resolved for the moment, I called Boogie's brother's house next. His brother tersely informed me that Boogie had moved out recently and was now living a wild and sinful life under the care of some cocaine freak from Tokyo named Prince Genji.

"You could say he's doing real well," Boogie's brother said sarcastically. I knew he had never liked me anyway, and I'd long ago stopped worrying about it. "I'm sure he'd love to hear from you. Maybe you can help him out on his project."

"Project? Boogie's working?" I was amazed.

"You could call it that. Here—" his brother said, giving me Boogie's new phone number. "Give him a ring. And don't forget to say hello to him for me."

I cheered up. "Why sure. I'll be glad to—"

"George," he interrupted, "you can also tell that *bakla* brother of mine that I'm through. His whole family washes their hands of him. You understand? We never want to see him again."

This time, Boogie's brother hung up on me first.

Welcome to de Ghetto

From my new apartment window, I watched Silver Daddy stroll down the street. He wore a leather cowboy vest that accentuated the paunchy belly that jutted out as he walked. There was something grand about the way he swaggered, in spite or because of his weight. Like a futuristic Santa Claus so sure of himself he sees nothing, he stopped under my window and called up to me, his icy blue eyes twinkling and his silver moustache gleaming. Ho-ho-ho.

"Are you the new tenant?"

"Yes. My name is George Sand."

"I know," Silver Daddy said. "Stanley told me. This is all very interesting. You must come to dinner this evening and meet my family."

I seemed to have no choice in the matter. We arranged a suitable time, and he strolled away, turning around halfway up the block to tell me that my new neighborhood would be a good education for me.

"Bleeding bodies happen almost every day in America," Silver Daddy said ominously. "You simply must face up to it, George."

Persimmons

Tinkerbelle, Silver Daddy's secretary-companion, led me into the dining room of Silver Daddy's spacious ghetto penthouse. A wooden refectory table was set for four people with earth-toned ceramic bowls and ivory chopsticks. A slender vase filled with white chrysanthemums stood at the center of the table. Chinese masks and cubist paintings by Silver Daddy hung on the walls. Navajo baskets and Nigerian carvings were strewn haphazardly but deliberately around the room.

Tinkerbelle watched me as I wandered around, politely studying Silver Daddy's rather bland attempts at painting. Tinkerbelle was in her early thirties, a small-boned woman with shoulder-length brown hair and horn-rimmed glasses. She was wearing her standard uniform: nondescript plaid skirt, white Ladybug shirt, and a conservative cardigan sweater. Everything about her was mousey, but she emitted a certain nervous energy as she scurried around the room, chain-smoking Gauloise cigarettes. Bored with the paintings and artifacts, I decided to be friendly and start a conversation.

"Are you the one helping Silver Daddy out with the translations?" I asked her.

Tinkerbelle seemed rather miffed. "Have you been talking to the tenants? If so, you've been grossly misinformed. I am Silver Daddy's secretary —his right hand, so to speak. I sometimes also do the cooking for him," she added, primly.

"Oh," I said, immediately intimidated by her Dame Edith Evans manner.

"Silver Daddy is a gourmet chef, among other things," Tinkerbelle continued, with a great deal of pride. "He taught me how to cook international dishes. I hope you like sushi."

"It's actually one of my favorites."

"Good. We're offering a complete Japanesque menu tonight: miso soup, sushi, sashimi, and daikon. Silver Daddy's on one of his kicks."

Suddenly, Silver Daddy's precocious fourteen-year-old daughter grand-jetéed into the room. An aspiring ballerina with feline green eyes and long dark hair pulled back into a ponytail, she wore a pink tutu, pink tights, and pink satin toeshoes. She held out her hand and spoke with a puzzling accent that constantly shifted from French to Bela Lugosi pseudo-Hungarian.

"Good evening," she said. "You must be George. My name is Porno. I'm Silver Daddy's teenage daughter."

I shook her hand. "Pleased to meet you," I said, somewhat startled.

"AND HERE HE IS, LADIES . . . AMERICA'S OLDEST LIVING LEGEND: MY ESTEEMED FATHER, SILVER DADDY!!!" Porno announced brightly, like an emcee in some decadent Berlin cabaret.

Tinkerbelle bowed as if on cue, and I followed suit. Silver Daddy sauntered into the room, wearing a long black kimono with a red sash tied around his sumo wrestler waist.

I handed him a gift-wrapped package, trimmed with origami birds. "I brought you some persimmons."

He sized me up slowly with his icy blue eyes. "DELIGHTFUL! Remind me to tell you one of my persimmon anecdotes someday. You know what they taste like, don't you?"

"No," I said, shaking my head.

"**Japanese pussy**, of course!" He chuckled at his own joke. Porno and Tinkerbelle clapped their hands and laughed along with him. "Shall we sit down and have dinner?" Silver Daddy gestured toward the table. "You must tell us all about yourself, George."

We all sat down except Tinkerbelle. She flitted about like a dragonfly, serving the food, bringing dishes in and out of the room, taking long drags off her pungent cigarettes.

"You're named after *the* George Sand, aren't you?" Silver Daddy asked me.

"Actually, my parents thought they were being funny. I don't think they had any idea who she really was," I replied.

Silver Daddy frowned. "How *painful*. Have you ever read any of her novels?"

"No."

"Oh, you *must!*" Porno chimed in. "I read all her work by the time I was twelve."

Unimpressed by his daughter's enthusiasm, Silver Daddy pointedly ignored her. "At least read her biography," he advised me. "There are some good ones available these days. You may find it illuminating. She was a most interesting personality—particularly when she ran around with that musician Chopin!" He paused. "I hope you brought your work."

I hesitated before answering. "I did. I wasn't sure if I should, but—"

"Don't be silly," Silver Daddy interrupted. "*I expected you to.* How do you like the miso soup? Tinkerbelle made it herself, from scratch."

"It's organic," Porno said, with the same enthusiasm. "Soybean's the best thing for you. I was raised on it. Wasn't I, Daddy?"

"Yes," Silver Daddy sighed. He turned to me. "Her mother was a health food fanatic. Died at an early age."

"No she didn't!" Porno declared, visibly annoyed. "You're always saying that! Mama is alive and well in Arizona. Your *first* wife died at an early age. In childbirth, I believe."

"Having a baby is like shitting a giant watermelon," Tinkerbelle suddenly intoned, sitting down at the table. She nibbled at her sushi.

"I wouldn't know," I murmured, blushing.

"Well, that's all right," Porno said, " 'cause Tinkerbelle knows. Tinkerbelle likes to think she's an authority on all subjects—don't you, Tinker dear?"

"It's your father's influence," Tinkerbelle replied coolly. "Have some more sashimi, Porno."

In a mournful, basso profundo voice, Silver Daddy began chanting:

> *There was a young man*
> *from St. John's*
> *who went out to bugger*
> *the swans,*
> *when up stepped the porter*
> *who said, "Take my daughter—*
> *them swans is reserved*
> *for the dons."*

Once more, Tinkerbelle and Porno applauded and giggled. "Daddy, you're getting more academic in your old age," Porno said.

"It's difficult having a movie star for a daughter," Silver Daddy said stiffly.

I looked at the smiling Porno. "I didn't know you were in the movies."

"We don't talk about it much around here," Porno said. "Daddy forbids it."

"I only forbid it because I'm not sure of my feelings," Silver Daddy snapped. "You're only fourteen years old. What would your mother have said if she knew? She's probably turned over in her grave by now."

Porno began pouting, her full, luscious lower lip trembling with emotion. "There you go again. Mama's not dead. Your first wife is dead. Mama lives in Arizona. And she doesn't care about me one way or the other."

Gazing at me with her green cat-eyes, she said, "Daddy likes to think he's ahead of his time, but he can't cope with the fact that I make pornographic movies."

"Is that how you got your name?" I asked, losing my appetite.

"Yes. It's my stage name. **I hate my real name.** Can you imagine someone as hip as Silver Daddy calling his daughter RUTH?"

"May I have some more sushi, please?" I asked Tinkerbelle, trying to conceal my embarrassment. All I'd wanted was a good meal and a positive start in my career.

"Have as much as you want," Silver Daddy said grandly. "I love young girls with hearty appetites."

"You certainly do," Porno said.

"RUTH!" Silver Daddy barked, his icy blue eyes crackling. "You're getting out of hand. I wish you'd *shut up.*"

I started to get up from the table. "Maybe I should leave. . . ."

Tinkerbelle was horrified. "You can't do *that*. You haven't finished your dinner."

"Certainly not," Silver Daddy agreed. "**I won't allow it!** Don't let family intrigues spoil the evening for us, George." He took a deep breath. "NOW—it's time for my persimmons."

I sat back down. Tinkerbelle handed Silver Daddy the bowl of persimmons.

Silver Daddy attacked the persimmons, slurping noisily and lasciviously. Once in a while he would look at me meaningfully. Porno watched her father eat the fruit with a dreamy look in her eyes.

"Daddy, do you know the title of my next film?"

He never stopped eating. "WHAT?" he grunted.

"*Persimmons!* I thought of you right away." She paused, but when her father didn't react she began directing her comments to me. "I'm going to star in the loveliest film," she began, in her childlike, faraway voice. "I shall lie spread-eagled on top of a concert grand piano, and my mouth shall remain open throughout the entire movie. See my mouth? I've been told I have the most sensuous mouth since Ingrid Bergman in *Notorious*—don't I, Daddy?"

Silver Daddy reached for another persimmon.

"Two Arabian stallions prance around the room, their luxurious manes occasionally brushing against my extremely sensitive nipples," Porno said, a slight smile at the corners of her mouth. "The opening scene will be shot in slow motion, of course, with lots of diffused light and all that sort of thing. Then Van Cliburn enters the room, totally unaware that I'm lying naked on his grand piano, and proceeds to play an extremely tacky rendition of 'Moonlight Sonata.' "

"Hmmm. One of my favorites," I murmured.

"Would you like some tea, or coffee?" Tinkerbelle asked me.

"Coffee."

Tinkerbelle dashed out of the room, puffing on another Gauloise.

"As I writhe sinuously atop the concert grand," Porno went on, by now lost to us, "a leering Aubrey Beardsley–type dwarf waddles into the room, carrying a dome-covered silver platter. He removes the dome to reveal a quivering asthmatic anteater. The anteater, of course, has no idea what's going on. He crinkles his snout in the direction of my gaping, nubile honeypot."

I was so mesmerized by this scenario that I was unaware of Tinkerbelle at my elbow, pouring coffee in my cup. Porno seemed to be going deeper into a trancelike state.

"I lift up one leg in agonizing slow motion, as the anteater's tongue slithers slowly out. The whole thing is going to be choreographed like an excruciating, torrid ballet—by me, of course. . . ."

"I didn't realize you were so talented," I said.

She ignored me. "The sticky tip of the anteater's tongue explores my swollen clitoris, and I arch my supine back as the leering dwarf giggles. Van Cliburn sweats as the music crescendos, his hair in electric shock reminiscent of Elsa Lanchester in *Bride of Frankenstein*. The anteater, disappointed at having found no ants, turns away from my juicy honeypot and is suddenly grabbed by the leering dwarf, who by this time has an enormous hard-on."

She paused, and for a moment her cat-eyes focused on me. "You know, little men have the biggest dicks, sometimes."

She said this with a combination of innocence and matter-of-factness that reminded me of my friend Boogie.

"This leering dwarf pulls down his knickers and buggers the struggling anteater, who can't escape the dwarf's powerful embrace," Porno said, panting excitedly. "Van Cliburn, oblivious to everything around him, is still crescendoing as five West Indians calypso into the room."

I gulped my coffee.

"Ahhh," Silver Daddy said, sucking on another persimmon, "*neocolonialism*! The fucker and fuckee."

Neocolonialism

"The first West Indian has a dick that's long and thin, like a buffalo's," Porno said breathlessly. "He enters me in the usual missionary position. I moan. He comes fast, like a junkie. The second West Indian has a dick that's pointy, like a Masai spear. He turns me over—quickly, quickly—and enters me from behind, humping me like a horse. No, no," she gasped, "not like a horse! Like an angry wolf!"

"An angry wolf *in heat*," Silver Daddy added solemnly.

Porno nodded in agreement, her green eyes glittering. "He pulls out and comes all over Van Cliburn's elegant, brand-new tuxedo. Van Cliburn doesn't care, he continues his 'Moonlight Sonata' crescendo. The third West

Indian has a dick that's not too long, but rather thick and awesome. I can't wait. He wraps my legs around his broad shoulders and proceeds to fuck me DEEP, with long, masterful strokes. By this time, the leering Beardsley-esque dwarf has rolled underneath the grand piano, grunting like a sow as he buggers the terrified anteater. Meanwhile, the fourth West Indian places his hook-shaped dick into my luscious, foaming, strawberry mouth."

"More coffee?" Tinkerbelle poured me a second cup.

"Thank you," I said. "It's very good."

"It's Blue Mountain coffee," Tinkerbelle informed me. "Silver Daddy orders it especially from Jamaica."

Porno had shut her eyes, looking more ethereal than ever. "The fifth West Indian is a beautiful, degenerate faun—the only other *star* in the film. He sucks my prominent, aching nipples as he beats off his dick, which happens to be the longest, thickest, most cobralike dick anybody would ever want to see. By this time, I am shrieking and gasping for breath—in between dicks and tongues in my mouth, my honeypot, and God-knows-where-else!"

She opened her eyes. "The fifth West Indian finally comes—like Niagara Falls—a never ending stream on my breasts, my eyes, and my warm creamy belly. He wipes his dick in my long straight hair, murmuring endearments in Spanish, Portuguese, French, and patois. Van Cliburn finally collapses like a rag doll on his piano stool. The leering dwarf reaches a violent orgasm, strangling the puzzled and terrified anteater."

Silver Daddy smiled at no one in particular. "Salvador Dali enters the room, unlocking a cage filled with yellow butterflies—"

"Yes!" Porno exclaimed, radiant. "The butterflies hover over my sleeping body in the still, now empty room. The film ends."

No one said anything much after that. Tinkerbelle had settled into a smoke-filled reverie of her own, and Silver Daddy retreated into his bedroom with my manuscripts. After my fourth cup of coffee I excused myself and went downstairs to my apartment. They didn't bother to say goodnight.

My apartment was really a one-room studio, with a dingy closet of a kitchen and a gloomy bathroom where the roaches liked to hide. The best thing about it was the bathtub, a massive boat with lion's paws that had definitely seen better days. I loved filling it with warm water and just sitting in it for hours, thinking. Unhappy with the mattress on the floor I was using to sleep on, I had even considered turning my wonderful bathtub into a bed.

I had left the apartment pretty much in the same state I had found it —the floor littered with papers of every shape and size, including newspapers. Almost all the papers belonged to the poet Paolo, although lately I had gotten in the habit of discarding my poems and stories in the same way—using the sheets of paper as rugs, haphazard decorations on the floor that floated in the air when the wind blew through the apartment.

I had taken to tacking some of my poems, finished and unfinished, on the walls next to or on top of the poems Paolo had glued on like wallpaper. In an eerie way, it made me feel safe and comfortable.

I called Boogie and invited him to see my new home. He seemed highly amused by my surroundings as soon as he walked through the door. I was impressed by his appearance—Boogie had always been very pretty, and his looks confused a lot of people. He could pass for Latino, Asian, even Native American. His eclectic way of dressing never betrayed the toughness behind the elegance, and I loved the way his beauty drove men and women crazy. Nothing seemed to disturb him, an attribute that could sometimes make me angry. But when I was feeling good about myself, I could think of no one else in the world whose opinion mattered more.

Boogie in the Palace

Boogie came from a hardworking, lower-middle-class family that always found it difficult to make ends meet. I suppose that's why he was so clever at putting old clothes together into what he called his "costumes." I stared curiously at the expensive silk scarf around his neck and the custom-made snakeskin boots he wore on his feet. He sat down on a stack of books. "Really, George. It amazes me how you can live here," he said with a smile.

"It's my own place, Boogie. I've never had one."

"Hey, remember the first time I met you? In that fucked-up high school we went to?"

"Yeah. How can I forget, you asshole?" I said, lounging on the mattress next to where he sat. "You called me a cunt."

We both laughed. "Hey, I thought you was such a fox," Boogie said. "*Really*. You're one of the few women I've ever considered fucking."

"Oh, *please*," I groaned. "The way you talk, you'd think you were a million years old. You don't even know that many women!"

"Okay then, maybe you're the only woman I've ever considered fucking—and I'm eternally grateful for the passing desire."

"I'll bet."

"Anyway, I saw you sashaying down the hall carrying your books and lookin' so outta place. . . . 'Shit,' I said to myself, 'that looks like another Pinoy!' I was so sick of bein' the only Filipino in that goddam school . . . y'know what I mean? I wasn't even fashionable!"

"You haven't changed. Is that all you care about?"

"Seriously, George," Boogie said, "bloods were *in* that year. Remember? Civil rights, Martin Luther King, and all the white girls fucking the black dudes? Remember Pamela Wolfe's birthday party?"

"I wasn't invited," I said, "but I went with you. You were so popular."

He was obviously pleased. "Of course I was! Life of the party, best dancer in school—"

"The most promising musician," I said, remembering our high school yearbook.

"Pamela Wolfe referred to us as 'spades'—I guess cuz we hung around the bloods all the time. 'Oh, Boogie,' " Boogie mimicked Pamela Wolfe's whiny voice, "you've gotta come to my party!' She was always pushing her big tits in my face. . . . 'Bring all your James Brown records and all the spades you know!' God! The nerve of that woman," he said, enjoying himself.

"It wasn't so long ago," I said. "You talk like it was ages and ages ago."

"Well, it is to me," Boogie retorted sharply. He got up and started pacing around the room, wired. "If I never see those people again, I'll be just fine," he muttered. "Especially Pamela Wolfe."

"She was a real liberal," I said, in an attempt to lighten up his sudden change of mood. His expensive clothes and temperamental nature were all new to me.

"Yeah, but it was all a game to her. Let's not talk about her anymore. It's boring," he said.

His brusqueness hurt my feelings. "No one knew you were a fag then," I said sarcastically. "They just thought you danced well."

Boogie stopped pacing and looked at me, smiling again. "You cunt."

"THAT, I believe, was the first word you ever said to me. You walked up to me in the hallway and stared me up and down. Then you flashed that famous smile, showing me your pearly white teeth. 'PUKI,' you said to me in Tagalog."

"That's right, sweetheart. I wanted to get a *reaction*."

"So where'd you get all the fancy clothes?" I suddenly asked, taking him by surprise.

A full-length mirror hung on my closet door. Boogie stared at his reflection. "I thought you'd never ask," he said. "This involves you—so pay attention. One day, as I was prowling the streets looking for some action, a car pulled up. It was a little sportscar driven by a young woman who looked just like Billie Holiday. She even wore a gardenia in her hair. She introduced herself as Cinderella."

"Cinderella?"

"Uh-huh. She was very pleasant, George—and soft-spoken. She seemed to know all about me. And *you*."

"Weren't you paranoid? Maybe she's a cop."

Boogie looked annoyed. "Oh honey, STOP. I know a cop when I see one—better than you ever could. I've been dealing with them all my life," he said with pride. "You don't know nothin' about that, where you come from."

It was my turn to get annoyed. "And what the fuck is that supposed to mean?"

Boogie put his hands on my shoulders, massaging them gently. "There you go again. Relax," he said. "Is it true, or isn't it true that maybe your daddy plays golf with the president back in the islands every once in a while?"

"He can't stand the president, too, you know—" I said, angry with myself for feeling guilty.

"I'm sure he can't, but for all the wrong reasons. The president probably can't tell the difference between a salad fork and a soup spoon. Remember that story you once told me? Your father got invited to some official function at the palace and he refused to go—what was it he said?"

I started giggling. "He said—'My dear, I've been invited by a better class of people, in my time.' "

"Exactly!" Boogie declared, a look of triumph on his face.

"I was disappointed," I said. "I thought it would make a good story. Father goes to banquet with corrupt politicians. Gossips with Lady Macbeth, compliments her on her jewels."

"Of course you were, George. And don't give me that shit about your writing! You wanted your father to go to the palace for the same reason we all want to go to the palace! To rub elbows with some real *power*—"

"That's not true." I shook my head slowly. Boogie stopped massaging my shoulders and sat next to me on the mattress.

"You're lying again, George. Don't think I don't know. Your mother would admit it. She doesn't mind being crass."

"But I do," I said, in a small voice.

He put his arm around me. "That's all I'm trying to tell you, sweetheart. Even your mother knows more about this shit than you do. She came from a poor family and married into money, right? That's why she hates me. I remind her of her family."

"How do you know? You were born in America. You've never even been home," I said.

"All I have to do is listen to my father talk in his broken English," Boogie said wearily. "Look at his worn-out hands. See my mother's shy and frightened face whenever she gets on a bus. They're permanent immigrants in this lousy place, and I've stopped asking myself why they even bothered coming here. I *imagine* the Philippines. I have a fertile imagination, George. You always used to say that."

I said nothing. Boogie tightened his grip on my shoulder for a second, then let me go. "I've hurt your feelings. I'm sorry—and all I wanted to do was tell you how I got these clothes," he said, with a sad smile.

Guerrillas

I ignored Boogie's attempts to soothe me. "When I go home, back to the islands to visit my father, the same movie unfolds in my head."

Boogie prodded me gently. "What movie?"

"The one where they're gonna come and kill everyone in the house. And I'll just happen to be there, by chance—except deep in my heart I know that it's all part of my destiny." I paused, looking at Boogie's chiseled, inscrutable face.

"There are three bedrooms in my father's house," I said, "and my grandmother, who is paralyzed, sleeps in the first bedroom at the top of the stairs. My grandmother is totally helpless, so a nurse has been hired to remain at her side twenty-four hours a day. My grandmother is fed intravenously and shits into a sack that's attached to her side. She clutches a rosary in her gnarled, arthritic hands—mumbling incoherent prayers to herself. No one understands her, but everyone goes on about what a true saint she is. Her eyes are glazed, and she doesn't seem to recognize any of us."

Boogie took my hand. I held on to his tightly.

"It's true," I said. "I'm not lying this time, Boogie. I like to imagine that my grandmother's already left her skeletal body, that she exists on a high spiritual plane. In my movie, they kill the nurse first, but they never touch my grandmother. In fact, they seem to be afraid of my grandmother. After the massacre she's the only survivor left—bobbing up and down in her wheelchair, mumbling and clutching the rosary beads in her hands."

"Who are *they*, George?" Boogie asked, although he knew.

"The revolutionaries. The guerrillas—yes, I prefer calling them guerrillas. It's so much more accurate." We sat in silence for a while, and I didn't let go of his hand. "I sleep in the second bedroom. I hear them in the next room, killing the nurse quietly and efficiently. I lie in my bed, sweating and staring at the door. Should I try to escape? I ask myself over and over again. I can hear the leaves rustling. The night is alive with insects chirping and lizards hissing outside my window. It's unbearably hot, even in the middle of the night. I am unable to move, sweating and trembling underneath my thin blanket. I hear soft movements in the next room, one low and muffled cry. I go over the movie again and again in my head. The night the guerrillas come to my father's house. I even imagine the face of the killer."

"Stop it, George. I can't listen to this anymore," Boogie said, letting go of my hand and getting up from the bed. He walked over to the mirror and stared at his reflection once more. His face was like stone, and he could see me reflected, on the mattress directly behind him.

"But you must," I said, "because it's all true. A vision of the future."

Boogie walked over to the window and stared out at the street. "No. You're wrong. It's one vision of the future, and it's your own particular paranoia that's taken you there."

"The killer is a beautiful young man. He looks like you, Boogie. High cheekbones, smooth copper-colored skin, straight blue-black hair. His lovely eyes pierce the darkness in my bed as he finds me, cowering. He bends his sullen face toward mine. I am gazing into his glistening eyes, thinking of my father sleeping in the third bedroom. I am sure the young man is going to kiss me, but he slits my throat instead. Quietly and efficiently. I've been spared hearing my father die—"

Boogie was visibly shaken. "Jesus Christ! I think you've taken too much acid. Don't be so hard on yourself! Listen, everyone has a choice." Boogie said, trying to convince himself. "To see what they wanna see. To be what they wanna be. It's all very simple. I mean, I know what you're talkin' about—but I don't wanna be reminded of it **all the time!**"

"I'm sorry."

He grinned. "It's okay, it's okay—we're both tripping heavy, that's all."

"Hey, you want some coffee?" I asked, smiling back at him. "It's all I have."

"No, thanks. Maybe I should run out and get us a bottle of wine. Calm you down," Boogie said.

I started crying very quietly. He took me in his arms. "Oh God," I said, my face pressed into the collar of his fancy new shirt, "I feel so silly."

"You shouldn't feel silly. And I'm sorry for saying those things about your parents. It was cruel and stupid," Boogie said.

"Sometimes I think I'm in love with you," I confessed, tears streaming down my face.

Boogie kissed my wet cheek. "I think I'm in love with you too—sometimes. Feel better? Want me to get you some water?" He seemed nervous about what he'd just said and rushed out of the room, busying himself in my pathetic little kitchen. He came back with a glass of cloudy water.

"Tell me where you got your clothes," I said.

"Well, it's all very convoluted, but I've got this patron right now, who I met through Cinderella. He has me working on a project."

"What kind of project?"

"It's really *our* project, George—that's why I was so glad when you finally called me up tonight! I'd been thinking about you, but I didn't want to call your house and get your mother on the phone. I want you to get involved in it. It could be the biggest break in our lives." He pulled a small vial out of his shirt pocket. "Here. I got something for us."

"How'd you manage to pay for this?" I leaned over as he put the silver spoon up my nose.

"My benefactor. You must meet him—he's a very generous man. Our favorite drug—" Boogie chortled with glee. "This should bring you up. Really, George. I don't like seeing you morose like this. It's creepy."

"I'm not being morose," I retorted, snorting more. "I'm just being dramatic."

"Well, save the drama for our project," Boogie said, excitement mounting in his voice. I didn't know if it was the coke, but I hadn't seen Boogie excited like this in a long time. Except maybe the time we saw Jimi Hendrix.

Guitars / Shooting Stars

The first time we saw Jimi Hendrix perform, we thought we were hallucinating—watching him slash his burning guitar onstage, making love to it as if it were a woman.

It might have been his face or hair, I'm not sure. Or the way he looked slightly uncomfortable onstage, holding his guitar awkwardly, yet playing it with the clarity and authority of one who knows his instrument completely, inside and out.

We were in our last year of high school—1967. I had gotten very close to Leopoldo Makaliwanag, who called himself Boogie. He invited me to hitchhike to Monterey for the Pop Festival with him, with maybe fifteen dollars between us. No tickets to any of the concerts, but a lot of faith.

I wanted to be there for the sun and the crazed, Technicolor atmosphere. Boogie was there for the music. He was ready to offer his services to the festival promoters, in exchange for free tickets to the concerts. Cleanup guy, security guard, gofer, anything . . .

At night we huddled in a sleeping bag next to the Hell's Angels campsite. No one took us seriously, not even the bikers. We were two wayward Filipino kids in torn jeans and tattered velvet shirts. Our secondhand coats offered no protection against the fierce Monterey nights, but what did we care? It was a chance to see and hear Otis Redding—plus a new band from England led by some guitar player named Jimi Hendrix.

They were scheduled for the last night of the festival. When Jimi came out onstage, we couldn't believe our eyes. People stood on their folding chairs to get a better look. Who was this outrageous black man with the dangerous hair and those two foreign-looking white boys in the background as his *sidemen*???

He wasn't Otis Redding. Everyone felt safe about loving him.

He wasn't even Little Richard. Everyone could dismiss him as some legendary rock 'n' roll faggot.

He was Jimi Hendrix—sticking his pretty pink tongue out at all the women in the audience, maybe even the men. It was 1967. Flower-power time. Not the time for ambiguous sexual dilemmas.

Boogie and I stood up on our chairs to get a better look, like everyone else. Jimi's hair stood out from his head like a crown of flames.

Boogie was mesmerized by this black apparition piercing the cold night air with the silver arrows of his guitar. "He's afraid they won't accept him," Boogie whispered in my ear. "That's why he's overdoing it." Then Boogie sighed. "Ooh, I can't stand it," he murmured. "This music is terrifying."

"Isn't he lovely?"

We both agreed.

Boogie and I took countless turns snorting up the blow. I could tell he was enjoying having excellent drugs at his disposal and enough cash in his pocket to take taxis everywhere and buy me bottles of wine and cognac.

"You'll never believe it, George—it's too grand." Boogie laughed. "Like I was saying earlier, I met this mysterious woman, Cinderella. Turns out she knows all about us—how talented we both are. I figured she was some big freak who hung out in the music scene and liked young boys. But she's not—not at all! She's a free-lance agent of some sort. For this prince."

"What kinda prince?"

"A prince named Genji. Lives in this palatial flat downtown. He's young, and oh-so pretty." Boogie sighed, a sly smile on his face. "Buys me all my clothes. Pays the rent. Loves to get high."

"Sounds too good to be true."

"Nothing wrong with it, George. It's legit. I work for him, in a sense. He wants to finance a musical, see. And I've been commissioned to write the music. You're the perfect person to write the lyrics and the story. Genji's got the concept. We're gonna blow everybody's minds—y'know what I mean?"

How could I resist? I told him I'd be over to meet the prince the next afternoon.

Gardenias

Cinderella picked me up in her innocuous little green sportscar. She had been sent to take me to Prince Genji's house. "Get in," she ordered, her face obscured by the rhinestone-studded veil of a velvet pillbox hat. She was distant but polite, smiling at me occasionally as she drove expertly down the freeway.

"Prince Genji is eager to meet you," she said smoothly. "I'm sure you'll get along with him quite well."

112

"I can't wait."

"The most important thing is to remember how committed the prince is to this project, and how much he expects out of you and Boogie."

"I really don't know much about it," I said.

"The prince will be happy to tell you everything," Cinderella said. "I only work for the prince."

Somehow when she said that, I didn't quite believe her, but I decided not to say anything. We drove along in silence the rest of the way, and I studied Cinderella stealthily. Something about her—the way she sat up straight, for example, holding her head like a swan—made me quiet and somehow put me in my place. She reminded me of some imperious facets of my mother. Two gardenias were pinned to the bosom of her silver dress.

Prince Genji

The butler led me into Prince Genji's opulent living room. Jimi Hendrix's "Are You Experienced?" was blasting through the giant speakers. A grand piano stood in one corner, next to huge bay windows that looked out into a garden. The floor was covered with plush, thousand-year-old Persian and Chinese rugs. Emerald-green plants hung from the ceiling, and cobra orchids filled the black vases scattered around the room. A collection of gold and silver fans was displayed on one wall, and the marble-topped coffee table was littered with cocaine and assorted paraphernalia: razor blades, straws, packs of matches, and tiny spoons.

Prince Genji was lounging on the sofa, lazily watching Boogie dance to the jagged metallic music through half-open eyelids. Occasionally he nodded his head in time to the music, but Genji was obviously in a stoned stupor—a half-smile on his serene, girlish face.

They were oblivious to our presence, and for the longest time the butler and I stood in the doorway.

Boogie flaunted his hips in front of the sleepy-eyed prince. "OOH— will you listen to that, Genji! Have you ever heard anything so low?"

"Certainly not."

"A vision for the future, Genji! A vision for the universe!"

Prince Genji looked bored. "I'm nodding out."

"You mustn't nod out, Genji—it's too early! For godsake, I'm all hyped up! I'm about to give birth to an idea. Shit, that's what's wrong with you people!"

Prince Genji shot Boogie a warning glance. "Are you going to bring up the war again?" he asked defensively.

"I was talkin' about aristrocrats, fool," Boogie retorted, dancing over to the record player. He played the same song by Hendrix over and over, as if he couldn't get enough of it. "You constantly bring up these projects, Genji—wonderful projects, I might add—but when you get right down to it, you're just blithering away, at my expense," Boogie added cockily.

"**At your expense?** Who's paying the rent around here? Who's giving you a place to stay? Who clothes you and feeds you? Who believes in your musical talents?" Prince Genji demanded.

Boogie stopped dancing and looked at the angry prince. "You do."

"And don't you forget it."

The tense silence was broken by Boogie, who sat next to the prince and smiled seductively at him. "Well, as I was saying, Genji, we've got to get started on this musical. My head is just swimming with ideas."

The prince yawned. "Why don't you snort some heroin and cool down? There's plenty of time for all that." Genji bent over and touched Boogie's face, ready to kiss him.

The butler cleared his throat, his eyes fixed on the floor.

Genji looked up, annoyed. "Yes, Esteban. **What is it?**"

"You have a guest, Prince Genji," the tuxedo-clad eunuch announced. "Cinderella dropped her off. She claims to be a friend of Señorito Boogie's, whom she keeps referring to as *Leopoldo*."

"That's my Christian name, dear," Boogie said coldly.

Prince Genji was amused. "Calm down, Boogie. GOODNESS! I'm sure Esteban didn't mean to offend you. Did you, Esteban?" The butler was silent. "Well, Esteban, show the young lady in."

I was shy and nervous, intimidated by the luxuriousness of the surroundings. The beautiful young men stared at me, like two preening leopards purring before the kill.

"You are prettier than I expected," Genji cooed, suddenly kissing me on the neck. He pulled up my shirt and kissed my belly. "I love to kiss. Kissing is the most exquisite movement of the mouth. Have you had lunch?"

"I'm sure food is the last thing on her mind, Genji! Let's talk business," Boogie snapped.

Genji was tickled by Boogie's jealousy. "Certainly, Boogie. Come, dear George. We don't want to offend your friend. Pull your shirt down."

"Let's get high," Boogie said.

Genji pulled on a bell cord, and the butler entered the room. "Esteban, bring me my potions." The butler bowed and exited. "George, come sit down next to me. Boogie tells me you're quite the poet."

"She is," Boogie gushed. "George, show him some of those lyrics we were working on."

I handed Genji my notebook, and the three of us sat in silence as he flipped through the notebook casually. "My, my . . . you have such a way with clichés, George," he finally said. "You make them palatable."

"I like working with the obvious," I said.

"And the not-so-obvious," Boogie added.

The butler brought in a silver tray laden with bottles and little boxes and glassine envelopes. As quietly as he came, he swished out of the room.

"My potions!" Genji was delighted. "Finally. I can't work without them." He looked at me with a disconcerting warmth. "You wouldn't happen to know any riddles, would you? I love riddles. They keep my mind active."

Boogie was snorting away and getting bitchy. "Riddles? That's a new one. I thought having houseguests gave your life meaning—"

"**Mind your manners, young man!** You don't know to whom you are speaking." Genji turned back to me. "I don't know how you put up with him. He's beautiful, but he really lacks breeding."

"I'm sure he didn't mean it."

"I'm sure he did," Genji retorted. "I may seem sheltered, but I'm not stupid."

Boogie got up and went to the piano. He sat down and stared at the keys for what seemed an eternity. Then he started playing.

"*Smokey Robinson?*" The prince spit out the name with contempt. "Is that all you know?"

"It's part of my Apollo Theater concept," Boogie said. "For the musical."

"Well, I wanted original tunes. That's what the public wants," Prince Genji said. He directed his next remark to me. "Boogie *thinks* he knows what the public wants. But what does he know about Broadway? He's never been out of California."

"Boogie didn't mention Broadway to me." I was surprised.

"That's typical. What did you think, my dear? That I was going to all this trouble just to finance some little-theater project?"

"Why us?" I asked. "We don't have any experience."

"Precisely. But you have the potential," Genji replied. "And that's what I'm banking on. Fresh meat. Young blood."

"Actually," Boogie said to me from across the room, "it's because he doesn't know anyone else."

I could barely suppress a giggle. Genji ignored us. "I want a combination of kabuki, the Folies Bergère, Busby Berkeley, James Brown at the Apollo, and pornography. I want masks in red and black, and chorus lines of young virgins with blond marceled hair singing 'You Can't Take That Away from Me.' I want levels of meaning, most of all," Genji emphasized, his black eyes shining, "esoteric, obvious, spiritual, and vulgar—all at once! I have the means to produce this extravagant dream, but I don't have any connections."

"This is kinda wild," I said hesitantly. "I mean, I've never been asked to do anything like this."

"Of course not, George!" Boogie said, growing impatient with me. "This is a major break. Don't listen to her, Genji. She's shy, but she can do it."

It was my turn to get angry. "STOP APOLOGIZING FOR ME. I'm trying to understand why."

Prince Genji looked puzzled. **"Why, what?"**

"Why you're doing all this," I said. "I mean, with your kinda money, you could invest in a sure thing. Musicals are so—"

"Chancy." Boogie finished my sentence for me.

"Yes," I agreed, "chancy. I mean, how do we know it's gonna work? What if you lose all your money in such a risky venture?"

"Risky venture, *indeed!*" Genji sniffed, giving me a haughty look. "Would you rather I invested in oil, perhaps? Or coffee beans? No one knows it, but the price of coffee is going UP. And we're going to have an oil crisis very soon. And how about commodities. Pork bellies and winter wheat. Grain futures. *Invisible things.* Don't you think I've done all that already? Pet food, for instance. Did you know that's a safe and sound investment? I'm surprised at you, George Sand."

"Why?"

"Because you're being so mundane this evening." Prince Genji and Boogie started laughing. I stared at them in disbelief, then got up from the couch.

"I'm leaving," I said. "I don't have to listen to this shit."

"Come on, George!" Boogie needled. "Can't you take a joke? You used to have such a sick sense of humor."

"Humor? You call his insults humor?" I looked at the smiling prince. "Thanks for an unpleasant evening."

"George, don't leave," Boogie pleaded, a frantic look in his eyes. "PLEASE."

"I don't know why I let you get away with so much shit," I said to him wearily. Resigned, I sat back down. The prince offered me some more coke.

"George, I must apologize for my bad temper," Genji said. "It's the drugs, I'm sure. I get carried away sometimes. Don't I, Boogie?"

"Yeah. I was meaning to speak to you about it."

"You're quite a liar," Genji said, still smiling. "But we'll discuss that some other time. Now, George, will you participate in this glorious project and stop worrying about the risks I'm taking? That's none of your concern, really. You should write, let your imagination run free, and enjoy yourself. We're going to make artistic history."

"Think of the fun we'll have," Boogie said, "collaborating on a musical about people like us."

"It's never been done before, you must admit," Genji said.

I felt pressured and exploited. "All right. But I'm still a little confused about it." I sighed.

"How do you think I feel, being the bastard son of an emperor who is no longer fashionable?" Prince Genji gazed into my eyes. "My mother was a hostess at the Queen Bee Cabaret in Tokyo. My supposedly invincible father surrendered his country. My mother was paid off. I was sent to Europe to learn the Western ways of life—Paris, Florence, London, and even Budapest!" He laughed. "Do you know who I am? I guess Boogie never told you, but I know you, George Sand. I know what's going through that head of yours—your little nightmares about Daddy. Don't you know I understand it all too clearly? We are quite alike, you and I."

"No, we're not."

"You'll find out, soon enough," Genji said. "Both of you remember this—there are reasons why we all came together. I could be skiing somewhere in Switzerland, you know."

"Why don't you, then?" I asked him. "Skiing's easier than dealing with us."

"DO NOT ABUSE ME," Genji said coldly. "You may have talent, according to your friend here, but you don't know anything. You don't understand me, because you refuse to face your nightmares. And that's what this musical is all about. Our American nightmares." He chuckled. He left the room, leaving a chill behind him.

I was frightened and anxious to leave.

"Boogie—" I touched his arm.

Boogie was still staring off into the distance. The butler came into the room, dimming the lights and cleaning up the coffee table. Boogie patted my hand absentmindedly. "Don't worry, babe. Everything's gonna be all right . . ."

Tender Vittles

"Rover, Rover . . ." I called out softly. "This cat that is sometimes an animal and sometimes a man—where are you, Rover?"

Rover appeared suddenly, lounging like an alley cat on the fence next to my apartment building. I hadn't seen him since our first encounter, and I missed him terribly. He leaped down nimbly off the fence, landing directly in front of me and grinning.

"Oh, Rover, where've you been? I've got so much to tell you."

"Really? Hey, George, I got somethin' for you. Somethin' very important to me." He grabbed me and pulled me toward him, startling me at first. Then we started dancing around wildly on the sidewalk. I was puzzled by his behavior, but then I got caught up by the sheer exuberance of the moment.

"I know why I love you," Rover said, kissing me passionately.

"Why?"

"I'll never tell."

"I love you back," I said. "I need to see you more. So much has been happening since I last saw you. I'm working on this musical project."

"Tell me about it," Rover said playfully.

We went upstairs to my apartment and made love for hours. I fell asleep. When I awoke, the room was dark and Rover had disappeared, leaving his white guitar behind him. A sheet of music paper lay on the pillow next to me.

Loving You Was Better Than Never At All
by Rover The Cat (BMI, ASCAP, MEOW)

A new song. I was overwhelmed by a sudden, terrible loneliness. I never had the chance to tell him about my musical project, and I was afraid I would never see him again. I got up from the disheveled bed, looked for my notebook, and began to write.

Cinderella

A roomful of snow-white angora kittens / mirrors / Little Richard's silver boots / Lady Murasaki combing Dorian Gray's hair / Aluminum-foil palm trees / Lupe Velez holds a bullwhip in one delicate hand, cracking it over her head as a chorus line of male Cuban dancers, pre-Castro-Havana-Ricky Ricardo style, shimmy and shake—Hawaiian shirts tied in a knot at their gleaming, well-oiled chests.

I was writing in my studio when a coach pulled up in front of the building. I heard Stanley Gendzel three flights down, cursing and throwing a general fit. The elegant coach was driven by rodents wearing lace-cuffed velvet jackets and sequined knickers. Satin ribbons were tied to their tails.

"RATS!" Stanley shrieked. "**RATS DRIVING A COACH**! They'll copulate and multiply all over the building!" He began sobbing. "This is all I need."

The rats remained calm, ignoring Stanley's outbursts. They didn't seem to have the slightest interest in copulating all over tenement halls.

There was a knock at my door. A footman entered, wearing an oversized Halloween rat mask. "I have been sent by Cinderella to give you this," the footman said, handing me a vial of cocaine. "She wishes to thank you for the work you've done so far, on behalf of Prince Genji, her dearest client. She urges you to keep on writing."

"Thanks," I mumbled, staring at the large vial in my hand.

"Always remember," the footman said, "the best is yet to come."

He exited with a flourish, gracefully and quietly. I was stunned. Pure coke. The best in the West. Better than any joint shared furtively in high school toilets. Better than any blot of acid from Stanford laboratories. Better than any heroin balloon. Better than so-called love. Better than dancing. Better than poetry. Almost as good as music, and almost better than real love. "Oh, Cinderella," I said to myself, "my guardian angel, Cinderella."

The Sphinx Winks

The coke made me fidgety and nervous—my heart beating wildly and my head brimming over with ideas, like an outer-space washing machine spinning round and round. I managed to walk over to my makeshift desk and type.

> Dancers glide through the room, dressed like Carmen Miranda. Their glistening, parted red lips are frozen in eerie, perpetual smiles. They kick their legs high up in the air to silent music. The young men in loud Hawaiian shirts enter stage left. They are barefoot and shake rattles and maracas at the audience, as if casting a spell.

A frenetic, soundless movie. The insides of my wired mind. In spite of my growing anxiety, I couldn't stop snorting more coke. Jimi Hendrix warbled,

"And the gods / made love." I collapsed on the floor. My radio was on. The Temptations followed Hendrix.

> *Ooh baby baby*
> *ooh baby, ooh baby . . .*

The diabolic disc jockey, Ding Dong Daddy, hissed and cooed on the airwaves. "THAT WAS IT, BOYS AND GIRLS—A RUNAWAY HIT BY THE TEMPS! THE TIME IS EIGHT SECONDS TO ONE, AND THIS IS YOUR NUMBER ONE DJ, DING DONG DADDY, PLAYING THAT MUSIC TO YOUR HEART'S CONTENT, ON THE GRAVEYARD SHIFT OF YOUR MIND. HEH-HEH-HEH . . . A NUMBER ONE DJ WITH A RUNAWAY HIT . . . AND THE TIME, BOYS AND GIRLS, IS ONE O'CLOCK IN THE A.M. AND IT'S TOO LATE!" He laughed maniacally. "IT'S TOO LATE!"

I tried to sit up, but rolled over on the floor instead, drool forming on the edges of my mouth. A giant orange cat entered my room, sniffing around me as if looking for something important. The door to my studio opened quietly, and Cinderella tiptoed in, carrying a huge bowl of food for the huge orange cat. The cat growled and began tearing each fish-flavored kernel apart with his fangs.

Cinderella bent over me, slapping me awake. I could smell the faint odor of gardenias.

"Rover . . ." I murmured. "Where's Rover?"

"You're going to be all right," she said, watching me carefully with her lavender-painted eyes.

"My nose hurts."

"That's what you get for being so greedy."

"I got carried away," I groaned. I sat up, gingerly feeling my aching head, my arms, my back. "I was trying to finish this incredible scene with my exploding imagination, but I think I got ahead of myself."

Cinderella straightened up and headed for the door. "I must go now. You'll feel better in a little while. Wash out your nostrils with warm water and take some vitamins. I certainly hope you've learned your lesson. As for me, it's way past my bedtime, and I can't stay."

Her satin skirt rustled as she shut the door behind her. The big orange cat finished eating. He climbed out my window and perched on the ledge, watching me languidly, like some guardian of the tomb, through the night.

Letters from Home

May 10

My dearest daughter:

I am writing you from the rain forests of Mindanao, where I've decided to stay and continue my search for rare species of dragonflies, monarch butterflies, giant praying mantis, and tsetse flies. Everything here is black, black—even the butterflies. I never thought I'd see anything like this, except in Brazil or Africa.

How are you? I hope you are attending church regularly and keep in constant touch with your mother. She keeps sending me telegrams in the jungle, worrying about you.

If you ever decide to return to the islands, let me know and I'll send you a plane ticket. The guavas are exceptionally sweet this year.

Fondest regards,
Dad

June 4

Dearest Dad:

I am in the midst of writing a Broadway musical. Can you believe it? You always said a college education wasn't necessary.

I've been rather sick lately, but I think I'm okay now. Must've been something I ate. Oh, well.

I phone Mom from time to time, but lately I've been so busy, it's been difficult.

I don't feel like coming back to the islands. I also haven't been to church since I was thirteen, but of course you can't remember that far back.
     Write soon.

Love,
George

June 6

Dearest George:

Why haven't you called me in over a month? I'm worried sick, and so is Auntie Greta. You can thank your lucky stars *and* Auntie Greta that I haven't called the police to check on you!

This is a ridiculous situation for a woman of my stature, and you're really being *inconsiderate*. Move out of that ghetto. Get a telephone. For godsake, don't you think of anyone else but yourself and that friend of yours?

You know WHO I'm talking about!

Love,
Your Mother

P.S. Auntie Greta sends his best. He hasn't been doing too well lately.

(Enclosed with her letter were newspaper clippings: "**DRUG-CRAZED STUDENT JUMPS OUT WINDOW / THINKS HE IS GOD!**" "**JIMI HENDRIX DEAD!**" I left the clippings on my desk, and the headlines glared at me for several days. I finally threw them in the trash and felt better.)

The Gangster of Love

I went over to Prince Genji's flat to show him the first draft of the script. The butler ushered me into the living room and informed me that the prince was getting dressed to go out. "He'll be with you shortly. Please make yourself comfortable."

I noticed a tall, lean man in his thirties sitting in the shadows, puffing quietly on a hookah.

"How do you do, George? My name is Doctor T." His voice was soft and enticing, eyes concealed by dark sunglasses. He made me uncomfortable.

"I'm here to see the prince," I said curtly, ignoring his introduction.

"Mind your temper. Why don't you sit down?"

"No thanks."

"You're afraid of me, aren't you?"

"Of course not."

He put the pipe aside. "What're you afraid of?"

"Nothing. Listen, I don't know why you're being so presumptuous," I said, "but I'm here to see the prince on business!"

"So am I. What's wrong? Think I'll sink my teeth into you? Exploit you? Treat you with disrespect?"

He was flirting with me. I decided to give in to his strange charm and flirted back. "Yes, I'm sure you're capable of all those things."

"Do you find me charming, George? I find you charming. I've heard a lot about you from Genji—"

"Really?"

"You'll come and see me sometime, won't you?"

"Why should I?"

"Because it will be a memorable experience, for both of us."

Prince Genji made his entrance, perfumed and decked out in colorful silks. He surveyed the situation. "WELL, I see you've made yourselves at home. Did you bring my package, T?"

Doctor T nodded, his face bland and expressionless. I could feel his eyes boring into me behind the dark sunglasses.

"And what have you brought me, George?" Genji asked.

"The first draft of the script. Is Boogie here? I'd like him to see it."

"No, he went out shopping," Genji said, with a hint of irritation. "That boy knows how to spend money—"

"She's really more than you described, Genji," Doctor T said, as if I weren't there. "Quite a young woman."

"You've always known I had good taste, T. Now, let's see what you've got," Genji said to me, putting on a pair of rose-tinted reading glasses.

I handed him the script, and he read out loud.

A poet dying in a bathtub. Smokey Robinson swaying and crooning in a blue spotlight, stage left. Women with elephant masks, stage right. A giant hypodermic needle carved out of bamboo is lowered onto this tableau. A young man dressed in a cat costume begins an electric guitar solo . . .

"WHAT'S THIS???" Prince Genji looked at me, shocked.

"Blackout," Doctor T said.

I smiled. "That's right."

"It's wonderful," Doctor T said.

Genji was unimpressed. "Wonderful? How could you say that? I can't see it."

"Well, I can." Doctor T shrugged his bony shoulders.

"And I can," I said, encouraged by T's support.

"Don't you think it's a little too different? I'm not paying you to write surrealistic bullshit!" Genji exclaimed. "The public won't understand."

"I thought that's what you wanted," I said. "Our American nightmares."

"You went too *far!*"

"You're beginning to sound like a typical producer," Doctor T said. "Stop worrying about the public. I thought you were trying to be different!"

"Of course I am! BUT, I'm not too sure about that giant hypodermic needle."

Doctor T and Genji gazed at each other. Some kind of understanding passed between them.

"Well, it's your money," Genji said.

"And *yours*," Doctor T said.

"*You* seem quite taken with it."

Doctor T was casual. "I am. I have confidence in this young woman's abilities."

"I'll bet."

"**Stop!!**" I threw my hands up. "If you don't like it, Prince, just say so."

"My dear," Prince Genji said coolly, removing his glasses, "my co-investor in this project seems quite satisfied, so I won't argue with him—for the moment."

"I've written more, but I thought I should show you the first draft before I got too far," I said.

"**Indeed**. Well, I think I'd better dip into my vials and clear up my mind," Genji said, getting up from the sofa.

"I left the package with your butler," Doctor T said.

"Wonderful. It's been such a trying day." Genji threw his head back and looked at me. "You may leave the script here. I'll look at it again later." He walked out of the room, his scarves and scents trailing behind him.

"I don't think he likes me at all," I said. "I wonder why he even bothers . . ."

"That's not for you to worry about," Doctor T assured me. "Just remember what a rare opportunity you've stumbled into."

"Boogie got me into this. Have you met him?"

Doctor T seemed disinterested. "Yes, I have." He got up and put on his jacket. "I have to go. Would you like a ride home?"

"No, thank you."

He held out a slender, beautiful hand. "I hope to see you again."

I surprised myself with my boldness. "I'd like to go to your house instead," I said, taking his hand. He didn't say anything and led me to the driveway where his chocolate-and-cream limousine was waiting, driven by Jerome, an ageless-looking man with a basset hound face.

The Milky Way

I could almost see my mother swoon when I called her a few days later from the pay phone. "Darling," she moaned, "I've been trying to contact you for *days*! It's all over the papers—"

"*What's* all over the papers? What happened?"

"The most horrendous thing. Auntie Greta has been *murdered.*"

I felt sick. "What for? Who'd want to kill him?"

"How should I know? For his antique candelabra, probably. He was always courting danger, bringing home those boys he picked up on the street. He never listened to me. Maybe he was getting senile, but even after that last burglary, he kept running off to those bars as if nothing had happened."

"My God."

"It's shameful. He was brutally murdered at the age of fifty, and the police have no clues. That could've been ME!"

Dear Auntie Greta, with his crystal goblets and cheap red wine, his dapper suits, his Chihuahuas, and his vacuum cleaners. He was a sweet man, spick-and-span and deeply religious, confused by his deadly attraction to young, muscular boys with corrupt hearts and ethereal faces. He went to church for Sunday mass and afternoon novenas. At night, in spite of my mother's persistent nagging, he haunted the bars and the streets.

"I'm having a nervous breakdown," my mother said. "You'd better attend the memorial service. I made all the arrangements—with no help from his family, mind you."

"Aren't they coming?" I asked.

"Hell, no! They're embarrassed by all the scandal and refuse to have anything more to do with him."

"That's very kind of you. Auntie Greta would've appreciated what you're doing," I said, paying my mother a rare compliment.

She acted as if she didn't hear it. "It's just awful. We aren't going to bury him in the proper way. We're having him cremated. His corpse, if you'll pardon the expression, looked so depressing I just couldn't stand it. What a nightmare!" She took a deep breath. "The memorial service is tomorrow night, and Greta's father confessor will officiate. All of Greta's weird friends are going to be there."

"I won't miss it," I promised, fighting back tears.

"Have you heard from your father?"

"Not lately," I said.

"Hmmm. Wonder if he's found any insects lately. Oh, well"—my mother sighed—"look your best, dear. Remember, Auntie Greta would've wanted it that way."

I hung up the phone and locked myself in my studio. I refused to answer the door when Stanley knocked, demanding the rent. "Open up! I know you're home," Stanley said. "Wait till I tell Silver Daddy! He'll throw you out in the street!"

I didn't care. Finally Stanley went away, muttering loudly. I sat in the darkness for most of the night, unable to think or write, a numbness creeping over me.

At one point Silver Daddy banged on my door. "My dear, are you all right? Is there a tragedy in your family? Let me in," he begged. "I'll console you. Don't worry about the rent! I understand about the ups and downs in an artist's life. GEORGE! DON'T DO ANYTHING RASH!"

I couldn't take it anymore. Pressing my face against the door, I said as calmly as possible, "I'll be all right, Silver Daddy. *Just leave me alone.*" I was finally left in peace, tears streaming down my face.

The End of the Queen

Auntie Greta's father confessor led the prayers. Hundreds of people were there: hairdressers, waiters, couturiers, actors, bartenders, mimes in white-face, aging whores, cabdrivers, pharmacists, musicians, successful gigolos, ditchdiggers, poets and novelists, weightlifters, backup singers in sequined dresses, sixteen-year-old basketball players in sweatpants and sneakers—and, of course, my mother.

The flowers that had been sent by Auntie Greta's numerous well-wishers and grieving cohorts glowed mystically in the semi-darkness of the chapel. The large room was stuffy with burning frankincense mixed with the scent of jasmine oil, tea rose perfume, sandalwood fans, and sweat. "I knew Auntie Greta quite well," Father Confessor began. "Are you aware that he died on the night of the full moon???" He struck a dramatic pose.

I thought it was a rather odd way to begin services for such a famous personality, especially when the entire row of poets and novelists began to snicker.

"Auntie Greta died suddenly and violently by the light of a full moon," Father Confessor continued, ignoring the poets and novelists, "and so his only heir—a ten-year-old Chihuahua named Revenge—inherited all that was left of Greta's belongings: a nine-by-twelve-foot frayed Persian rug and a set of gold candelabra from Barcelona, recently recovered by the police."

Father Confessor turned his gleaming eyes in my direction. "I believe your mother gave the precious candelabra to Auntie Greta during one of his frequent and suicidal bouts of depression . . ."

A murmur went through the crowd. My mother smiled graciously as we both stood up. A spotlight came out of nowhere and beamed down on us, just like the Academy Awards on TV.

"Like mother, like daughter," my mother said, obviously delighted to be the center of attention. "As I'm always telling my daughter, 'charity begins at home.' You know how these homosexuals can get despondent," she said, to my embarrassment.

The young basketball players stopped dribbling long enough to perk up their pretty puppy ears and listen.

"WELL," my mother went on, fluttering her wonderful Minnie Mouse eyelashes, "whenever Auntie Greta got sentimental, he'd always phone me to say goodbye. I'd always say, 'GOODBYE, WHAT?' And the old bag would sniff and snort and moan and announce that he was going to kill himself. I went through this melodrama with him every time he drank. 'OH, PUH-LEEZE!' I would sigh. 'STOP FEELING SORRY FOR YOUR-SELF!' There's nothing quite so loathsome as self-pity, wouldn't you say?"

She directed this question at Father Confessor, who nodded solemnly.

"*Indeed*," Father Confessor agreed, his alcoholic's face flushed and glistening with sweat, "nothing quite so loathsome."

My mother pursed her bright red lips in satisfaction. "YES, I tried to tell Auntie Greta over and over again—*killing yourself won't solve any of your problems!* No one cares. I mean, *I* care. And Auntie Greta cared. And sometimes my daughter George cares, when she isn't wrapped up with that sleazy friend of hers, Boogie, who's going to come to a bad end too, mind you. BUT, no one else cared, and Auntie Greta just wasn't being responsible. His hairdressing career was finished. Sailors mugged him constantly, and he drank too much! His liver was in shreds. In and out of the hospital he went, paying off medical bills with money he borrowed from ME. His only true friend.

"It's like I tell my daughter: 'As you get older, you'll see how lonely life really is!' Even your children turn on you," she said sweetly, giving me and the audience her most effective *mater dolorosa* routine.

"My daughter fancies herself an artist—a poet, to be exact. Isn't that wonderful?" my mother said. "I always encouraged her, with no help from her father. He's just an airmail letter and occasional check to her, if you know what I mean. ANYWAY, I've always believed in encouraging people to be themselves. Especially my only child, who's a poet. Or so she says. Although I try to be realistic about the situation. Like I tell her, it's okay to write all that mumbo jumbo stuff, but why not write something that makes money and save all that hocus-pocus for the weekend?"

I was cringing in my seat, but I realized my mother was carried away by her own "stuff." She fanned herself grandly with a stiff palm leaf as she went on.

"Times haven't changed *that* much, and I just don't understand why my daughter's so uncooperative with me. She's always getting in and out of strange vehicles, consorting with riffraff, writing strange and confusing curses she refers to as 'poems.' Her so-called friend Boogie encourages these mystifying convolutions. I sometimes think he's also responsible for a large part of them, but I could never say that to her face.

"My daughter certainly has her pride. She wants to be given credit for everything she does. I guess she gets that from me," my mother added, smiling. "I keep warning her over and over again, just like I did Auntie Greta, about her lifestyle and her friends. Boogie's nothing but a lazy drug addict fronting himself off as a piano player. But no, she won't listen to her own mother," she said with disdain.

"**Drugs.** My daughter thinks I don't understand about the nuances of such things. She thinks I'm not *worldly*. But I've said to her often, 'There's nothing new under the sun, and you can't fool your mother!' Blood is thicker than water, and her so-called friends are going to turn on her in the end. Mark my words! I'm always right!"

The crowd held its breath in reverence and awe of her. The heat and the silence in the chapel were oppressive. We all watched in fascination as my mother swayed, her body locked into some kind of marvelous trance.

"What have I done to deserve this convolution as my child?" she asked no one in particular. "Not that I don't love her, mind you! No one knows how to love her like I do! But she doesn't understand *that*, yet. Who are these furry, dark creatures I see her mooning over? They'll never do her any good. They have no breeding! All they know how to do is make noise—and they have the nerve to call themselves *artists*! What's the world coming to, when *animals* have the arrogance to try to be like human beings, and vice versa???"

She paused, giving the mesmerized audience enough time to catch its breath.

"I don't see the order in it, do you? I'm all for affirmative action and all that sort of thing, but I can't go for these tomcats acting like they're *men*, sticking it in my daughter and her having kittens for babies. They'd end up drowned in a sack, in some canal on the South Side of Chicago! And *then* what? What are those poems and so-called plays going to get her? Who would've guessed I'd have a POOR-IT for a daughter? Not a poet mind you, but a poor-it?" My mother gazed at me lovingly. "And now, my dear," she said, not missing a beat, "why don't you recite us a poem? Show us how talented you are!"

Another murmur went through the crowd. Suddenly, they all began to clap, politely at first. Then the clapping became louder and more persistent, the crowd rowdier. I was humiliated and terrified by what my mother had asked me to do.

"Tell us a poem!" the basketball players cheered.

"Tell us a poem!" the gigolos whistled.

"Yes, yes! Tell us a poem!" the hairdressers and waiters pleaded.

"Chirp it to us, sister!" the backup singers crooned.

"Tell us a poem! Show us! C'mon. Don't be an ass!" the weightlifters and cabdrivers shouted, laughing and making obscene gestures.

"Whip it to us!" the poets and novelists demanded, last but not least.

Telephones began ringing as more spotlights beamed down on me. Roses showered from the ceiling, and the crowd's roaring never ceased. My mother kept bowing and blowing kisses to the grateful, bloodthirsty audience.

It was probably the grandest memorial service Auntie Greta could ever have imagined. Hysteria, melodrama, and pandemonium—Father Confessor and my mother Consuelo basking in their glory. They were oblivious to the fact that I hadn't responded to their request and was in fact heading out the door of the chapel, gritting my teeth in helpless rage. Father Confessor growled at me with some compassion, but no one else paid any attention.

"I've had it with your insults and innuendos," I said to my mother. Her eyes were shut, and she was rocking back and forth, totally unaware of my presence. "I'm sorry it had to be this way. GOODBYE."

No one tried to stop me, and I ran out of the chapel without looking back. I packed up my few belongings and took one last look at my little apartment. All in all, I had accomplished a lot of work in that cramped space. But it was time for me to move on. I owed two months' back rent, Stanley was on my case, and I couldn't stand any more of Silver Daddy's obsequious patronage. I tiptoed down the stairs in the dead of the night, past Stanley's door, and snuck out into the street. Standing on the corner, I took a deep breath and savored the growing excitement in the pit of my stomach. I had made my decision, and I felt quite adult about it. I was moving in with Doctor T, in his gloomy mansion up in the hills.

Toots Suite

The beginning of my relationship with T was the end of my relationship with the elusive Rover, who had fled to the mountains of northern California with his guitar. Occasionally he'd send me packages of vitamins—A, B, and C—plus shark liver oil, cod liver oil, avocado cream, and placenta cream. He worried about my health and wrote me righteous little notes:

George—

I know you're living with
a gangster. Don't be led around
by your nose. Eat right and keep fit.
I'm watching you.

Love,
Rover

"You don't need that kind of love," Doctor T would say, stuffing my nose with snowflakes. "If love were ever really love that way . . . he's just a dream. A furry face in the night. A kid who doesn't know how to fuck. Where is he when you need him, I'd like to know???" Doctor T was a master at raising doubts and suspicions.

Rover wrote me again:

> Up above the world you fly,
> like a tea tray in the sky.
> Who's that gangster in the hat?
> Makin' like a superstar . . .
> ruining your life and looks,
> when you should be writing books!

I wrote him back:

. . . None of what you say is true. I've never been more productive.

I led a slow, leisurely life in Doctor T's mansion. Jerome, T's valet-chauffeur and trusted assistant, watched over me like an unassuming hawk. He had a subtle way about him of being in a room and watching you carefully, yet never making you feel that anything was out of the ordinary. I suppose that was his greatest talent. After a few weeks in his constant, low-key company, I even started to like him.

"Jerome is one of the only people I trust," Doctor T said. "He doesn't just work for me. He's also a friend and an assistant in all my serious undertakings. Do you understand? Don't let that doggish manner fool you. Jerome is no basset hound."

In many ways, I sought Jerome's silent approval. When I got dressed to go out, I always made sure Jerome saw what I was wearing. If he didn't say anything, that meant everything was all right. If he cleared his throat or rolled his eyes, I knew I was in trouble.

The more dependent I became, the better T liked it. "We're looking out for your interests, George. And sometimes the truth is so plain you can't even see it. Don't worry about anything—we'll take care of it."

Jerome brought in some coke, arranged it on the table, and left the room. He never got high with us. I used to wonder if he was secretly contemptuous of my drug-ridden relationship with Doctor T.

"Stop frowning, George," Doctor T chided me, as he helped himself to some lines. "It doesn't suit you."

"I was just thinking."

"About what?"

"Jerome. What goes on inside his head."

"They call him the Roamer, George. That's all you need to know."

"Jerome the Roamer."

"Yeah, that's right."

The Doctor's imagination had no end. After we got high, he'd do it to me in the hallway, sitting on a chair, in the garden, in front of mirrors, with or without music, on the kitchen table, on the kitchen floor, in the bathtub, in the shower, in front of a movie camera, with a tape recorder running, in the morning, in the afternoon, in the evening, in the sleek slick-dick car, and with Jerome watching. Once, we even pretended to be ordinary people and got on a Greyhound bus bound for New York City. Doctor T stared out the window casually, wearing his trademark sinister sunglasses. I put my head in his lap and pretended to fall asleep, giving him the best blow job imaginable. The thrill was unforgettable.

Sexuality replaced writing in my life. Like Doctor T, I became a master of erotic ease.

Once in a while I'd phone Prince Genji and say I was busy doing "research" for the musical.

"I'll bet," the prince would retort, knowing better. My excuses were getting weaker, and the prince was getting more hostile. One day, while T was napping, I asked Jerome to drive me to Genji's flat so I could visit Boogie.

"**Where is my musical?**" the prince demanded. "Am I supporting a couple of parasites? I can't keep paying all these bills and have nothing in return! All I've seen so far are notes and poems that mean nothing to me. **Nothing,**" he repeated emphatically. "I can't go to Broadway with a bunch of poems in my hand! I've got to show them something new! Something innovative! Something that's gonna make money!"

The prince turned to Boogie, who was sitting across the room, his eyes downcast. I was worried about him. I hadn't seen Boogie in weeks, and he looked smaller and thinner than I remembered. His skin had a jaundiced tinge to it.

Genji pointed a finger dramatically at Boogie. "AND YOU! Boogie, Mr. Boogie Man, where is my music? I haven't heard you play the piano in ages! I clothe you, I feed you, I fuck you when you're lonely and play host to your shady friends, but what do I get in return??? I should've known better! I never should've listened to Cinderella!" The prince was so furious, he practically pulled out his hair.

Boogie remained silent, and I was shocked by his passive response. How could he let the prince insult him? It was disgusting.

I got up from my chair and nodded to Jerome. "Let's go, Jerome. *I've had enough.*" I glared back at the prince. Now that I was associated with Doctor T, Genji knew better than to fuck with me. "Why don't you calm down?" I said to him. "You might develop ulcers, with all that hollerin' you do."

Boogie lifted up his head and smiled at me wanly. "Are you going so soon, George?" he asked wistfully. I took his cold hand as he followed us like a lost orphan to the front door.

"You mustn't let that fool treat you like shit! Why do you do this to yourself?" I said, squeezing his hand. I threw my arms around Boogie. I hated to see him like this.

He quickly disentangled his frail body from my embrace. He was still wearing that vacuous smile.

"Oh, George, the prince is right. I'm full of shit. I'm living off him, and I don't do anything to earn my keep."

"I'm sure you've done your share," I said. "At any rate, we're not under contract to him, you know! Nothing says we *have* to produce. Why don't you pack your stuff and come with me?"

Jerome looked askance in my direction, but I ignored him. "C'mon, Boogie. You need to get away from this dungeon."

Boogie shook his head. "No. Not today. I'm not ready yet. In spite of what you think or say, I owe Genji *something*. If it weren't for him, I'd be nobody. I'm glad you're safe and happy. As for me, I've got accounts to settle."

I kissed him on the cheek. "I'll call you in a few days."

Safe and happy, indeed! If only Boogie knew the truth, I thought, as Jerome drove up Doctor T's long and winding driveway. T was standing on the front steps, wearing one of his caftans. I knew he was naked underneath.

"Where have the two of you been?" he wanted to know. "I was getting worried."

"She asked me to drive her to Genji's," Jerome said, deadpan. "Genji pulled another one of his famous scenes and treated us *rudely*. Something should be done about that madman."

The Doctor took me in his arms, and I snuggled up to him. He nibbled softly on my ears. "Did Genji treat you rudely, my dear? Are you upset?"

I nodded.

"Oh my, I guess we'll have to do something about that, won't we?" T murmured. He led me into the house and up into the bedroom.

I got in bed and crawled under the covers. "T, I'm worried about Boogie."

T had his back to me as he sat on the edge of the bed, mixing some new concoction for us to snort. "What is it, darling? Has the prince turned your friend into a junkie?"

"I get the feeling you don't think much of Boogie."

"He's frivolous," T said, grinning. Even when he grinned, there was a coldness in his eyes that unnerved me. He had asked nothing of me in the beginning, only that I sit back and enjoy the luxuries he had to offer, give him the benefit of a doubt, and snort up to my heart's content. When he started feeling rushes of paranoia, he asked me to stay up all night and play dominoes with him. I was the better domino player, and the most "intelligent" fuck (as he put it) he had ever had. He even asked me to read my poems and stories to him before we went to bed—a vulnerable, whimsical side of his personality no one else was allowed to see. Not even the trusted Jerome.

It was easy for me to love Doctor T, but I couldn't understand how he could be so cruel about my only friend. It was a source of constant friction between us.

"Why do you call him a junkie?" I asked. "What's the difference between him and us?"

"What do you mean by that question, George?" T handed me the dope.

"Well, here *you* are, turning me on to this and that, while Genji turns Boogie on to that and this. What's the difference?"

"The difference, George, is in the *quality* of this and that. I'm afraid your friend is off into the deep end."

I was horrified. "You mean needles and heroin and all that sort of thing?"

T said nothing.

"I still don't understand," I blithered, "the difference between him and us. I mean, I'm just as strung out on you, aren't I?"

In fact, the Doctor's detachment was making me horny. Or was it because I was high? I didn't care anymore. The hell with Rover, who was just another memory! The hell with art!

T looked pained. "You ask too many questions, George. Sometimes I just can't deal with your questions. What do you want of me? Don't I love you enough?"

I couldn't stand to see him upset. Gazing into his snakelike eyes, hypnotized and loving it all the way, I licked the center of the palms of his hands, very slowly, the way the Beast licked water from Beauty's hands in the 1939 movie I once saw and never forgot.

"Of course you love me," I whispered, higher than a kite, higher than a rocket on its way to the moon, higher than anyone could be if they'd just finished a musical. . . .

It was Boogie who said that the trouble with us was, we weren't even niggers. "I mean, what are we selling, and who wants to hear it?" he'd say, his wasted eyes skimming over my halfhearted attempts at a script. "They already got niggers to entertain them. What's so interesting about us?"

I didn't understand him, but what he said disturbed me deeply. I knew Boogie was seeing something clear and terrifying, that summer of splendor in Genji's Gothic palace.

The prince was pressuring Boogie tremendously, tired of having Boogie on the payroll, perhaps even tired of Boogie himself. Boogie had nowhere else to go, no other piano to play. Off to Doctor T's house he would run, seeking whatever kind of solace I could offer him. He wouldn't leave Genji's place until it was dark, claiming the sunlight hurt his eyes.

"I'm okay," Boogie would say with a grin, seeing the worried look on my face.

T put up with Boogie only because I demanded it of him, and Boogie was sensitive to this. It made for long and uncomfortable silences whenever T came into the room, which he often did just to intimidate Boogie.

I made Boogie cup after cup of Constant Comment tea sweetened with honey. I forced him to eat the gourmet hot links T would grill on Saturday nights. We sat down to awkward, formal dinners set by fussy Jerome with candles and fresh flowers, eating our hot links smeared with Dijon mustard and sipping Dom Perignon champagne.

I dragged Boogie to the movies with us, but more often than not he nodded out through most full-length features. The only movies he'd stay awake for were cartoons. Bugs Bunny made him crack up hysterically whenever he said, "What's up, *Doc?*"

As a musical team, we felt abandoned. Toyed with and cast aside. In desperation I clung to my romantic fantasy with Doctor T. Boogie, on the other hand, clung to me.

One night, very late, when Doctor T and Jerome were out making one of their sinister "deliveries," Rover phoned. It was one of the few times T had left me alone. I was nervous and jumpy, knowing he was capable of slithering into the bedroom at any moment.

"Are you all right?" Rover asked, in his most official tone of voice.

In his inimitable, feline way, he sensed something was wrong. That made me feel better, somehow.

"No, I'm not," I said, staring absentmindedly at the ceiling. Cobwebs formed lacy patterns on the antique chandelier. "How'd you get this number, Rover? It's unlisted."

"I have my sources too, you know! What about this hoodlum you're living with? Does your mama know about him?"

"I'm old enough to do as I please," I answered, highly insulted. "She doesn't know where I am, in answer to your question."

"A girl of your breeding should know better," Rover said. "You know, your breeding is what attracted me to you in the first place. Plus your latent talents. I thought you'd be different from all the other bitches, if you'll excuse the expression."

"That's just too bad, isn't it! I didn't measure up to *your* high expectations!"

"I know what's happening with you, George. That's why I left town. I've retreated to my hideout in the mountains, where the stars are real and gangsters are something you read about in the papers."

"Stop calling him a gangster."

"Face it, George—that's no doctor! And he doesn't have long to live," Rover said. "He's too upwardly mobile for his own good—and he isn't as slick as he thinks he is. I've heard all about it, on the subterranean grapevine. He's got people out looking for him, George. *Watch out.*"

Abruptly, he hung up.

T was mad, of that I was quite sure. He slept with a gun by our bed. Sometimes I'd wake in the night to find him padding softly around the house with a flashlight, checking all the doors and windows, making sure everything was locked up tight.

"You never know," he'd say, when I asked why he was so paranoid.

He professed disdain for people who used needles, but he'd recently acquired a new habit—furtively shooting up coke when he thought I was asleep. He locked himself up in the little room next to the kitchen that he referred to as his sanctuary. Jerome and I weren't allowed in that room without his permission. When they were out on "business," the room was padlocked.

T would say, with a sad smile, "A lot of people don't like me, George. You know that, don't you?"

I agreed with everything he said. It was less trouble, and it seemed to take so little to appease him—in the beginning.

Jerome placated him by being available for T's every whim and desire: long, aimless drives by the ocean or trips to the movies on the spur of the moment. Doctor T had no other way of relating to the world. He enjoyed sitting in a dark theater with crowds of teenagers hooting at the screen. It made him feel "alive," and yet above it all. Otherwise, he would go into a rage and lock himself in the little room for days. All we could hear were groans and the sounds of objects being thrown around in a fury.

Soon after these increasing fits of lunacy began, I realized that I was practically a prisoner in this mansion. The ever faithful Jerome had been assigned to keep an even more watchful eye over me and monitor all my phone calls.

T accused me of knowing too much. He kept a tight and painful grip on my arms and shook me like a rag doll. "Who told you people were after me? **How did you know?**"

"No one. No one told me anything. I never said that!"

I watched as he switched on the flashlight and looked under the bed. "What are you doing, T? This isn't necessary."

"You don't know about these things," he muttered. "Your name isn't on a list."

"*What* list? Come on, T, let's go to bed. You haven't been to sleep in days. You need rest."

"Ah, George. You care about me, don't you? Yes, I know that about you. We're like two guitars in love—so in tune with each other. Don't ever leave me, George."

"I'm here, T. You don't have to worry. Get some rest. I'll watch the house," I said.

T suddenly laughed. "You bitch! I know what you've got on your mind! Slip me a few downers so I pass out. Then you can climb out the window

140

and meet that pussy friend of yours—what's-his-name, Rover the Cat! Or maybe it'll be that faggot Boogie, who's been dying to fuck you for years. Yeah, that's right. He's been masquerading as a faggot. MY GOD! I NEVER THOUGHT OF IT BEFORE! OF COURSE! THE PERFECT COVER-UP!"

He went on ranting and raving, gripping me tightly and bringing tears to my eyes. When he saw my tears, he would stop and hold me close to him, stroking my hair. "I'm sorry, baby love. Be patient. I'm going out of it again."

I wasn't really afraid of him then. It was just so awful to see him fall apart. Usually Jerome would come in the room and discreetly rescue me from further harassment by distracting T with business suggestions or offers to go to nightclubs or the movies. As T became crazier, however, he shunned public places. Even Jerome became subject to T's suspicions. He accused us of conspiring against him.

"I know Jerome wants to fuck you," T would say, his eyes gleaming like a wolf's in the dark.

How wild he looked, and yet I loved him even in his delirium and wanted only to make him better. I told him over and over I loved him, and held him like a child. We would cry and make promises to each other, then end up fucking so passionately I'd get dizzy with his smell, the feel of his tongue licking the salt on my skin. When he wearied of me, finally, he would drift off into a nervous sleep.

One night he sat up with a jolt on the bed. I could feel his eyes on me, but I kept my breathing steady and pretended to be fast asleep. He turned the flashlight on my face, whispering, "Are you under the bed, George? *Are you under the bed?*"

Occasionally I phoned my mother. She always went into hysterics at the sound of my voice. "Is it you? Is it really you? Oh God, I've got the police out looking for you."

"Good grief, Mama."

"Where did you run off to after Auntie Greta's memorial service? Where are you staying now? Are all those rumors true? *GEORGE*, if you don't tell me the truth, I'm going to write your father a nasty letter."

"It's okay, Mama. I already wrote him a letter telling him not to worry. It's exactly what he wants to hear."

"GEORGE! Don't think you can go on like this forever! How can you do this to me? I'm having a nervous breakdown!"

After a few more of the same kind of conversations, I stopped trying to talk to my mother at all. T became the center of my life. Whatever I wanted, he gave me—except the freedom to come and go as I pleased. At first, he was so fascinating and consuming that I really didn't mind. He never bothered me when I wrote, and I was even close to finishing the script for Prince Genji. Only when he interfered with my friendship with Boogie did I realize that things had gotten out of hand.

"I don't like the way he looks," T said. "I never liked junkies. They're disgusting."

I'd had enough of his righteousness. "And what do you call yourself? I know you're shooting up in that room when I'm asleep," I blurted out.

I knew I'd gone too far, as soon as I said it. Jerome wasn't home, and I had no one to defend me.

T stared at me for a moment with astonishment. "How wonderful you are, George. How you amaze me, with your perception. Darling, darling! How did you guess?"

He began slapping me around my head and my face. As I tried moving away from him, he hit me anywhere he could—on my sides, on my belly, on the arms I threw up to protect my face.

"STOP IT!" I gasped. "STOP IT!" I was screaming and crying, but it didn't matter to Doctor T anymore.

I loved him, and I couldn't understand why. He was a frenzied animal, and he just kept on hurting me.

Rice Congee: Dubious Treasures

I was a mess. I hadn't been sleeping or eating, keeping up with T's hallucinations. After he beat me, he fell on his knees and wept, begging my forgiveness. Then he ordered Jerome to drive me to the hospital. They treated my bruises and didn't ask any questions.

I stayed in bed for days, reading comic books and scribbling in my journal. My condition seemed to take T's mind off his paranoia. He seemed like his old solicitous self, serving me meals in bed and encouraging me to finish the play. He got me high when I complained about my aches and pains. I remember giggling with him about it, and trying to fuck afterwards—except everything hurt too much, and I went to sleep instead.

I thought the nightmare was over. I finished the play and convinced myself that T was under a lot of pressure and consequently had "overreacted" when he beat me. I didn't want to think about it anymore. I wanted to go on living my fairy tale life, lying to myself.

T was giving me a sponge bath with scented water when the invitation to Boogie's party arrived, via Jerome.

I glanced nervously at T.

"Open it," he smiled. "I know you miss him."

I tore open the envelope. "Oh, T!" I squealed. "It's Boogie's birthday, and he wants to celebrate my finishing the play!"

"How delightful. Isn't that delightful, Jerome?" T said. "Maybe the boy's straightening out."

Jerome was silent. T dried me with a towel. "Well, baby, do you want me to go?"

"Of course I do! And you too, Jerome!" I said, throwing my arms around T.

I couldn't believe the sudden turn of events. Maybe everything was going to be all right, after all.

This was no ordinary birthday party, and I worried about what to give Boogie as a present. I had written him a poem, but was dissatisfied with it:

> *dying fawn*
> *sun of anubis*

yr corrupt song
is choreographed
by the supremes

   the white bandit
   holds you by the neck
   on a diamond-studded leash
   or is it the silver conch belt
   of jimi's corpse?

"How morbid," Jerome said, after reading it.

I thought Jerome had impeccable taste, so I asked him if he would go shopping for me. "Pick out a piece of jewelry for Boogie—a bracelet, a necklace, anything. I'll give it to him with the poem."

Jerome left that afternoon to go shopping. T had been in his little sanctuary all day, but I wasn't worried. He even had the door unlocked.

At T's request, Genji had brought me back a formal silk kimono from Japan. I tried it on in front of the mirror, wondering if it was too outlandish to wear to the party. As I stared at my reflection, T suddenly appeared behind me. Electric Miles Davis was playing on the stereo, and T danced around to the dense and sinister rhythms.

He thrust his pelvis in my direction, stepping here and there, snapping his fingers and moving his head from side to side.

"Feel good, don'tcha?" He leered.

I tried to kiss him, but he avoided me. Thinking this was a new game, I grabbed his arm. He giggled, pushing me away.

"What're you up to?" I asked, confused.

"Feel good, don'tcha?" he repeated, whirling around the room. He danced up close to me and stuck his pretty tongue out, in a pose that would've lit up Broadway.

"Yeah, I feel good," I said, leaning up toward his face for a kiss. He spit at me instead.

I was stunned. For a long while I just stood there, not sure it had really happened until I felt his saliva dripping down my cheek.

He grinned. "Feel good, don'tcha?" He spit on me again.

I backed out of the room, slowly.

"WHERE DO YOU THINK YOU'RE GOING? Don't you want a kiss? I thought you wanted a kiss—"

"You're crazy."

"Yes, George! That's what they say," T sang, in a falsetto reminiscent of all that was good about Detroit.

"You've been shooting up again."

"Yes, George! You're absolutely right!" T agreed, coming at me.

I ran out of the room, but he caught up with me in the hallway and pushed me up against the wall. "Don't worry about your friend, George," he said, panting heavily. "I've got a nice present for him, and we're all going to have a good time."

"I'm not going with you."

He laughed. "That's too bad, isn't it? You have no choice, George. You have no choice. . . ."

Silver Daddy was there—and Tinkerbelle, smoking her inevitable Gauloise. Porno wore a lavender jumpsuit and pink dancer's leg warmers. Momma Magenta was carrying a sketchpad and her black portfolio. Cinderella stood demurely in the shadows, a corsage of gardenias on her wrist and a shimmering gold net veil masking her face.

"Are you all right?" Momma Magenta asked me, looking concerned.

I nodded, avoiding her eyes. T had a grip on my arm, and I didn't want to cause a scene.

The living room was lavishly decorated for the party. Prince Genji was busy lighting the candles on Boogie's piano-shaped birthday cake. Jerome was standing next to him.

"Jerome!" I called out. "Did you get the present for Boogie?"

He looked uncomfortable as T answered for him. "Of course he did, darling. Jerome's a responsible man."

"What did you end up getting him?" I asked Jerome, trying to ignore T.

Jerome shrugged his shoulders. "I'm not sure," he stammered. "T had it all wrapped up. I didn't even have to go shopping. As a matter of fact, I just gave it to Boogie."

"The present's from you and me, darling," T said.

I looked around the room for my friend. "Where is he?" I asked Genji.

"How should I know? That boy's so irresponsible."

Porno pulled an ivory comb out of her silk purse and began combing her hair. "Yes, he is rather irresponsible, isn't he?" she agreed.

"How do you know? You've never even met him!" I said to her, annoyed.

"He should never have gotten into buggery so young," Silver Daddy intoned, sipping the *sake* the tuxedo-clad butler poured him.

"I don't think we should be criticizing him at his own party," I grumbled, freeing my arm from T's viselike grip. He was too busy whispering into Porno's ear to notice what I'd done.

"Well, if he doesn't show up soon, I shall blow out his candles for him!" Porno declared, licking her glossy red lips. She fluttered her lashes at me. "George, you look different. Are you well? Did you ever finish your project? I must tell you about my latest movie. You'd love it."

I ignored her narcissistic blitherings.

"Where's Boogie?" I repeated, for the benefit of everyone in the room.

They stared at me as if I were crazy. Then the chattering resumed.

"Have some wine," Prince Genji said.

I looked at him blankly. "It's his birthday party, and he should be here. Don't you think it's a little strange?"

"Your hair wants cutting," Tinkerbelle said to me suddenly.

"You should learn not to make such personal remarks," Silver Daddy reprimanded her. "It's very rude."

He turned to the rest of us. "Why is a raven like a writing desk?"

Genji clapped his hands. "A riddle, a riddle! I love riddles! Riddles clear up the atmosphere! Riddles break the ice! This is going to be a grand party—I just know it!"

"I certainly hope so," Momma Magenta said. She pulled out her Rapidograph pen and began to draw.

———

Doctor T was kissing Porno's wrist, and she was blushing. Cinderella was conferring with Jerome in one corner. Porno cast a furtive glance in my direction. I grinned back at her.

"Do you know where Boogie is, Porno dear?"

"NO, I DON'T!" And I do wish you'd stop asking that question." She offered T her other wrist to kiss.

He began slowly sucking on her fingers, while gazing at me. I was furious.

Genji rushed over to where we sat. "T—it's so good to see you! Would you like some wine? How about some sake? No? Well, I've got some champagne chilling, just for you!"

I tapped Genji on the shoulder. "When was the last time you saw Boogie?"

Genji threw his arms up in exasperation. "WHO CAN REMEMBER TRIVIAL DETAILS? I'm not sure about anything, at this point!"

Jerome cleared his throat. "I believe he's taking a shower."

"A shower? It's nearly midnight," Silver Daddy remarked.

"You might just as well say 'I see what I eat' is the same thing as 'I eat what I see,' " Tinkerbelle said.

"You might just as well say 'I like what I get' is the same thing as 'I get what I like'!" Silver Daddy added lasciviously.

"It is the same thing with you," Porno said to him, and everyone stopped talking.

At that instant, the butler Esteban broke the silence by hitting a brass gong with a large mallet. Prince Genji ushered everyone into their chairs, then clapped his hands.

"Rice congee! Rice congee!" he chirped.

"Rice congee?" Cinderella inquired politely. It was the only thing she said all night.

"My dear, it's toothsome!" Genji assured her. "Toothsome and gratifying, in a most subtle way."

The candles were melting on Boogie's piano-shaped cake.

"But whatever is it?" Porno asked, her hand in Doctor T's lap.

"Some sort of porridge," Momma Magenta suggested.

"Some sort of stew," Tinkerbelle said, blowing Gauloise smoke in our faces.

"YOU'RE ALL WRONG, AS USUAL!" Silver Daddy proclaimed. "When I was in Asia, I had the pleasure of gormandizing rice congee *au table* each morning, in the company of defrocked Himalayan monks—"

"Not in the morning exclusively!" Genji sniffed, interrupting Silver Daddy. "A true devotee of *chinoiserie de luxe* learns to ruminate rice congee morning, noon, and *après le bain*, if you know what I mean!"

"Speaking of *après le bain*," I began, not really wanting to interfere with this sudden flow of esoteric knowledge, "hasn't Boogie finished his bath yet?"

"There you go again," Doctor T sneered. "Why don't you relax and eat your dinner? Boogie's probably primping."

"In the old days," Silver Daddy continued, undaunted, "the women of Chinese aristocracy blended powdered pearls with their rice congee to maintain their luxurious complexions."

"You might just as well say 'You are what you eat'!" Momma Magenta chimed in.

A huge silver tureen was wheeled into the room by the butler Esteban.

Genji was ecstatic. "Hmmm . . . rice congee with eight treasures! Can anyone guess what the eight treasures are?"

"A riddle! A riddle!" Porno squirmed in her seat.

"We've always *loved* riddles," Tinkerbelle said.

Genji turned to Silver Daddy. "Well, my dear authority, can you name a treasure?"

Silver Daddy cleared his throat and stuck out his chest. "It seems to me, if I remember Kyoto correctly, rice congee contained tree fungus, rat's ears, and dried lily flowers."

"**Wrong!**" Genji seemed to relish embarrassing Silver Daddy. "This is rice congee with eight treasures—my custom-made concoction ordered especially from Taiwan! Jerome? What about you? Take a guess."

"I wouldn't know," Jerome said, looking terribly out of place.

"Well then, you can't play the game, can you? PORNO, if you'd stop giving that man a hand job and give it a thought, I'm sure you can guess at least ONE of the treasures."

"BAH-NAH-NAH," Porno purred, without missing a stroke. T lay back in his chair, a dreamy look on his face.

"Excellent!" Genji beamed. "One treasure down, seven more to go! We can't eat until we solve the riddle. How about you, Momma Magenta?"

Momma Magenta dipped her pinky into the steaming tureen. "Gnats, boils, blood, death of the firstborn!"

Genji slapped her wrist with a jade-encrusted fan. "Wrong! This isn't Passover, dear. Not the plagues of Egypt on my house!" He sighed, tiring of his own game. "*Red beans and bananas, dates, lotus nuts, chestnuts and longan, grapes, and white gourd . . .* the eight treasures in rice congee, my friends."

The fragrant rice congee was served in delicate porcelain bowls. Genji sat at the head of the table, watching with immense satisfaction as his guests attacked the food.

I glanced at Momma Magenta's Mickey Mouse watch. It was past midnight, and there were still no signs of the guest of honor.

I got up from the table. "I'm going to look for Boogie."

Everyone stopped eating.

"You can't do *that*," Tinkerbelle said.

"You can't do *that*," Porno agreed.

"It's rude!" Silver Daddy was offended. "*Artists may be artists*, but manners are always important!"

"She's never been too *social*," Genji said, giving demure Cinderella a meaningful look.

T ignored us all and went on eating.

"I'll go with you," Jerome said suddenly. I was taken aback by the kindness in his voice but didn't say anything. We left the room and started up the winding stairs toward the bedrooms.

"I'm not sure," Jerome said, "but I think this has something to do with that present I brought him."

"*What* present? You mean what T gave you? Why didn't you bring him my poem? Why didn't you buy him a bracelet, like I said? WHAT HAVE YOU DONE?"

"I'm guilty of a lot of things, but I'm not a *killer*."

I was horrified. "What was in that package, Jerome? Don't you know?"
He avoided my eyes. "I thought you were in on it."

I ran down the hall opening doors to bedrooms and closets, frantically searching for my friend. Towels and sheets fell on me, Siamese cats meowed and hissed as I ran in and out of rooms. Genji's caged jungle birds were in an uproar, flapping their wings and shrieking. They seemed to sense my mounting panic. I was dizzy with the heavy odor of incense perfume, thrown off guard by the numerous mirrors reflecting my every move.

Nearing the sound of water running, I walked slowly in the direction of Genji's bedroom. I motioned to Jerome. "Come with me," I said. "I don't want to go in there alone."

The door to the bathroom was ajar. The sound of running water was deafening to my ears. I worked up my nerve and pushed open the door, Jerome hovering anxiously behind me. We were unable to see at first because of the steam, but it soon became all too clear. Boogie lay crumpled up in the shower—his face blue and serene, the remains of a mighty fix scattered on the floor around him, blood and water flowing down the drain.

Roller-Skating on Saturn's Rings

Everyone, of course, had an alibi: They were downstairs in Prince Genji's dining room having rice congee for dinner.

"**Heroin**? My goodness! We never touch the stuff!" Prince Genji said to the lieutenant who was interrogating us.

After the police finished asking their questions, the ambulance came and took the corpse away. T and I got into the limousine. He wanted to take Porno home with us, but I slammed the car door in her face. T never said a word.

Jerome drove us home. We were suffering from exhaustion and a vague uneasiness with each other. As soon as we arrived at the mansion, T locked himself in his little room. I lay on our bed and wept.

———

Jerome came into the bedroom, nattily dressed in a navy-blue pin-striped suit. "I've packed my bags and given notice," he said. "I can't stay here any longer."

I felt extraordinarily calm. "Where are you going?"

"Hollywood. Maybe I'll go into the music business."

"Don't be too hard on yourself."

"It's true, isn't it? I'm just a glorified gofer." He lowered his voice. "Do you want to come? He's locked up in that room again."

"Don't worry about me. I'm not afraid of him anymore."

"I'll leave the front door unlocked." He blew me a gentle kiss and left.

It was still dark outside. I hadn't turned on the lights in the house, or the heat. I stayed, sitting on the bed, shivering and numb with grief. The phone rang.

"It's me," Rover said.

I could barely talk. "**YOU**. Is it, really?"

"Yup. It's me—with some news for you. A few minutes ago, Genji's place went up in flames. Some say it was arson. Nothing remains."

"I'm sure it was arson, and I'm sure it was committed by a ghost," I said.

"They're coming to take the gangster away. He can't pull this one off and get away with it."

"I know."

"Well, what're you gonna do? Who's gonna take care of you now?"

"I'll take care of myself."

"Do you love him?"

"Yes."

"**GEORGE**, you've blown it again!"

It was my turn to hang up.

I decided not to take anything with me except my notebooks and one or two drawings. I left the manuscript on the bed.

The night was stunningly beautiful, with a full, orange moon—a painted backdrop on the set of an innocent movie where all you had to do was dance a watered-down version of the rhumba and sing Cole Porter tunes to be happy, accepted, and free.

T was standing on the balcony. He howled at the moon, reaching out with his slender arms as if the moon were his to possess.

"How lovely you look," I said, knowing he would still be there when the sun came up, knowing he couldn't see me.

My bones ached, and I felt a sudden rush as I walked down the street.

It was always that way with me when it was time for me to go.

THE WOMAN WHO THOUGHT
SHE WAS MORE THAN A SAMBA

the woman who thought
she was more than a samba
rode underground trains
dressed up for dancing,
as usual

never mind
that she looked good
succulent like peaches
tattoos on her skin
enough to make
most men sigh

rats
strung out on methadone
rode underground trains
with her,
rats in a trance
scratching
balancing oblivious children
on their laps

rats in a trance
scratching
asleep
ears glued
to radios blaring
city music
metallic abrasive
hard city music

the woman who thought
she was more than a samba
rode underground trains
terrified

she'd forget
how to dance

her dreams
were filled with ghosts
young men she knew
who danced
with each other
consumed by
ambiguous dilemmas

grinding their narrow hips
to snakelike city music
metallic abrasive hard city music
grinding their narrow hips
against her sloping,
naked back
like buffaloes
shedding their fur
against a tree
whispering—"it's a shame
you aren't a man . . .
you have so much man
in you"

in brazil
the women samba
only with their legs
their faces are somber
and their upper torsos
never move

in haiti
people draw themselves
without arms

and don't seem
to dance at all

exuding matinee idol ambience
the young men she knew
wore white
and sported moustaches
"we are a tropical people"
they reminded her,
"the most innovative
in the universe"
they gyrated desperately
and stayed drunk in bars
"we're **in,** this year"

it's a shame
i weren't a man
and who's the woman here?
she often asked herself
sometimes she screamed:
i'm older than you think
i'm getting so sick of you
i can't even remember your names
you all look the same . . .

she fell in love once
and the wounds never healed
it was romance
old as the hills
predictable in its maze
what medieval tapestry he wove
to keep her still

gazelles loped
past their window

and veils kept out the sun
she had her own take on things,
her perfume-scented version
of the story
never mind that
he always won,
leaving unfinished poems
under her bed
orchestras strung upside down
from the ceiling
traces of blood as souvenirs
of their exclusive
combat zone

the woman who thought
she was more than a samba
carried her solitude around
in pouches made of chinese silk
changing her jewelry
with each new lover
insisting they move
with sullen grace
stressing the importance
of style
on a dance floor
how arrogantly they might
hold up
their leonine heads

her dreams were filled with ghosts
perched on her bony wrists
grinning gargoyles
who menaced her every step
and wouldn't
let her go

she longed to be
her mother
in a silver dress
some softly fading memory
lifting her legs
in a sinuous tango

I WENT ALL THE WAY OUT HERE
LOOKING FOR YOU, BOB MARLEY

but you left this island
of bananas and poinsettias
i imagined was so much
like my own
how could you leave
before my arrival
you must've known
your songs got the same
english madness
i got stuck with

and here we are,
spending christmas
in your country
and you aren't even here
and these lovely women
drive us around
to dull intellectual parties
just like california
and i ask about you
cuz i figure
there are some very influential types
present
and they must know
your phone number and address
possibly even arrange
the grand rendezvous
of all times

but as soon as i mention
your name
they smile and shake their heads
"no, he's not here," they say
"he left the country . . ."

and my friend suggests
taking a plane to your new house
i mean after all
we came all the way out here
to have this conversation and dance
with you

but the intellectuals
shake their heads and are bemused
"he lives somewhere
between the bahamas and london . . ."
then they say
"sometimes he visits new york"

the bahamas is okay with me
but london is incapable
of exciting my imagination
and i know your mama
lives in new jersey
or wilmington delaware
or maybe miami
but i don't see you
walkin' down eighth street
in the snow
or emerging from
abysmal subway stations
my own extraterrestrial
prehistoric futuristic
man

how could you do this to me
there are so many questions
i need to ask you
like who "they" and "them" are

everybody in your country
keeps talkin' about

are they horsemen of darkness
descending from blue mountains
in the middle of the night
or malevolent spirits
cutting open children's vaginas
to facilitate rape
because children don't align themselves
with the right party

and who are they
lying there with balls cut off
because they don't belong
to anything
and do women fear
walking home
and who are they
blocking the streets
with all this music
telling me about them
who drive me around
in their cars
and instigate terror
with their theories

all i know is
them don't got your records
in their houses
and they don't live
in the hills
and them are genteel
and offer me homemade sorrel brew
and pimento liqueurs

and peacocks are caged
in their gardens
and they don't speak english too well
and them can read
and they can't
and them can write
and they can't
and them work
and they don't
and them are leaving the country
in droves
and they can't or won't

and this just isn't fair
because you are the only one
i trust
i have to know
were you shot in the arm
like they said
and don't they know
they can't kill music like that?

they should take heed
from america
and relegate you to the
sheraton hotel's junkanoo lounge
as a malnourished dance band

and this just isn't fair
because you are the only one
i trust
and i haven't even met you yet
and i am
waiting

Kingston, Jamaica, 1977

such a strange girl / chiquita / hangin' out with the likes of terra nova / a
man / woman / what polite people refer to as transvestite / terra nova /
bundled up in technicolor crocheted doily shirts / outdated sixties bell-
bottoms / dressed in the outdated chic / of rock stars' old ladies / like
chiquita remembered seein' / in the backstages of fillmore east and fillmore
west / when jimi hendrix was still alive / some shy young man with blown-
out hair everyone ignored / in those days

but jimi was dead / and terra nova reigned / in the streets of new york
city / carrying her bundle of technicolor clothes and opalescent jewelry /
new york city / the only city that mattered / in terra nova's serene opinion

"it's not as if i haven't traveled" / she would say / "it's not as if i
haven't been to kansas–st. louis missouri–grand rapids michigan–new
jersey–or cicero illinois . . . i've even given california a whirl . . . some
old man took me to paris for a one-night stand near the folies bergère! but
i couldn't stay . . . everything was too historical and they kept egypt
locked up in some museum basement . . . san francisco's too slow for me
. . . oakland too much to handle . . . los angeles far too spatial! i like to
walk at night . . . but l.a. cops are trigger-happy in the wrong way . . ."

and terra nova would flash her famous smile / at chiquita / whom she
now accepted as a friend / after all / it was chiqui who named this spirit /
new earth / a found poem / in rags / they haunted streets / together /
sometimes peering into cars / parked along the river / in the late night /
watching men / jack off men / languidly / nervously / or desperately.

but **jimi was dead** and what about transsexuals? chiqui often asked
her friend / terra nova was proud of the fact that she was not one / or the
other

"i hesitate to speak on the subject" / terra nova replied / "only because
one never knows, one never knows . . ." like the weather / one of terra
nova's favorite subjects

chiqui and terra nova would lean against a car / parked on christopher
street in the early morning / and discuss last night's tv news / terra nova
had a crush on ed bradley / and was a fan of CBS / "he seems so kind and
unapproachable / **a real man**" / she would sigh / but it was the weather
report that infuriated her / snide and smug weather men and women who
predicted sunshine / five days in advance

"how could they know?" / terra nova cried / "**how could they know!
and how dare they disturb my atmosphere with BAD NEWS**" / BAD
NEWS / terra nova had no room for that / in her life

and whenever chiqui asked about transsexuals / which she often did /
bein' a young and fascinated woman / curious about silicone breasts /
artificial vaginas / and stitched-on penises / terra nova would refer to one of
her cherished movies / "frankenstein" / any version would do.
"now / you think about that / GIRL / you
think about that" / was all terra nova murmured
closing large almond-shaped eyes and nodding her head slowly / her
disheveled mass of curls / shaking this way / and that / how melancholy
overcame her as she marveled at the world and **jimi hendrix dead** so
many years

once / when chiqui had some money / she bought terra nova a new
wig / a royal peacock-blue wig / and terra nova threw back her head and
laughed and laughed and embraced the smiling chiquita / "my chiquita
banana" / terra nova crooned

terra nova wore her new electric-blue wig to washington square park
and danced for a giggling crowd / sang stevie wonder songs out of tune /
but didn't care / was joyful even when the rain came down and the crowd
dispersed

chiqui and terra nova collected more quarters and dimes than any
hustler in the park that afternoon / strolling down the streets arm in arm /
like tropical apparitions / only visible to a few

YOLANDA MEETS THE WILD BOYS

After the paradiso and the milky way and the kosmos, seeming
as if we had all been sent to gig at some celestial city—
which, despite what some folks think, AMSTERDAM IZ NOT—we
strolled along some canal in the late night in search of that
nebulous JAZZ which might be happening in a garage
masquerading as a nightclub. I turned to lorenzo and said
(—or was it lewis? we were all walking together stoned and
speeding and exhausted)
                              "Shit—this is almost as bad as the jazz life . . ."
            what david murray refers to as the jazz life
y'know . . . and I *should* know, all of us here
like grinning creatures of the underworld,
poeticizing to young zombies asleep in the deep hashish maze
of netherlands bliss, borrowing from katmandu and goa,
in love with japanese hair, the waterfalls of africa,
and what would my mother say if she knew? That i
shoulda had a job, vuitton luggage, a bathtub
in the george cinq hotel.
      Not this yolanda, screeching back to the wild boys
of romance, wild boys lurking in the shadows of the grimy
paradiso balcony, wild boys chanting "BULLSHIT BULLSHIT"
to all the weary poets, while yolanda yells back
                              "fuckyoutoo, jack!"
tensely awaiting a confrontation that does not come.
      THE YOUNG PUNKS OF AMSTERDAM play follow-the-leader,
coming alive only when their band appears. They grab each other's
crotches, and it's an all-male show, the women highly made up and
strangely passive. I'm feeling too old for this and don't believe much of
what i see: wearing black, young blond boys writhe around the stage floor
deliriously anti-rhythmic at the feet of their rock 'n' roll idol, who leaps
about and throws his hips in their faces.
                  "HEY THERE MUTHAFUCKAS
            I'LL SHOW YOU SOME REAL ROCK 'N' ROLL!"
yolanda sings in english.
      The boys don't seem to care or understand. They want their

band! She pulls out
her folsom st. whip and whirls the silver microphone above
her head, like a space-age cowgirl in a rodent rodeo.
"SAY BOYS, CAN YA ONLY GET IT UP
        FOR EACH OTHER?" yolanda teases, rolling her eyes
and cracking her black whip. "HERE'S SOME REAL BLACK
                    FOR YA—some san francisco
        boys' town action!"   The crowd is transfixed
as yolanda slashes the whip across their idol's back,
ripping off his t-shirt and drawing blood.
            "YOLANDA WANTS TO KNOW—can you
            handle it, or are we merely playing?" she grins.

        They grab each other's crotches
            and it's an all-male show,   the women
                highly made up
                    and strangely passive.

(i ask harold norse
    about marlon brando
        as we breakfast on eggs and coffee and jam that's too sweet.
        "He'd fuck anything that moves," harold replies,
                with a certain authority.   I wonder
about myself, and jeanne moreau . . . we could elope together
in the south of france and make movies . . . does patti smith spit
    every time she performs? . . . ntozake and her appetites—how
        we compare notes . . . would we really have
                            any children?)

Yolanda throws back her head and laughs, strutting defiantly
across the amsterdam stage. The stage
is littered with paper cups, hurled by the wild boys from the
balcony. She picks one up and throws it back
at a bewildered audience, the boys still writhing and delirious.
        "WHERE'S THE GLASS?" yolanda wants to know,
        "THE BROKEN SHARDS OF GLASS? WHERE ARE

THE HALF-FINISHED BOTTLES OF BEER? DON'T THEY
ALLOW THEM HERE?"

She shows them her high-heeled boots
and flicks her tongue like a desert lizard.
"LORD . . . CAN YOU
GET IT UP, JUST SO
YOLANDA CAN SEE?" She can't seem to stop laughing,
shaking her long fingers
like lacy fans:

europe / europe / what
a creature / all dis history /
and no future . . .

The crowd becomes enraged,
pushing toward the stage. The young blond boys
climb up, running toward yolanda . . . she's standing still,
a half-smile on her glistening ruby-red lips.
Yolanda sways in snakelike motion, holding the angry boys
at bay by some sort of musical hypnosis . . . her small, clear
voice singing:

europe / europe / what
a creature / all dis history /
and no future . . .

The young boys remove their leather jackets and black t-shirts.
The band stops playing. IT'S YOLANDA'S SHOW, FINALLY—and she
motions for them to unzip their tight black pants.
(Some did it mockingly. Some did it cursing all
the while. Some did it aggressively.
Some did it with a certain surprising shyness.
But *they all did it.*)
Yolanda turns to the young girls in the audience, who seem

to be watching all this with a deep and mournful curiosity.
"NOW LADIES," yolanda says,
very slowly and deliberately, "IS IT SEX,
OR IS IT DEATH—or could there
be anything in between?"

She repeats this question several times, her voice
getting louder and louder. "IS IT SEX, OR IS IT DEATH—
or could there be anything
in between???"

"Music!" a young girl shouted.

"Nothing!" another one cried.

"Metal!" the women roared, mascara streaking
their pallid faces and mingling with a sudden flow of tears.
Even yolanda's eyes are wet, but she keeps grinning
as she looks at the waiting boys
some with hard-ons
some with semi-hard-ons,
others without . . . their dicks
flaccid and pink,
like sleeping baby mice.

Yolanda orders the flaccid ones to drop to their knees and work on
the semi-hard-ons with their mouths. The boys who are already erect
begin touching each other, enamored with each other's obvious virility.

Most didn't seem sure of their position. TO BEND OVER and be
loved, or to DO THE LOVING.

Some tried to touch and grab yolanda, who easily jumped out of
their reach, gracefully avoiding the wild-eyed boys, dazzling the entire
room with her intricate r & b choreography.

"TELL THE TRUTH TO YOURSELVES," yolanda says
to no one in particular. "TELL THE TRUTH TO YOURSELVES,
and remember what your women have told you . . ."
With this, all
the women rose up in magnificent and beautiful fury,
screaming:

"MUSIC!" "NOTHING!" "METAL!"

Yolanda disappeared into the night and caught the first available pan am flight back to new york.

I ran into her strolling down eighth street. Walking past me, she smiled and murmured in a sweet hoarse voice:

"BLACK / BLACK . . . A JOB WELL DONE."

MING THE MERCILESS

dancing on the edge / of a razor blade
ming / king of the lionmen
sing / bring us to the planet
of no return . . .

king of the lionmen
come dancing in my tube
sing, ming, sing . . .
blink sloe-eyed phantasy
and touch me where
there's always hot water
in this house

o flying angel
o pterodactyl
your rocket glides
like a bullet

you are the asian nightmare
the yellow peril
the domino theory
the current fashion trend

ming, merciless ming,
come dancing in my tube
the silver edges of your cloak
slice through my skin
and king vulgar's cardboard wings
flap-flap in death
(for you)

o ming, merciless ming,
the silver edges of your cloak
cut hearts in two

the blood red dimensions
that trace american galaxies

you are the asian nightmare
the yellow peril
the domino theory
the current fashion trend

sing, ming, sing . . .
whistle the final notes
of your serialized abuse
cinema life
cinema death
cinema of ethnic prurient interest

o flying angel
o pterodactyl
your rocket glides
like a bullet
and touches me where
there's always hot water
in this house

New York
peep show:

1982–1992

THE MUMMY

Montana,
you beat your fists
against museum doors
your bronze dress
shimmering
in the starless night.

The doors are locked,
Montana
dreaming
of snow-white mice
cluttering the shelves
in your kitchen,
snow-white mice
inside the oven,
snow-white mice
clogging
your shiny aluminum sink,
their corpses curled up
like piles
of fluffy cotton.

Mosques are desecrated
and altars overturned
outside the museum's
cool stone walls.
Border skirmishes
seen and heard
in the distance,
delicate bursts
of poppy-red flames.
The wars go on and on,
invading
your dreams.

The mirror reflects
a young man's body
dangling
from a rope
and you gasp:
"O, my brother—"

The doctor
finally lets you in,
unlocking the door.
Forbidden to touch you,
he stares straight ahead,
avoiding your curious glance.
"You're partly Egyptian, aren't you?"
The doctor inquires.

You stalk
the dark museum halls
calling out the name
of your dead lover,
the name of a man
unspoken
since the siege of Troy.
"How did you guess?" You growl,
"Do you have to open graves
to find girls
to fall in love with?"

The doctor smiles,
averting his gaze
from your ravaged face.
He longs to trace
your fish scale dress
with his slender fingers.

Montana
scarlet
shameless
Montana,
you stalk
the dark museum halls
in a rage.

Ripping
your satin gloves
to shreds
you pry open
coffins;
reading
between the lines
you decipher
hieroglyphics
on tombs.
"Any message would do,"
you say,
tiny jeweled tears
permanently etched
in the corners
of your eyes.
The doctor sighs,
his impotence
ancient
as the curse
that immortalizes him,
the terrible secret
that pursues you.

Montana
on the night
of a full moon

you are a perfumed woman
in a bronze dress
who shatters glass
with a vengeance,
searching in vain
for signs and clues
among the rubies
and emeralds
that litter
museum floors.

THE MUSEUM WORKS FOR SCIENCE
NOT FOR LOOT,
the doctor tells you.
You laugh at his bandaged face,
the sad, smoldering eyes—
the only things visible
beneath the gauze.

"You can't tell the blood
from the paint
splashed on these walls,"
you say with contempt,
reaching out for his arm
in spite of yourself.
He moves away.
"I dislike being touched,"
he whispers,
"pardon me—it's an
Eastern prejudice."

You never see his anguish;
he won't allow it.
His pride

is what keeps him
going.

Exhausted,
you lie amid the rubble.
The mummy
guards your body
and you dream
of straddling
your sleeping lover's back
like a dolphin
you ride underwater

safe
within the confines
of deserted museum halls.

ARTS & LEISURE

i read your poem
over and over
in this landscape
of women

women purring
on balconies
overlooking
the indigo sea

my mother's
blue taffeta dress
is black as the sea

she glides
out my door
to the beach
where sleek white boats
are anchored
under a full,
luscious moon

still
i am still
the wind
outside my window
my mother's ghost
evaporates
in the long
atlantic night

i listen to the radio
every chance i get

for news
of your city's
latest disaster

everything *here*
the color of honey and sand
everything *there*
verges on catastrophe
a constant preoccupation
with real estate

everything *here*
a calm horizon
taut bodies
carefully nurtured
oiled & gleaming
hair & skin

i read your poem
over and over
turning my head
from prying eyes
the low hum
of women singing
in another room

i switch stations
on the radio
turn up the volume
i almost touch

the air
buzzing electricity

james brown "live at the apollo"
the smooth female d.j.
interrupts bo diddley
groaning "i'm a man"

it is a joke here
in this baby-blue resort
where art
is a full-time hobby
art
is what everyone
claims to do

women sprawl
like cats
on each other's laps
licking the salt
off each other's skin

and i walk
in search
of the portuguese fishermen
who hide
in the scorched trees
the bleak, blond dunes
that line the highway

i imagine
you asleep
in another city

i take your poem
apart
line by line

it is a love letter
we wrote each other
some time ago
trying in vain to pinpoint
that first, easy
thrill.

THE SONG OF BULLETS

Formalized
by middle age
we avoid crowds
but still
love music.

Day after day
with less surprise
we sit
in apartments
and count
the dead.

Awake,
my daughter croons
her sudden cries
and growls
my new language.
While she sleeps
we memorize
a list of casualties:

The photographer's brother
the doctor is missing.
Or I could say:
"Victor's brother Oscar
has been gone for two years . . .
It's easier for the family
to think of him dead."

Victor sends
a Christmas card
from El Salvador:
"Things still the same."

And there are others
who don't play
by the rules—
someone else's brother
perhaps mine
languishes in a hospital;
everyone's grown tired
of his nightmares
and pretends
he's not there.

Someone else's father
perhaps mine
will be executed
when the time comes.
Someone else's mother
perhaps mine
telephones incessantly
her husband is absent
her son has gone mad
her lover has committed suicide
she's a survivor
who can't appreciate
herself.

The sight
of my daughter's
pink and luscious flesh
undoes me.
I fight
my weakening rage
I must remember
to commit
those names to memory
and stay angry.

Friends send postcards:
"Alternating between hectic
social Manila life & rural wonders
of Sagada . . . on to Hong Kong and Bangkok—
Love . . ."

Assassins cruise the streets
in obtrusive limousines
sunbathers idle
on the beach

War is predicted
in five years
ten years
any day now
I always thought
it was already happening

snipers and poets locked
in a secret embrace
the country
my child may never see

a heritage
of women in heat
and men
skilled at betrayal

dancing
to the song
of bullets.

HOMESICK

Blame it on the mambo and the cha-cha, voodoo amulets worn on the same chain with tiny crucifixes and scapulars blessed by the Pope. Chains of love, medals engraved with the all-seeing Eye, ascending Blessed Virgins floating toward heaven surrounded by erotic cherubs and archangels, the magnificent torso of a tormented, half-naked Saint Sebastian pierced by arrows dripping blood. A crown of barbed-wire thorns adorns the holy subversive's head, while we drown in the legacy of brutal tropical generals stuffed in khaki uniforms, their eyes shielded by impenetrable black sunglasses, Douglas MacArthur style.

And Douglas MacArthur and Tom Cruise are painted on billboards lining Manila's highways, modeling *Ray-Ban* shades and Jockey underwear. You choose between the cinema version starring Gregory Peck smoking a corncob pipe, or the real thing. "I shall return," promised the North American general, still revered by many as the savior of the Filipino people, who eagerly awaited his return. As the old saying goes, this is how we got screwed, screwed real good. According to Nick Joaquin, "The Philippines spent three hundred years trapped in a convent, and fifty years in Hollywood . . ." Or was it four hundred years? No matter—there we were, seduced and abandoned in a confusion of identities, then granted our independence. Hollywood pretended to leave us alone. An African American saying also goes: "Nobody's *given* freedom." Being granted our independence meant we were owned all along by someone other than ourselves.

I step off the crowded plane onto the tarmac of the newly named Ninoy Aquino Airport. It is an interesting appropriation of the assassinated senator's name, don't you think? So I think, homesick for this birthplace, my country of supreme ironies and fatalistic humor, mountains of foul garbage and breathtaking women, men with the fierce faces of wolves and steamy streets teeming with abandoned children.

The widow of the assassinated senator is Corazon Aquino, now president of the Republic of the Philippines in a deft stroke of irony that left the world stunned by a sudden turn of events in February 1986. She is a beloved figure, a twentieth-century icon who has inherited a bundle of cultural contradictions and an economic nightmare in a lush paradise of corrupt, warring factions. In a Manila department store, one of the first souvenirs I buy my daughter is a rather homely Cory Aquino doll made out of brown cloth; the doll wears crooked wire eyeglasses, a straw shoulder bag, plastic high-heeled shoes, and Cory's signature yellow dress, with "I Love Cory" embroidered on the front. My daughter seems delighted with her doll, and the notion of a woman president.

Soldiers in disguise, patrol the countryside . . . Jungle not far away. So goes a song I once wrote, pungent as the remembered taste of mangoes overripe as my imagination, the memory of Manila the central character of the novel I am writing, the novel that brings me back to this torrid zone, my landscape haunted by ghosts and movie-lovers.

Nietzsche once said, "A joke is an epitaph for an emotion." Our laughter is pained, self-mocking. Blame it on *Rambo, Platoon,* and *Gidget Goes Hawaiian.* Cory Aquino has inherited a holy war, a class war, an amazing nation of people who've endured incredible poverty and spiritual loss with inherent humor and grace. Member of the ruling class, our pious president has also inherited an army of divided, greedy men. Yet probably no one will bother assassinating her, as icons are always useful.

My novel sits in its black folder, an obsession with me for over ten years. Home is now New York, but home in my heart will also always be Manila, and the rage of a marvelous culture stilled, confused, and diverted. Manila is my river of dreams choked with refuse, the refuse of refusal and denial, a denial more profound than the forbidding Catholic Church in all its ominous presence.

Blame it on the mambo and the cha-cha, a cardinal named Sin, and an adviser named Joker. Blame it on a former beauty queen with a puffy face bailed out of a jam by Doris Duke. Blame it on *Imeldification.* Blame it on children named Lourdes, Maria, Jesus, Carlos, Peachy, Baby, and Elvis. Blame it on the rich, who hang on in spite of everything. Blame it on the same people who are still in power, before Marcos, after Marcos. You name it, we'll blame it. The NPA, the vigilantes, rebel colonels nicknamed "Gringo," and a restless army plotting coups. Blame it on signs in nightclubs that warn: NO GUNS OR DRUGS.

Cards have been reshuffled, roles exchanged. The major players are the same, even those who suffered long years in prison under one regime, even those who died by the bullet. Aquino, Lopez, Cojuangco, Zobel, Laurel,

Enrile, etc. etc. Blood against blood, controlling the destinies of so many disparate tribes in these seven thousand islands.

I remember my grandmother, Lola Tecla, going for drives with me as a child down the boulevard along Manila Bay. The boulevard led to Luneta Park, where Rizal was executed by the Spanish colonizers; it was then known as Dewey Boulevard, after an American admiral. From history books forced on me as a child at a convent school run by strict nuns, I learned a lopsided history of myself, one full of lies and blank spaces, a history of omission— a colonial version of history which scorned the "savage" ways of precolonial Filipinos. In those days even our language was kept at a distance; Tagalog was studied in a course called "National Language" (sic), but it was English that was spoken, English that was preferred. Tagalog was a language used to address servants. I scorned myself, and it was only later, after I had left the Philippines to settle in the country of my oppressor, that I learned to confront my demons and reinvent my own history.

I am writing a novel set in contemporary Philippines. It is a journey back I am always taking. I leave one place for the other, welcomed and embraced by the family I have left—fathers and brothers and cousins and uncles and aunts. Childhood sweethearts, now with their own children. I am unable to stay. I make excuses, adhere to tight schedules. I return, only to depart, weeks or months later, depending on finances and the weather, obligations to my daughter, my art, my addiction to life in the belly of one particular beast. I am the other, the exile within, afflicted with permanent nostalgia for the mud. I return, only to depart: Manila, New York, San Francisco, Manila, Honolulu, Detroit, Manila, Guam, Hong Kong, Zamboanga, Manila, New York, San Francisco, Tokyo, Manila again, Manila again, Manila again.

ALL SHOOK UP

Chorus:

did you know?   oh-oh
did you know
there are no   oh-oh
no no bananas
in France?   uh-oh!
Josephine's skirt *was* imported.

c'est soir, les noires
uno, dos, tres
isa, dalawa, tatlo
ang tatay mong kalbo!
BON SOIR!

no good bananas in France?
absolutely. no, none.

did you know? uh-oh!
Otis Redding's new album
is not available?

death is death
recordings are forever . . .

    1.

"the king" is dead
but the real deal
has never been forgotten.

pulp songs stupefy some,
awaken others.
revolution's sentimental,
after all.

2.

confessions of an exotic exile:

"the definitive tango definitely took place
in Paris . . . years ago, strange fun at the Hotel Intrigue . . .
Little Algeria, the Latin Quarter—baby, couscous balungus,
every night!"

considered avant-garde,
the lovers partied hard . . . much too ahead
of their time.
they caressed & cajoled
their quivering prey:
"ménage à trois is so french,
doncha think?"

those were the days! love me tender,
fierce celebrations of the Western Empire's
decline. That fuckin' curse worked every time—
"you plundered the planet, darlin'!"

VIVA LAS VEGAS! Elvis puffs up.
love decays so sweetly.

confessions of an exotic exile:

"après le bain, en la grande cama de la
pequeño hotel room, the homely young musician
spreads her beautiful thick legs with reluctance.
a working-class Parisian, she is an experiment;
by the way, I never listen to Elvis."

a working-class Parisian,
she is an experiment; the exotic exile's

first and only white woman. Such thighs!
the panting lovers sigh:
"you taste like the moon! you smell like
new-mown hay!"
or a cow, shy & moony—
the exile thinks, bending to kiss
her other lover.

    3.

"the king" is dead
but the plagues
are now upon us.

build a fort
make soup
set fires
only pack what you can carry!

we're all shook up.

Paris is a stinking racist town
Argentinians refuse to serve
us steaks we don't even want—
WE WANT CAFE! CAFE OLE! THAT'S
ALL WE WANT YOU NEO-NAZI EXPATRIATES!

arbitrary & arrogant
gendarmes demand
i.d.
in crowded subway stations

we whip out passports
trembling with rage.
we dream of singing
right up in their faces

but we know better.
you know the rap—
"je suis une ugly américaine, bébé!"
hiss that secret litany,
protection against evil spirits:

little richard,
fats domino,
chuck berry
otis uno
otis dos
otis tres,
fontella bass.
we're international citizens,
you understand.

    4.

otis blackwell
always said
you were a smart girl
(better call him up).

another otis,
sugar.
otis,
some name
otis
elvis's favorite flame
of black r & b mythology.

i tell you
that was many years ago
paris still a racist town
but the subways are licked clean
by Algerians & Viet Cong

glass cases along tiled walls
displaying leftovers from the Louvre.

Manila's racist too—
don't let them tell you different.
it's always "mestizo" this
or "Amerikano" that—
the anxious watch for dark skin
and aboriginal noses.

what do we do?
too many rotten Spaniards
in the stew—
the Elvis Presley of the Philippines
a half-breed pretty boy
1959   1963   1965
now passé
Eddie Mesa is alive & well
in Brooklyn
Otis Blackwell
too
somewhere in Brooklyn
(better call him up)
he always said
you were smart

I'm shook up
I'm in love
I'm in love

1956   1957   1959
Cora Aguilar
so tough,
swiveling her hips
just so

the right snarl
on her pouty lips

Cora cuts her long black hair
into a perfect polynesian pompadour
lacquered with cheap pomade,
her dazzling rooster's crown.

far more perverse & memorable
she is the "female elvis of the philippines"
more man than Eddie
more Elvis than Elvis
swollen & immortalized
on his bed of plastic roses.

divine pulp
& corny love
the nasty drawl
& innuendo
of your delicious poetry
Otis

she masters phonetically
and spits out with passion
swaggering behind
her suggestive guitar
Cora
all brown and muscular blaze
sinuous onstage—
a natural.
her guitar was the real thing,
electric

Otis.

5.

is an old rule,
some say.
"you got to be hungry
to hip hop."
you got to be hungry
to rock 'n' roll.
everything else
pales by comparison.

elvis—
the same rules apply.

who wrote the song?
who gets the credit?
what's in a name
but the world—Elvis

"el vis" so pseudo-french
so possibly spanish—the sound of it bastardized,
redneck tender and cruel.
no big deal in a racist world

where art is art
in spite.

TRAVELS IN THE COMBAT ZONE

Where is my fine and feathery friend, that poised and gentle creature? Last seen in the combat zone, mulling over a better-than-average meal in an all-night cafe.

She's in a trance, dreaming of catching the mystery train back to the tropical landscape of her memories. The waiter presents her with a fortune cookie. She cracks it open; there's nothing inside. What's this? An omen, no doubt. She is terrified. She's a North American casualty, unsure of her real identity, if a "real" identity even exists.

The waiter shrugs. He's seen it all before. "No news is good news," he announces cheerfully.

"I saw a dead man this morning—sitting up in a doorway, like he was taking a nap," she tells the waiter. "I saw a man on the subway with no eyes. I saw a woman kicked through the turnstile. I saw the same woman run screaming through the subway cars, begging for help. I saw the man follow her with a confident look on his face. I saw the Queen of the Nile push a shopping cart filled with bottles up 147th Street and Broadway. I saw a man with blue-black skin shave off his invisible beard with a knife, using only the sky for his mirror . . ."

The waiter presents her with a bill. "When you gotta go, you gotta go," he says.

Where is my fine and feathery friend, that poised and gentle creature? Last seen in flight from the plague-ridden cities of the combat zone, clutching a list of the dead and dying in her hand. Last seen fighting off despair in an all-night cafe, where old Chinese men sip black tea at three in the morning. She sits at her table long after the bill has been paid, long after the waiter has retreated into the sanctity of his own impatient dreams.

In the landscape of her memory, she's in Zamboanga—in an open market surrounded by grinning women. They call out her name, holding up bolts of cloth and elephants carved out of seashells. "I am one of you," she tells the women. "I am not an American, I have no money." The women mock her with laughter; they don't believe her lies. She's a perpetual foreigner, at home in airports—an exile within, homesick for what she can only imagine.

Against a backdrop of billboards advertising DUNKIN' DONUTS and KIKKOMAN SOY SAUCE, gold-and-white mosques are built next to rice fields. Where is my fine and feathery friend? She's in a dusty paradise, walking slowly on an unpaved road. Suddenly, the sky turns black, the burning sun eclipsed by a flock of black swans in flight. Swans of mourning, their bleak formation hovers over her in a graceful arc, a trail of sorrow which vanishes in an instant. An omen, no doubt. She can hear the waiter in the North American cafe warning her: "You can run, but you can't hide."

No longer terrified, she clutches the list of the dead and dying in her hand. She will commit their names to memory, she will remember to stay angry.

The sun is blazing. She keeps walking.

TEENYTOWN

Once, there was a teeny tiny town ruled by a teeny tiny mayor. Teeny tiny goats roamed abandoned buildings and teeny tiny parking lots strewn with rubble and teeny tiny garbage. Everyone was always hungry. You could see it in their tiny anxious faces and their teeny tiny eyes. (Including the mayor.)

Teeny tiny boys and teeny tiny girls lived in teeny tiny mousetraps and ate cheese. Five days a week, some of the more ambitious ones went to teeny tiny offices, smoked teeny tiny cigarettes, and slaved at part-time jobs where they never got to use their tiny minds. No small matter. Two days a week, all the other teeny tiny boys and teeny tiny girls dreamed teeny tiny dreams which they diligently recorded on teeny tiny scraps of paper. A slight ripple on the dim horizon. A faint explosion from a distance. But a shit-stirrer, nevertheless.

To squelch rumors and prevent exotic and desirable aliens from ruining the neighborhood, the wily, teeny tiny mayor called town meetings on a monthly basis. Everyone was encouraged to complain at the same time, and when the noise died down, everyone always went away feeling much better.

At teeny tiny parties where no one was invited, teeny tiny poets compared dreams. They were always amazed at the similarities in length and content; of course, it had been the same old teeny tiny town ever since anyone could remember—and they liked their dreams that way. When the party was over (when the party was over), the teeny tiny poets fed their scraps to the ravenous, rabid goats who bleated, barked, and wailed in the squalid alleys outside holes they called "windows."

Days and nights passed in dissonant, familiar harmony—teeny tiny sunless days that turned without warning into terrifying moonless nights that seemed to go on forever. The teeny tiny townsfolk took small comfort in promising each other that teeny tiny terrors could always be kept at bay. You know how the song goes, the old song, the one about dreaming: "You can be, if I can be . . ."

SKULL FOOD

THE FATHER:

You what?
NO.
Don't do that.
Behave yourself.
Why are you eating that yogurt? After this, why don't we go
somewhere and get something for you to eat.
Some real food.
That's what you need.
PUT THAT YOGURT AWAY.
Do you have any food in the house?
Any real food? Is George
cooking for you tonight?
But you can't be sure, can you?
After we get out of here, I'll get you
some real food.
You need some real cooked food,
that's what you need.

THE SON:

*I've been coming here for months. When I come, I bring my Caravaggio. I
live in my Caravaggio. Then I bring my Van Gogh. The doctor loves Van
Gogh. Then he looks at my book. You know my folks can't handle me being
sick like this, being sick like this, being sick. You've got to put a bucket next
to my bed. DAD. I am doing my best. I am doing the best I can. Dad, I
keep promising him I'm going to Fort Washington to see Mary. Paul's scared
to come near me, this is not my fault. You know you can buy tons of
marijuana, Paul told me. He's walking on his way to work, and there's all
these people. You know Paul and I used to take acid together, yeah when we
were fifteen didn't I tell you about it? Don't you think I'm doing good for
being damaged? I've got to get to Fort Washington soon and see Paul and
Mary I promised them. I've done everything to help myself, this isn't my fault.
I'm going to lie down. I'm going to lie down on the floor. I've been here for
hours . . .*

SKULL FOOD #2

This city is demented.
There are big holes in my head.
Sunshine works in Times Square
Tamboo drives buses for the MTA
takes my money
tells me
you look pretty too.

Thank you,
I say.
There are big holes in my head.
My memory has become too selective
and I hate this city.

Sunshine meets her
man Psycho
in the park.
Sunshine is a beauty
thick ankles
albino ringlets
a nose for trouble.
I remember hundreds of
fifteen-year-old girls named Sunshine
in 1967.

Sunshine
I call out
from the back of the bus
is that you?
She doesn't hear me
of course
she only has eyes
for her main Psycho
but Tamboo hears me
though I'm mute.

"Say, can I eat your pussy
for ten bucks and a bag of groceries?"
RIGHT NOW?
I am amazed.

Sunshine
gets off the bus
ahead of me
disappears into the dark
city park
calling to her drifter lover:
"Psycho! Hey Psycho!"
She sings.
De de dementia
I whisper back,
half in love
with her melody.

It's the same girl
twenty-two years ago
but now the escalator works
in the underwater train station.
The city's submerged,
but everyone asks me for directions.
How should I know where you're going?
I'm from New York.
Liar.
You smell like you're from Oakland.

De de dementia
Ferdinand Marcos sits
two rows ahead of me
and at the next stop
Imelda rushes in.

How would you want to be remembered?
How would you want to be?
How would you want?
Dan Ackroyd interviews
Jose Napoleon Duarte of El Salvador
animal torture
animal abuse
animal neglect
in Norte America

For us
it's not a question
of slaughter
it's a question of torture.
I've got big holes
in my head
big lapses
and polka dots
of memory.

As for me,
Duarte replies,
I am a fighter
who confronts
destiny.

VULVA OPERETTA

In my dream, sweaters are referred to as "vulvas." They are mohair or angora wool, of a soft, warm texture—gray, bleeding into a deep, rich red—similar to Japanese raku pottery.

We wear these sweaters.

People say things like: "It's hot. I think I'll take my vulva off."
Or: "It's cold. I think I'll put my vulva on."

Foppish men and women ask each other questions like: "Where did you get that BEE-YOO-TEE-FULL vulva?"
Followed by remarks like:
"I think I'm gonna put my vulva in the closet. I think I'm gonna put my vulva in the closet. I think I'm gonna put my vulva. I'm gonna. My vulva. I."

CARNAL

Third day of my visit to San Francisco, I am overwhelmed by another attack of arbitrary passion. I stand counting pennies, waiting for the J-Church streetcar to make its appearance on Eighteenth Street and Guerrero.

Right across the tracks I see the flat where my poet used to live. Crab soup, fried plantains, crushed garlic in peanut oil. Fireworks, betrayal, constant hunger. The poet and I knew how to play.

I have just visited a filmmaker who once made a movie of me standing motionless and droning my rhymes to a restless audience. "A rapper before your time," the melancholy filmmaker remarks, with some sadness. I rush out of the filmmaker's apartment, pretend I have an appointment.

And this horniness that keeps getting in the way . . . And this hunger! I'd brought the filmmaker a box of manju from Japantown. Pink beancakes. Bubblegum pink, sticky sweet. We ate and watched the grainy movie in silence. If only the poet were still in the country, if only my mother . . .

Her is the name I've given myself on this particular visit. Small *h*, almost invisible. I don't mind seeming to disappear in this way; it is the voyeur in me incited to rebellion, the living poet ghost who joins my mother fading into the furniture.

Actually, if you ask me—I'm always starving. Even in New York. But this ritualistic, Catholic horniness is even worse than hunger—and seems peculiar to San Francisco. It is arbitrary, a void—I can't name a single person or object of desire . . . A desire invoked by nostalgia—for perfume, food, the clanging of the J-Church streetcar . . . It envelops me as soon as I disembark from the airplane. Into a dark tunnel, and out into the murky bay. In little crazy ways at first, desire swoops and buzzes, much like flies used to descend on an ex-lover.

Unlike the poet, the doctor was stupid and beautiful, with a deadly fear of flies. There were plenty of reasons for me to leave him, but the flies and stupidity were the main thing. He was studying to be a surgeon, determined to rise up out of the depths of his neighborhood. He loved California, and said he never wanted to leave it. I often said, with a hint of real affection in my voice: "If you could've performed neurosurgery with your tongue or penis, you would've been brilliant."

Instead, he killed flies every chance he got. In intimate, pseudo-French bistros at the foot of Nob Hill. In barbecue joints on Fillmore and Divisadero. In the emergency rooms of Oakland hospitals. In my shiny blue car. He swatted the little creatures with rolled-up issues of *Time, Newsweek, Black Enterprise.*

I read to him from Emily Dickinson: "A Fly Buzzed When I Died." It was my favorite Dickinson poem, but he didn't care. "Very nice," he muttered, as he kept on killing. Swoosh, swoosh. Swat. Goddammit.

"A bed is for sleeping," I told him, showing him the door. I handed him his chic doctor's bag, his genuine antique alligator satchel—the one bulging with scalpels, stethoscopes, vials of Dilaudid, liquid cocaine, and transparent Band-Aids.

What to do? My mother was slipping, inch by inch, into the furniture.

"No one's as good-looking as they used to be," she sighed, shrinking slowly into her own skin. It was hard to watch.

As my mother's only daughter, I found it impossible to stay. It was time to abandon a sinking ship and all the pretty boys trying to swim. The doctor took me to the airport in his burnt-orange Renault. Asked me to marry him. "I'd rather die," I confessed.

Years later, my mother still hung on by sheer stockings. Everyone else I knew curled upward in spirals or sent coded messages from distant clinics; outpatients like my mother, hanging on by the skin of their canines . . . so quiet in their madness as they swung from dusty chandeliers, dogs, dogs all my memories a melancholy snarl.

And there are more dying than I care to think about, so many I stop dreaming and keep grocery-shopping, stocking my shelves with . . .

My mother sleeps through the next big earthquake.

Time to clean house. I've obviously stayed away too long and decide to save her. She stares at me with cloudy eyes, calls me by my cousin's name. Another time she says, "You know, you remind me of my daughter."

I hire a live-in nurse to catch my mother before she falls—more and more, she's in danger of falling, forgetting to breathe, being forgotten. I count my pennies; there's just enough. My dreams fade slowly in, fragments of color at first, puddles of mud oozing back into my landscape.

The nurse calls himself Bienvenido—he's a weightlifter with wisdom, works out all his urges and desires in the gym. Bench-presses to euphoria, until there's nothing left. I wish I could learn from him, sweat out my nonspecific longings while toning up my thighs. *Just look at him glow . . .* He sweats, makes jokes, is gentle with my mother—cooks vinegary pork adobo and forces her to eat. "Remember," he whispers to the old woman, "isn't it delicious?"

I learn to feed her with a spoon, like a baby—
I learn to feed her with my hands—
whatever it takes I do, returning over and over again
to this city of too much memory. She makes faces and complains
in a wan voice, "But there is no flavor." Her final questions to me
are: "But where have you been? Why are you so late?"

San Francisco, CALAFIA. I'm home, in spite of myself. This is the city where I have lived half my life. I use up my nickels and dimes, make no connections. Wanna eat dinner together? Anybody home? The poets work for the post office now, or drive buses, or brag about the cultural impact of their roles as arts administrators. They worry about their children's impoverished education, they argue about censorship and funding, they are bored with being labeled multi-anything; they've grown too fat or too thin, their hair is falling out, their gums bleed.

The only one I still trust warns me: "You can't keep smelling doo-doo everywhere you go."

I long for an authentic, Mission District burrito. Starchy and soothing. The kind you buy under a freeway overpass, the kind that used to cost only $2.95 but now has tripled in price. Rice, beans, barbecued beef, guacamole and jalapeño peppers, fiery kisses. *Sour cream.* A fresh, fat tortilla rolled up like a hot white towel. A cheap, forbidden meal in itself. *Flesh.*

LOS GABRIELES

*The journey begins, a journey of dreams and seductive memories, a journey
of doorways and detectives, a journey of streets with names like* Paseo de
Recoletos, *and* Street of the Moors, *and towns with the names* Ronda, Jaen,
Granada . . .

The painted women of La Fiesta de Paloma dance their dainty, erotic
sevillanas. *I am smothered by the scent of their sweat and sandalwood perfume.*
"Daughter," they greet me gaily. "Join us and remember."

*Pepa, my cigar-box señorita, wakes from her fitful sleep. She strolls down
the aisle of our 747. We are on our way to Madrid, via Ireland. I stare at
tinted photographs. My mother in a flowered dress, her head tilted. Then
another one, faded black and white: 1958, she is in San Sebastian with my
father. Next to them stands a midget in a sharkskin suit.*

*Pepa, my bizarre beauty. Big lioness head, dwarfish body, smoky-blue
eyelids, spiteful mouth. Sleepwalking down the aisle of our crowded 747, she
is a young girl cursed with the face of a widow, a young girl born with a
scowling face.*

*In her lilting, scornful Spanish, she speaks to an old man in a rumpled
white suit. I am an insomniac on airplanes. I pretend I know everything there
is to know about the old man and the scowling señorita. He is Pepa's abuelito,
and this is his last trip home. On his lap lies a battered briefcase, inscribed
"Transamazonia."*

As soon as we disembark in Madrid, I lose sight of Pepa and Abuelito.
The airport is teeming with exhausted travelers and hysterical relatives. Kisses
are exchanged—boisterous greetings, hugs, more kisses. Children are wor-
shiped in this country—lifted high up in the air, made to laugh, held close.
Men and women weep with joy and chain-smoke elegantly, oblivious to
death. They smoke and smoke, they gesture emphatically with their cigarettes
and fans, they talk in their language of hands and anguished music. I reek
of tobacco, enveloped in a delicious haze of flowers and flying kisses.

*"And so I danced and danced," my mother told me, eyes bright with
memory. "It was your father's birthday, and I hired the trio of flamenco
guitarists. I danced on wooden tabletops, I danced even after the musicians
fell back from utter exhaustion, I danced until the sun came up and only
Candelas was left with her voice cracked, but still singing . . ."*

An Irish expatriate tells me the Spanish and the Irish possess kindred souls. It is the same, he tells me—the penchant for melancholy, exuberant sensuality, and anguish. Again, that word which explains so much and which I love. The expatriate defines the anguish behind the smile as Lorca's persona. It is also inherently Filipino, I inform him, but he doesn't seem to be listening. We get drunker as we go from bar to bar; we take drunken photographs of each other. I tell him about my mother and the gypsy she met named *Candelas de los Reyes*.

The expatriate pities me, he pities all Americans, especially New Yorkers and their obsession with money. "You must come back to Spain," he tells me sternly when I say goodbye. "You must investigate your roots!"

Roots? I want to laugh and say: "I was born in the Philippines, I'm a quincentennial bastard, my roots are dubious."

But the night is old and he has slipped into the dark.

I visit a very old woman named Concha who lives in the famous Neighborhood of Fascists. Concha the widow, *viuda de los Blah Blahs*. She's got a ten-room apartment, very grand, with the works—balcony, oil paintings of homely ancestors, piano with fringed shawl, heavy velvet drapes. She was born in Manila and almost married my father, but settled for a *real* Spaniard instead. The Pope, she informs me over homemade gazpacho, is in Spain. Would I like to stay after dinner and watch him say mass on television?

"Like most Catholic women, Concha dreams of fucking the Pope," my mother used to say.

This is the story of threes. Three friends named Luis, Renee, and Jessica drive to the province of Malaga under a full moon. The landscape is pure Goya—arid and awesome, or so Jessica thinks, half awake and dreaming. The scent of olives permeates the air. Every third day on this journey south, they meet three different Gabriels. One has the face of vice—vacant and beautiful.

My dreams are unfolding triptychs, haunted by archangels and goats.

Luis and Renee attempt to dissect my nightmares; we lounge on our beds by the ocean, staring at the black sky. "It's a painting you saw in a museum," Renee assures me. "Something you've buried and forgotten."

"Tres tristes terrible," Luis sighs. I go back to sleep.

At a cafe, three gypsy women approach us. Two are barefoot and one is suckling an infant. They are too proud and fierce to beg; they demand food and money. We give them bread, what's left of a potato omelette, and a bottle of water.

El Museo Chicote. "Your mother and father must've come here," Luis says. "This is where Ava came with her bullfighter Dominguin." We slip into a booth to speculate on the ancient waiters and eavesdrop. Three men sit in the booth in front of us. One stabs the air with his cigar. "This is the best thing in my life," the old man declares to no one in particular. "I will die if I no longer have my cigar." It is ninety degrees outside and we are wilting, but the old man is impeccable down to his two-tone shoes. I imagine him to be the widow Concha's resurrected husband, Hector. I imagine him to be my father's father, Federico. In the soothing green afternoon gloom of the Museo Chicote, the forbidding man preens for our benefit and barks at his friends.

Down the street from the Chicote, we see a sign which I interpret as the Cafeteria for Masochists. Delighted, I imagine a bustling restaurant where the food is always bad, and one could go at any time of day or night to get shouted at, slapped around, or simply ignored.

At the Plaza de Toros, a bull is stabbed repeatedly by men on horses but keeps charging the young matador. Luis refuses to watch this gory spectacle and leaves us to fend for ourselves. The matador is gored in the thigh and carried away. The men on horses return to circle the bull and finish him off. *Something my mother described to me once. Was it Dominguin or El Cordobes she went to see in this very place? Ava Gardner was sitting nearby in a special box reserved for celebrities, with a bunch of Hollywood types. "She had a foul mouth," my mother said, with admiration.* The crowd cheers the dying bull. It is too long and festive a death, much longer than I expected. Blood and dust are everywhere.

———

In a tavern called Los Gabrieles, I recuperate from a night without dreams. I study another black-and-white photograph. Did my father take this picture? My mother sticks her tongue out at the camera, posing in a saucy halter dress, catlike sunglasses shielding her eyes. Again, the midget stands next to her, spiffy and solemn in that same sharkskin suit. Only his tie is different. What was his name? He followed her everywhere, she told me once. My mother laughed and laughed as she told me the story. Standing off in the background to the right is another woman. Darker, younger, and more beautiful than my mother, the gypsy Candelas averts her gaze from the camera. Was she in love with my mother too? My father didn't seem to mind, my mother said. All that attention, all those people, such melancholy music.

Free of guilt, pursued by phantoms from the not-too-distant past, I follow telltale signs and note the omens as I go, lured by the somnambulant invocations of Lorca, lured by the serenade of effeminate, deadly gangsters with slicked-back hair, lured by the furious specter of Ava Gardner in a halter dress, cussing out an even drunker Ernest Hemingway, lured by the music of fans snapping open and shut, lured by the anguished faces of doomed bullfighters in their suits of lights.

ESSENTIALS
of Accounts Payable

Essentials Series

The Essentials Series was created for busy business advisory and corporate professionals. The books in this series were designed so that these busy professionals can quickly acquire knowledge and skills in core business areas.

Each book provides need-to-have fundamentals for those professionals who must

- Get up to speed quickly, because they have been promoted to a new position or have broadened their responsibility scope

- Manage a new functional area

- Brush up on new developments in their area of responsibility

- Add more value to their company or clients

Other books in this series include the following:

Essentials of Capacity Management,
by Reginald Tomas Yu-Lee

Essentials of Corporate Performance Management,
by Franklin Plewa and George Friedlob

Essentials of CRM: A Guide to Customer Relationship Management,
by Bryan P. Bergeron

For more information on any of these titles, please visit www.wiley.com.

ESSENTIALS

of Accounts Payable

Mary S. Schaeffer

Editor of
IOMA's *Report on Managing Accounts Payable*

WILEY

Copyright © 2002 by John Wiley & Sons, Inc. All rights reserved.

Published by John Wiley & Sons, Inc., New York.
Published simultaneously in Canada.

This publication is designed to provide accurate and authoritative information in regard to the subject matter covered. It is sold with the understanding that the publisher is not engaged in rendering legal, accounting, or other professional services. If legal advice or other expert assistance is required, the services of a competent professional person should be sought.

Library of Congress Cataloging-in-Publication Data

Schaeffer, Mary S.
   Essentials of accounts payable / Mary S. Schaeffer.
     p. cm. -- (Essentials series)
   Includes index.
   ISBN 0-471-20308-4 (pbk. : alk. paper)
    1. Accounts payable. I. Title. II. Series.

HF5681.A27 S33 2002
657'.74--dc21   2001046538

10 9 8 7 6 5 4 3 2 1

for my wonderful, talented son
Benedict Ronald Ludwig

Preface

A common misconception about accounts payable is that it is not very complicated or sophisticated. "What's the big deal?" the skeptics ask. "The accounts payable department just pays bills." Anyone who knows anything at all about accounts payable knows that it *is* a big deal. When the accounts payable function is not handled correctly, duplicate payments abound, check fraud thrives, costs skyrocket, discounts are lost, vendor relations falter, and certain state regulatory agencies may arrive more frequently to perform an audit (unclaimed property and/or sales and use tax). And that is just the tip of the iceberg.

Unfortunately, some accounts payable associates have done a poor job in educating their bosses about the complexities of the accounts payable functions and responsibilities, and the business and financial press has virtually ignored their contributions, as well. The purpose of this book is not only to change those perceptions, but also to provide a solid foundation for those just starting out in accounts payable. Because we've included some brand new areas, including Extensible Markup Language (XML), the Internet, imaging, and more, more seasoned accounts payable professionals will benefit from the book as well.

The book begins with a quick review of the accounting and bookkeeping functions as they relate to accounts payable. It also shows how accounts payable information fits into the big picture and provides some of the foundation information for the company's financial reports.

Because virtually all accounts payable departments pay bills, the chapter on invoice handling is quite thorough in explaining how

corporate America handles its invoices and writes its checks. These once-routine chores have now become quite complicated, and if they are not handled correctly, problems will abound. Best practices in both areas are discussed.

Despite accounts payable associates' best efforts, inevitably some invoices need to be processed outside the normal time frame. Exception handling and the Rush check issues are examined in detail. Although it is not possible to completely eliminate Rush checks (Wouldn't that be wonderful!) there are ways to limit the numbers of these annoying items and also limit the problems they create.

Third-party audit firms continue to thrive, collecting duplicate and other types of erroneous payments made by companies everywhere. If duplicate payments were prevented before they occurred, companies would not support this thriving business. The chapter on preventing duplicate payments recommends the best ways to do this. In fact, it contains tips from several well-regarded professionals who make a rather attractive living chasing the duplicate payments made by companies of all sizes.

One of the biggest causes of duplicate payments are payments made when the original invoice cannot be found. Although refusing to pay is not a reasonable approach—after all, mail does get lost—there are ways to pay from a copy without greatly increasing the odds of making a duplicate payment. Chapter 6 looks at the best ways to pay a lost or missing invoice without creating additional problems, that is, making a duplicate payment.

The purchasing–accounts payable relationships in many companies leaves much to be desired. These two departments often do not get along. This is unfortunate because they both benefit from smoother relations. Chapter 7 suggests ways that the accounts payable associate can make this tenuous relationship work even under the most trying of circumstances.

Few companies give their master vendor file the attention or care it deserves. We take a look at the statistics regarding how corporate America treats its master vendor files, the problems that can arise from inadequate care and controls, and ways that companies can best maintain their master vendor file.

Early-payment discounts are near and dear to the hearts of many corporate controllers. It falls on the accounts payable department to ensure that all the discounts are taken. In fact, one accounts payable professional says the only way to get the controller at his company angry is to lose one of these discounts. Chapter 9 explains how these discounts work, why they are so important, and who takes them and under what circumstances. It also examines the deduction issue and the effects of taking unauthorized discounts. This chapter suggests how to work best with suppliers when taking discounts and lists deductions that might be unfamiliar.

Handling travel and entertainment (T & E) expense reports typically falls under the accounts payable umbrella. For many, it is a thankless function that is time consuming and adds little value. Chapter 10 evaluates current processes and recommends ways to make the traditional function operate just a little smoother.

T & E is one of the areas in accounts payable that is experiencing much change. As hotels look for ways to increase income, they have developed some unique ways to increase revenue without appearing to be raising their prices. They are identified so accounts payable associates will be aware of them when they encounter them. Similarly, phone charges have gotten out of hand, and there are ways to fight these excess fees.

Finally, the chapter on T & E in the twenty-first century takes a look at the phenomenon of cell phones and how these instruments are changing the corporate landscape. It also reviews current cell-phone policies and discusses how companies are paying for this new device.

Electronic Data Interchange (EDI) had been around since the late 1970s. Although current projections for future growth are no longer off the charts (thanks to the Internet and XML), most experts believe that this stodgy electronic methodology will be with us for years to come. Thus, most accounts payable associates will need to have some basic understanding of EDI and its impact and use in accounts payable. Chapter 12 addresses these and other related EDI topics.

The Internet has invaded accounts payable departments everywhere, radically changing the way many perform their day-to-day functions. Chapter 13 takes a look at how companies are using the Internet in accounts payable. It also contains many Web site addresses that illustrate many of the points.

XML is revolutionizing the way companies report and share data. Chapter 14 provides accounts payable associates with the basic XML information they need to understand the process and its impact on accounts payable. This is an area that will grow rapidly in the next few years, and it is important that accounts payable associates get in on the ground floor.

P-cards, also referred to as corporate procurement cards, have made a major impact on accounts payable, drastically reducing the number of invoices for companies that make effective use of these cards. Chapter 15 reviews some of the basic data related to p-cards and shares some advice for getting the most out of them. It also evaluates the types of data currently available for general ledger updates.

Fraud, especially check fraud, is a growing problem in corporate America. Companies that do not understand the dynamics and learn how to protect themselves will find themselves victims of the unscrupulous. Chapter 16 reviews some of the more common types of accounts payable fraud and offers suggestions for companies that wish to protect themselves against hucksters looking to take their money.

A number of new technologies, including imaging, interactive voice response units, encryption, and digital signatures are being used very effectively in accounts payable departments. Chapter 17 discusses these technologies and presents a number of case studies that demonstrate how real-life companies have integrated these approaches into their accounts payable departments.

Sales and use tax, escheat, evaluated receipt settlement, benchmarking, audit firms, value-added tax (VAT) recapture, and 1099s are just a few of the other issues handled in a growing number of accounts payable departments across the country. These and other high-level accounts payable concepts are explained in Chapter 18.

Eventually, after working in accounts payable for a number of years, most accounts payable professionals will be given the opportunity to manage a group, first perhaps as a supervisor and then eventually as the manager of the department. Chapter 19 provides an overview of the skills and requirements for that challenging position.

Accounts payable is changing rapidly. The skills and education needed to survive in the past simply won't cut the mustard. Chapter 20 takes a look at the brave new accounts payable world in the twenty-first century and tells our readers what to expect and what they need to do to prepare to be an accounts payable survivor in the next decade.

Good luck—it will be a challenging, yet exciting time.

Acknowledgments

Throughout this book you will see mention of a company called IOMA (Institute of Management and Administration), a New York City–based newsletter publisher. It is the company I work for and is the publisher of, among many others, a monthly newsletter called *IOMA's Report on Managing Accounts Payable*. In my position as editor of this publication since 1995, I have had the opportunity to interact with hundreds of accounts payable professionals and the vendors who provide accounts payable services. It is from these interactions that I am able to develop new material—not only for the newsletter each month, but also for this book.

When we started the newsletter, there was very little published on the topic. IOMA stepped in to fill this void and today those who want information can find it, not only in the newsletter but also in our books, on the Internet, and at conferences. IOMA also produces valuable research for the accounts payable profession. Throughout this book, you will find a smattering of benchmarking statistics. These come from a biannual survey of more than 900 responses from the accounts payable community. They provide a snapshot view of what is being done in today's accounts payable departments in companies of all sizes and in all industries. They are presented to guide the reader toward current best practices.

Without the backing from IOMA in the accounts payable research, neither the newsletter nor the books nor the valuable benchmarking information would be possible.

Contents

Contents

CHAPTER 1

Some Accounting and Bookkeeping Basics

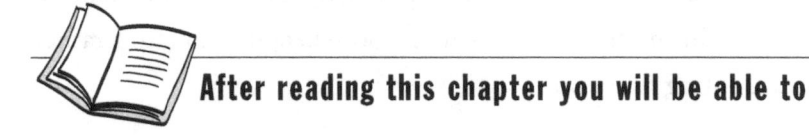

After reading this chapter you will be able to

- Understand accounting and bookkeeping as they affect accounts payable and where accounts payable fits into the big financial picture
- Recommend good internal controls for accounts payable policies and procedures
- Avoid common accounting mistakes
- Use common accounting and bookkeeping terminology when discussing accounts payable related issues

In order to fully understand why matters are handled the way they are in accounts payable, it is a good idea to know a little about accounting and bookkeeping. Much of what is done in the department has strong accounting implications. By understanding basic accounting and bookkeeping as they relate to accounts payable, associates will instinctively understand the reasoning behind certain actions. They will also be able to avoid common mistakes that arise from a lack of understanding of the difference between debits and credits. Remember, accounts payable is a lot more than just paying bills.

What Is Bookkeeping?

Bookkeeping is the first step—the recording of all activities and transactions. It is the first step in the accounting cycle. In fact, some of the processes that are commonly referred to as accounting are actually bookkeeping. For example, balancing a checking account statement is actually a bookkeeping function, although it usually falls under the accounting umbrella. Many consider gathering backup information, such as is done in the three-way match, a bookkeeping function rather than an accounting function.

What Is Accounts Payable?

The *accounts payable* figure on the financial statements of any company represents the company's unpaid bills. It is the money owed by the company to its suppliers and other creditors. Accountants break the money owed by the company into two groups: *current liabilities* and *long-term liabilities.* They consider accounts payable a current liability. Current liabilities are those obligations that must be paid in less than one year. Other current liabilities might include taxes and salaries. These are separated from items such as long-term debt repayments that have longer due dates.

Is It Bookkeeping or Is It Accounting?

Don't waste a lot of time trying to determine whether something is an accounting function or a bookkeeping function—it doesn't really matter what you call it. To use an old Shakespearean quote, "A rose by any other name smells just as sweet...." As long as the function is performed correctly, its classification really doesn't matter.

Liabilities

A company's *liabilities* are its obligations. They include items such as bank loans, money owed to vendors (also known as accounts payable),

employees' salary, and any other expenses that might arise from the business operations. Typically, liabilities are broken into two categories: short term and long term. Short-term liabilities are typically those that must be paid in the next 12 months while long-term liabilities are those that are due after 12 months.

Thus, accounts payable is almost always a short-term liability. Interest on bank loans is typically considered short term while the principal repayment is classified as long term—until the year they become due.

Assets

The opposite of a company's liabilities are its *assets*. One hopes to work for a company whose assets exceed its liabilities. For accounting purposes, the company's assets are everything it owns. These, too, are broken down into two groups: current and fixed. *Current assets* are items that can be converted to cash rather easily. They include accounts receivable, inventory, and prepaid rent.

Fixed assets are items that are generally not held for resale purposes. This includes items like machinery, real estate, and furniture. Although it is true that most of these items could be turned into cash, this could not be done easily, so they are not considered current or liquid assets.

When analysts look at assets and liabilities, they not only study the relationship between the two, but also look closely at the comparison between current assets and current liabilities. If current liabilities exceed current assets, there can be serious financial consequences.

Expenses

Expenses can be classified several ways:

- *Pre-paid expenses* are monies paid in advance for a product or service. They are actually considered an asset until the expense is incurred. The most common pre-paid expense is insurance, which can sometimes be paid as infrequently as annually.

3

- *Current expenses* are expenses that have been incurred (and thus are considered a liability) and will be paid within the current period.
- *Accrued expenses* are expenses that a company has incurred but has not been billed for yet. Many companies accrue accounts payable expenses at the end of each month and virtually all accrue them at the end of the fiscal year for financial statement purposes. It is not uncommon to hear accounts payable associates talking about doing accruals at month end.

Using accruals allows the company's executives and bankers and—in the case of public companies, its investors—to have a realistic picture of the company's financial position and obligations. These numbers can be especially meaningful in the case of those companies that employ payment timing or stretching practices.

Accruals

Accounts payable associates will sometimes indicate that they are doing accruals. As just indicated, this is usually done at the end of some sort of a reporting period. Typically, what the associate is doing is calculating the expenses that have been incurred but for which no invoice has been received. This is not done in every accounts payable department but is performed in many.

Chart of Accounts

When accounts payable associates record information, they must have a category with which to associate the information. To do this, most companies assign a reference number or an account number. The list of all these account numbers is called the *chart of accounts*. It is sometimes referred to as the index of the general ledger. Each company develops its own chart of accounts. The number of accounts is limited only by

the imagination of the company's accountant and the company's detail requirements. There can be as few as 50 accounts for a small company, or many more. A few nimble accounts payable associates end up knowing the account codes of their most common transactions by heart and rarely refer to the chart of accounts.

General Ledger

The entire chart of accounts for a particular company and all its related information is called the *general ledger.* It is referred to in accounting literature as the GL, sometimes written G/L. It is the information pertaining to the actual accounts, and great care is given to who has access to it and who can update information in it. In fact, there is often great debate about outside information being fed directly into the G/L. Some auditors recommend against this unless strong controls monitor the outside input. Others prefer these updates be done to some sort of a suspense account, with the company doing the update after the outside information has been reviewed.

Debit and Credit Memos

This area sometimes leads to confusion in accounts payable—the results of which can be pretty strange. A *debit memo* is a convenient way of letting a creditor know that the company wants to debit the vendor's accounts payable account for a return, a price reduction, or some other matter. In an ideal situation, the creditor will confirm this reduction by issuing a *credit memo.* As you might have guessed by now, reality is not always so smooth. Sometimes, the supplier will realize it was overpaid and issue a credit memo—which it doesn't give to the customer. The credit balance sits on the account. Eventually, the vendor may simply write off the amount, never giving it to the customer.

How General Ledger Information Is Used

In addition to special company management reports that are produced from the G/L, most companies produce three very important types of reports that are used by lenders, outside investors, and others considering lending money to a corporation.

1 *Balance sheet*—The balance sheet, also referred to as the statement of condition or the statement of financial position, shows the status of the company's assets, liabilities, and owner's equity at a given point in time. Balance sheets are sometimes unofficially called a snapshot view of a company's financial health. Like a snapshot, the view can change seconds after it is taken.

2 *Income statement*—The income statement, also referred to as the profit and loss statement (P & L), summarizes the revenues, costs, and expenses during a given period.

3 *Statement of cash flow*—This report summarizes the organization's cash inflows and outflows for a given period.

Taken together, the balance sheet and income statement make up a company's financial statement. Thus, when a firm is asked to provide its financial statement, it must supply its balance sheet and income statement. Traditionally, the financial statements had been the main tools used to analyze a company's financial performance. However, given some of the gimmicks and one time or extraordinary gains (or losses) that companies sometimes post on financial statements, a number of analysts now also focus on the statement of cash flow.

In the worse-case scenario, the vendor does send the credit memo to the customer and the accounts payable associate, not understanding debit and credit memos, *pays* the credit memo. Now the company has double paid the vendor an amount it never owed in the first place. This, unfortunately, is not an uncommon occurrence, and is one of the reasons accounts payable associates need to understand rudimentary accounting.

Sometimes you will see debits abbreviated as dr. and credits as cr. The abbreviations come from the Latin terms from which the terms are derived, *debere* and *credere*.

Adjusting Entries

When the books are closed, usually at the end of the month, often times adjusting entries will be made. These are generally for items that cannot be recorded in the daily transactions. Many companies close their books several days before the end of an accounting period so they can get all the necessary work completed by the end of the period (usually a month). Additionally, at year-end the books may be kept open to the last possible moment in an attempt to get in every last item.

GAAP

Companies are under great pressure to produce the best possible numbers in their financial statements. If there were no guiding principles, some might be tempted to fudge the numbers. To make sure their statements meet regulators standards, companies must complete their accounting using generally accepted accounting principles (GAAP) standards. This also makes it possible to compare financial reports from one company with those from another. Expect to hear about financial statements prepared using GAAP or according to GAAP guidelines.

The goal of GAAP is to prevent companies from using a variety of creative accounting techniques to make the numbers look better than the company actually does.

Year-End Window Dressing

Companies that rely heavily on their year-end financial statements will sometimes take great pains to make sure the numbers make the company look as good as possible. There is absolutely nothing wrong with this as long as the year-end manipulations are done according to GAAP. For example, a company that normally stretches its payments may decide to pay within terms to avoid showing a large accounts payable balance. Some might view an unusually large accounts payable figure with a skeptical eye, thinking it indicates a problem. Conversely, other companies might decide to stretch payments longer at the end of a fiscal period to show a large cash balance in that period.

Audit Trails

Accountants are famous for talking about audit trails—and with good reason. They make a lot of sense. Whenever possible, make it very clear why and how certain actions were taken. For example, if an invoice is to be short paid, indicate the reason in the file. To make the issue even clearer, some companies pay the entire original invoice and then issue a debit memo to cover the difference. The exact methodology is less important than making the reasoning clear to anyone who comes along. Putting a note in your files might work for the accounts payable department, but if that information is not available to others who might need it, your audit trail might not be very clear.

Suspense Accounts

Sometimes it is not clear to what account an item should be booked. Rather than delay the processing of the item, it is booked to a *suspense*

account to be researched further at a later date. The theory behind suspense accounts is that they allow the work to proceed and are to be cleaned out shortly when the proper accounting is determined. However, researching items in a suspense account is not at the top of anyone's list, so items often stay in suspense much longer than the company's accountants and controllers would like. Left up to their own devices, many professionals would not use suspense accounts. However, they are a necessary evil if one wants to run an efficient accounts payable department.

Summary

From this very brief review, accounts payable associates can see how very important it is that the company's accounts payable functions are performed and recorded accurately. If not, the company's financial statements will not be accurate and investors and potential lenders could be misled.

CHAPTER 2

Invoice Handling: The Three-Way Match and More

After reading this chapter you will be able to

- Understand all the documents needed to make a payment
- Know the proper procedures for handling invoices
- Identify the problem areas related to invoices
- Handle problem invoices
- Use statements correctly

At the very lowest level, accounts payable's chief responsibility is to pay a company's bills. On the face of it, this might seem simple, but it is not, really. Those who say, "What's the big deal—you get a bill and then you pay it," show no understanding of the corporate accounts payable world. Yes, accounts payable pays the bills—but no, the staff does not just get a bill and pay it. It only does so when proper controls are in place and when the payment is approved.

Payment Process

Three documents normally govern a corporate payment: the invoice, the purchase order, and the receiving documents. We look at each of these in detail in this section.

Invoices

Simply put, an *invoice* is a bill. Invoices can be simple or complex. For example, a bill for a magazine subscription usually has one item on it and is pretty straightforward. Now, think about a charge card bill. If your charge card bills are like mine, they have many charges on them. Each item purchased is listed separately so you can identify the goods you bought. In the business world, a bill is known as an invoice, and each of the lines representing an individual purchase is referred to as a *line item*.

In addition to information about what was purchased, the invoice will ideally contain this information:

- Where to send the payment
- When the payment is due
- What the payment terms are; that is, whether a discount is available if a payment is made early
- Any special instructions

Unfortunately, all invoices are not the same. Not all invoices spell out the required information clearly, and certainly not all companies use the same format. Worse still, many invoices are confusing, and a few are even misleading. Thus, one of the many roles of the accounts payable department is to check the invoice to see that it is accurate.

One of the common methods for judging performance of accounts payable associates is to measure the number of invoices processed in a given period of time. Since one invoice may have one line item while another can easily have hundreds, this method of comparison leaves much to be desired. Even those companies who have taken the measurement concept to a more reasonable level and measure line items processed instead of invoices can run into trouble. Why? Some invoices, regardless of the number of line items, are easier to process than others.

Some companies are good at preparing clear, accurate invoices, while others are not. After you have worked at a particular company for a while, you will come to know which vendors provide easy-to-process invoices and which vendors should be avoided like the plague.

Purchase Orders

The purchasing department sends a *purchase order* (PO) to the supplier when ordering goods for the company. Ideally, it will show not only all the details relating to the purchase (i.e., quantity, price, and so on), but also any special terms that the buyer may have negotiated. All too often, the purchasing department negotiates a great deal and then forgets to notify the accounts payable department. Then, when the vendor "forgets" to use the negotiated price and sends a bill with the original price, accounts payable has no way of knowing and ends up paying the original price—so much for the great negotiation.

In an ideal world, the purchasing department would send along a copy of all completed purchase orders to accounts payable. In reality, accounts payable does not always receive copies of purchase orders. Also, in many organizations the PO is not completely filled out, so even if accounts payable receives the PO, it does not have all the information it needs to verify purchases.

Receiving Documents

Before paying an invoice, most companies want to make sure the goods were received. Additionally, they want to know whether everything that was ordered was actually sent. In some industries, suppliers are permitted to ship within tolerances of, say, 5 percent. In other words, the supplier can ship anywhere from 5 percent below the amount ordered to 5 percent above it. Thus, before paying the invoice, it would be imperative that the accounts payable associate knows the quantity received.

The fact that the receiving documents are used in verifying information before a payment is made should put additional pressure on the staff that works on the receiving dock. However, some receiving departments don't check the goods received against the receiving documents.

Traditional Method of Handling: The Three-Way Match

In an ideal world, where all documents were checked and completed and sent to accounts payable, paying invoices would be rather simple. The accounts payable associate would take the three governing documents— the invoice, the purchase order, and the receiving document—and compare the three. They would all agree and the invoice would be processed for payment. In reality, the first-time match rate (sometimes referred to as a first-time hit rate) at many companies hovers in the 50 percent area.

That's right—only half the invoices that come in for payment match the purchase order and the receiving documents. Many companies have first-time hit rates that are much higher. But if you ask accounts payable professionals in the trenches, they will tell you that the biggest problem is with the invoices.

In order for the vendor to be paid on a timely basis, all the documentation must be received in the accounts payable department in some sort of a reasonable time frame. This can be difficult if the invoices are sent willy-nilly all around the company. For this reason, some companies have a policy of directing all invoices to accounts payable. This works well if accounts payable either has a purchase order for the invoice or knows who placed the order. If not, it is a real problem. Where to send the invoice also revolves around the approval issue.

Not all companies use the three-way match for handling payments. Other approaches are discussed in Chapter 18.

Approvals of Invoices

In theory, if all the documentation is filled out correctly and if it all matches, the accounts payable department should be able to pay the invoice without input from any other party. However, few companies are at this point. Even at those companies where the documentation is good, management often demands that the original purchaser get involved and approve the invoice for payment. Why? That's a good question.

Getting approvals on invoices before payment can lead to a multitude of problems. The following is just a few of the things that can go wrong:

- The invoice is not addressed to anyone in particular and floats around the company, eventually landing on the desk of the right person. In the meantime, the vendor looking for payment makes several calls to the accounts payable department, forcing an accounts payable associate on a wild goose chase looking for the missing invoice.

- The invoice is missing for so long that the vendor eventually sends a second one addressed to the accounts payable manager, who immediately forwards it to the appropriate party for approval and then speedy payment. Eventually, the initial invoice shows up, is approved, and is sometimes paid. Thus, eventually the vendor gets paid twice—not a bad deal for the vendor, but not such a good option for the customer.

- The invoice is sent to the accounts payable department, which forwards it to the approver. This usually entails making a copy of the invoice, keeping a log of who was sent what, and when it was sent. If the approver is not a details-oriented person, the approval of invoices is likely to be a low-priority task and the invoice can sit waiting for approval for weeks. At least in this scenario, the accounts payable associate can identify where the invoice is when the irate vendor calls.

15

- Invoices are directed to the original approver, who then forwards them to accounts payable with the necessary approvals ready for payment.

All of these approaches are common in corporate America today. Leading-edge companies insist on complete documentation, and some allow payment, without further approval, if the three documents match.

Companies that use imaging and workflow are starting to bring that technology into their accounts payable departments. In these companies, all invoices are sent to the accounts payable department, where they are imaged—scanned and turned into a computer-readable attachment. The invoices are then forwarded using workflow technology and e-mail to the appropriate person for approval. With the approval in place, the invoice is then returned to accounts payable for payment, assuming, of course, no discrepancies.

Who Can Approve?

At most companies, only certain people can approve invoices for payment. Most companies limit this ability by rank, job responsibility, type of purchase, and sometimes even the dollar amount. In the best of circumstances, the board of directors should have given these approvers authority and accounts payable should have copies of these board authorizations. You notice we said, in the best of circumstances. Not all companies are this organized.

However, even if there are no board authorizations, accounts payable should have a list of who can approve what purchases. A high-level executive at the company should sign off on this list. Otherwise, it is exceedingly easy to have fraud, and accounts payable could end up taking on a responsibility it should not. Copies of the list should be given only to those who need it, and in all cases should be filed away carefully. The list should not be hung on the wall for easy reference or

left lying on a desk where anyone walking by could see it and easily make a copy. When the list is updated, as it periodically will be, old copies of the list should be destroyed.

If you want to be super careful, new copies of the list should only be exchanged for the old ones, and all the old ones can be destroyed together.

Signatures

Just because an invoice arrives in accounts payable with a senior executive's signature on it does not mean that the senior executive actually approved the invoice. To protect the accounts payable staff, the department should have signature cards in accounts payable containing the actual signature of anyone authorized to approve invoices. And, it should be the executive's real signature—the one he or she uses everyday and not the Sunday-school signature. More than one executive has taken the time to sign a signature card carefully, when in actuality everything else has an illegible scrawl on it. In these cases, the signature card should have the illegible scrawl, as well or the accounts payable associate might suspect fraud when the signature cards are checked.

We are not suggesting that these cards be checked for every invoice that shows up. However, spot checking once in a while is not a bad idea. And, obviously, if a suspicious-looking signature arrives on an invoice, the signature cards should be checked immediately. One accounts payable associate reports receiving an invoice with an illegible scrawl that could not be identified. After checking the signature cards and finding no match, she bounced the invoice to the secretary who had sent in the invoice. It seems that the treasurer, someone who rarely approved invoices, had approved this particular invoice. He was one of the culprits who had supplied his Sunday-school signature rather than his real one. Luckily, he was good-natured and re-signed a signature card

using his real signature. However, more than one accounts payable professional has uncovered internal fraud by simply checking signature cards.

Other Invoice Issues

Unidentified Invoices

Often an invoice will show up in the accounts payable department with no identification as to who ordered the product. Sometimes by looking at what is included on the invoice, a savvy accounts payable associate will be able to figure out who the likely purchaser is and will then forward the invoice to that person for approval. However, that is frequently not the case, especially in the case of generic goods.

Some companies simply return those invoices to the vendor, instructing the vendor to forward the invoice to whomever they shipped the goods. Their managers think that it is not the responsibility of their accounts payable department to play detective. This may be a good approach for another reason, and that is fraud. More than a few companies out there prey upon overworked accounts payable departments. They send along invoices for goods not ordered, knowing full well that these small dollar invoices will be paid without authorization. For more information about this type of fraud, refer to Chapter 16.

Invoices Without Invoice Numbers

Most, but definitely not all, companies put an invoice number on all their invoices. This is a unique number and identifies that particular invoice. It is a critical number, as it is used as a reference by all parties involved. The vendor uses the invoice number to make the cash application when payment is received and the customer (that's you) uses the invoice number to track the invoice, relate it to a particular purchase order, and—most importantly—to make sure that the particular invoice

in question has not already been paid. When the customer goes through its computer files, it will search to see if the particular invoice number has been paid. Additionally, most accounting programs require an invoice number in order to generate a payment.

So, invoices without invoice numbers present a real problem for accounts payable associates. To get around the issue, most companies simply assign an invoice number. This must be done with great care, or else the system will regularly dump out a large number of payments when any duplicate payment check programs are run.

Using the date to assign an invoice number is likely to cause problems, as you will probably end up with duplicate invoice numbers. Some use a combination of the vendor number and the date. Again, this can cause trouble if you receive more than one invoice from the same vendor on the same day.

Another ploy is to use a combination of the account number. Be careful with this if the account number bears any relation to the tax identification number or a person's social security number. There have been instances where unscrupulous employees (yes, there are a few of those) have taken the social security numbers and used them in an unscrupulous manner.

The best technique is probably to make up a dummy number that includes some unique identifier to the vendor—for example, a combination of digits from the vendor's phone number and a running total.

Summary Invoices

Often a company will receive many small dollar invoices from the same vendor. In the case of an overnight shipping service and a Fortune 500 company, the number of invoices involved could be astronomical. In these cases, some companies request that individual invoices be suppressed and the vendor send one invoice summarizing the purchases for

a given time period, usually a week or a month—hence, the term *summary* invoices. These are especially appropriate for shipping companies, office supplies, and temporary help agencies.

Remittance Advices

When most companies print their checks, they print identifying information on the accompanying remittance advice. The most important piece of information usually is the invoice number (hence the problem when an invoice has no invoice number). Now, this remittance advice is usually of no importance to consumers, but to companies it is vitally important. It gives the vendor the information it needs to apply the cash to the correct account.

However, certain companies send along a stub with their bills. They require that this stub be returned with the payment. This is so the vendor can apply the cash payment correctly. The most common of these relate to utility bills, such as the phone or electricity bills. When you make your own utility payments, you typically include the stub with the payment so the utility company can apply the payment to your account. The utility company wants the same stub with your company's payment. Unfortunately, this presents a problem for accounts payable.

Many companies print and mail their checks without ever returning them to accounts payable. Some even have a machine that prints, signs, and seals the check. Thus, special arrangements must be made for checks that require special material to be included with the payment.

When Invoices Are Short-Paid

When an invoice is paid for the exact amount, there is rarely a problem. The issue is that, unfortunately, it seems that invoices are rarely paid for the exact amount. Deductions are frequently made, for various reasons:

- Discounts for early payment
- Short shipments
- Damaged goods
- Advertising allowances
- Prior credits
- Insurance or freight incorrectly charged
- Pricing adjustments
- Overshipments
- Advertising allowances

When the credit manager at the vendor's office receives the payment, he or she does not know what the deduction was for. Inevitably, the invoice remains open because it has only been partially paid—at least in the manager's eyes. The credit professional then calls the accounts payable manager, and an attempt is made to reconcile the difference. Unfortunately, by the time the call has been made, the accounts payable manager has long forgotten the reason for the adjustment and must pull the file to find out exactly what happened.

A better approach is to include the reasons for the deductions with the payment. The vendor might not agree with all the deductions, but at least it will know the reasons for the reduction. Several companies include a checklist form that allows the accounts payable associate to check off the reasons for the deductions. This approach at least documents the cause and gives the credit professional the information needed to research the problem on the other end. Often, this simple form eliminates the problem completely.

Blanket Purchase Orders

When companies make the same purchase over and over again, say for office suppliers or rent payments, the need to complete a purchase order does not seem as relevant—to some. Some companies have taken to writing one purchase order to cover multiple purchases or payments. This is referred to as a *blanket PO,* and it generates a lot of controversy. People either love them or hate them. Often, corporate philosophy and culture will dictate whether they are used.

Payment Issues

Late Fees

Some vendors have taken to charging their tardy customers a late fee for payments that arrive after the due date. Most accounts payable pro-

TIPS & TECHNIQUES

Blanket Purchase Orders

If blanket purchase orders are used, care should be taken to make sure that they are not misused. At a minimum:

- A dollar limit should be included. This can be an overall limit or a periodic limit, say $1,000 per month.

- In the case of repetitive periodic payments, say for rent or equipment leasing, the blanket order should have an expiration date. More than one company has used a blanket purchase order to cover a lease and then continued to make the lease payments after the lease has expired and the equipment has been returned.

- Blanket POs should be reviewed at least annually to make sure they are still relevant.

fessionals feel that this is above and beyond what is necessary. "Dispute all late fees" is a common practice. Before paying such fees, determine if the issue of late fees is addressed in the contract your company has with the vendor. Most contracts are silent on this issue.

Most accounts payable professionals refuse to pay these fees, especially if the payment is only a few days late. The truth is that most vendors who charge late fees do not expect to collect them. They add the fees to their invoices in order to send a message to the customer that they intend to be paid on time. Many of these vendors charge the late fees, see what they can collect, and then as a matter of course, write them off.

However, some vendors deduct the late fees from rebates, if rebates are payable for volume purchases. Typically, these rebates are payable annually, and the late-fee issue is not raised until it is deducted from the rebate. Then the discussion is not pleasant.

Others accounts payable departments refer the late fee matter to the purchasing manager who can negotiate it when a new purchase is being contemplated.

Statements

"Never pay from a statement" is usually good advice. However, that does not mean that accounts payable should not get statements from all vendors at least once a year. These statements should not be used for payment purposes but to track how the account is doing and to ensure that the accounts payable department has received all the invoices sent.

When asking for statements, make sure that you insist that the statement show all activity. More than one crafty credit professional has produced statements that show outstanding invoices only. The main reason for getting statements, in addition to monitoring invoice activity, is to check for outstanding credits. When these are identified, the accounts payable professional should ask for a check for these amounts.

If the vendor is reluctant to write a check, and many are, then the credit should be applied to the next invoice paid. Receiving the payment is best, not only from a cash flow standpoint, but also because it is less likely to confuse matters later. If the credit is applied to an open invoice and a payment is made for the remainder of the invoice, confusion could ensue. This is most likely to happen if the person handling the cash application on the other side is not proficient and records the payment as a partial payment.

If the credit is to be applied to an outstanding invoice, make sure your documentation is clear. Include in your file any back-up documentation so when you are questioned about the matter 12 to 24 months later, you will be able to figure out what you did.

A Note about Open Credits

A few accounts payable clerks with a weak understanding of accounting will actually pay a credit. Not understanding that the open credit is money owed *to the company* not money owed *by the company,* numerous accounts payable clerks have paid open credits.

Invoice Due Dates

Accounts payable professionals and their company's vendors have conflicting agendas. Accounts payable professionals want to hold on to their company's money for as long as possible while the vendor wants to get paid as quickly as possible. Sometimes credit professionals will make what they call a courtesy call to the accounts payable manager a week or so before the invoice due date. This is most likely to happen with large-dollar invoices. The purpose of these calls is to make sure that everything is in order and that the invoice will be paid on time—a reasonable approach.

The beauty of these calls, at least from the vendor's perspective, is that any problems can be resolved before the due date and the payment can be made without interruption. Additionally, if the invoice has not been received, for any reason, a copy can be supplied and the payment can still made within the agreed upon time frame. Although some accounts payable professionals welcome these calls, others find them a nuisance and a few refuse to take them at all. Those refusing to take

TIPS & TECHNIQUES

Invoice Handling

1 Check the math on any invoice that does not appear to be computer generated.

2 Date-stamp invoices the day they arrive in the accounts payable department.

3 If an invoice must be sent out for approval, keep the original in the accounts payable department and send the copy out for approval.

4 When sending invoices out for approval, keep a log of who the invoice was sent to and when it was sent.

5 Highlight key information on invoices, especially those that are not clear.

6 When a photocopy of an invoice, or a copy marked second or duplicate invoice, appears in the accounts payable department for processing, follow the procedures in Chapter 6.

7 When paying many small-dollar invoices to the same vendor, ask for a summary invoice.

8 Consider p-cards for all small-dollar payments (see Chapter 15).

them typically work for large companies where there is a policy of not addressing any vendor issues until an invoice is 30 or more days past due.

A few enterprising vendors have taken these "courtesy calls" to a new level. They will call up and ask the accounts payable associate for a payment for an invoice they claim was due the prior week. Don't necessarily believe everything you hear on the phone. Before you drop your work and rush their payment through, make sure they are telling the truth and the payment is actually past due. Once you get a phone call from such a vendor, add their name to the list of pushy vendors who will stretch the truth to lure an early payment from an unsuspecting accounts payable department.

Error Rates

Not all payment errors are due to mistakes made by the paying company. Many invoices are not calculated correctly to start with. Whether the error is an intentional attempt on the part of the vendor to collect funds it is not owed or is an honest mistake is irrelevant to the paying company. Its accounts payable staff must deal with these errors. Ideally, the mistakes are found before the payment is made. Exhibit 2.1 presents the latest statistics from the *IOMA Managing Accounts Payable Benchmarking Survey* showing the percent of invoices that arrive with errors. As you can see, it is a hefty 5.2 percent.

What is clear from these statistics is that companies looking to improve their overall efficiency will be able to do that by focusing on invoice processing. As you will see as you read the upcoming chapters, invoices and the way they are handled in corporate America will change—and in many cases, change radically. In order to make the best decisions regarding potential changes, it is imperative that accounts payable associates have a good understanding of the basics of invoices. After all, you have to crawl before you can walk, and as you will

EXHIBIT 2.1

Invoices that Arrive with Errors

By Company Size

Up to 99	4.7%
100–249	4.6%
250–499	6.0%
500–999	6.3%
1000–4999	4.4%
5000 & up	5.1%
Grand Total	5.2%

By Industry

Manufacturing	5.8%
Financial Services	4.4%
Transportation/Communications/Utilities	3.9%
Government	5.2%
Wholesale Trade	7.1%
Retail Trade	5.5%
Health Care	5.1%
Education	4.3%
Services (Business, Legal, Eng.)	3.5%
Other	7.0%

see toward the end of the book, the changes in invoice handling could be radical.

Summary

Not all invoices are created equally. Proper handling involves following company policy and procedures as well as understanding what you are dealing with and what problems you may encounter with the invoices from various vendors.

CHAPTER 3

Checks: The Traditional Payment Mechanism

After reading this chapter you will be able to

- Establish the proper procedures for printing and handling checks
- Set up strong internal controls for check handling and signing
- Make appropriate recommendations regarding check signing
- Set up appropriate procedures for ordering and storing checks

Some readers may be thinking, "A whole chapter on checks—what can she possibly have to say that will take up a whole chapter?" I could have written twice as much.

Check Printing

Once an invoice has been approved for payment, and the accounts payable department has verified all the documentation and mathematics, it is time to actually print the check. In order for this to happen, the item has to be scheduled for payment and the check has to be *run*. Large companies typically run checks every day, but smaller and even large mid-size companies are more likely to run checks at most several times a week. In corporate America, checks are rarely handwritten anymore. Manually produced checks are written only in cases of extreme emergency.

When the checks are printed, they may or may not be facsimile signed, depending on the corporate policy and the dollar amount of the check. After the checks are printed, they should be mailed to the intended recipients, not returned to the person requesting the check.

Returning Checks to Requestor versus Mailing Checks

When checks can be returned to the person who requested them, it makes it easier for an employee to defraud the company. Thus, most internal audit departments, along with outside auditors, will insist that checks are mailed to the recipient and never returned to the person requesting and/or authorizing the payment. In addition to the fraud concerns, additional problems can crop up if checks are returned to the requestor:

- The accounts payable department wastes time creating a log and getting signatures of the person picking up the check.

- The person who retrieves the check may lose it.

- There may be a delay between the time the check was retrieved and the time it is delivered to the recipient. In this lag, the vendor may call looking for its money and a duplicate payment may be made.

- The accounts payable associate responsible for returning checks to the requestors will be continually interrupted as checks are picked up.

- The accounts payable department must sort out the checks that have to be returned to the requestors from those that must be mailed, adding another step to an already labor-intensive process.

- Many requestors send their secretaries to pick up the checks. The secretary then leaves the check on the boss's desk. If the boss doesn't see it, the check might get buried under paper-

work. Sometimes months later, when the check is uncovered, it is then mailed or delivered long after a duplicate payment had been issued.

- The person to whom the check is delivered either loses it or fails to deliver it to the proper credit department in a timely manner. Again, a duplicate check is issued and eventually, long after the fact, the first check surfaces and is deposited.

Types of Checks

Most people are familiar with checkbooks. In their simplest form, these checks are bound in a small book and handwritten. This is what most individuals use to pay their own bills. Companies take a more sophisticated approach, using multipart checks that can be printed in one of two ways—either in a continuous format or individually usually using a laser printer.

Continuous Checks

Continuous-format checks typically are preprinted with the appropriate bank account information, along with the company name, logo, and mailing address. There are usually two, three, or more copies of each check printed. This type of check stock has to be kept in a secure location, and access must be severely limited. Additionally, a log should be kept of the checks used each time there is a check run. A calculation should be made using the number of checks printed, the last check number used and the ending check number. This is to ensure that no checks slip through the cracks and that no checks are unaccounted for. Accounts payable must also account for voided and damaged checks.

The controls for this type of check are numerous—and tedious, given the technology now available. Companies are moving away from this type of check in favor of using laser produced checks.

Laser Checks

Laser checks are printed on laser printers identical to the ones used by most personal computer owners. Many of the brand-name laser printers most readers are familiar with can also be used to produce checks. In the best circumstances, checks are printed on blank paper that has certain security features imbedded in it. See "Security Features in Checks," in this chapter for additional information about security features. The beauty of using blank paper is that no special controls have to be used to store it or monitor the stock—other than to make sure that the company always has an adequate supply on hand.

The software used by the company will print the entire check, including the Magnetically Incoded Character Recognition (MICR) link, the company logo, the check number, the dollar amount, and all other related information. The remittance information is printed on the check stub at the same time. The printer must have a special MICR cartridge to handle the MICR line, and it can also be outfitted to put a facsimile signature on the check at the same time the printing is done.

If a facsimile signature is used, proper care must be taken with the *signature plate*. Most companies keep the signature plate in their safe, bringing it out only when checks are run. Typically, the person who has the combination to the safe has nothing to do with requesting or approving checks.

Many companies reserve a special printer for printing checks only. This can lead to sloppy practices if the facsimile signature plate is left in the printer and the printer is not kept in a secure location. One accounting professional we know observed a client with lax controls. To make his point, he printed a million-dollar check made out to himself and left it for the CFO of the company. The CFO got the message quickly, and the company immediately implemented better controls surrounding its check printer.

The beauty of laser printers is that they allow an accounts payable associate to print a check whenever desired. However, most companies shy away from continual printing, as it is disruptive to the accounts payable department. Still, it does allow the company to produce a professional-looking check at a moment's notice, should it be required.

Frequency of Check Runs

Even companies that print checks every day usually do so at a set time—especially if the facsimile signature plate is locked away in a safe. This allows the accounts payable department to operate most efficiently. However, many companies do not have check runs every day and may schedule them as infrequently as once every two weeks. The *2001 IOMA Benchmarking Survey* of more than 900 professionals shows that less than 30 percent of all companies print checks every day.

IN THE REAL WORLD

How Often Companies Run Checks by Company Size

Number of Employees	Daily	Weekly	Twice a Week	Three Times a Week	Biweekly	Two Times a Month	Monthly
Up to 99	10.3%	51.3%	17.9%	5.1%	2.6%	10.3%	2.6%
100–249	7.1%	55.4%	14.3%	8.0%	8.0%	6.3%	0.0%
250–499	15.5%	53.4%	21.4%	5.8%	2.9%	0.0%	0.0%
500–999	22.1%	47.8%	22.1%	5.1%	0.0%	2.2%	0.0%
1000–4999	39.6%	32.4%	17.4%	7.2%	1.4%	1.9%	0.0%
5000 & up	60.9%	12.0%	14.3%	12.0%	0.8%	0.0%	0.0%
Total	29.8%	38.4%	18.8%	7.4%	2.3%	2.7%	0.3%

The frequency of check runs at your company will depend on many things, including the company's needs, the corporate culture, and the company's approach to payment stretching.

Check Signatures

It is important to differentiate between those authorized to sign a check and those authorized to approve a payment. Typically, people who can sign checks do not approve payments. Check signers are generally members of the treasury and/or accounting departments as well as very senior-level company executives. Each bank will require a signature card for each signer for each account, as well as a board resolution authorizing the person to sign on behalf of the company. In some instances, companies will delegate the authority to senior-level executives allowing them to designate other employees as authorized signers. In those instances, that documentation is supplied to the bank in place of the board resolution.

Some companies limit the dollar amount for which certain employees can sign. For example, a company might allow an employee at the manager level to sign checks up to $10,000 but require that a higher-ranking executive sign checks for larger amounts. Additionally, checks above a certain dollar amount will sometimes require two signatures. These limits and requirements are set by the company and must be given to the bank.

Although some people see it as an honor to be allowed to sign checks for a company, those charged with the task quickly realize that it can be a royal nightmare—especially in those companies that issue many emergency checks. If a facsimile signature is used on checks, it will be one of the authorized signers' signatures on the plate. This section looks at the various types of signatures and the security issues surrounding them.

Proper Controls of Check Signer Information

The information regarding who can sign on which bank accounts and for what dollar amount is typically compiled in a report used by those who need the information. This report will also indicate whether one or two signatures are required on checks and at what dollar level a second signature would be required. The distribution of this information should be limited and the reports kept in a safe, secure place. This would be valuable information to someone intent on using checks to defraud a company. Thus, anyone who has a copy of this report should keep it in a desk and not lying around where anyone walking through the department can see it.

Additionally, the information is usually periodically updated. When this occurs, new reports are distributed to those who need the updated information. At that point, either the old reports should be collected and destroyed or a cover memo should be put on the report asking the recipients to destroy their old copies.

Rubber Signature Stamps

In this day and age, rubber signature stamps are a terrible idea. Fraud using one of these stamps is laughably easy—so easy, in fact, that use of a rubber stamp makes a company liable for any check fraud committed using the stamp. Not only are the stamps easy to use once thieves have gotten their hands on a sample signature, but the crooks can also make their own stamps using the company's signatures once they know that rubber stamps are used at the company.

Facsimile Signatures

These are signatures made by a machine that match a real signature. They are used by most mid-size and large companies and are the signature of a high-level authorized signer. In those instances where two

35

IN THE REAL WORLD

Who's Really
Signing the Check?

Few executives like to sign everything themselves. In fact, when they are out of the office, they let their secretary use a rubber stamp to sign checks with their name. This is ridiculous. The secretary is signing the checks, so why not make her an authorized signer and protect the company from possible fraudsters?

signatures are required, most companies will allow one of those signatures to be the facsimile. Typically, the treasurer or controller's signature is used for the facsimile plate.

The signatures used in annual reports are typically not the actual signatures of the officers involved. The reason for this is that crooks figured out many years ago that they could forge checks by making a reasonable copy of the signature in the annual report. Now, most companies use an artist's rendition of a signature in the annual report.

Manual Signatures

Handwritten signatures are being used with much less frequency in corporate America. Typically, they are now used only on very-large-dollar checks or emergency checks. However, with the advent of laser printer technology that can encompass a facsimile signature, even the number of handwritten emergency checks is declining.

Double Signatures

Double signatures are generally required on all checks over a certain dollar amount. What that dollar amount is will vary from company to company. A few companies with very good controls will allow all

checks to go out the door with only one signature, and that signature is generally a facsimile signature.

Most firms, however, require two signatures when the dollar amount of the check is large. The definition of *large* depends on the company. Some set the limit for one signature as low as $10,000 while others have it as high as $1 million. We know a few that require a second signature for all checks over $1,000.

Accounts payable departments looking to have the limit raised and facing resistance should try to do it in a stepped approach. For example, an accounts payable manager trying to have the limit raised from $1,000 to $100,000 might first try getting the limit raised to $5,000 or $10,000. Then when everyone is comfortable at that level, seek to have it raised again. Eventually, you will reach the desired goal.

Getting Checks Signed

Should checks require a manual signature, someone will be assigned the responsibility of tracking down the authorized signer and making sure the checks are signed. Usually, before signing the check, the authorized signer will check the documentation that supports the check to make sure that the check should be issued—otherwise, you should be using a facsimile signer! This is part of what makes getting checks signed manually such a labor-intensive process.

After the checks are printed and before they are given to the signer, they must be reattached (usually with a paperclip) to the back-up documentation. The signer should check the documentation and then make sure the check is made out to the correct party, for the correct amount, and on the correct bank account. Additionally, the signer will want to ensure that the proper authorizations are in place. Although this checking can be done relatively quickly for one check, if there are many checks it can take some time.

Thus, checks are often left with the signer. This can and often does present a problem if the check signer isn't prompt in signing the checks. The checks might sit around for several days before being signed and returned to accounts payable or treasury for mailing. The problem arises when a check is waiting for signature and the vendor calls looking for its payment. If a log isn't kept of who has what checks at all times, time is wasted as accounts payable runs around and tries to find the check. Worse still, if confusion reigns, a duplicate check will be cut, signed, and given to the vendor—with no guarantees that the original check will be destroyed when it eventually finds its way back to be mailed.

It is a much better practice to have strong up-front controls and use a facsimile signer. Alternatively, checks should not be taken to the signer unless he or she is ready to sit down at that very moment and sign the checks.

Filing Checks

Some checks come with a copy of the check. Typically, the copy is marked "copy" and is printed on thin onion-skin type paper—usually pink or yellow. Many companies attach a copy of the check to the original request and documentation and then file the whole batch away in the vendor's file. This is a labor-intensive practice that may not be worth the effort. Although it is true that the backup must sometimes be pulled, it does not have to be pulled from the vendor files.

If your computer system is capable of tracking, then the copies of checks can be filed separately. Also, once the check is cashed, a copy of the cancelled check is more likely to be required than the check copy. Some companies no longer print the check copy.

Cancelled checks are typically held with the reconciliation. Many companies hold onto cancelled checks for seven years, which takes up a lot of storage space. However, with the advent of imaging, many

IN THE REAL WORLD

A Horror Story

One conscientious executive didn't want to waste time in the office so he would take the checks home with him at night in his briefcase and review them and sign them while watching television. Needless to say, all the backup for the checks went with him. One day, his briefcase was stolen—along with all the backup (original invoice, packing slip, approvals, and purchase order). That one incident was all it took to prove to the company that this practice could no longer be tolerated. Checks and the backup should never leave the premises.

companies no longer hold onto cancelled checks, relying instead on the imaged copy.

Protecting the Check Stock

The check stock used should incorporate a number of the security features described on page 40. If preprinted check stock is used, it should be stored in a secure location with access limited to a few authorized employees. In no case should an authorized signer be the person responsible for securing the check stock. A log should be kept so that at all times it is possible to determine which checks are in the secure location. Periodic audits should be made of the check stock, and occasionally these audits should be surprise audits conducted by the internal audit department.

Care should be taken when ordering checks. Price should not be the primary consideration. A reputable company should be used. Take a close look at the box in which the checks are mailed. One company used to mark its boxes with a big sign that said, "CHECKS ENCLOSED." Why not put a sign on the box that simply said, "STEAL ME"?

TIPS & TECHNIQUES

When New Checks Arrive

1 Immediately check the box to see that it hasn't been tampered with. If it has, make a note to that effect and notify the appropriate personnel.

2 Check the beginning check number and the ending. Is this the sequence that you ordered? Are any checks missing?

3 Log the checks in and immediately store them in your secure locations.

Security Features in Checks

In order to thwart check forgers, it is recommended that several of the following security features be incorporated in your check stock. Common sense will dictate the number and which ones are appropriate for you. A high-quality secure check stock with antifraud features can reduce the likelihood of incurring altered check fraud and can reduce or eliminate your liability if check fraud should occur. In response to the growing check fraud problem, the check-printing industry has developed security features for checks. The following are some common security features offered on security check stock. If you want to have a little fun while reading this, take out your personal checks and see if you can identify which of the following are used on your checks.

- *Void pantographs*—A pantograph is a design that is not clearly visible until a copy has been made, when such words as "VOID" or "COPY" become visible, making the copy nonnegotiable.

- *Watermarks*—Watermarks are subtle designs of a logo or other image. Designed to foil copiers and scanners that operate by imaging at right angles (90 degrees), watermarks are viewed by holding a check at a 45-degree angle.

- *Microprinting*—A word or a phrase printed on the check so small that to the eye it appears as a solid line. When magnified or viewed closely, the word or phrase will become apparent. Copiers and scanners can't reproduce at this level of detail so microprinting when copied will appear as a solid line.

- *Laid lines*—Unevenly spaced lines that appear on the back of a check are part of the check paper. This design makes it difficult to cut and paste information such as payee name and dollar amount without detection.

- *Reactive safety paper*—This combats erasure and chemical alteration by "bleeding" when a forger tries to erase or chemically alter information on the check, leaving the check discolored.

- *Special inks*—Highly reactive inks that discolor the ink comes into contact with erasure chemical solvents.

- *Color prismatic printing*—A multicolor pantograph background is extremely difficult to duplicate when using a color copier or scanner.

- *Special borders*—These borders on the check have intricate designs that, if copied, become distorted images.

- *Warning bands*—These bands describe the security features present on a check and alert bank tellers or store clerks to inspect the check before accepting it. They may also act as deterrents to criminals.

- *Thermochromic inks*—These are special, colored inks that are sensitive to human touch. When activated, they either change color or disappear.

- *Toner grip*—This is a special coating on the check paper that provides maximum adhesion of the MICR toner to the check paper. This helps prevent the alteration of payee or dollar amount by making erasure or removal of information more difficult.

Advances in Check Monitoring

IPS of Boston is known for its laser check products. In addition, it is the company that developed DoubleCheck, software that makes positive pay possible for virtually every company, regardless of size, financial wherewithal, and systems capabilities. We asked its president, Gary McNamee, to comment on how far check-printing technology has come in the last 10 years and to list advances, if any, he expects in the next 5 years. Here's what he had to say about the past and the future of laser check printing.

Ten years ago the concept of laser check printing was very misunderstood. The idea of printing your checks while you wrote them was usually met with a quizzical look asking, "What's the difference?" Today, laser check printing is not only an *accepted* means but also an *expected* means of disbursements in both large and small organizations alike. The technology was adopted initially in A/P departments followed by Payroll when the improved security, efficiency, and cost savings became apparent. One major benefit of laser check printing was the transition of the data on the preprinted check to an electronic format. This was a major obstacle in the conversion to electronic payments for most organizations.

In the next few years, more and more companies will embrace the next step in the payment evolution; electronic payments. Laser check printing has acted as a catalyst in this process. The advent of the Internet will only enhance this transition. On the consumer side, it is being noticed already in the form of e-checks, where paying by check over the Web has become as easy as using a credit card. In corporations, the information that accompanies the payment, that is, invoice, remittance and so forth, will further pull electronic payments along. Finally, where the government goes, corporations generally follow. With the government's widespread use of ACH transactions, the wheels have been set in motion for electronic payments becoming the future standard in commerce.

TIPS & TECHNIQUES

Monitoring Checks

1 Sequential numbering for all accounts should be used regardless of the type of check stock—preprinted or blank. This helps guard against fraud and aids in the reconciliation process.

2 All mutilated checks should be voided. This can be done by either writing the word *VOID* across the face of the check or tearing off the signature portion of the check.

3 Voided checks should be accounted for in the reconciliation process.

4 Most experts recommend that each company use only one type of check stock regardless of how many different accounts or applications they may have. This makes it easier for the bank and your employees to identify fraudulent checks. Some companies like to use different-colored checks for different applications, but this makes the control issue more difficult.

5 If cancelled checks are held at the company, they should be stored in a secure location. Why? Thieves can get all the needed information to prepare fraudulent checks from cancelled checks—so don't make it easy for them.

Reordering Checks

Most companies have established policies and procedures for reordering checks. For starters, the existing supply should be monitored and an order should be placed for additional checks well before the existing supply runs out. The printer should have instructions listing the few employees that are allowed to reorder checks. Finally, there should be limitations on who can change the "ship to" address for new orders.

When the order is placed, the employee placing the order should ask to be notified when the checks are shipped. A tracking number

should be obtained if UPS or FedEx is used, and the shipment should be monitored. This is extremely easy to do on the Internet. If the shipment is missing, the bank should be notified immediately. Stop payments can be placed on the check numbers in the missing batch or the account can be closed, if that is deemed appropriate and not too disruptive.

Although these measures might seem extreme to some, given the extent of check fraud and the potential financial damage that can be done with unauthorized checks, no action is too extreme when it comes to guarding the check stock.

Other Controls Regarding Check Stock

A blank check is an invitation to a thief to raid a bank account. Thus, correct care of the check stock is imperative. The previous Tips & Techniques box highlights some procedures for protecting the check stock.

A Check-less Society

Many futuristic publications predict a check-less future. Yet, this never seems to happen. Worse, the number of checks written continues to grow—although the growth might not continue as McNamee indicates. We asked Don Wittmer, director of Sales & Marketing for Express Management Services (a firm that helps companies recover duplicate payments) about a check-free future. Here's what he had to say.

> The payment process, whether for government or private industry, will always have a certain element of paper checks. Every firm has a number of small vendors that perform necessary services that do not have the sophisticated banking relationships to accept a wire transfer or an EDI payment. Second, many people are still not comfortable even in today's electronic commerce unless they can physically hold and touch a check. Even considering the risk of loss, thousands of social security checks are issued each month. Third, many transactions must be

completed between multiple parties, and the check seems to still fill this void. Consider a closing between parties for a parcel of real estate. The seller's real estate agent, the selling party, the purchasing party, the purchasing party's real estate agent, and the title company all have a vested interest in being paid "on the spot." Lastly, miscellaneous purchases, where credit cards may not be accepted, leave only cash or a check as the alternative payment vehicle.

Summary

Policies and procedures regarding all facets of checks are not as simple as it may appear at first glance. Handled appropriately, a company will run into little trouble. Ignored or managed sloppily, a company can run into major problems. A well-informed accounts payable staff is the first deterrent against such an unfortunate occurrence.

CHAPTER 4

Exception Handling and Those Dreaded Rush Checks

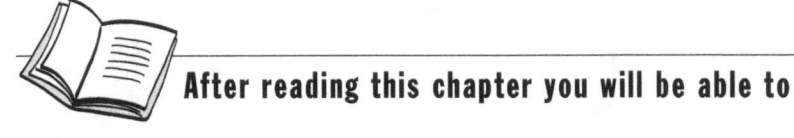

After reading this chapter you will be able to

- Understand why exception handling should be a concern
- Recommend ways to limit the number of checks issued outside the normal process
- Convince management to back your efforts to limit Rush checks

Two big concerns for virtually every company are duplicate payments and check fraud. Any time a check is issued outside the normal process, it not only increases the work in the accounts payable department, it puts the company at greater risk for making a duplicate payment and for check fraud. This is not to say that Rush checks should be completely eliminated from the corporate landscape; in most companies, that is just not possible. There are legitimate emergencies. However, companies should do everything possible to hold the number of checks issued outside the normal cycle to a minimum. The impetus for this move usually comes from the accounts payable staff, on whose desk these rush requests usually land.

What Is a Rush check?

A *Rush check* is any check produced outside the normal check production cycle. Companies that run their checks from a mainframe com-

puter are often forced to either use a typewriter or handwrite a check that is produced outside the normal cycle. On top of all the other problems discussed in this chapter, a handwritten check looks unprofessional and does not send a good message to your vendors.

Today, many, but not all, companies use laser printers to produce their checks, both regular and Rush. This eliminates the problem of unprofessional-looking checks but does not negate the other, much larger problems that are caused whenever a check is produced outside the normal check cycle.

Every company has a different name for Rush checks. You will hear them referred to as any one of the following:

- Rush checks
- Emergency checks
- ASAP checks
- Manual checks
- Quick checks

Why Are Rush Checks Such a Problem?

The main reason accounts payable associates dislike Rush checks so much is that it disrupts the normal routine of the department. When a request for a Rush check comes in, the associate has to stop whatever work he or she was doing and attend to the new task. This means reviewing the documentation to make sure everything is in place, dragging out a checkbook or firing up a new program on the computer, and then chasing down one or more authorized signers to sign the check. On a good day, this can take 15 minutes; if there is difficulty in locating an available signer, it will take much longer. Then the accounts payable associate has to make sure that the information is entered into the accounting system so records are updated. And, if positive pay is

being used (see Chapter 16 "Fraud: Vendor, Employee, and Check," for a discussion of positive pay), the accounts payable associate must make sure that the issued check file is updated to reflect this item.

In addition to causing a lot of extra work for the accounts payable department, there can be negative financial implications for the company as well. An inordinate amount of duplicate payments are checks that were Rush checks. Why? Sometimes the check has been cut and is somewhere in the process waiting to be approved, signed, or mailed.

IN THE REAL WORLD

Rush Checks: A Taxing Problem

One accounts payable manager, who for obvious reasons prefers to remain anonymous, relates the following story about Rush checks at her company. She says that against her wishes, field locations have checkbooks, which they use to handle emergency items. One of the field locations was negotiating with local taxing authorities. When its negotiations were complete, the local executive wrote a seven-figure check and gave it to the tax authority. He neglected to tell the home office. It is possible that he simply had a memory lapse, but more likely, he wanted to write the check himself and the home office would have insisted that a check that large go through normal processes.

The interesting thing about this story is that there would have been adequate time for the check to go through the standard procedures. Anyway, because the home office was not notified, it never included the check on the checks-issued file it gives to the bank each day to guard against check fraud. When the check showed up at the bank, no one, either at the bank or at the home office, knew the check was legitimate—so they bounced the check. As you might imagine, there were a few angry discussions that day.

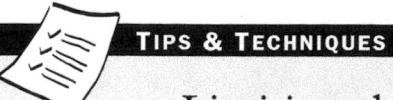

Limiting the Number of Rush Checks

1 Publish your accounts payable schedule. Let everyone know what the cut-off points are for getting a check. This schedule can be sent around in a memo and put on the company's intranet site.

2 Each time a Rush check is produced for someone, give that person a copy of your timetable to avoid future mishaps.

3 Develop a set of procedures to handle invoices from the receipt of the bill until the final payment goes out the door. Make sure that these are shared with everyone who might need a check.

4 Produce an accounts payable policy and procedure manual to be used by the entire company. Whenever a PO, check request, expense report, or other item is submitted incorrectly, photo-copy the appropriate page from the manual and return it to the submitter, along with the incorrectly filled out form.

5 Require everyone to follow set procedures. Do not make exceptions for favorites or friends.

6 Take advantage of the changeover to reevaluate and stream-line current procedures when putting in a new computer sys-tem.

7 Develop standard forms for use within the accounts payable department and by those requesting information or checks from accounts payable. Print the cut-off times on this form.

8 After publishing a corporate policy and procedures manual, measure and report findings to reduce exception items and costs.

TIPS & TECHNIQUES CONTINUED

9 Improve communications with other departments by reviewing procedures and streamlining them so the new measures work for both departments.

10 With management's support, "Just say no." If the reason for the request is carelessness on the part of the requestor, refuse to cut the check. Inevitably, the requestor will try to go over your head. What ensues won't be pleasant, which is why you need management's support. However, this particular requestor will get the message, as will others in the company. As long as management is behind this initiative it will work extremely well. If the accounts payable associate takes this action and is not supported by management, the results will be counterproductive.

11 Most accounts payable associates know who the culprits are. By working with these departments or individuals, you may be able to improve procedures to reduce the number of times these individuals have to come to you for an emergency check.

12 Sometimes, even though accounts payable knows who the offenders are, the individuals involved are offended when encountered about their check request behavior. To counter this reaction and to substantiate your claim should you have to go to their manager, keep a log of all Rush checks issued in the department. In this log, document each request, who requested it, the department, and the reason why the check did not go through the normal check cycle. Armed with hard numbers, the culprits will be hard pressed to refute your claims.

Inevitably, both checks get cashed. Using Rush checks also increases the chance that the company will be exposed to fraud.

Getting Management on Your Side

Everyone who works in accounts payable knows that Rush checks are inefficient, costly, and prone to duplicate payments and fraud. Unfortunately, management often doesn't understand what the big deal is. By putting your request in terms management can relate to—like money—you will greatly improve your chances of success. Here's how several accounts payable professionals got management on their side:

- *Figure out how much staff time is devoted to Rush checks.* Calculate the time spent producing the check, getting it signed, and then entering the data into the accounting system. Convert this to a human equivalent. One large company averages 30 Rush checks each day. The manager there conservatively calculated that it took 15 minutes of extra processing time to handle a Rush check. That meant that 8.5 hours of the accounts payable department's time was devoted to Rush checks each day—that's more than one full-time employee doing nothing but handling Rush checks. When the company demanded staff cutbacks, this accounts payable manager saw the opportunity. Staff reductions meant the department would have to be more efficient—and what better way to improve productivity than to get rid of Rush checks.

- *Calculate what it costs to process a Rush check.* This takes the above approach one step further. Once the time has been calculated, convert that to a dollar cost by using the average salary of the staffers who handle the process. Then calculate, on average, how many Rush checks are issued each day. Convert that to an annual figure. "Once I showed higher management how much it cost to do manual checks," explains one accounts payable specialist, "I never had a problem with the

change." Sometimes, this number alone is enough to make management sit up and take notice.

- *Focus on duplicate payments.* Count the number of duplicate payments that were manual checks. If you use a third-party audit firm, it may even have these figures for you. Also add up the dollar amounts on these duplicate payments. Then, calculate what you had to pay the audit firm to find these payments. Bring this number to management's attention. Let's say your company made 125 duplicate payments, for a total dollar amount of $175,000 that involved manual checks. Depending on the size of checks and the contract you have with the audit firm, your company would pay between $60,000 and $85,000 to recover that money. That's an expensive way to pay for sloppy corporate habits—that is, allowing Rush checks in the first place.

  Caveat: Many accounts payable professionals are reluctant to use this approach because management often blames them for the duplicate payment. Thus, it is imperative that good documentation be gathered to show that the problem arose because of the Rush check, not poor controls in the accounts payable department.

- *Keep management in the loop.* A number of accounts payable professionals have had success by requiring that a high-level executive sign off on Rush check requests. This tactic alone often causes the rest of the company to modify its behavior, as few are willing to explain to management on a regular basis why they need a Rush check—especially when the requestor is the cause of the problem.

- *Inconvenience management, as well as accounts payable.* This approach must be used delicately. However, a number of accounts payable professionals have succeeded by asking a high-level executive sign Rush checks. When high-level executives are constantly interrupted, they begin to understand

the inconveniences suffered in accounts payable. Make sure they understand that you would not bother them if you could avoid the problem—but you must have the check signed.

- *Involve several departments in recommending change.* Management is likely to back an initiative that comes from several departments. In addition to the management backing, the other departments are likely to honor procedures they had a hand in creating. As much as accounts payable managers may not like it, the group that works out the new procedures should include the worst offenders, if at all possible. Not only will the compliance be higher, but by including them in the process reengineering task force, you may ultimately mend broken fences and gain a greater understanding of the problems they encounter that lead to the Rush check requests. Your eyes may spot a solution they do not see, and vice versa.

The accounts payable professional's goal is to modify procedures so that the number of these annoying Rush cheks is minimal. Support from senior management is an essential step to achieving that goal. Adopting one of the techniques discussed here just may help accounts payable professionals achieve that goal.

IN THE REAL WORLD

How to Convince Management to Say No

Here's what happened at one company where the controller thought the accounts payable manager was making too big a deal about Rush checks. The controller could not understand what the problem was, but in an effort to meet the accounts payable staff halfway, he agreed that all Rush checks would come to him first. What effect did this have? The company now has a "Just say no" policy.

TIPS & TECHNIQUES

Designating a Handler of Rush Checks

Here's another approach that sometimes works. Do you have some-one on staff who is very efficient but also someone the rest of the company would rather avoid? If you can persuade this person— without telling them the real reason you have selected them—put them in charge of Rush checks and watch the number of requests dwindle! Whatever you do, don't give the assignment to the softie in the department.

What Else Can Be Done to Limit Rush Checks?

For starters, realize that in most cases, Rush checks will never be com-pletely eliminated. The simple reality is that most companies occasionally do have true emergencies where a check must be drawn. By working with other departments, especially those that seem to always have dire emergencies, the accounts payable associate may come to understand the circumstances that lead to Rush checks and, consequently, may be able to devise solutions to eliminate the problem.

Read carefully the chapter on working with purchasing and other departments. As you get to know other departments and they get to understand your requirements, you may be able to come together to devise workable solutions. Many Rush checks are simply a result of misunderstandings of the others' requirements.

Also, if you accommodate someone who is really in a bind, he or she might appreciate your help and be more considerate in the future. There is a downside to this approach, so use it very carefully. The "give them an inch and they'll take a mile" crowd will take advantage of your good nature. Also, what you do for one, you should do for all. Avoid

doing "special favors" for friends in other departments and then refusing to do the same for those you don't like as much. Although it is natural to like some people more than others and to try and help those you consider friends, not treating everyone equally can cause problems.

Not only can it cause problems, but others will quickly figure out who you will cut a Rush check for and who you won't. If you are receptive to Sarah in purchasing, before you know it, purchasing will be sending Sarah down with all its Rush check requests.

Summary

Rush checks will never go away completely. The goal of the accounts payable associate should be to minimize the number of such checks, find the most efficient method possible for handling them, and then institute as many controls as possible to make sure duplicate payments don't occur as a result of a Rush check.

CHAPTER 5

Preventing Duplicate Payments and Other Common Errors

After reading this chapter you will be able to

- Pinpoint the problems that cause payment errors, be they duplicate or erroneous
- Implement procedures to improve payment accuracy
- Effectively deal with discrepancies and disputes
- Implement effective controls to minimize duplicate payments

Errors in accounts payable–related activities cost companies millions of dollars each year. The mistakes lead to nonpayment, duplicate payments, excess payments, and insufficient payments. Each of these outcomes results in extra work for the accounts payable department, sometimes for the purchasing department as well, and usually deteriorated customer relations. What few outside accounts payable realize is that duplicate payments are a huge problem for most companies—regardless of size. It is in everyone's best interest that these mistakes be minimized.

What Causes Errors?

Just about anything under the sun can cause an accounts payable mistake. However, most of the mistakes are a result of incomplete infor-

mation. Deductions and discounts are lost when purchasing fails to keep accounts payable in the loop or when it fails to fill out a purchase order with all the details. Many suppliers send vague or misleading invoices, the result of which is that an incorrect amount is paid.

And occasionally, accounts payable does make a mistake. However, even though accounts payable may get blamed for most of the errors, the reality is that most of the mistakes come about because of poor communication or misinformation from other departments. That's why it is imperative that good communication channels be established and relationships with other departments be good. Many accounts payable departments have to work on improving their ongoing relationships with other departments—especially at those companies (and there are many of them) where the purchasing department and the accounts payable department would like to cut each other's throats. Well, this may be overstating the problem slightly, but you get the idea.

Most Common Types of Errors

One of the most basic causes of errors in accounts payable are the errors introduced when data are re-keyed. This can occur in many, many places. When the purchase order (PO) is filled out and sent to the supplier, the vendor takes information from the PO and uses it to prepare an invoice. This is the first possible place for a keying error. Once the invoice is received, the associate in accounts payable takes the information and re-keys it into the company's accounting system, providing another opportunity for a keying error. Thus, any move to an electronic transmission of POs and/or invoices takes a stab at this problem. Use of EDI, electronic invoicing and/or imaging should reduce error rates.

Other common errors include improper calculation of discounts, misapplied deductions and allowances, improper freight calculations, insurance charges, and incorrect due dates. The statistics in Exhibit 5.1

EXHIBIT 5.1

Error Statistics

No. of Employees	Payment	Invoices
Up to 99	1.8%	4.7%
100–249	1.5%	4.6%
250–499	2.3%	6.0%
500–999	2.0%	6.3%
1000–4999	1.4%	4.4%
5000 & up	1.3%	5.1%
Total	1.6%	5.2%

show the average error rates reported in the *IOMA Managing Accounts Payable Benchmarking Survey* for payments and invoices. You will note that the error rates on invoices are much higher than the error rates in payments. Both error rates reported probably understate the problem. Why? There are two basic reasons:

1. People tend to low-ball their error rates. No one wants to own up to a 10 percent error rate, even if that is the case.

2. People can only report the errors they catch. Thus, the reported figures do not include those cases that "got away."

Accuracy

Obviously, improving the accuracy of input will reduce errors and minimize duplicate payments. Lack of accuracy is also one of the major reasons for mismatches in the three-way match. Some companies have found that by using keystrokes instead of a mouse, speed and accuracy are improved. It might take a little bit of adjusting to get used to using keystrokes when you instinctively reach for the mouse, but with a little bit of training, accuracy and speed will improve.

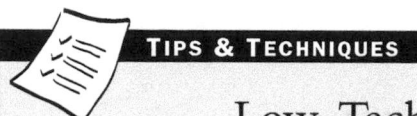

TIPS & TECHNIQUES

Low-Tech Solutions

1 Send along a letter explaining why an invoice was short paid.

2 Don't pay from copies without stringent controls.

3 Check large payments against the files to make sure that the invoice has not already been paid. The definition of large will vary from company to company.

High-Tech Solutions

1 Use batch totals to verify the input of groups of invoices.

2 Accept invoices in some form of electronic environment so no re-keying is required

3 Use workflow and imaging to process invoices

Tolerances

The subject of tolerances can provoke a debate among accounts payable professionals. There are two schools of thought:

1. *It is a waste of time to try to resolve small dollar differences.* Some companies set a limit, say $5. If the three-way match is off by less than this amount, they simply pay the invoice as billed and don't spend time trying to resolve the difference. They claim it is a waste of everyone's time and money to resolve such petty differences. The level of allowable discrepancies will depend on the nature of the business and the corporate culture.

2. *Small differences may be the result of two larger problems, each going in the opposite direction.* This group believes that all discrepancies

should be resolved. Furthermore, they maintain that unscrupulous vendors will figure out your tolerance level and then build that amount into all future invoices.

This is a matter that should be resolved at the management level. Some companies take the middle road, allowing a very small tolerance level for discrepancies, such as a dollar.

Handling Discrepancies

Accounts payable is a very poor place to resolve discrepancies. The accounts payable staff had virtually nothing to do with the transaction and does not have the needed information to resolve the discrepancies. The decision as to where to handle discrepancies must be made at a very high level. People from other departments must be involved. The most efficient way to resolve the problem is to refer it back to purchasing. All accounts payable associates can do is to point out how they do not have the necessary information to resolve the problem. If management determines that accounts payable will handle the matter, it then becomes imperative that accounts payable be given complete and accurate information.

Timeliness

Payment timing has become a big issue as companies look for ways to hold onto their cash. Most companies realize that the extra interest income they earn when holding onto their money flows right to the bottom line. Likewise, those experiencing cash-flow crunches can manage the tightness a little bit by simply delaying payment. What's more, some suppliers tolerate the practice, thus inducing their customers to delay payment even further. Is this fair? Probably not, but since few companies actually pay their bills within terms, it might be necessary in order to remain competitive.

In any event, the issue of payment timing is a management consideration and should be left to the executives who make these global decisions. Accounts payable associates who take the liberty of paying late without specific direction of management put themselves in jeopardy when a valued supplier complains or puts the company on credit hold. At best, the associate will end up with a tarnished professional reputation within the firm; at worst, the associate will be out of a job. Don't make this decision yourself. Look to management for formal guidance on the issue.

Duplicate Payments

It is a dirty little secret that most in corporate America prefer to ignore —but companies make duplicate payments all the time. Exhibit 5.2 provides the latest numbers from the *2001 IOMA Managing Accounts Payable Benchmarking Survey.* However, the actual numbers are probably higher. Why? For starters, few like to admit they make mistakes, especially errors of this sort. And then there is the fact that companies can only report those duplicate payments that they discover. Many go undetected, and thus don't make it into the statistics.

EXHIBIT 5.2

Percentage of Companies Reporting Errors in Specified Ranges

Range	Percent of Companies
0%	7.0%
Less than .1%	71.2%
0.1–0.5%	16.4%
More than .5%	1.0%
No response	4.3%

Reasons for Duplicate Payments

Bob Metzger, president of RECAP, Inc., a firm specializing in the recovery of duplicate payments, comments on the most common reasons for duplicate payments in corporate America. Here's what this pro has to say:

> Virtually all duplicate payments are due to two sets of invoices or an invoice and a statement being sent by a vendor and approved by someone who send both to accounts payable to be processed. All accounts payable software is limited in terms of the checking that is performed to detect a duplicate payment. Typically, the Invoice Number and Vendor Number are checked to see if a transaction with that information is already on file. If the same vendor is on file more than once, the duplicate check will fail if a "different" vendor is selected. Even if the same vendor is selected, the test may fail because the actual invoice does not have an invoice number and one is made up by the data entry person. Forty percent of all invoices do not have invoice numbers, making this a significant problem.

> To reduce the likelihood of duplicate payments, vendor files should be reviewed regularly for duplicate names and changes in names. Rules for assigning invoice numbers to invoices without invoice numbers should be developed and followed. Track and analyze duplicate payments that are caught; a few vendors and a few approvers typically account for most duplicate payments. Before posting, carefully review all large dollar invoices against previously paid invoices. Invoices for more than $10,000 account for less than 4 percent of an organization's total transaction volume but 70 to 90 percent of the total dollars paid and 70 to 90 percent of the total amount of duplicate payments.

Stopping Duplicate Payments

Completely eliminating duplicate payments may be an impossible dream, given the realities of today's hectic business environment. However, severely reducing the number of such payments is possible if the proper procedures are put in place. Business Strategy Inc.'s Beverly Brando recommends these strategies to put a crimp in the number of double payments:

1 Set up a policy for consistently creating invoice numbers for invoices without invoice numbers. The guidelines should include rules for logically creating invoice numbers. All personnel should be instructed on the invoice number protocol. The rules should not use dates by themselves or the account number.

2 Establish a policy when paying from copies rather than original invoices. These procedures should include flagging payments made from copies and invoices over 30 days old. Require high-level approval for each such payment and pay only after a thorough search has been made of the paid invoice file.

3 If payments are made from statements, implement a strong policy for researching each item before the payment is made. It is imperative that consistent entry be made for the statements to be consistent.

4 Maintain a log of all prepayments and deposits. Additionally, keep a copy of the contract or agreement in the paid invoice file. Managers should regularly review the payment history of those vendors that require prepayments.

5 Eliminate duplicate vendor numbers. This is probably the number one cause of faxes and second copies of invoices getting paid. Time spent purging the master vendor file will reap big dividends. And, of course, there should be only one master vendor file.

6 Cross-reference payments between entities. One of the easiest ways for a duplicate payment to slip through is to have one of the payments made to a related entity.

7 Verify that all entities receive the best available terms and conditions. Two subsidiaries should not be receiving different terms or conditions from the same vendor. Both should take advantage of the best offered.

8 Discount vendors should receive the highest priority. Compare the receiving date from the receiving department with the date the invoice is received, not the invoice date. Then calculate the discount period using the most favorable date. This is important, as apparently a few vendors hold large invoices for an extra day or two before mailing them to make it difficult for the purchaser to qualify for the discount.

9 Do not repay discounts simply because the vendor claims you did not qualify for them. Verify these claims and make sure the vendor is not simply holding the invoice, making it impossible for you to qualify.

10 Do not request credits. If for some reason a vendor owes you funds, have a check sent. Allowing the vendor to issue a credit is just asking for trouble down the road—assuming the credit is even given.

11 Create a better working relationship with purchasing. By obtaining a thorough understanding of the responsibilities of purchasing, you will be in a better position to resolve discrepancies and anticipate problems. Similarly, if they understand the accounts payable process, they will be better able to take actions to avoid practices that inevitably lead to a duplicate payment.

12 Consider using an outside audit firm. Not only will they recover the duplicate payments that were made in the past, they will identify the holes in your procedures—loopholes that you can close so that future duplicate payments will be minimized. This will be discussed in more detail later in the chapter.

Improving Control Measures

Brando says most duplicate payments are the result of inadequate control measures. For instance, whenever discrepancies are discerned during the invoice audit process and payment is withheld pending approval, the chance that a duplicate payment can be made is increased immeasurably. The approval process quite often includes the need to either copy or fax the invoice to the approving authority. In addition, payment delays will sometimes result in the vendor sending additional invoice copies to the accounts payable department. If one adds to this scenario a general failure to update and review the master vendor file on a regular basis, resulting in the possibility that individual vendors could have more than one vendor number, computerized duplicate-payment blocks are rendered useless, thus allowing the multiple invoice copies to be approved and processed for payment without detection.

Therefore, the single best technique for preventing duplicate payments would be to review the master vendor file on a regular basis, eliminating any vendor duplications, and pay all invoices according to the best terms available, either purchase order or invoice. This method of control eliminates the need for the costly follow-up procedures inherent in the approval method and increases accounts payable productivity by reducing the number of times an invoice has to be handled.

Handling Missing Invoice Numbers

Another leading causes of duplicate payments is invoices that have no invoice numbers. The reason for this is simple. One of the ways that companies track which invoices they have paid and which they have not is by referencing the invoice number. If one doesn't exist—well, you don't have to be a rocket scientist to figure out that this will increase the odds of a duplicate payment.

Compounding the problem is the fact that many invoices without invoice numbers are for repetitive payments, or payments that are made on a regular basis. A perfect example of this might be the rent or the monthly Internet connection charge. Although it is less likely that the rent would get paid twice because the dollars involved are usually large, smaller invoices might easily be paid twice. Thus, it is a good idea to assign invoice numbers to those invoices that arrive without one. This should be done in a systematic way to avoid using the same invoice number twice. This implies that using the date as the invoice number is not a good idea, as several invoices could arrive on the same day.

Accounts payable should devise a numbering scheme that incorporates your own requirements and then make sure that everyone uses it when assigning an invoice number. Some companies use a combination of the vendor number and invoice date—assuming that they receive no more than one invoice per day from any vendor (which might not be true in the case of companies like Federal Express) and that their invoice number field has an adequate number of fields.

Outside Audit Firms

Outside accounts payable audit firms are a wonderful resource for companies that know how to use them correctly. The firms review past payments, recover duplicate or erroneous payments, and recommend procedural changes to eliminate payment errors and increase controls. Their fee for this service is usually a percentage of what they collect. This appears to be a can't-lose proposition for the company hiring the audit firm. Yet, many still do not use them. Why not?

For starters many companies believe they never make a duplicate payment—and some are right. If they are correct in their assertion, then having the audit firm in costs nothing and ensures their peace of mind. If they are wrong:

- They collect money that they did not know was theirs.
- They plug the holds and change procedures to eliminate the problems in the future.
- They don't lose any more money due to the inefficiency or weak controls.

Sometimes, accounts payable associates are reluctant to use an audit firm because they usually get blamed for the erroneous payment. This is inappropriate, however; the blame for duplicate payments should not end up in accounts payable unless it belongs there. Especially if accounts payable knows the problems are elsewhere but cannot get the problems addressed internally, an outside audit firm can be their best friend. These auditors can be objective in pointing out weaknesses in the current system that permit the erroneous payments. Annoying as it may be, management might listen to an outside consultant or auditor when it turns a deaf ear on its accounts payable staff.

How To Be Your Own Auditor

Duplicate payments can be discovered before they go out the door. This section takes you through three phases in preventing duplicate payments.

Phase One

Most accounts payable professionals know who their problem customers are. They also know which ones are likely to receive duplicate payments. Prepare a list of such vendors. Then, ask the information technology (IT) department to run three reports by vendor. These reports should show payments made to each vendor by *invoice number, dollar amount,* and *invoice date.*

A manual review of these reports will allow the accounts payable professional to identify those payments that should be investigated further. While this research is being done, the accounts payable professional

should collect information as to why the duplicate payment was made. This will be used for two purposes. It helps identify weaknesses in the current processes and it pinpoints the individuals causing most of the problems.

The recovery work should not begin without approval from the accounts payable supervisor. This is where accounts payable professionals sometimes run into trouble. Instead of applauding the person for finding the funds, management might criticize the accounts payable department for making the second payment. It is crucial that this issue be handled appropriately, and it offers an excellent chance for accounts payable professionals who want to improve their stock with upper management and tighten procedures.

Phase Two

Once the first cut has been thoroughly analyzed, it is time for the next step. Many accounts payable managers believe they know to whom the duplicate payments are going. They may or may not be correct. Thus, it is recommended that the process be conducted for all large and possibly even mid-size vendors. There may be additional revenues to be had from these sources.

Phase Three

Many companies do a very poor job of cleaning up their master vendor files. The same company could be in there several times under slightly different names. This is one of the leading causes for duplicate payments. The accounts payable manager can request a list of all the vendors in the master vendor file. Review the list carefully to determine which vendors are actually duplicates.

Then group the information from the list of suspected problem cutomers and the list of large and mid-size vendors and compare them

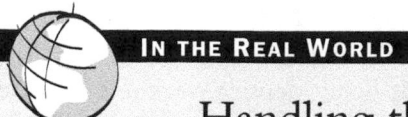

Handling the Criticism

Unfortunately, when it comes to duplicate payments, accounts payable associates are often in a no-win situation. If they uncover a duplicate payment and report it to management, they are often blamed for the mistake—even if they made the second payment at the explicit instructions of a senior executive. Business Strategy Inc.'s Beverly Brando offers superior advice on turning this potential bomb into a great opportunity. The accounts payable professional who has gathered the backup information for each duplicate payment has taken the first step to avoiding blame. Analyze the reasons for the duplicate payments. In some organizations, a few weak links cause the majority of the problems. Rush checks, for example, are often at the root of duplicate payments.

Identify these weak links and include them in a report to management. "Not only will this information protect the accounts payable department," says Brando, "but it gives the accounts payable manager the ammunition needed to force change." When an accounts payable manager has documentation that shows the company made $2 million in duplicate payments because of Rush checks, management will suddenly pay attention.

Money talks, and there is nothing like some of the company's hard-earned cash walking out the door to get management's attention. Once you have it, be ready to recommend procedural changes to fix the weak links.

The advantage of handling the duplicate payments in-house is that third-party audit fees typically run as high as 50 percent. Thus, a company with $2 million in duplicate payments could pay the outside firm as much as $1 million to recover the funds. The cost if the accounts payable department does it is much lower. If there is a significant problem, the company will still be ahead of the game financially, even if one or two people had to be added to the staff to handle the work.

to the master list of vendors to further identify duplicates. This step alone may provide the accounts payable manager with the ammunition needed to finally get the master vendor file cleaned up.

By quantifying the losses due to duplicate payments, accounts payable professionals will be armed with the ammunition needed to change those procedures that cause problems. Best of all, the company will be able to recover 100 percent of the duplicate payments for itself.

Summary

Duplicate and other erroneous payments can be a big problem for all companies. Most who claim they never make a duplicate payment are probably not taking a realistic evaluation of the problem. By employing best practices, minimizing errors, and paying within the appropriate time frame, companies will be able to reduce the number of payments made in error. Those who employ payment-stretching techniques need to be especially careful about the duplicate payments in their organization.

CHAPTER 6

Paying Lost or Missing Invoices without Creating Additional Problems

After reading this chapter you will be able to

- Understand the problems created when paying from an invoice copy

- Evaluate realistic policies and procedures to use when paying missing invoices

- Make recommendations to eliminate the risk of a duplicate payment when paying a missing invoice

- Minimize the likelihood of paying a *lost* invoice twice

Unless you have worked in accounts payable for some time, lost or missing invoices may seem like no big deal. Here's what happens —over and over again. A vendor calls up looking for a payment that was due two, three, or more weeks earlier. A search in undertaken, not only of accounts payable but also of any other department where the unpaid invoice might be. Typically, this would be purchasing. After this exhaustive investigation is made, it is decided that the invoice is indeed lost forever and the supplier is instructed to send in another invoice. Many times the vendor will fax the invoice in order to expedite the already-late payment. The second invoice may even be marked copy or duplicate. Payment is made, and everyone is happy.

Now, a few days or weeks later, the original invoice shows up. Because of the enormous workload in most accounts payable departments, no one realizes that this is the same invoice as the one paid earlier. Complicating the matter even further, this second, but original, invoice is probably approved for payment. So it is paid. Whether the original invoice was lost in the U.S. mail, inter-company mail, or a pile on someone's desk is irrelevant. The vendor has now gotten paid twice—and only a very efficient and very honest vendor will return the second payment.

Is It Realistic to Never Pay from Copies or Faxes?

Given this scenario, it is easy to see why many companies are loathe to pay from anything that is not an original invoice. In fact, the problem has gotten so bad that many companies refuse to pay from anything that is not an original invoice—including fax copies. The statistics "In the Real World: Percent of Companies that Will Pay without Original Invoices," taken from the *2001 IOMA Managing Accounts Payable Benchmarking Survey*, show that only slightly more than half the companies participating in the study say they will pay from a copy.

Unfortunately, it is probably not realistic to *never* pay from a copy. We all know of instances when the U.S. mail delivered letters or cards weeks or even months late. Even in the most efficient organizations, papers—including invoices—get lost. Therefore, most accounts payable departments establish guidelines for dealing with payments made when the original invoice is missing. Marking the second invoice as a copy or stamping it duplicate does not really help when the original invoice shows up. Most accounts payable departments are overworked and understaffed, so they are unlikely to devote the time to isolate invoices that are finally showing up for the first time, after the second, or copy, has been paid. This chapter looks at guidelines for dealing with missing invoices.

IN THE REAL WORLD

Percent of Companies that Will Pay without Original Invoices

By Size of Company	Percentage
All Companies	54.5%
Up to 99	43.6%
100–249	41.4%
250–499	47.6%
500–999	60.7%
1000–4999	56.4%
5000 & up	66.7%

Industry	
Manufacturing	53.4%
Financial services	45.2%
Transportation/communications/utilities	68.9%
Government	68.4%
Wholesale trade	70.4%
Retail trade	59.5%
Health care	51.6%
Services (business, legal, engineering)	49.1%
Education	75.0%
Other	42.4%

Instituting Controls

Obviously, the best control—never paying from a copy—is not realistic in most cases. Telling the utility company or a valued supplier that you do not pay unless you have the original invoice is likely to bring about undesirable consequences, such as no electricity or being put on credit hold and not being able to get needed supplies—something management at most companies would not find acceptable.

This policy is not realistic for another reason: If the vendor is told, "Produce the original invoice if you want to get paid," the vendor will just produce another "original" invoice. From the supplier's perspective, it has acted in good faith, and is simply following the customer's policy. But this policy actually increases the odds of duplicate payments, as the customer could eventually receive two original invoices. So it is better to allow copies, but establish policies and procedures to control the circumstances under which payments are made.

The next best step, then, is to make it difficult for those who try to pay from copies. Why? Some people would much rather call the vendor and ask that another copy of the invoice be faxed over than actually sort through their desk to find the missing invoice. The accounts payable associate, with management's approval, needs to make it easier to look for the invoice than to get it paid from a copy. This can be done in several ways:

- Require two or more additional signatures on copies of invoices from higher-level employees—say, the requestor's supervisor and the controller.

- Only pay from a copy after the invoice is 30 or 60 days old.

- Require that a manual search of the files be made to ensure the invoice was already paid.

- Hold on to the invoice for an additional five to seven days to see if the original "mysteriously" appears. You'll be surprised how often this happens.

The Lousiest Way to Avoid a Duplicate

In responding to various IOMA surveys, more than a few companies indicated that way they guard against duplicate payments is to rely on the memory of the accounts payable associate. This is outrageous. If a purchasing executive can't remember which invoices have already been

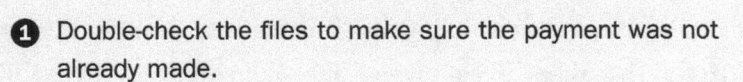

TIPS & TECHNIQUES

Best Techniques for Preventing a Second Payment

1 Double-check the files to make sure the payment was not already made.

2 If the request was made by purchasing, demand that a valid PO and an unmatched receiver be provided.

3 Make sure the duplicate is marked copy or duplicate and filed immediately.

4 Run the information through a search routine based on the invoice number and dollar amount.

5 Require an explanation for the lack of an original invoice with the payment request.

6 Review requests for payment without an original invoice and make a determination on a case-by-case basis as to the advisability of paying. Make sure to get your manager's input before rejecting a request.

7 Have the payment request signed by the individual who has the primary relationship with the vendor.

8 Pay from a copy only if the invoice number is completely legible —if not, ask for a clean copy so that you can check against other invoice numbers.

approved, how can a company expect the accounts payable associate who sees 10 or 20 times as many invoices as any one executive to remember? Fortunately for the companies involved, these associates are able to catch many duplicates but, obviously, not all. It is outrageous that a company would expect this.

Paying from a Statement

The answer here is simple—DON'T. Statements are wonderful for reconciling accounts and identifying missing invoices. However, paying from a statement will certainly increase the odds of a duplicate payment with one exception (see the following "In the Real World"). The reason for this is that there is no invoice to put in the file. Paying from statements can lead to major problems and duplicate payments.

The exception is in those rare instances when a company pays its vendors strictly from the monthly statement. This is not the normal course of things. However, sometimes when a company has many invoices, say from an overnight shipping company, they may choose to pay once a month, from the statement, rather than from the individual invoices. Usually, this is only done with the concurrence of the vendor, but it is a good solution when there are many small invoices from the same vendor.

Some reading this may be thinking that too big a deal is being made out of this issue. Consider some of the real-life episodes illustrated in the "In the Real World."

What Does the Vendor Do with a Duplicate Payment?

Still not convinced that paying from a copy is a problem? Do you believe that vendors return duplicate payments as soon as they realize what has happened? Some do, once they get around to reconciling their accounts. However, even the most well-intentioned supplier is not going to put returning your money at the top of its list. In most companies, cash that is received is put into a miscellaneous income account and researched when time is available. Remember, the longer the vendor holds onto the money, the more interest it can earn on your funds —and no vendor returns duplicate payments with interest.

IN THE REAL WORLD

Duplicate Payment
Horror Stories

❶ A senior purchasing executive approved for payment two copies of the same $138,758 invoice—three days apart. Two years later, when the duplicate-payment audit firm found the second payment, he blamed accounts payable. Luckily, the accounts payable supervisor at this company was able to retrieve both copies of the invoice—with his signature on them. However, it took several hours of work and two heated discussions before the matter was dropped.

❷ The secretary of the president of a mid-size manufacturing company screeched into accounts payable, at the president's direction, with a copy of a two-month-old invoice, demanding that a check be cut immediately. The supplier was threatening to stop shipments if the old invoice was not paid immediately. A quick inspection of the files showed that not only had the invoice been paid, but the supplier had also cashed the check. Further discussion with the supplier and investigation on its part revealed that the supplier had received the check but applied it to another customer's account. If it had not been for the cool head and quick thinking on the part of the disbursement manager at this company, a second check would have been written. Although the professionals involved in this case believe the demand on the part of the supplier was an honest mistake, it still would have resulted in a duplicate payment but for the competent accounts payable professional.

❸ In reviewing payments after the fact, one company discovered that it had paid a $150,000 invoice twice. The supplier in this case was a Fortune 50 company that had sent a second invoice—but neglected to mark it "second notice." When the accounts payable manager called the supplier, he was told that the supplier had realized it had been paid twice and

79

intended to repay the customer, however, it would take another three weeks to have a check request drawn, approved, and the check cut. This company was lucky—it got its money back after a month. However, it lost whatever investment income it could have earned on that money for the month. One has to wonder how long it would have taken the vendor to notify the customer of the duplicate payment without being prompted. There were two rather disheartening issues in this case. First, when the two invoices were pulled, they did not look alike. They had different formats. Second, they also had different invoice numbers. Thus, those relying on the memory of the accounts payable associate or a duplicate payment program that matched invoice numbers would not have been able to catch the duplicate payment easily!

4. On more than one occasion, a nasty supplier has taken a duplicate payment and returned the check—not to the accounts payable department but to the company's chief financial officer, president, or some other high-ranking executive with a cryptic note about the lack of controls at the customer's back office. You can imagine how well those notes are received.

Here's the dangerous part. Many companies (there are no statistics on this, for obvious reasons), when they cannot apply the funds to the correct account, simply write the amount off to miscellaneous income and forget about it. The money is never returned. That is one of the reasons that duplicate-payment audit firms thrive. Many companies believe they never make a duplicate payment because none of their vendors have ever returned an excess payment. In these cases, the money is usually gone for several years.

Those familiar with the escheat laws are probably thinking that the vendor should turn these funds over to the state, and they are correct. However, companies rarely escheat their credit balances. For more on escheatment refer to Chapter 18, "High-Level Accounts Payable Concepts."

Summary

Invoices can and do get lost or mislaid. It is an inevitable fact of life. Payments must occasionally be made without an original invoice. The goal of the accounts payable associate is to ensure that this happens as little as possible, and when it does, to try and ensure that a duplicate payment does not arise as a result. Those companies that establish realistic guidelines for paying from copies are in the best position to minimize the risk of a duplicate payment.

CHAPTER 7

Improving the Relationship with Purchasing

After reading this chapter you will be able to

- Understand the purchasing–payables issues and dynamics
- Find ways to make the relationship work—even if it means taking the first step
- Identify the problems that purchasing has with accounts payable
- Develop an ongoing, sound, working relationship with purchasing and other departments

Although it is important and beneficial that accounts payable get along with all other departments, the relationship with purchasing is often the most crucial—and unfortunately, is often the most tenuous. Traditionally, but definitely not at all companies, accounts payable and purchasing were at each other's throat—each feeling that the other didn't understand their requirements and was making their own jobs difficult. Because the two groups have to work closely together, the smoother this relationship can be made, the better it will be for the individuals who work in both departments, as well as the company as a whole. I am happy to report that there are numerous companies where accounts payable and purchasing work well together. Also, over

the last few years anecdotal evidence suggests that there has been a marked improvement in the rapport between the two groups.

Interaction between Purchasing and Accounts Payable

Purchasing provides accounts payable with the most crucial piece of information it needs to pay an invoice—the purchase order. The purchase order (PO) spells out the agreement that the company has made with a particular vendor. In theory, if the PO is filled out correctly and completely (the first problem), accounts payable should not have to contact purchasing as long as the invoice matches the PO and the receiving department checks off the receiver and indicates that everything was received. However, this is not how it works at many companies. The invoice is often sent back to purchasing (or is mailed directly to purchasing), and accounts payable only pays it after a purchasing executive has approved it. Why is this approval necessary? That's a good question.

Of course, in many organizations, the purchase order is not filled out completely, the invoice doesn't match the purchase order, and/or the quantities or quality of goods on the receiver does not match the purchase order. Resolving these discrepancies is no fun and is not high on anyone's list of priorities—until the supplier is refusing to ship additional needed goods and everyone is up in arms. Of course, I'm presenting the worst-case scenario, but even one half as bad is bound to lead to frayed nerves, mistrust, and bad feelings. It's no wonder many accounts payable/purchasing relationships are frayed.

Why Getting Along Is So Important

For starters, resolving discrepancies requires cooperation. Although it is true that the primary responsibility for resolving discrepancies falls at the purchasing department's feet, it is accounts payable who has to deal

with the fallout of poor or late research. It is in both parties' best interest to get these errors resolved quickly and efficiently while keeping the vendor as happy as possible.

If the relationship is good, accounts payable is much more likely to be able to get purchasing to complete its purchase orders completely so accounts payable has the information it needs to process payments quickly and efficiently without bothering someone in purchasing to help resolve a discrepancy. Thus, while it is in everyone's best interest, accounts payable ends up the biggest winner as they are eliminating many of their problems, freeing them to work on more meaningful work.

Points of Contention

There are five main problems that arise between accounts payable and purchasing—at least from the accounts payable viewpoint:

1. *Missing information on purchase orders*—One of the biggest complaints many accounts payable professionals have with purchasing is that some purchasing personnel do not completely fill out the purchase order. Then when an invoice shows up, the accounts payable professional does not have the information needed to determine if the invoice is correct. Even sending the invoice to purchasing for approval does not always solve the problem. Many executives will routinely approve an invoice without checking the details. Thus, the company may end up spending more than it had originally anticipated. But, if this is the case, there is little that the accounts payable associate can do other than pay the approved invoice—certainly not an ideal situation for any company.

2. *Misinformation about discounts*—Purchasing departments are sometimes quite adept at negotiating special deals that give their companies price breaks or other favorable terms. For example,

sometimes toward the end of a period, be it a quarter or a fiscal year, a supplier will offer extended terms in order to get the sale on its books. The customer is then not required to pay for the merchandise until the end of those terms—which, in certain instances, can be as long as six months. This is a great cash-flow enhancer for the customer and should either increase its investment income or decrease its interest expense. In either case, the impact on the company's bottom line should be positive.

However, often just the opposite occurs, as purchasing never informs accounts payable of the special deal. Then when the invoice shows up, it is scheduled for payment according to the standard terms and the money goes out long before it should. The company then ends up with lower investment income or higher interest expense—the direct opposite of what was planned.

Similarly, if the special negotiated prices are not communicated to accounts payable, it will pay the invoice as it shows up, especially if it has been approved. Often, the communication at the vendor is equally as poor, so the invoice that is presented does not show the special prices. Thus, with no one giving the special pricing information to the accounts payable department, the old prices are paid—probably for a larger quantity than would have been ordered under the existing price structure.

Accounts payable associates need to find ways to get information about special pricing or term deals. The source of this information is the purchasing department. Duplicate payment firms love these problems as it means additional income for them when they recover funds due to missing pricing information. Unfortunately, they cannot recover lost investment income.

3. *Delays*—Delays in processing invoices in purchasing often mean extra work for the accounts payable department. Many accounts

payable departments waste valuable time chasing down invoices that are either out for approval or out waiting for someone in purchasing to resolve a discrepancy between the invoice and the purchase order.

4. *Lost discounts*—The delays discussed above can also lead to the loss of an early payment discount. If purchasing does not turn around invoices quickly or resolve discrepancies in an expeditious manner, the company will not qualify for the early payment discount. Even though some vendors look the other way when a customer takes the early payment discount a few days late, not all are so generous. The amount of lost discounts can add up at firms that make substantial purchases. As one accounts payable professional says, "The only mortal sin in our organization is missing an early payment discount."

5. *Rush checks*—Rush checks are a nightmare for accounts payable and can lead to other problems such as duplicate and/or fraudulent payments. Thus, most accounts payable departments work assiduously to eliminate them. Delays in the purchasing department often lead to a demand for a Rush check. This is especially true in the case of a valued supplier threatening to put the company on credit hold. Unfortunately, many outside the accounts payable department don't understand not only how much extra work a Rush check causes accounts payable, but also the additional risks that cutting Rush checks entail.

What Can Be Done to Improve the Interaction

Getting along with purchasing is just one piece of the pie. The truth is that accounts payable needs to strengthen relationships with all departments, purchasing being the most crucial. There are several ways this can be done.

Education

Many of the problems with other departments come from the fact that there is no understanding of what goes on in accounts payable and what its constraints are. Educating the rest of the company—not necessarily an easy task—is the best way to address this issue. Start by sharing accounts payable's time schedule. For example, if checks are run every Tuesday and Thursday afternoon, spread the word. If approved invoices and check requests must be received by noon on those days, make sure everyone is aware of this. Then when someone arrives with an approved invoice on Thursday at two in the afternoon, there will not be an argument. A memo with the schedule can be sent to all affected parties and the point can be reemphasized every time a Rush check is requested.

Communication

Simply talking to the professionals in purchasing can help. Once they understand what your concerns are and you understand what their issues are, you will be in a much better position to resolve some of the differences. Along the same lines, if problems persist with one or more individuals, it might be time to sit down and have a one-on-one chat with the person. Perhaps there is a misunderstanding that can easily be cleared up, or perhaps accounts payable can adjust some of its requirements to help solve the problem. The important thing to do is to start talking in a nonaccusatory manner. Having lunch with your peers in purchasing is not a bad idea. When you become friendly with those on the other side of the fence, it becomes easier to resolve errors and discrepancies and to get them to understand your problems.

Role Reversal

Walk a mile in their shoes. The best way to get purchasing and accounts payable to get along better is to each try out the other's job for a short

period. This might mean spending a day with a purchasing professional and then having a purchasing associate spend a day with you. In each case, the professional should go through their normal daily routine and allow the other to observe all the problems they encounter. The beauty of this approach is that both professionals come to understand the problems and issues the other encounters. Once they have this understanding, they might be able to suggest alternatives to make the relationship between the two work smoother. Remember, purchasing occasionally has some complaints about the way accounts payable handles what it considers to be sensitive issues—and occasionally, they have a legitimate complaint.

Working for Purchasing

Never, you say? Well, the reality is that some accounts payable departments already report to purchasing, and the trend will continue in certain industries. Right now it occurs primarily in nonmanufacturing companies—typically, but not always, when the two departments are combined. Usually, it is the purchasing manager who ends up as the head person. Accounts payable might not like this, but when management makes this decision, accounts payable's opinion does not matter.

Think about this issue from a selfish standpoint. Isn't it better to develop a good working relationship with purchasing before you are forced to report to the head of purchasing? Should there be a rancorous relationship between the two groups, what do you think is going to happen when accounts payable gets moved under the purchasing umbrella? However, if the two get along and if accounts payable has even made some suggestions that have made the purchasing operation work a little smoother, the move to purchasing is likely to be less rocky.

Now, you might be thinking, "This will never happen at *my* company!"—and you might be right. In 2001, only a small number of

accounts payable departments reported to purchasing. However, some experts expect this number to grow—especially with the advent of e-marketplaces and other process improvements that will reduce the number of professionals needed to handle the purchasing function. Accounts payable won't get off scot-free, either. There will be a reduction in the number of associates needed to address the more clerical issues. Thus, forward-looking accounts payable professionals will make sure that they strengthen their working relationships with all other departments, especially purchasing.

An Accounts Payable Gift for Purchasing

In many organizations, purchasing information is all over the place. This is unfortunate, because the more information purchasing has, the better job it can do negotiating pricing breaks for the company. Accounts payable usually has the information purchasing needs. It knows how much the company spends each year and it knows where every dollar goes. By working with purchasing, it is typically very easy to design reports that provide purchasing with needed and extremely useful aggregate data that can be used to strengthen negotiating positions.

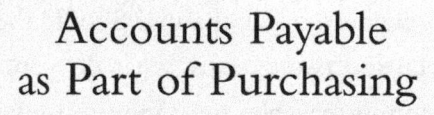

IN THE REAL WORLD

Accounts Payable
as Part of Purchasing

At a recent accounts payable conference, the prediction was made that by the end of 2006, approximately 25 percent of the accounts payable departments would report to purchasing. Several in the audience disagreed with this premise—they thought the number would be higher. No one argued that it would be lower.

These data also allow purchasing to consolidate its supplier base from thousands to perhaps several hundred. Instead of having 56 vendors supply a given commodity, the company might concentrate its activity with the 5 to 8 that will provide the best price and service. Companies have been able to wring impressive concessions from suppliers when they promise to buy significant amounts of product.

Many purchasing organizations have been surprised when they began working with accounts payable to find out how many different suppliers the company was actually using in different locations. By consolidating the purchasing of key items, they have been able to save their companies millions of dollars—money that flows right to the bottom line. This money could not have been saved without the data input from accounts payable.

Those accounts payable associates looking for a way to bridge a gap with purchasing might recommend to their superiors that they find a way to work with purchasing on this all-important issue.

National Association of Procurement Professionals

In an interesting twist on the payables/purchasing dynamic, the National Association of Procurement Professionals (NAPP) has gone out of its way over the last few years to include accounts payable professionals and issues in its annual conference. The event, held each January on Marco Island in Florida, focuses on separate purchasing and accounts payable issues, as well as items that affect both groups.

What this event signifies is the recognition that the two should work together and are often affected by the same matters. Purchasing professionals often invite their accounts payable colleagues to accompany them to this event. (More information about this event can be obtained from www.nappconference.com or payables@aol.com.)

Key Issues Often Overlooked by Accounts Payable when Dealing with Purchasing

Walking in someone else's shoes means realizing that there are other concerns besides the accounts payable ones. We asked Barbara R. Kuryea, president of AP Consulting Services, to comment on the purchasing issues that accounts payable fails to consider. She brings a special expertise to this subject, as she is the NAPP payables advisor. Here's what she had to say:

> Remember that there are always two sides to every issue or problem. Therefore, accounts payable must keep an open mind

TIPS & TECHNIQUES

Improving the Purchasing/Payables Relationship

Jim Heard, the director of shared services for Dana Brake and Chassis, has a lot of experience dealing with purchasing, and he has made it work. A few tips that he recommends to those who want to improve that ever precarious relationship include:

❶ Switch jobs for a week or two to truly understand each other's needs.

❷ Screen all problems prior to sending to purchasing to minimize their need to get involved.

❸ Simplify their participation in the process by whatever electronic means are available (even e-mail gives them a simple reminder and easy way to respond).

❹ Work at having a satisfactory personal relationship with purchasing individuals. This will make the business relationship come off without a hitch.

and be willing to listen to purchasing's side of the story. Other problems may arise because of conflicting strategies. In fact, purchasing's strategy may be in conflict with accounts payable's strategy when the two report into different management teams.

In real-life situations, purchasing sometimes must react quickly to the businesses' needs; therefore, in these cases, accounts payable may be the last to know about a new supplier relationship. On the surface, this may appear to accounts payable as if purchasing is purposely keeping accounts payable out of the loop, when in fact, this is not the case. The actual reason may be that there was no time to bring accounts payable on board prior to contracting with this supplier.

Accounts payable often blames the purchasing group for mismatched invoices. However, industry statistics of mismatched invoices reveal that there are a large number caused by "no receipts," which obviously are not purchasing errors.

Management must recognize the importance of accounts payable and purchasing working together to create cost-effective and efficient purchase-to-pay processes. Accounts payable needs to focus its attention on supporting purchasing and on becoming value added to the business.

Summary

Getting along well with all departments is important, as it allows accounts payable to ease in its own requirements. However, working well with purchasing is crucial, especially in a manufacturing environment, for the accounts payable associate who wants to survive and thrive in the twenty-first century. Not only will the partnership make for a smoother, error-free environment, the accounts payable associate will be well situated should his or her company make the move of placing accounts payable under the purchasing umbrella.

CHAPTER 8

Master Vendor Files: An Often-Overlooked Function

After reading this chapter you will be able to

- Understand the importance of good master vendor file policies

- Eliminate duplicate entries in your master vendor file

- Set up a naming process so that duplicate entries will never be made

- Set up master vendor policies that will minimize the opportunities for both employee and vendor fraud

Proper control and maintenance of the master vendor file can minimize many problems in accounts payable. This chapter discusses this oft-ignored vendor file in detail.

What Is the Master Vendor File?

The master vendor file contains all the needed information about a particular vendor. Each file should have identical information. Generally, a master vendor file is set up when a company embarks on a relationship with a particular vendor. What defines a relationship varies from company to company. Some will establish an entry in the file after three transactions, while others require five or more. The exact number is typically set by company policy.

Other times a company will be set up in the master vendor file if a serious purchasing contract has been signed. The file might contain information such as the following:

- The exact company name

- The mailing address where payments are to be sent

- Contact information in case there are problems—this might include both sales personnel and members of the credit department

- Payment terms

- Tax identification numbers

- Officers of the corporation

- Additional information, as determined by the company

The company will probably also want to set a policy as to what investigation should be done on a company before it is entered into the master.

Duplicate Payments and the Master Vendor File

It is imperative that the master vendor file be set up according to strict guidelines if duplicate payments are to be avoided. Let's look at the simple example of IBM. If it is set up in the master vendor file as IBM, I.B.M., and International Business Machines, invoices can be misplaced. Let's say an invoice is sent to accounts payable and paid under the vendor number for I.B.M. After being paid, the invoice is filed in the I.B.M. folder. Now, several days after the invoice has been processed and the check is mailed, but before the payment arrives at IBM, a second invoice appears for the same amount. This often happens if invoices are not processed in a timely manner, as vendors are quick to send out a delinquency notice.

This time, the associate handling the invoice notes that the correct name for IBM is International Business Machine and checks that master

vendor file. The invoice does not show up as paid in that file, and so the associate goes ahead and pays the invoice. This is one of the most common causes of duplicate payments.

This case was rather easy to decipher because the names are so similar. Occasionally, the names are not that similar, especially in the cases where a company is doing business as (DBA) another more common name.

Duplicate entries also occur when dormant entries are not eliminated from the master vendor file. Not to pick on IBM, but it is a classic. Let's say your company hasn't done any business with IBM for several years and then begins a new relationship. Well, not realizing that there was already an IBM in the master vendor file, someone might set up a new account for I. B. M. or for International Business Machine, thus perpetuating the problem.

Controls

Most companies do not give unlimited access to the master vendor file to just anyone. The potential for fraud and errors is just too high. The few people who can update or edit the file are given strict instructions on how to update the file. For example, they might be told never to use abbreviations, never to use the word *the* in front of a company name, and so on. The company itself determines these guidelines.

Another safeguard is to run a report periodically, but no less frequently than once a month, of all changes made to the master vendor file. Someone in senior management should review this report to make sure that all the entries made to the master vendor file were legitimate.

Set-up Procedures

Obviously, more than a few people can make recommendations for new entries to the master vendor file. In fact, in most organizations, many people will need to have vendors added to the master. The most

efficient way to do this is to develop a form that must be completed by whoever is requesting the entry. The form should be signed by the requestor and then approved by someone authorized to approve such entries. This is very important in preventing fraud. In some companies, a vendor cannot be paid unless it is set up in the master vendor file.

Accounts payable generally has a difficult time with certain vendors submitting their taxpayer identification number. The best time to get it, and the time when accounts payable has the most leverage, is before the first payment is made. By refusing to cut a check unless the taxpayer identification number has been provided, accounts payable significantly increases its odds of getting that number. Otherwise, year-end rolls around and accounts payable is not only inundated with 1099s and other year-end tasks, it also has to chase down vendors for their taxpayer identification numbers. And, you know how helpful a vendor is likely to be if the end result means it has to pay higher taxes. (This is more of an issue with independent contractors than with corporations.)

One-Time Vendors

Companies face the conflicting issues of trying to keep the number of vendors in the master vendor file to a minimum while simultaneously requiring as many ongoing vendors be included in the file. Thus, the issue arises as to what to do about one-time vendors. Many companies do not enter them in the master vendor file. As already indicated, some have a requirement of three or more payments. Yet, not entering them in the file can mean that getting 1099s together at year-end will be difficult—although it doesn't have to mean that.

Some accounts payable managers keep a file for miscellaneous vendors. All important information related to these infrequent vendors is kept in this file—including those elusive taxpayer identification numbers.

There is no right or wrong answer as to when to include a vendor in the master vendor file as long as a policy is set and adhered to uniformly for all vendors.

Naming Conventions

One of the best ways to minimize the number of duplicate entries in the master vendor file is to use a naming convention and then make sure that everyone who enters information into the files adheres to it strictly. Again, there is no right or wrong way to do this, as long as it is consistent. Jon Casher, chairman of RECAP Inc., a company that not only collects duplicate payments for corporations but also helps those firms with their master vendor files, recommends answering the following questions:

- How many characters does your system allow for a vendor name?

- Does your system allow more than one line for a vendor name?

- Does your system allow for a different name to appear on the check than on a 1099?

- Can you look up a vendor based on a short name, full name, or "sounds like?"

- When you look up a vendor and a list of vendors is displayed, how much of the vendor's name and address are displayed so that you can select the correct vendor?

- Are there limits as to how many characters/lines of a name can be printed on checks, fed to other systems, appear on reports or screens, or appear in window envelopes or mailing labels?

- Can you link vendors under a common identifier with an address qualifier to allow multiple addresses for the same vendor?

RECAP's Naming Convention for Master Vendor Files

1 If the name is a corporation that includes Corp, Inc, or LLC, include that in the name when you set up the vendor.

2 If the name of the vendor begins with an article (*The, A,* etc.), do not include it in the name when you set up the vendor.

3 If the name is an individual, consistently include or exclude prefixes such as Mr, Ms, Dr.

4 Avoid using periods (.) within vendor names; use one space after each initial.

5 Avoid using apostrophes in vendor names or in abbreviations of words in vendors names.

6 Avoid abbreviations, or be consistent in their use.

7 Enter vendor names beginning with a number as specified. However, names that begin with a changing year, such as the 1999 U.S. Open, should be set up without the year prefix.

8 If abbreviations are used, a short table of allowable abbreviations should be prepared and provided to people who are authorized to add vendors, as well as to people who have to find vendors based on a name. For example, American can be abbreviated either Am or Amer. Decide which you will use and include it in the list.

9 If the vendor is *doing business as, trading as,* or *known as,* use the vendor's actual name and DBA, TA, or KA, followed by that name on the second line of "name" or first line of the "address."

10 If the vendor asks that you pay a factor, set up the name for the vendor and put the name of the factor as the second line of the name or the first line of the address.

11 If the vendor is a taxing authority, set up the name of the taxing authority as the name. Put any qualifiers, such as department, division, and so on, on the second line of the name or on the first line of the address. Despite instruction on many property-tax bills that specify that you make a check out to the name of an individual as tax collector, the check will be cashed if you make it out to the name of the taxing authority as the first part of the vendor's name to indicate no data are missing.

12 If your system does not support two-line names, consider using the first line of the address for the continuation of the vendor's name. If the vendor's name fits completely in the name field and the first line of the address is required, put a period in the first line of the address.

With the answers to these questions and the suggested policy in the Tips & Techniques box, you will be able to devise a naming policy for your company that will eliminate duplicate files for the same vendor.

Reports

Many companies overlook the necessity to produce reports about their master vendor file. As already indicated, however, producing a monthly report about updates and edits to the master vendor file for management is one of the first steps to preventing vendor and/or employee fraud. In addition, by manipulating the data, you may be able to produce a report of all inactive vendors. This can be reviewed and used for purging the file when doing a master vendor file cleanup.

Simply obtaining a count on the number of entries in the master vendor file will give you an idea as to whether your files need to be purged. By comparing your numbers with those produced in the *2001*

Number of Vendors in the Master Vendor File

Percentile	No. of Vendors
90th	500
75th	3,000
25th	35,000
10th	75,000

IOMA Managing Accounts Payable Benchmarking Survey you will be able to determine if your files are too large. Compare your numbers to the information provided in Exhibit 8.1.

Preventing Fraud

Lax attention to the master vendor file can lead to fraud. Here's one of the easiest ways for an employee to manipulate the master vendor file for fraudulent purposes. Let's say that anyone can go in and update the file. An unscrupulous employee goes into the file and changes the mailing address for one or more vendors. This employee is, probably, not stupid enough to use his or her own address but rather, an innocuous post office box. Then when invoices work their way through the system, the checks are drawn and signed and mailed to the incorrect address. The employee picks up the checks, closes the post office box, cashes the checks, and then goes into the master vendor file one more time and changes the mailing address back to the correct address. Other unscrupulous employees have been known to create fictitious vendors in the file and then send invoices from the phony vendor.

Now, when the vendor complains that it did not receive payment, it is next to impossible to tell what happened—unless management had

been looking at regular reports showing what was changed on the file and who made those changes. Thus, limiting the ability to edit the file is a best practice. Yes, the purchasing manager could probably check it fairly easily—but why expose the company and the employee to the potential problems?

Who Controls the Master Vendor File?

In real life, the responsibility for the master vendor file can lie either in accounts payable or in purchasing—occasionally, it lies in both departments. *Both* is not a good answer, because then no one is ultimately responsible. Some companies actually have two master vendor files, one in each department. More often than not, maintaining the master vendor file is an accounts payable function. In any event, the two departments must work closely on this matter because both have a stake in the information included in the file.

IN THE REAL WORLD

Frequency of Master Vendor File Cleanups

How often are master vendor files purged? Not often enough. Look at the statistics from the *2001 IOMA Managing Accounts Payable Benchmarking Survey:*

Monthly	3.3%
Quarterly	2.0%
Annually	27.7%
Every two years	17.0%
Every three years	14.1%
Never	31.5%

Cleanup

Purging the master vendor file is one of those annoying and time-consuming tasks that many companies never get around to doing. In fact, it is a dirty little secret in corporate America, but according to the *2001 IOMA Managing Accounts Payable Benchmarking Survey,* over 30 percent never purge their master vendor file.

Results of Poor Master Vendor File Policies

"What's the big deal?" you ask. Most accounts payable departments have a lot more important things to do. Ignoring master vendor file maintenance routines will ultimately cause corporation's problems. RECAP's Casher addresses this issue.

"When a vendor master file is not maintained properly," he says, "a company is exposed to several risks as well as lost opportunities. The risks include: duplicate payments, uncashed checks, fraud, and tax liability. The lost opportunities are in leverage, discounts and processing efficiencies."

Risks

A major cause of duplicate payments is multiple records for the same vendor (see Chapter 5). If addresses are incomplete or inaccurate, payments may not be delivered and checks may never get cashed. Uncashed checks may have to be stopped, voided, and reissued. If they are not, the company will need a process to find the payee and to escheat the funds, if the payee is not found. If there are inadequate controls for adding and updating vendor information, fraudulent transactions may be processed. If taxpayer identification numbers are missing or inconsistent with the taxpayer name, the IRS might send B-notices (notification by the IRS that information provided by the company is

not consistent with IRS information). If you are unable to get a valid taxpayer ID, your organization will be liable for taxes that should have been withheld.

Lost Opportunities

If related vendors are not linked, you may not know how much business you are doing with a vendor and could therefore lose leverage opportunities. If your vendor file does not have appropriate terms specified, you may be losing or not taking discounts. If you can identify your high-volume vendors, you can decide which of those are candidates for EDI or other forms of electronic invoicing. If you can identify your low-volume vendors, you can determine who might be candidates for elimination or conversion to p–cards.

Summary

Master vendor file policies and procedures are often overlooked in overworked accounts payable departments. By understanding the problems that lax policies can cause, the accounts payable associate is in the best position to implement changes that will limit a company's potential losses due to fraud, duplicate payments, and extra work.

CHAPTER 9

Discounts, Deductions, and the Problems They Cause

After reading this chapter you will be able to

- Calculate whether to take a discount for early payment
- Recommend a policy regarding early payment discounts
- Evaluate methods for updating vendors regarding deductions made on invoices
- Discuss payment timing issues

D iscounts for early payment are a touchy issue in accounts payable. Many suppliers offer their customers a discount for early payment. The best-known early payment terms are 2/10 net 30. What this indicates to the customer is that the full payment is due in 30 days. However, if the customer will pay in 10 days, it can take a 2 percent discount. Thus, a company with an invoice for $100 could pay only $98 if the invoice was paid within 10 days or the full $100 if it was paid at 30 days. Although 2 percent might seem like a small amount of money, it can add up fast and is a very high rate of return for a company on its money.

You will note that we did not indicate when the clock starts running for the 10 or 30 days. The supplier would like it to be 10 days from the invoice date, while most customers start the clock running the day they receive the invoice. Thus, the two parties rarely agree. It should be

noted that if electronic invoicing takes hold, there will no longer be any controversy over when to start the clock. Some suppliers start the clock running on the earlier of the invoice date or the date the goods are received by the customer.

Terms of Sale

2/10 net 30 is not the only discount term used. Certain industries have their own terms. For example, terms in the food industry are much shorter. They might be, in an extreme case, 2/7 net 10, although more common is 1/10 net 11. In both these examples, the suppliers think that if the customer can't pay within the discount period, it must be experiencing some financial difficulties. After all, why would a company not pay within the discount period if it had to pay a greater amount only a few days later?

Vendors that make many shipments to the same customer, usually for small dollar amounts, sometimes move to what is called *prox terms*. The terms are then aggregated and payments are made once a month for everything ordered in the prior month. Payment might be due on the 15th of the following month in which goods were ordered. Then, instead of having, let's say, 2/10 net 30 on a variety of invoices, with payments going out many times during the month, only one check is mailed. On average, everyone comes out equal.

Should the Discount Be Taken?

Deciding whether it makes sense to take the discount is a financial calculation. As a general rule of thumb, unless interest rates are very high, it makes financial sense to take the discount. The calculation to use to determine the effective interest rate for taking the discount is:

$$\frac{\text{Amount of discount}}{\text{Discounted price}} \times \frac{\text{Number of days in the year}}{\text{Number of days paid early}} = \text{Return on Investment}$$

Going back to the hypothetical $100 2/10 net 30 example, the numbers work out as follows:

$$(\$2/\$98) \times (365/20) = 37.24\%$$

Now most companies don't earn 37 percent on their money, so they should take the discount and make the payment early. Even if the discount were only 1 percent, and the rate of return was about half that, the discount should probably be taken.

For some companies, however, taking the discount is more than a financial issue. There are other issues, the most obvious being cash flow. Companies just starting out or others with slim margins or cash concerns simply may have to pass on the discount because they don't have the cash to pay early.

The other matter that occasionally prevents companies from taking the early-payment discount is their own internal processes and procedures. Some companies simply cannot get the paperwork turned around quickly enough to earn the discount. Thus, they forgo the discount because they are not able to get the check cut quickly enough.

At the other end of the spectrum is one of those dirty little secrets that companies don't like to talk about. Some companies "give themselves a few extra days" when qualifying for the early-payment discount. Thus, they may take the discount even though the payment doesn't go out until a few days after the discount period has ended. And that's not all. Some companies take the early-payment discount *regardless* of when they pay the invoice and what their cash-flow situation is. In the *2001 IOMA Managing Accounts Payable Benchmarking Survey*, respondents were asked about their policies regarding payments and the taking of discounts. The results are presented in Exhibit 9.1.

Unauthorized Deductions

When paying an invoice, accounts payable professionals often reduce the invoice amount, usually at the direction of someone in purchasing

EXHIBIT 9.1

Company Policies Regarding Discounts

Policy for Taking Discounts	Percentage
Take all discounts offered, even if payment is past terms	33.3%
Take all discounts offered, within limits of terms	43.2%
Take some of the terms offered based on our cost of funds	14.7%
Refuse all discounts offered	6.2%
No response	2.5%

or some other executive. Occasionally they do it themselves in order to pay for a partial shipment. When vendors do not approve these deductions in advance, they refer to them as *unauthorized deductions.* Unauthorized deductions often cause a lot of problems—for both the buyer and the seller. Here's what happens.

Let's say an invoice for $20,000 shows up approved for payment for $19,750. The purchasing manager deducted $250 for an advertising allowance. This may be a legitimate deduction. In fact, experts in the recovery report that between 85 and 90 percent of all unauthorized deductions are eventually allowed—emphasis on the word *eventually.* Anyway, the accounts payable associate does as instructed and pays the invoice for $19,750.

When the payment is received, the vendor does not know why the deduction was taken or that it was legitimate. So, the accounts receivable associate credits the customer's account but leaves an outstanding balance of $250. Then, either someone from the vendor's collection department begins calling accounts payable trying to collect the $250 or the accounts

---

TIPS & TECHNIQUES

Getting Discounts

Some suppliers, especially on large invoices, don't want their customers to qualify for the discount—it's a lot of money and they would prefer having the funds in their own pocket. Thus, they hold the invoice for a few days before mailing it, making it next to impossible for the accounts payable associate to get the invoice processed in time to qualify for the discount. There are two responses to such tactics.

❶ Date-stamp everything as it hits accounts payable, and then start the clock ticking from the date stamp.

❷ If you suspect that a supplier is pulling this trick on your company, save the envelopes with the postmark. Then, when you have built a case, approach the vendor and look for ways to eliminate the practice. But don't be accusatory. Some companies review all large-dollar invoices before mailing in order to make sure they are correct. These well-intentioned companies don't realize that in doing this they are making it difficult for the customer to meet the early payment date.

---

receivable associate calls trying to uncover why the $250 was deducted from the invoice. Or, even worse, the customer gets put on credit hold because the invoice remains unpaid for an extended period of time.

Whatever the outcome, the calls don't start until days after the invoice has been paid and the accounts payable associate must check the files, because by then, the reason for the deduction is long forgotten. What a colossal waste of time for everyone involved. This problem has gotten so out of hand, especially in certain industries, that specialty firms have sprung up that do nothing but help vendors recover unauthorized deductions and unearned discounts.

Needless to say, accounts payable doesn't have the ability to resolve these, issues but accounts payable is where the calls come regarding short payments. Someone in accounts payable must then contact someone in purchasing to resolve the issue. As you might imagine, resolving deduction issues after the fact is not at the top of purchasing's fun-things-to-do list. In fact, resolving these issues leads to some of the friction between accounts payable and purchasing.

Additionally, the constant interruptions that these phone calls bring to the work of the accounts payable department is not a real productiv-ity enhancer. Most suppliers are not real thrilled about having to chase the customer for information or money, either. Thus, these phone calls can sometimes be contentious. In fact, resolving discrepancies after the fact is one of the least-liked parts of the function for most accounts payable associates.

There are, however, some ways to deal with this issue. The best answer is to give the vendor as much information as possible. While log-ically this sounds like a wonderful idea, it is not always as easy as it would appear. Most checks are printed and then sealed and mailed without going back to accounts payable for any attachments. This means that all

IN THE REAL WORLD

A Nifty Solution
to End Constant Interruptions

One innovative accounts payable manager found a way to relieve her staff of 12 of the annoyances associated with the constant inter-ruptions. She assigned one person to take all the deduction calls and work with purchasing to resolve the issues. How did this solu-tion work? She says she had 11 very happy staffers and 1 really dis-gruntled one.

the information provided to the vendor must be included on the check stub. Normally, companies try and include the vendor's invoice number and perhaps invoice date and maybe its purpose. After all, check stubs are not often that large and cannot hold reams of information. Additionally, there are often systems and programming constraints. The Tips & Techniques box on page 114 offers some solutions to this problem.

Payment Timing

Realizing the time value of money, some companies have taken a long, hard look at the way they pay their bills. Many have come to realize that if they pay a 2/10 net 30 day bill on the eleventh day and take the discount, their vendors will not complain—so they take the process another step further, and another and another. They are holding onto their money as long as they can. When large sums of money are involved, the extra income earned by delaying payments can be substantial, especially if it can be done for many days.

The trick is not to offend valued suppliers or hurt the company's credit rating. Some companies are concerned about their D & B Paydex number (it reflects how a company pays its bills) and thus are reluctant to pursue such a strategy. Some companies report, off the record of course, that they pay those reporting into D & B within the appropriate time frames while stretching payments on other vendors who do not report in and are not critical to the long-term viability of the firm.

Some do stretch payments in a very organized fashion, even hiring professionals to advise them on the implementation of the practice. The decision to stretch or not to stretch is not one that should be made in the accounts payable department. It should be a conscious decision on the part of the company and should only be undertaken with the express approval of senior management. Otherwise, everyone will look the other way until a valued vendor complains or puts the company on

113

Dealing with Unauthorized Deductions

1 Send an e-mail with the deduction information to the appropriate accounts receivable person at the vendor.

2 Send a form letter to the appropriate person at the vendor detailing why the deductions were taken. Make sure to include the invoice number and the dollar amount of the payment.

3 Keep scrupulous notes in the files related to any deductions taken. Then when the calls start coming, refer to your notes for an easy solution.

4 Refer the calls to the appropriate purchasing executive. This is where the calls should go, but rarely do, in most organizations.

5 Limit the hours when phone calls will be accepted to resolve discrepancies.

6 Set up a separate phone number to accept phone calls regarding discrepancies. Instruct callers to leave all pertinent information, including:

- Vendor name
- Invoice number
- Amount paid
- Check number
- Check date
- Nature of the problem
- Phone number, fax number or e-mail address where information regarding the resolution of the matter can be sent

7 Develop a form to address these complaints. E-mail it to anyone with a problem, instructing them to e-mail the form back.

TIPS & TECHNIQUES CONTINUED

At the discretion of management, this form can be forwarded to purchasing or whoever authorized the payment for resolution.

⑧ Work with purchasing to establish a mechanism for informing vendors about deductions before the inevitable call comes regarding short payments.

credit hold. Then all sorts of havoc will break loose—none of it good for accounts payable.

The "Did You Get My Invoice?" Call

Let's face it—vendors want to be paid, and they want to be paid on a timely basis. In fact, if most had their way, they wouldn't even offer payment terms. They'd either get cash in advance (CIA) or cash on deliver (COD). Additionally, many are running on a tight budget and do not have a lot of spare cash lying around in case your company decides not to pay for a couple of extra days. Thus, to circumvent the payment-timing folks and to improve their own cash-flow projections, some credit managers have taken to calling their customers in advance of the payment date.

This is what is sometimes referred to as the good will or PR call. The credit manager calls the accounts payable manager to inquire if the invoice was received and if there are any problems with it. Now on the face of it, this might seem absurd. But, sometimes these folks have good reason to call. Some companies will not contact the vendor when there is a problem with an invoice. They simply wait until the vendor calls looking for payment—sometimes as much as 45 days after the due date—and then start discussing the problem. This is really not fair and is the root of these phone calls.

Thus, credit departments began calling in advance to identify and solve unresolved issues. Unfortunately, it has occasionally gotten out of hand with collection personnel calling all customers with large balances. What can be done about this intrusion into accounts payable? Here's how a few companies handle this issue:

- *Refuse to research these calls unless the invoice in question is more than 60 days past due.* Only the 800-pound gorillas will get away with this approach. Most companies will not tolerate this approach, especially with valued and needed suppliers.

- *Set up a Web site where the vendor can check its payment status.* Vendors can then be directed to the Web site with questions. Companies such as Intel have taken this approach and report it is very successful. This should improve vendor relations.

- *Set up interactive voice response (IVR) units with the same information.* These telephone calls operate in a similar manner and have been very successful for the companies that have installed such units.

- *Only accept such calls at a given hour on a given phone.* Once vendors learn that they can call, say, between 3 p.m. and 5 p.m., they will take advantage of the service. If an employee with access to the payment system handles the calls, he or she should be able to answer a large number of these inquiries while the caller is still on the phone.

- *Refer the calls to purchasing.* Purchasing will not be happy with this solution.

Summary

Unearned discounts and unauthorized deductions are two issues that cause conflict with vendors, despite the fact that most are ultimately allowed. Finding ways to eliminate this source of conflict will ultimately lead to a smoother relationship with the vendor and fewer interruptions from these vendors about short payments.

CHAPTER 10

Travel and Entertainment: The Traditional Functions

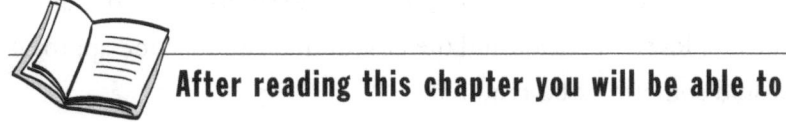

After reading this chapter you will be able to

- Understand the travel and entertainment (T & E) process
- Make intelligent recommendations regarding T & E paperwork
- Look at automation alternatives for the process
- Know how to evaluate value-added tax (VAT) and reclaim opportunities when international travel is undertaken
- Address the emerging T & E issues in the twenty-first century

Processing employee travel and entertainment reports can take a substantial amount of time if not handled efficiently. This chapter looks at the traditional functions of T & E; Chapter 11 covers emerging T & E issues.

Travel and Entertainment: An Overview

Travel and entertainment has come a long way in the last few years. Before technology and best practices made inroads into the T & E function, a traditional process typically took the following course:

1. Traveler obtained approval from supervisor for the trip. In some cases, this approval was written.

2. Traveler applied for and was given a cash advance. Often, this was for a significant amount of money if the traveler was to put the hotel bill and/or air charges on his own credit card.

3. Once the trip was complete, the traveler would submit a detailed expense report, including all receipts for the trip.

4. This report was presented to the traveler's superior, who approved the expense report for reimbursement. Depending on the employees involved and the cost of the trip, a second approval would sometimes be required.

5. Once all the approvals were in place, the expense report was forwarded to accounts payable for reimbursement with the next check run.

6. When the check had been produced and signed, the employee was called and asked to pick up the check. This caused all sorts of problems when the traveler wasn't around or the employee with the check was not around when the traveler came to pick it up.

7. The traveler would deposit the check and pay the credit card bill with the hotel, air, and other business-related charges.

This paper-intensive process required the cooperation of a number of different people. If there was a breakdown at any point, the employee could end up with a large credit card bill and no funds to pay it. When this happened, and it often did, an argument would ensue (usually in accounts payable), with the employee demanding to be reimbursed and the poor accounts payable associate with no ability to do it.

Today, few companies operate in this manner. For the most part, unless the circumstances are extreme, companies do not provide cash advances. The general feeling is that cash advances cause more problems than they solve. The traveler who has a credit card bill to pay is much

more likely to submit a report on a timely basis if he or she needs the company's money to pay the bill. This threat is reduced with the cash advance, and companies found that they had problems get the timely submission of T & E reports.

Most companies now offer corporate credit cards. Typically, these cards are either individual pay/corporate liability or corporate pay/ corporate liability. The other big changes relate to checking receipts, automation, and report and receipt handling.

As you can guess from this brief overview, it is vital that a company has T & E policy. Without a written policy, employees in different departments will be treated differently, and the accounts payable staff must simply rely on the managers' approval of all expenses. Accounts payable cannot enforce T & E procedures unless employees have a definite written policy. This chapter provides guidelines that can be used to create a T & E policy. For further information, you can also search the Internet for a sample policy and then modify it to meet your company's requirements.

Checking/Auditing T & E Reports

It is not cost effective for most companies to check every report and every receipt. The cost involved with such in-depth checking versus the amount of money saved is usually excessive—the dollar chasing a dime principle. Thus, it is now considered a best practice to only spot check T & E reports. Typically, reports are selected for checking under any of these circumstances:

- At random
- If they exceed policy guidelines in any area
- If the total expenses on the report exceed a certain pre-assigned level
- If the individual has been identified as one whose reports have been questionable in the past

Receipts

Receipts are a necessary evil for most companies when it comes to handling T & E reports. The trick is to find a way that makes the processing easier, while simultaneously satisfying both corporate and IRS requirements. Here are a few ways companies handle the problem:

1 Have all receipts placed inside an envelope and staple it to the back of the Excel-generated expense report so even the math is correct. Design the expense form with formulas (e.g., mileage) added in and frozen in their cells.

2 Check out automated systems, such as Concur Technologies, that can help you get to a near paperless state with expense reporting and the receipts required. Ask the IRS for a private letter ruling allowing you to use certain automated systems for the submittal of expense reports in conjunction with a data feed from the corporate card. This allows the company to recognize the data collected as valid receipts, except hotel bills, which will still need to be itemized electronically.

3 Have employees keep their receipts in an envelope. Spot audit a few statements each month, since the audit task is not really "value added."

4 Ask the employees to tape the small receipts to a standard size paper. They can write next to the receipts the purpose of expense or calculate the exchange rate, and so on. Then they staple it all to the back of their expense report. It saves a lot of time when the accountant has to review the receipts. It is also neatly organized, and the managers who approve the expense reports like it.

5 Consider implementing the electronic bar code scanning (e.g., IBM's Expense Reporting Solution). It works this way: Once a traveler finishes an expense report, and prints it out, the hard

copy has a bar code across the top of the front page and serves as a cover letter for the receipts. While the actual expense report goes via the Internet to the approver and to the accounting, the traveler mails the receipts. When the accounts payable gets the receipts, someone scans the bar code, which records a confirmation with the expense report in the system, that the receipts are on file in the accounts payable department. Presumably, the bar code can also help to retrieve the receipts for an audit.

6. Instruct employees to tape the smaller receipts to a sheet of paper and just staple it to the expense report.

7. Print out expense reports onto envelopes. The front is the expense worksheet and the back has a cheat sheet on what is and isn't reimbursable. Some travelers like this approach because it keeps each trip separate and gives them a place to store the receipts until they can work up the reimbursement.

8. Have bar-coded receipt envelopes printed and distributed throughout the company. They are pre-addressed and postage-paid. At the end of a Web-based expense report, the system asks for the bar code number to be entered. Upon receipt by accounts payable, the envelopes are scanned and filed according to received date (alphabetically, as their last name also appears on the outside of the envelope).

Companies that spot check audit anywhere from 5 to 25 percent of their employees' reports. Typically when a company moves to a spot check process, it starts at the 25 percent level. As the company gains comfort with the process, it progressively checks a smaller and smaller percentage.

Automating the Process

There are a number of big, expensive T & E systems that companies can buy. Implementing these systems can be time consuming and costly, in addition to the purchase price. As we go to print, some of these systems are becoming available through the Internet as an application service provider (ASP). This approach significantly lowers the up-front investment and simply requires the company to pay a set-up fee and usage fee for each report prepared.

Other, less costly approaches are also available. Some companies do remarkably well taking an Excel spreadsheet approach. The form is designed and the formulas are programmed into the form and locked in so the employee using the template will not be able to tamper with the formulas. The form is filled out and sent to accounts payable for processing.

Still another approach involves filling out the T & E form, either through an ASP or an internally generated form, and then passing the form around for approvals and payment using e-mails and workflow. Typically, the report is e-mailed to the supervisor for approval and then forwarded by the supervisor for payment. A few companies do after-the-fact approvals.

Another neat feature in some of the more sophisticated systems is the ability to automate escalating approvals. Thus, if a report is forwarded to a supervisor for approval and no action is taken, after a pre-set number of days the report is then sent to the supervisor's supervisor for approval with a notice to all parties that this is happening because no action has been taken by the first supervisor. This feature covers the cases of the first supervisor being unexpectedly out of the office. These systems also allow supervisors to update the systems when they will be out so reports are automatically forwarded to the next person up the ladder.

Getting Direct Deposit

Ask any manager responsible for T & E about using direct deposit for expense report reimbursements and you'll get nothing but positive endorsements. Yet, when these managers recommend direct deposit, they often run into a brick wall. Why? Since the cost savings are not overwhelming, it is difficult to cost justify the change to management. The problem is often exacerbated when other employees within the company fight the move to direct deposit. So, what is a manager to do? Here are a few cost justification techniques that work:

1. Cost justify the process.

2. Include the *costs* of answering phone calls asking where the check is. One company noticed a significant time and effort savings by knowing exactly where the payment was with electronic fund transfer (EFT). No more *the check is in the mail* and tracking down cleared checks.

3. Include the cost of losing the float on the money. Do the math and you may come up with significant savings and benefits by going to EFT.

4. Are your employees in the field or at headquarters? Customer satisfaction may be a cost for you. Sometimes if people are in the field and you direct deposit their reimbursement, they have no idea until they get the remittance in the mail. You may want to look into electronic remittance. Oracle and at least one third-party vendor (Bottomline Tech.) can send the remittance via e-mail. That way you get rid of the paper completely and your employees get their payment info quickly and easily. On the vendor side, it is much cheaper than FEDI (Financial EDI).

5. Look for a Web-based T & E system that will do direct deposits.

6. Don't forget the convenience factor. The direct deposit feature saves time and money in processing phone calls and placing stop payments on lost checks, not to mention how much happier the employees will be. People who travel extensively and have a hard time getting to the bank to deposit their checks really take to the direct-deposit concept.

EXHIBIT 10.1

Costs to Consider When Evaluating a Direct Deposit Option

- Check stock
- Envelope stock
- Time spent printing checks
- Time spent signing checks
- Time spent stuffing envelopes
- Bank reconciliation time
- Bank clearing processes
- Stamp ($0.34/check)
- Phone time regarding check status
- Lost checks

To help readers who wish to cost justify the move to direct deposit, Exhibit 10.1 lists some of the costs that can be included in that analysis. However, the big advantage of direct deposit is that it allows the accounts payable department to efficiently use its limited resources on more meaningful work. Remind management of this the next time there is a request for productivity-enhancing suggestions.

You may be able to identify additional costs that relate to the way checks are processed in your organization.

Value-Added Tax Reclaim

Value-added tax (VAT) is a consumer-oriented tax imposed on goods and services. A taxable entity incurring VAT for business purposes may be entitled to a VAT refund in many European countries and Canada. However, getting that refund is no simple task. The company entitled

to the refund must provide the original invoice, together with an application form and other supporting documentation, to the VAT authorities in the country where the expenditure was incurred. Typically, VAT reclaim is only an issue for companies whose executives travel to Europe and Canada extensively. Because the process is so technically complicated, many companies choose to outsource this function. However, even if the function is outsourced, the company must work with the outsourcer to make sure the proper documentation is provided.

Many companies reclaim the maximum allowable amount of their VAT payments because they know exactly what is reclaimable, and because they have the correct documentation.

Do We Have Enough to Worry About?

Reclaiming VAT payments is aggravating even for companies who use an outside service such as Meridian. Although these services do everything possible to make the process easy, a certain amount of effort on the part of the accounts payable staff is required.

Here's how Meridian VAT Reclaim's Sherri Gastelum says you can figure it out. Take half the amount spent on land travel and add that to half the amount spent on air. Multiply that by 15 percent (the average VAT charge). Figure out what percentage of your company's travel takes place in Europe. Then take that percentage and multiply it by the VAT calculation (see Exhibit 10.2). When you have your estimated VAT reclaim amount, you can decide whether reclaiming the VAT is worth the effort.

VAT levels are different from one country to another, and various items are recoverable in different countries. For example, Belguim does not allow business travelers to reclaim VAT on hotel costs, while the 17.5 percent charged in the United Kingdom and the 8 percent charged in Finland are reclaimable. VAT charges on meals are no longer

EXHIBIT 10.2

VAT Reclaim Estimating Worksheet

Average VAT charge =

$$\left(\frac{\text{Amount spent on land travel}}{2} + \frac{\text{Amount spent on air travel}}{2} \right) \times .15$$

Estimated VAT reclaim amount =

$$\text{Average VAT charge} \times \left(\frac{\text{Amount spent on European travel}}{\text{Amount spent on all travel}} \right)$$

recoverable in the United Kingdom. Visit Meridian's Web site (www.meridianvat.com) for updates.

Increasing Your Claim

VAT claims are often denied because documentation is not completed exactly the way the authorities require. To avoid that situation, Gastelum recommends giving the following instructions to your travelers in Europe:

- *Obtain original VAT invoices.* The authorities will not accept credit card receipts, copies of invoices, or statements of charges.

- *Request a VAT invoice for car rentals.* Otherwise, the invoice you get will not be usable for VAT reclaim purposes.

- *Avoid express checkouts.* Why? Because the invoices slipped under the door are not considered original invoices.

By sharing Gastelum's excellent advice to the company's travelers, the accounts payable professional will increase the odds of getting documentation that the VAT authorities will have no choice but to pay.

How Amazon.com Brought Scalability to the T & E Process

Some rapidly growing companies find that they outgrow the wonderful new T & E system implemented just a few short months earlier. The key to avoiding such problems is to focus on the scalability of software chosen. Speaking at an IOMA/IMI conference, Amazon.com's Frank McIntyre showed the audience how his department selected a T & E program that was flexible enough to handle exponential growth without increasing the size of the accounts payable staff or traumatizing the group with an overwhelming number of transactions.

Caveat

When looking for a scalable solution, managers need to exercise some caution. Cost is always a consideration. Truly scalable systems can be quite expensive. Sometimes, companies may find solutions that appear to be scalable on the front end, but on the back end the results are far from pretty. McIntyre warns against creating a back-end monster. He pointed out that results experienced when installing a new T & E system often don't meet expectations. No solution solves every problem. However, the solution selected should address most of the common problems in the organization. In reality, he says, nothing is truly scalable.

T & E executives are also cautioned to look out for hidden back-end costs. If extensive IT help is needed to implement a new system, the expense can be formidable not only in terms of dollars and cents. Getting the necessary IT personnel allocated to the project could delay implementation or draw limited resources from other projects.

Background

To put the matter in perspective, McIntyre shared some Amazon.com statistics:

- Sales increased 1000 percent from 1998 to 1999.

- Headcount at the company went from 2000 in March 1999 to 7000+ a year later.

- The accounts payable staff increased 0 percent in the same time frame.

As the company grew through aggressive product launches, the following two slogans became the company mantra:

Get Big Fast.

Just Do It.

As McIntyre laughingly noted, the last can cause problems in accounts payable, especially when it comes to T & E reports.

Solution

It was pretty clear to McIntyre that the T & E solution would have to be scalable. He uses a definition from Dictionary.com to explain what he means by scalability. It is "how well a solution to some problem will work when the size of the problem increases." He says that from a business perspective, scalability means a solution that minimizes or eliminates incremental costs as volume or activity increases.

There are a number of ways to "scale" a process. For starters, it is possible to make additional resources available. This can come from cross-training or contingent staff. Innovative uses of personnel can also help. At Amazon.com, mentally challenged individuals are employed to fold checks and stuff envelopes. Outsourcing is another possibility, as is enabling technology to help with the process. McIntyre was also looking for one other attribute. As much as possible, he wanted to get rid of the paper.

Old Amazon Process

Before Amazon.com searched for a new T & E solution, its expense reporting process was cumbersome.

- It was paper based.

- It required receipts.

- It was 100 percent audited in advance.

- Employee reimbursement occurred after approval, auditing, and processing.

- Reimbursement was by check only.

- Turnaround time averaged four to six weeks.

The problems were exacerbated by the increasing numbers of new employees who traveled extensively.

The New Solution

The implementation of a new system also allowed Amazon to put into place some best T & E practices and get away from the old mindset. It selected a Web-based expense submission, which was tied to its financial reporting system. Oracle Web Expense was chosen. Not only did the new system take a giant step away from paper, it also

- Made payment upon approval

- Audited after the fact and at a graduated depth

- Used a transaction feed from the travel card

- Had a single point of entry for credit card reconciliation coordinated with a procurement card program

Guidelines

McIntyre offers some guidelines for those wishing to emulate the changes made at Amazon.com. He suggests setting key objectives for the project at the start of the process, with input from key stakeholders. With these guidelines in place, the manager responsible for the project should model the existing process and then the new desired process. From these two models, the manager can identify the nonscalable aspects and where the risks to the system are.

Summary

The T & E process exists in virtually every company. A strong policy and intelligent procedures will minimize the impact that the process has on the accounts payable department. By utilizing automation and some of the third-party software on the market today, a company can minimize its T & E processing costs and limit the amount of staff time needed to handle the function. However, even without the purchase of expensive third-party software, a company can still effectively handle the function if a strong policy is enacted.

CHAPTER 11

Travel and Entertainment in the Twenty-First Century

After reading this chapter you will be able to

- Identify the new T & E issues—including Web airfares, online booking issues, cell phone charges, and outrageous hotel surcharges for a variety of items, including phone calls and energy

- Craft solutions to deal with the new issues

- Make recommendations to management regarding issues not previously included in the company T & E policy

- Advise company travelers on the best ways to reduce or eliminate some of the new "hotel" surcharges

If this book were written just a few short years ago, most of the issues discussed in this chapter would not have been included. The Internet has changed many accounts payable applications and procedures, with T & E being at the top of the list. Although it has improved the processes and made information much more readily available, the Internet has also introduced issues that simply did not exist in the very recent past.

Web Airfares

Travel agent or Internet? That is the question facing cost-conscious managers when it comes to getting the lowest possible airfare for busi-

ness travel. There are issues beyond grabbing the lowest price. Once upon a time, travelers were beholden to their travel agents and were forced to take whatever fare the agent quoted with no opportunity to uncover lower ticket prices. This is no longer true. The Internet gives the average traveler readily available access to the cheapest airfare— regardless of what information the travel agent chooses to provide. The problem is that many of these fares are available only if booked over the Internet or directly from a consolidator.

This limitation can be an issue for those companies whose T & E policy mandates that all company travel arrangements be made through a particular travel agency. Nevertheless, conscientious employees everywhere are checking the Internet and uncovering airfare bargains. These individuals are simply highlighting the price, not necessarily a bad focus when management is hell-bent on reducing costs. But such an approach ignores these issues:

- Control
- Potential for abuse
- Overall lower airfare costs due to negotiated rates based on volume
- Convenience
- Time (is this what companies want their well-paid executives spending their time on?)
- The ability of a travel agent to occasionally bend the airlines' rules to get a lower fare

Unfortunately, many T & E policies were written before use of the Internet was commonplace. Thus, they are silent on the booking issue.

Web Fare Realistic Solution

Here's how several managers have attacked the Web fare problem:

1. Bring the issue to management's attention and ask for a standard policy.

2. Once the issue has been decided, write up an addendum to the policy addressing how airfare ticketing is to be handled. If the decision is made to insist on using the designated travel agent, make it clear that the company will not pay for tickets purchased outside this channel.

3. Have the senior official in your company with the overall responsibility for enforcing T & E policy sign off on the policy.

4. Distribute the written policy to everyone who might be affected.

This is not a matter that the accounts payable associate can resolve. It is a management decision. However, the associate can and should bring it to management's attention. After all, they are the ones getting the expense reports containing Internet airfares.

IN THE REAL WORLD

Getting the Most from Internet Data

Companies that choose to book through a travel agent can still make use of the Internet. Some managers regularly checks flight times, prices, and other information at www.expedia.com. When the travel agent can't match the Expedia price, the manager simply prints the page off the computer and faxes it to the travel agent. Alternatively, the manager could copy the information and send it as an e-mail to the travel agent. Either way, the travel agent may be able to handle the details of booking the flight, and the traveler still gets a better deal. For the traveler, it is the best of both worlds.

Some Airfare Web Sites

On any given day, any one of the sites listed in Exhibit 11.1 could give you the lowest fare. New sites regularly appear, and company mergers or buyouts often eliminate dot-com companies. However, this list is a good place to start when looking for discount airfares.

A recent study by Stanford University's business school (and audited by KPMG) found Hotwire.com to offer the lowest fares. Hotwire paid for the study, however, thus making the results suspect. Many people find sites that require users to log in with a user ID and password a real hassle, and that is one of the requirements to use the Hotwire site.

Potential Problems When Using Internet Tickets

Many well-meaning employees adept at shopping on the Internet are posing a new problem for those responsible for controlling both the T & E process and its costs. The problem is that travelers now have access to the most accurate data when it comes to travel and can book

---

EXHIBIT 11.1

Common Airfare Web Sites

www.cheaptickets.com   www.priceline.com[b]

www.counciltravel.com[a]   www.qixo.com

www.expedia.com   www.sidestep.com

www.hotwire.com   www.travelocity.com

www.lowestfare.com   www.ukair.com[c]

www.orbitz.com

[a] For students and youths under the age of 26

[b] Name your price auction type bidding

[c] For airfares to and from the United Kingdom only

---

the travel themselves instead of going through the corporate travel office. On the face of it, this approach may seem reasonable. However, it can cause unforeseen problems:

- *Unused tickets*—Unused tickets become an even bigger problem when the travel office has no record of the initial purchase of the ticket.

- *Missing or lost receipts*—It is often difficult to obtain an acceptable receipt for trips booked online. If the receipt *is* obtained, it is important that the traveler not misplace it. Replacing a lost receipt can be difficult without the established travel-office connections.

- *Problem resolution*—This can become a nightmare should plans change or an error occur with the ticket. Airlines are more responsive to travel agents who bring them tons of business than to individual travelers who have problems.

- *False economy*—The actual savings may not be as great as the traveler thinks especially if the traveler is a high-level executive whose time would be better spent focusing on corporate issues. The few extra dollars may be insignificant when compared to diverting the executive's attention from more important issues. Additionally, many airlines tack on a $10 fee if a paper ticket is requested when an e-ticket is available. Many online bookers willingly pay this fee, further eating into potential cost savings.

- *Reduced leverage with travel agents*—When booking an individual ticket, the traveler often ignores the big picture. Companies often are able to negotiate substantial discounts based on the number of trips booked through a particular service. The traveler who books on his own diminishes this effort and puts the company in a less competitive situation when the contract comes up for bid.

- *Control*—It is difficult to monitor travel policy compliance of those who book outside the company travel agent.

Those reading this will probably realize that some of the issues raised here also apply to e-tickets, which airlines are pushing heavily, as it reduces their costs.

Internet Airfare Policy

Getting management to make a decision on the airfare booking issue is the first step to having a workable T & E airfare purchase policy. Whether Internet fares are permitted will depend somewhat on the company size and on corporate culture. Companies that don't have extensive travel budgets and therefore do not negotiate discounted airfares might be happy to allow employees to save the company some money by purchasing online.

If the company decides to allow online purchases, procedures should be written and distributed to all affected parties. Either way, once the decision is made, the T & E manager must enforce the policy uniformly and fairly.

Even if the company policy does not allow online purchases, the Internet data might still be helpful. Many executives routinely check the travel sites for timetables. At the same time, the price information is displayed. Some travelers forward this information to the travel agent, allowing them to make the booking (see "In the Real World," page 133). The only time it does not work is when the airfare displayed is available only if the ticket is purchased online without a travel agent.

There is no right or wrong answer to this dilemma. The important thing for those responsible for travel costs is to identify the issue, bring it to management's attention, and see that a corporatewide policy is adopted. With a firm policy in hand, the manager responsible for T & E cost containment will have the tools to do the job properly.

Online Booking

Online booking is one of the newest means for corporate America to cut its travel and entertainment expenses. While in theory the process should be relatively simple, real-life implementation has not been so smooth at many companies that have gone this route.

Management support is imperative to the success of any program. Without it, an online process is likely to wither on the vine. Why? Overall corporate adoption rates are low—approximately 9 percent in the United States, and much lower elsewhere. With vigorous management support, however, several companies have successfully gotten as much as 75 percent of their bookings online. The key is to have a senior-level executive who demands that employees use online bookings and then stands behind that proclamation.

At this point, a usage rate much higher than 75 percent is unlikely, for two major reasons:

1. Some senior-level executives will refuse to use the new online systems.

2. Not all airlines are online.

IN THE REAL WORLD

E-Tickets:
A Cultural Revolution

Getting people to change in the corporate environment is often difficult, especially when that change involves new technology. For many, the idea of online booking and an electronic ticket is revolutionary. They like the comfort of talking to a travel agent and the confirmation of a paper ticket. The idea of going to the airport without a ticket is unnerving. "You have no idea," reports one exacerbated travel professional, "how many times I am asked, 'What if my name isn't in the computer?'"

Selecting the Product

The marketplace for online booking systems is still in a state of flux. Not all products offer the same services, and there is no standard for the loading of private fares. These issues need to be thoroughly investigated before the vendor is selected. "We have several unclear airfare pricing issues," explains one harried executive. She says these include

- Whether the airlines or travel agencies are responsible for the loading of private fares
- Problems with making online changes to existing bookings
- Employee training

Those selecting a system are also advised to select one that will integrate preferred suppliers and that has the ability to interface globally in the case of international travel. The company selling the product should make the necessary commitment both financially and in terms of manpower.

Employee Training

Even if a great product is selected and there is superior management support, an online booking process can still bog down if the employees don't know how to use it properly. More than a few companies have learned this lesson the hard way. One of the surest ways to get buy-in from the employees (aside from having strong management support) is to see that the travelers and those responsible for making their travel arrangements know how to use the system.

"Once we started our employee training process," explains one manager, "both employee use of the system and employee satisfaction increased." How can this professional be so sure that the employees were satisfied? She says the answer to that question is simple. Since the inception of the online program, she has tracked the number of employee complaints made via telephone and e-mail and they have decreased dramatically.

A Help Desk

Those rolling out large programs have found that they can increase both the usage of the program and employee satisfaction by having a help desk. This assistance is available to any employee having difficulty using the online booking system. Sometimes a little personal attention, walking the employee through a rough spot, can make all the difference when it comes to the employee enthusiastically embracing a new system.

It might be necessary to put several additional employees on the help desk when the system is first rolled out. After it has been operational for several months, however, most companies are able to reduce the number of employees running the desk.

Mid-size companies may not need to have a full-blown help desk but will get the same results by assigning the "help function" to one or more employees who also process T & E.

User Surveys

Once a system is up and running and the employees trained, many companies are tempted to move on to the next project. There is, however, one more step that some firms take to ensure the success and user-friendliness of their online booking system. They take a satisfaction survey measuring the responses from all users and use the results to identify any weak or rough spots in their processes. Several companies have reported that they received suggestions from end users that, when implemented, made the process more manageable.

Online Booking and Electronic Tickets

Online booking does not necessarily mean electronic tickets—although the two often go together. Many travel agents and airlines issue e-tickets. A number of companies have pared their T & E costs by simply moving to an electronic ticket format. Nevertheless, even in an online booking

environment, some travelers are not comfortable with e-tickets, especially if international travel is involved. This is definitely a case where you can have one without the other and still see cost savings.

Online booking is here to stay, and its use will grow in the coming years. Those who are not already using it are well advised to learn all they can about the new process—it is only a matter of time before it will come to your company.

Hotel Surcharges

Hotels have found another way to supplement their income. Rather than raising their prices (that would be too obvious), they add new charges to their bills. The most understandable, perhaps, are the energy surcharges that hotels began adding when fuel prices went through the roof. The implication is that the surcharges will be removed when the fuel prices subside. What is bothersome about these fees is that in all likelihood, it will take the hotels quite some time to remove them as fuel prices go down. Also, when fuel prices dip, hotels never bother to give travelers a rebate for the money the hotels saved on their fuel bills.

The second, more troubling type of fee is something referred to by various names including luxury fee, resort charge, and so forth. Some hotels make these fees mandatory, while others will remove them if the guest objects. These daily fees tend to run anywhere from $10 to $20 per day. The hotels say they cover items such as

- Parking (regardless of whether the guest actually has a car!)
- Use of the gym
- Unlimited local calls
- A free copy of *USA Today*
- Free 800 phone calls

and a variety of other perks that travelers may never use.

You may wonder why the hotels don't simply raise their rates, and that is a legitimate question. There are several reasons. Being able to quote a lower price makes them more competitive in a bidding situation. Also, it allows the traveler to squeak in under company pricing limits, which puts it on more companies' lists of allowable hotels. Finally, relying on surcharges gives the hotel the appearance of having lower prices than it actually does, snagging customers who like "bargains."

Whatever the reason, many hotel bills are starting to sport these charges. Travelers in a hurry might not even realize that they can opt out of these fees in some cases. In any event, the accounts payable associate, when reviewing travel receipts, should realize that not all of these luxury fees are an extravagance on the part of the traveler. The fee may simply be the hotel's way of lining its own pocket without appearing to charge a higher price.

Hotel Surcharges for Phones

The outrageous fees some hotels are charging for phone calls has gotten out of hand. For starters, phone calls made to 800 numbers are not always free when made from a hotel room. Almost all hotels charge a fee ranging from 85¢ to $1.25. Most travelers know this and are not overly concerned about this small amount. What they don't realize is that a number of hotels start charging if the phone call lasts more than 60 minutes. This is an especially important issue to those companies that give their employees an 800 number to use to call the office when traveling. The company ends up paying for the call twice if the call should exceed one hour, as many to the office do. Also, if many short calls are placed to an 800 number, the bill can add up quickly. One executive ended up with a bill in excess of $100 for such calls.

Long-distance calls can really hurt. One harried executive expecting to pay about a dollar a minute for long-distance calls was horrified

to find out that the hotel actually billed him at the rate of $3 a minute. This kind of hidden surcharge violates FCC regulations.

A 1998 FCC rule requires that "people away from home be told in advance what rate they would have to pay and how to reach a company they usually use." Is this being done? The FCC made calls from 1,700 hotel and motel telephones and coin phones. *Result:* Three large telephone services were fined.

The American Hotel Association distributes a guide for hotel use that lists FCC's requirements. In boldface, the flier says it is not enough for a hotel to put information about its phone service into the usual tabletop portfolio, or even in a drawer. The information, including how to reach other telephone companies, must be posted "on or near the telephones used by guests or the public." The flier also says that guests must be able to dial all three types of access codes: 800, 950, and 10-10 or 10-15 "dial around" codes that circumvent the hotels' preferred long-distance companies.

Should your travelers have any complaints about failures to adhere to the code, they can address their complaints to:

FCC, Consumer Information Bureau

445 12th St. SW

Washington DC 20554

Surprise Charges—When a Chain Is Not a Chain

Confusing the issue of hotel surcharges even further is the fact that most chains do not own or manage all the units that bear their name. T & E managers might think they know all the billing policies of a particular chain, only to be stung by a specific franchise. The fees quoted by hotels are generally only for those units owned or managed by the chain. Others can and do charge what they like.

Hotel Phone Horror Stories

Long-distance phone charges at most hotels are disgraceful. Few post the actual rates. Those that do rarely quote a dollar figure but show a percentage of their phone carrier's rate, indicating something like "125 percent of AT&T's long distance rate." Don't think this rate is ten cents a minute. In most cases, it will turn out to be something in excess of one dollar a minute. Many experienced travelers get around this ploy by calling their offices using an 800 number. Typically, hotels charge an $0.85 connect charge and several chains start their long-distance clock running after 20 minutes. The $0.85 only buys those first 20 minutes.

Some hotels automatically charge travelers for three minutes each time they dial long distance, whether or not a connection is made. The three-minute fee is also charged even if only a quick message is left on an answering machine. Pick up the phone, dial a long-distance number, and the meter starts ticking at $8.

Thus, travelers should be encouraged to review their bill for ridiculous surcharges before checking out. It is worthwhile to point out that a valet parking fee is not justified for the traveler who took a taxi from the airport. Likewise, it is worth noting that $3/minute is an excessive long-distance fee. Hotel managers will often reduce these charges when challenged.

Look at the hotel folio bills submitted by your travelers and you are likely to find some pretty outrageous phone fees. Even those eight- and nine-dollar entries may not be as innocuous as they appear.

Cell Phones

Another new issue to complicate the lives of the accounts payable associate is cell phones. Corporate road warriors live by their cell phones.

Phone Surcharges

① Before picking up the phone, read the hotel's phone charge policy. Most places either have a little card near the phone that states the policy or include it in their guest services book. If you cannot find a written statement, call the hotel operator and ask about the charges. Savvy travelers first got around the extreme charges by using 800 phone numbers, but some hotels have retaliated. Obviously, you can hang up every 20 minutes, but this is not always feasible, and it projects the wrong image.

② If the hotel's rates are excessive, collect calls are a reasonable alternative, as are corporate calling cards.

③ Prepaid phone cards can be given to travelers. These are currently available for 4.1 cents to 5.9 cents a minute. They are not quite as convenient as simply picking up the phone and dialing, but the amount of money saved more than offsets this minor inconvenience. As for tracking the calls made on these cards, it is almost not worth the effort.

④ A growing number of executives completely eschew the hotel phones and use cell phones to place their calls. Given the attractive cell phone rates offered in many parts of the country, they are reasonable perks for the traveling corporate executive. Each company will need to set its own policy on this matter.

⑤ Most hotels place bills under the door during the last night of the traveler's stay. Recommend that your travelers review their phone charges closely before checking out. If they have been charged for any calls that did not go through, they can demand that these charges be removed from their bill. In addition, if the charges for other calls seem out of line, don't just take it. When checking out, tell the clerk that you feel the

TIPS & TECHNIQUES CONTINUED

charges are unmerited. Many will automatically reduce the charges. One hotel automatically takes one-third off the phone bills of any guest who complains. If the clerk is unwilling or unable to reduce the phone charges, ask to speak to the manager or the person in charge. Explain your complaint politely, but firmly. Most will make some attempt at accommodating the guest. If enough travelers make it clear that they will not accept these outrageous rates, the hotels will probably look for some other means of making money. By sharing these tips with travelers, those responsible for T & E can help lower corporate travel costs.

Unfortunately, many accounts payable associates have experienced headaches over employee cell phone usage. These problems stem from a lack of policy, separating business from personal charges, complex pricing deals, sales and use tax issues, and billing woes.

A formal policy for cellular phones is therefore imperative. Otherwise there will be multiple contracts floating around—all at different prices. Also, with no formal policy, you will end up with the haves and the have-nots. That is, some departments will allow employees to have cell phones while other departments will not. A companywide policy eliminates this issue.

It is also important to develop a uniform rate. In most organizations, extensive use by employees of cell phones is so new that there is no uniform contract for everyone. Employees have gone out on their own to acquire their phones and contracts but, since some employees are better shoppers than others, the end result is chaos. As cell phones become more common, the rate matter should become less of an issue.

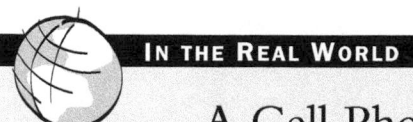

A Cell Phone Solution

As cell phones—and the new wireless Web phones—continue to proliferate, more and more of these kinds of problems will crop up. Companies with no overall plan in place can start fresh, but those with a variety of existing contracts will have a much harder time. Here is how one company addressed this problem.

The company negotiated reduced corporate rates for cell phone charges with a large cellular provider in the Los Angeles area. The company also decided which plan to offer based on an average monthly call volume. It then offered the employees the option of purchasing a new digital phone (required for the reduced rate) at the employees' expense and being reimbursed at the reduced rate, or keeping their own cell phone and plan, and receiving a reimbursable expense not to exceed the corporate rate. Most employees bought a new cell phone and went with the corporate rate because it was more attractive than any plan they could get on their own. If employees went over the corporate plan for the number of minutes, they would be responsible for paying the difference. Each employee signed an agreement detailing the plan.

The best way to ensure uniformity in contracts and rates is to have corporate negotiate a companywide purchase and provide phones to those who are authorized, in a manner similar to p-cards.

Summary

Cost and control issues related to T & E are rapidly changing with new products, technologies, and approaches. The accounts payable associate who continues to keep on top of these developments and who understands how these processes work will be in the best position to advise and monitor the T & E process.

CHAPTER 12

Electronic Data Interchange: The Key to a Paperless Accounts Payable World

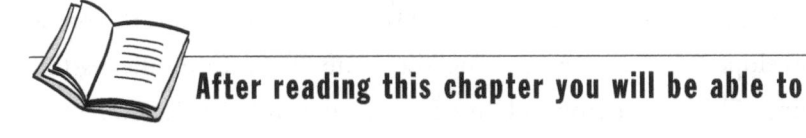

After reading this chapter you will be able to

- Have a basic understanding of electronic data interchange (EDI) concepts related to accounts payable
- Understand where EDI will fit into the big Internet picture in the future
- Understand accounts payable–related information in EDI transaction sets
- Make recommendations regarding the implementation of EDI and term renegotiations with vendors

Consider this a warning. This is probably not the most interesting chapter you will read in this book, but it is important. So, resist the temptation to skip to the next chapter, especially if the company you work for (or hope to work for one day) is very large or is a supplier to a giant such as Ford or General Motors. A number of these biggies are demanding that their suppliers use EDI if they want to do business with them.

What Is EDI?

The National Automated Clearing House Association (NACHA) offers the following definitions:

Electronic Data Interchange (EDI) is the application-to-application exchange of business information in a standard format.

Financial EDI (FEDI) is the electronic movement of payments and payment-related information through the banking system in a standard format between two parties.

Uniformity

What makes EDI work, despite its rigid standards, is that EDI standards were developed and everyone using the same "definition" means the same thing. The most commonly used standard is that developed by the American National Standards Institute (ANSI). ANSI uses the term *X12* to denote standards that cross industry, function, and company lines. Thus, the standards used for EDI are often referred to as ANSI X12.

Many companies have huge EDI systems and are not willing to throw that investment away. Thus, it is likely that despite advances in Internet technology and the development of Extensible Markup Language (XML), EDI will be with us for some time to come. In fact, one of the newest developments in this arena is EDI over the Internet, which is discussed later in this chapter under "EDI Over the Internet."

The Data

There are numerous different types of data that can be transmitted from supplier to customer and vice versa using EDI. Each type, or *transaction set,* is precisely defined and has its own set of instructions. Each transaction set can be broken into three components:

1. The *header* contains data that pertains to the entire transaction.

2. The *detail* contains information that is applicable to one line item.

3. The *summary* is a small piece containing summary and control details.

All transaction sets begin with a header, called the *transaction set header* and end with a trailer, called, what else, a *transaction set trailer.* The detail section may have many lines, each containing relevant information.

Common Accounts Payable Transaction Sets

Although there are many different transaction sets, accounts payable associates will run into three types most frequently:

1. The transaction set called 850, which represents a purchase order

2. The set called 810, which represents an invoice

3. The set called 820, which are payment orders/remittance advices

Even those companies that make heavy use of EDI to transmit information are less likely to use EDI for purposes of sending funds. In fact, some companies will send the payment information on an 820 and the actual funds by check.

Companies that do not have the in-house expertise to handle EDI themselves often make use of value-added networks (VANs) and value-added banks (VABs). These are companies that do the EDI work for the company. Sensing a natural marketplace, some banks have gotten into the EDI business and help companies with their EDI transmissions. These are referred to as VABs.

Common Types of EDI

Many reading this may think EDI is some sophisticated and complicated concept that they have never encountered before. This is probably not true, as EDI touches the lives of many Americans. If your paycheck is automatically deposited in your bank account on payday, in all likelihood, the payment was made via the Automated Clearing House (ACH) using EDI. Many banks offer a slight discount to those applying for a mortgage if the borrower allows the bank to debit his or her bank

account each month for the mortgage payment. Most banks use EDI for this feature.

Similarly, if you know anyone receiving Social Security payments deposited in their bank account instead of by check, EDI is being used. In fact, the government is one of the biggest proponents of EDI, aggressively pushing its suppliers to submit invoices and receive payments electronically. Why? Because it is easier, cheaper, and once the system is set up, simpler.

Two Types of EDI Payments

Those reading this may have noted that receiving a paycheck electronically is very different from allowing a bank to take money out of their bank account each month for a mortgage payment. Payments can be done in one of two ways, as a credit or as debit. *ACH credits* are used when the payer deposits money into an account in payment of an invoice or for periodic payments such as paychecks, pensions, or annuities.

Alternatively, if the customer gives permission and signs the appropriate papers, the seller can automatically debit the purchaser's (or mortgagee's) bank account. This type of transaction is called an *ACH debit*. As you might imagine, many companies are reluctant to allow this type of arrangement.

It should be noted that only in the United States is there such strong resistance to the debit type of payment. Consumers in other countries routinely have their accounts debited not only for their mortgage payment but also for their utility bills and other regular payments. It is a way of life for them and they cannot understand the U.S. obsession with checks. Many average Europeans can count on one hand the number of checks they write in one year. Thus, when you look at figures for electronic payments, do not be surprised to see the United States at the bottom of the list.

Common Business ACH Debit Applications

In case you haven't guessed, there aren't a whole lot of companies that are comfortable with ACH debits. The idea of letting someone else go into their bank account sends shivers down the spines of most treasurers —and the bigger the company, the less likely they are to agree to this concept. There are, however, a few places where ACH debits are being used in the business environment:

- Certain tax payments
- Oil payments made to large companies on behalf of their station owners
- Interest payments made to financial institutions on behalf of certain debtors

EDI Over the Internet

The Internet has been a boon to many avenues of life, and EDI is no exception. Although many people either have trouble understanding all the gobbledy-gook associated with EDI or are simply bored to tears by the topic, most adults are comfortable with e-mail. It didn't take long for the powers that be to figure out that one way to reduce some of the horrendous costs associated with EDI would be to abandon costly VANs and move to transmitting data over the Internet. Yes, there are security considerations, but they are being addressed.

However, a number of banks have announced or are working on plans that will allow the transmission of EDI data over the Internet. Will the VANs go away? Unlikely. They will simply adjust and offer services to help those using the Internet.

Advantages of EDI

You may be wondering why companies go to all the bother of implementing EDI when it seems like it might be costly, rigid, and difficult to understand. Obviously, there are some compelling advantages:

- Fewer errors due to automated data entry
- Time savings due to the fact that there is no need to reenter data
- Time and cost savings due to the reduction in errors from keying mistakes
- Improved accuracy of data
- Decreased cost of paper supplies
- Reduced postage expenditures
- Fewer late payment charges
- A reduction in the number of lost discounts
- Improved accuracy of information shared within the company
- Data received more quickly, resulting in problems being uncovered sooner

Effect of EDI on Terms

One of the biggest excuses companies use for not moving to EDI, and more frequently FEDI, is float. Thus, in order to make EDI palatable to everyone involved, companies often renegotiate the payment terms with their suppliers so no one has even a "perceived" financial loss. This usually takes into account both mail and processing time and can result in an additional two to five days for the customer.

Trading Partner Directory

Despite the fact that EDI has been around for decades, use of it is limited. (see Exhibit 12.1) When your company makes the investment in EDI and begins to appreciate its benefits, it will want to add vendors to its EDI program. But how can you identify which suppliers are EDI capable? A company can query its existing vendors or check in NACHA's Trading Partner Directory.

EXHIBIT 12.1

Current EDI Users

By Company Size	
All companies	20.3%
Up to 99	10.5%
100–249	9.9%
250–499	8.8%
500–999	6.7%
1000–4999	22.5%
5000 & up	55.4%

What About the Future?

To see where EDI would go in the next five years, we turned to Harris Bank's EDI product manager, Greg Makowski. He spoke about how EDI changes affect the accounts payable associate:

> The good news, or the bad depending upon your perspective, is traditional EDI is not going away anytime soon. Large corporations—automotive companies, manufacturers, shipping, retail, grocers, etc. and organizations with large supplier bases—have invested heavily in EDI and have reaped the benefits of increased productivity and cost savings. EDI works well for them, they are satisfied and have no need to change.
>
> Furthermore, there is a plethora of new and very functional/easier-to-use EDI engines/translators on the market. That wasn't the case even two, three years ago, despite the fact EDI has been around for a long time. Until recently there weren't a lot of choices in vendors and the systems were very complicated and didn't have a good deal of flexibility (think any-to-any mapping).

Web-based EDI will obviously grow in the next two to five years as infrastructure changes allow more flexibility in sending/receiving and integrating EDI files with their applications. XML is still questionable until a solid standard is developed. There are over 3,000 versions of XML in use today. Most are developed and used between a large hub and its supplier base for POs, invoices, etc. Groups like DISA (Data Interchange Standards Association) and its ebXML should fill that void. Once DISA develops rules and a standard, XML should start taking off. For many organizations, XML will not completely replace EDI, but will be integrated along with and compliment EDI to reach smaller non–EDI-capable trading partners.

As for A/P applications, Web EDI and XML are still doubtful in the near future for the following reasons:

1. *Clients are still concerned about Internet security.* For large-scale XML payments, there still are many issues and concerns surrounding digital certificates.

2. *Many EDI payment files require just-in-time processing and are deadline oriented.* When clients use a VAN or send their EDI files direct, there is a strong comfort level ensuring that their payments will be made on settlement date. With the Internet, as it is today, there are a lot of concerns about timing.

3. *XML files are a minimum of 10 to 20 times larger than traditional EDI files.* Originating companies, originating banks, ACH operators (Fed), the receiving banks, and the receiving companies all will have to beef up their infrastructures to handle the tremendous volume and additional costs. There is a NACHA work group that is looking at the impacts of including XML within an ACH transaction (similar to an EDI CTX). Recommendations from the committee will be submitted to NACHA's steering committee by late summer

2001. If adopted, this will be a major ACH change and will take at least two to three years.

XML, however, is seen as a catalyst for more widespread adoption of electronic business practices. There are a number of factors such as the availability of standards, free tools, usability of XML over open networks, and the fact that XML is both human and machine readable concurrently. The future benefits of XML as it relates to the payment system are:

1. XML remittance information is carried through ACH with the payment.

2. XML data requirements for current stakeholders will add value to their customers.

3. XML payment order files provided by the originator to the originating bank that can be translated into ACH payments (required fields are needed for this to happen, however).

4. Ability to reach an extended audience, much larger that the current X12 installed base. This would include both business-to-consumer as well as B2B.

5. Value-added service for banks will provide Internet/XML remittance data to collection customers.

The long and short of it, however, is that you won't see anything happening with XML in the payment system (like EDI) for at least two or three years.

Summary

Although XML (see Chapter 13) may be the wave of the future, EDI appears to be here to stay for the foreseeable future. Thus, accounts payable associates should attempt to learn all they can about this subject.

Using the Internet in Accounts Payable

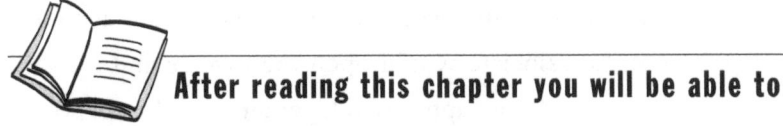

After reading this chapter you will be able to

- Understand how the Internet is being used in the average accounts payable department

- Know what advances are coming and prepare your company for them

- Find relevant accounts payable information on the Web

- Know what information to include in a company Internet or intranet accounts payable site

- Understand the advances and the limitations of e-mail and thus use it appropriately

The Internet has changed the accounts payable world forever. Information from vendors, service providers, and other accounts payable associates has affected the way the job is done today. Most experts believe that the revolution has just begun.

Most Basic Use of the Internet: E-mail

How did we ever survive without e-mail? Virtually all companies have given their accounts payable associates the ability to use e-mail with the outside. This is vital because most vendors not only correspond in this manner but are also starting to send invoices electronically. In the next

few years, the growth in invoices delivered over the Internet is expected to explode. While it is unlikely that paper invoices will ever go away completely, the wealth of new products on the market and the interest that corporate America has in cutting costs will feed this growth.

When combined with imaging, e-mail can become a powerful tool, eliminating much of the manual paperwork in accounts payable. Here's what's happening at some leading-edge companies. The paper-intensive approval process might have an invoice coming first to the accounts payable department. An associate would open the invoice and forward it to the appropriate party for an approval. Depending on the corporate culture, the original invoice might be sent or a copy of the original sent with the original held in accounts payable for safe keeping. That way, when the approver lost the invoice (or never received it), accounts payable had the original to make another copy to send for approval. (and you wonder why duplicate payments are such a problem?).

Eventually, after several phone calls, the approver would dig the invoice out from under an in-box, approve the invoice, and send it back to accounts payable using inter-office mail. If the approver were in the same building, the whole process could take as little as two days or as long as—well, your guess is as good as mine. If the approver were in another building or worse, across the country, the most efficient approvers might have the invoice back in a week, and the less efficient....

Enter imaging and e-mail. Now, the invoice when received in accounts payable can be imaged and the original hard copy either destroyed or sent to cold storage, depending on the company's policy. Then, using e-mail the image is forwarded to the approver for review and formal approval. There is now an audit trail for everyone to see. The send date is on the e-mail and the approver can no longer claim he didn't get the invoice, it was lost in the inter-office mail, accounts payable never sent it, or any other excuse.

If the approval is not received back in a timely fashion, the accounts payable associate can follow up using e-mail. Many companies have what is referred to as *escalating approvals*. They work like this. If after an agreed-upon number of days, say three or five, the approval has not been obtained, a reminder message is sent, usually automatically. If the approval is still not returned within a few days, the invoice is then forwarded automatically to the next-level approver—on an escalating basis. In theory, the invoice could eventually land on the president of the company's desk, but it is unlikely that this would ever happen.

The beauty of escalating approvals is that not only are they exceedingly efficient at removing an unpleasant task (the follow-up, please-approve-the-invoice phone calls) from the accounts payable department, they also cover vacation, sick days, and other emergency contingencies. After all, most bosses know when their subordinates are on vacation. There is also a subtle pressure on the approver. Once approvers realize that if they do not review invoices on a timely basis, the boss will know rather quickly, they tend to take the invoice approval process a lot more seriously.

Dealing with Discrepancies

E-mails to cover discrepancy resolution can be handled in a similar manner. Forms can be designed to make the process easier on everyone involved—and if accounts payable does not receive a response in the agreed-upon number of days, the e-mail can and should escalate to the next highest person on the list. This should not be done without the knowledge of everyone involved. It is an extremely efficient way of resolving the discrepancy and deduction issues.

A Word about Company E-mail Accounts

Some accounts payable associates are surprised to learn that their company e-mail accounts do not belong to them but to the company. That

means the company has the right to monitor any and all information that goes through those accounts. Many companies do this on a regular basis. Thus, you should have no expectation of privacy when it comes to that account.

Although some companies do not mind if their employees receive personal e-mails in their corporate accounts, it is wise to remember that corporate policy can change at a moment's notice. Do not have anything come into or go out of your company account that you do not want your boss to see—that includes off-color jokes, resumes, company secrets, and anything else that others might deem objectionable. More than one employee has lost his or her position due to inappropriate use of the Internet at the office. Some e-mails sent from European companies come with a warning footer noting that the e-mails are property of the company (and not the employee) and thus can be reviewed by a company official at any time.

Use of free e-mail (but not Internet access) from companies such as yahoo.com rocketmail.com and others is recommended not only for personnel communications but also as a backup, should your company's e-mail system go down. This account will provide you with an alternate means of communication should that happen. You do not realize how dependent you've become on e-mail until circumstances contrive to deprive you of the ability to communicate electronically.

Invoices Over the Internet

Are you ready to handle an infusion of invoices from your vendors over the Internet? Have you developed systems and procedures that will handle transactions being initiated not only on your company Web site, but also on someone else's? Think the Internet won't play such an intrusive role in business commerce for another 5 to 10 years? Well, think again. Both General Motors and Ford have announced massive

plans to become powerful players in the e-commerce arena—and we are not talking about selling cars.

By the end of 2001, General Motors expects to make all of its $87 billion purchases through its Web site. Whether it's steel for a manufacturing plant or pencils for its executives, the orders will be placed over the Internet. Ford Motor Company has similar plans. That's not all. Both companies expect their suppliers to purchase and sell excess inventory through the GM or Ford Web site. Since General Motors has approximately 30,000 suppliers—only slightly more than Ford—this will prove to be a massive undertaking. Even if you do not do business with General Motors or Ford, you may very well buy from some of the same suppliers who will have the ability to accept orders online in the new virtual marketplace.

What Accounts Payable Pros Can Expect

Although Ford and GM might not meet their aggressive targets, they will come close. Once their suppliers have invested the money to go online as required, many will like it and, in turn, will require that their suppliers go online as well. This will increase the number of companies participating in the automotive-based virtual marketplace. Other industries are sure to follow suit once the cost savings become apparent.

Most experts estimate that it costs approximately $100 for automotive companies to process a purchase order, but most of this processing cost can be saved using the Internet. This is just the beginning of the savings. With corporate America's zeal to cut costs, many other companies will begin participating in or developing their own virtual marketplaces.

Accounts payable professionals will feel pressure from purchasing and management to become e-commerce proficient and to find ways to modify existing systems and procedures to work under the new paradigm.

In theory, a commerce model with information passing between buyer and seller electronically should leave little room for human error. This *should* translate into fewer discrepancies as a result of pricing or other information errors.

On the plus side for accounts payable, the purchasing professionals using the new systems will also be responsible for inputting all information. Not only will they have to become e-commerce proficient, they will be monitored by their own companies to ensure that they do everything correctly. This may patch up some of the "black holes" into which needed information sometimes falls.

Action Steps

This is an area where accounts payable professionals can be the missionaries within their own organizations. By alerting management to the upcoming changes and recommending changes to accommodate electronic commerce within the accounts payable department, managers will be ready when electronic orders and invoices become the norm.

The accounts payable department will need to be staffed with professionals who are 100 percent computer- and related-technology-literate. This means not only knowing how to use the Internet, but also having a thorough understanding of the programming languages that will become the standard. XML is already a leading candidate in that field. Those who are ready for the change and can adapt quickly will not only survive, but thrive in the new electronic age.

There are several exciting new products on the market that make the invoices over the Internet a whole lot easier and put the capability within the reach of the average company. See Chapter 20, "Accounts Payable in the Twenty-First Century" for additional information.

Accounts Payable Web Pages

That's right, accounts payable departments everywhere are setting up their own Web pages. Some are doing it on the Internet for everyone to see. Others are limiting it to in-house folks and are putting them on intranet sites. Most are not hiring fancy consultants to do this but are doing it themselves.

On *intranet* sites, that might include these features:

- Answers to frequently asked accounts payable questions
- Accounts payable contact list with phone extensions and responsibilities
- Accounts payable deadlines for check requests
- Accounts payable policy and procedures manual
- T & E policy and forms
- Petty cash policy and forms—if a petty cash box still exists
- Purchasing card information
- All other accounts payable forms
- Copies of past issues of your internal accounts payable newsletter, if you have one

On *Internet* sites, that might include these features:

- Payment status of open invoices (password-protected, of course)
- Accounts payable contact list indicating responsibilities with phone numbers
- Company's invoice and supplier policies
- Companies W-9 policy for independent contractors

Those professionals who are curious about the Web and would like to design a home page but don't know where to start might try a company accounts payable Web site. What better way to pick up a new skill while

IN THE REAL WORLD

The Internet in Accounts Payable

What follows is a list of ways accounts payable professionals are now using the Internet along with Web sites that either provide information about the topic or present examples of how companies execute the strategies mentioned. This is probably a good place to reiterate what was said at the beginning of the book: The Web sites all worked at the time the book went to print. A few will probably no longer exist when you go to check them out. However, you may be able to find some that are even better to demonstrate the principles discussed.

1 *Ask questions.* If you need to know how to do something, try

- www.ioma.com/discussion/boards.html
- www.recapinc.com/ask_the_experts.htm

to get an answer from your peers or from an expert.

2 *Add frequently asked questions.* Do you get asked the same questions over and over again? Prepare a frequently asked questions (FAQ) sheet and post in on your intranet site.

- www.vcu.edu/procurement/apfaqs.htm

3 *Provide information within the company.* Prepare an in-house newsletter and post it on your Web site after sending copies to all employees.

4 *Use search engines.* When looking for information, be specific. Don't just type "a/p," for example. Use " ", +, and *not* to limit the results.

- www.dogpile.com
- www.google.com
- www.excite.com
- www.lycos.com

- www.ask.com
- www.altavista.com

⑤ *Locate p-card information.*

- www.americanexpress.com/cpc/pa/maintenance
- www.mastercard.com/ourcards.corporate/purchasing-card.html
- www.visa.com/pd/comm/purch/main.html
- www.purchase-card.com
- co.stanford.edu/payments/disbursements/credit-cards/pcard/manual/index.html

⑥ *Find the latest fraud prevention information.*

- Positive pay: www.positivepay.com/
- Phony Invoice Schemes: www.bbb.org/library/ba-inv.html
- Check fraud info from the Controller of the Currency: www.occ.treas.gov/chckfrd/contents.htm
- Frank Abagnale, a fraud expert and a fascinating speaker: www.abagnale.com/

⑦ *Find personnel.* Looking for a new employee? List your opening on any one of these sites:

- www.monster.com/
- careerpath.com

⑧ *Locate tax information.* For sales and use tax information, check the first three sites. For payroll tax and other information, check the next three sites.

- www.salestaxinstitute.com
- www.bna.com
- www.vertex.com

- www.adp.com
- www.payroll-tax.com
- www.paychex.com

9 *Find VAT information.* For information about companies that will help you reclaim VAT taxes paid by executives traveling overseas, check these sites.

- www.vrc-vatrefund.com/index.html
- www.autovat.com
- www.meridianvat.com/
- www.bizednet.bris.ac.uk/virtual/economy/policy/ tools/vat/vatws.htm

10 *Make use of education/professional organizations.*

- www.afponline.org
- www.aicpa.org
- www.aipb.com
- www.americanpayroll.org
- www.iappnet.org
- www.napcp.org

11 *Post on the Internet.* Reduce the number of calls into the A/P dept. Put invoice numbers and payment status info on the Internet (with appropriate controls as to who can see information).

- www.supplier.intel.com/dobusiness/ap/
- www.openinvoice.com/

12 *Learn about letters of credit.*

- www.avgtsg.com

simultaneously doing something job related? This would be something different to add to your resume.

Summary

Become as proficient as you possibly can when it comes to using the Internet. It is here to stay and will continue to make inroads into accounts payable. Those who thrive will be those who are adept at using the Web and who make it part of their everyday arsenal of tools.

CHAPTER 14

Extensible Markup Language: What Accounts Payable Pros Need to Know

After reading this chapter you will be able to

- Have a better understanding of Extensible Markup Language (XML)

- Understand where XML is going and how it fits into the accounts payable world

- Know where to go for additional information

- Know what accounts payable can do with XML

First there was HTML (HypertText Markup Language) for creating Web sites, and now accounts payable associates are starting to hear about a wonderful new language that will make their lives simpler and financial reporting a breeze (okay, that might be a slight exaggeration). XML is being touted as the next best thing since sliced bread.

What Is XML?

Extensible Markup Language (XML) is a meta language that allows the simple creation of a language or vocabulary. It is not a programming language or a formatting language like HTML. Users set up their own vocabulary and define the elements or objects they want the language to contain. XML processes these elements.

XML can also be called a *data wrapper* because it is used to wrap content, maintain structure, and provide compatibility between systems. It can be used to integrate data from different systems running on different platforms. This is just part of the reason the professionals are so excited about it.

XML can also be used to establish content for many users from one location, using style sheets to transform the data. As you will see in "A Sixty-Second XML Course" a little further on, XML is about describing data.

The fundamental hypothesis of XML is that it is *extensible,* which means you can create your own elements or tags. They are used to explain the content stored in the file. With XML you can

- Manage documents efficiently
- Develop your own vocabulary to describe data
- Create a structure so data can be moved from one location to another
- Separate content from display

A Sixty-Second XML Course

Terry Hinder, a senior manager for Covansys, is an XML expert. She provides a refreshing view of this exciting new concept. She begins with her own definition for XML, which she calls the glue that pulls e-commerce together.

If you only need to know a little about XML, Hinder says that all you need to understand is that it is formatted as tag-data-tag. An example of a well-formed XML document is:

<greeting type = "friendly">Hello, world!</greeting>.

Although you might not understand all the formatting that goes along with the sample, you certainly can understand the intent of the message. Additionally, Hinder says that legal XML documents, called

well-formed documents, describe logical trees. If a well-formed document conforms to an optional set of constraints (called a DTD, data transaction dictionary) it is also valid.

XML and Standards

One of the most frequent complaints heard about XML is that there is more than one kind of XML. That is only partially true. Currently, there are a few different XMLs, but they are all coming together as the different groups continue to work together. Hinder believes that in five years there will be a standard. However, accounts payable professionals cannot wait that long to get involved.

The emerging leader is something referred to as ebXML (electronic business Extensible Markup Language) which was created in November 1999 as a result of a NATO (North Atlantic Treaty Organization) meeting. Its charter, says Hinder, was to provide an open XML-language–based infrastructure enabling the global use of electronic business information in an interoperable, secure and consistent manner by all parties in an 18-month period.

Not only did this group meet its goals, but the major players in all current e-commerce initiatives have agreed to follow ebXML as their end state e-commerce standard. Or, as Hinder says, a standard becomes a standard when enough of the 800-pound gorillas agree to use it.

Accounts Payable's Role in Setting This Standard

Although they might not realize it, a number of accounts payable people reading this had a say in getting this standard set. Everyone who responded to the Electronic Invoicing and Electronic Payment Information Task Force survey (for the creation of a *standard* invoice) or who responded to the survey on the Internet had their "vote" counted.

171

The results of that survey were used to create the Rapid e-Invoice, which was ultimately presented to the ASI X12 committee as the "standard" for invoices. The Rapid e-Invoice is now available for use by anyone who wishes to use it. The form, along with much other related useful information, can be accessed through the Internet at www.sandia.gov/elecinvoice/home.html.

What Should Accounts Payable Do to Get Ready?

For starters, learn as much as you can about e-commerce, XML, and the new payment initiatives. Visit the following Web sites to learn as much as you can:

- www.w3.org
- www.xml.com/axml/axml.html
- www.microsoft.com/xml
- www.xml101.com
- www.xmlpitstop.com
- wwwxmlsoftware.com
- www.ebXML.org

At this point, there are only a few experts on these topics, but with a little effort you can become, if not *in* the loop, at least near it.

Find out if there is an exchange for your industry. You can do this by talking with the purchasing manager at your company or doing a search on the Internet. Simply go to www.google.com or one of the other search engines and put in your industry and the word exchange (e.g., paper + exchange).

Get involved. Find out what your company is doing. Many companies are already working on e-commerce initiatives and few even think to get their accounts payable managers involved. In fact, we know of several that have fallen apart because the payment piece was not addressed adequately (if at all!) at the planning stages.

Career Thoughts

Don't be surprised if you are rebuffed when you approach purchasing about its participation in e-marketplaces. Although these portals are magnificent for reducing costs and improving purchasing efficiency, they also can significantly reduce the number of people needed to handle a company's procurement needs. Thus, many in purchasing do not necessarily see exchanges as a good thing.

To be completely honest about the matter, these exchanges, if adopted wholeheartedly, will ultimately have the same effect on the accounts payable staff. With fewer invoices coming to a company, many will be able to reduce accounts payable staffs. This does not mean, however, that accounts payable professionals should fight the use of e-marketplaces—that would simply be a waste of time and effort and get you labeled as unprogressive and not receptive to change. "Don't go kicking and screaming," warns Hinder. You can lead the charge or be left behind —the decision is yours.

Business Prospective

When you think of XML from a business point of view, you really have to think of much more than just XML itself. XML is a tool that is analogous to a Universal or Master Key. XML will be the underlying enabler in industry electronic commerce, specifically in the account payable area in both strategic and tactical business processing.

First, let's begin at the highest level, which is the strategic level. XML has already begun enabling e-commerce, and will only expand in that direction in the next five years. Business will need to develop its e-commerce plan with an emphasis on collaboration. For accounts payable management, that translates to collaboration with business units, accounts payable, and suppliers. Note the word *collaboration* because XML and B2B e-commerce applications enable more than just

EXHIBIT 14.1

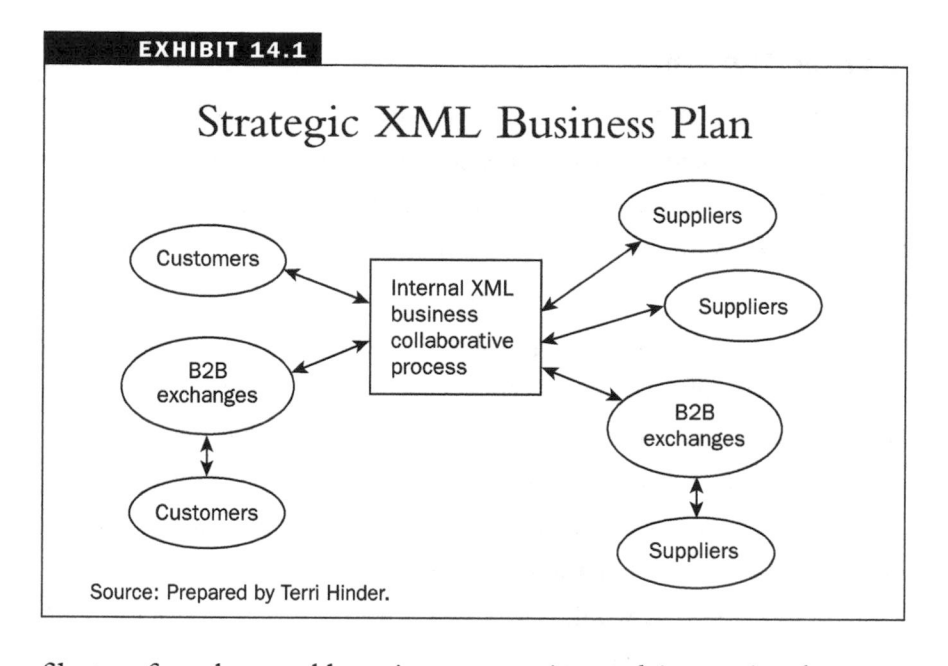

Strategic XML Business Plan

Source: Prepared by Terri Hinder.

file transfers; they enable active cooperation and interaction between business partners. Exhibit 14.1 shows a strategic plan using XML.

Second, while some are interested in the strategic picture, others would like a more tactical, business process (see Exhibit 14.2).

The model in Exhibit 14.2 shows several activities that are XML enabled:

(A) *Receiving receipts into the XML engine to send to A/P applications and other systems*—Buyers or others can easily be alerted as needed.

(B) *Alerts and visability to manage the business needs, such as discrepancy resolution*—The XML engine can allow visibility to accounts payable and other applications to view information for quick problem resolution. This also can be used to enable supplier collaboration for direct two-way conversation with suppliers for clarification. Business unit personnel can also be connected to the collaborative picture for joint viewing of same information for quick resolutions.

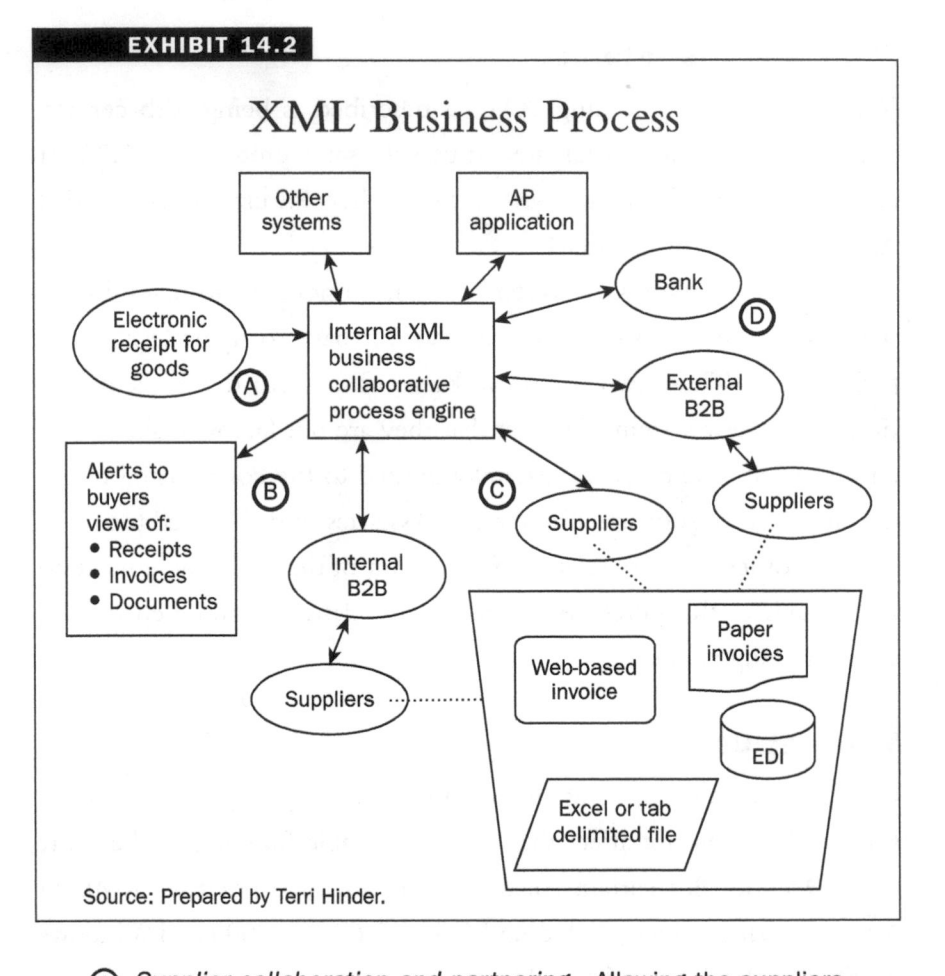

EXHIBIT 14.2

XML Business Process

Source: Prepared by Terri Hinder.

Ⓒ *Supplier collaboration and partnering*—Allowing the suppliers to view information from AP systems as well as have a plethora of options to use in invoicing.

Ⓓ *Payment ability electronically, EDI format if needed*—The Bank can then make electronic payment to suppliers.

XML is a powerful enabler of business tools. Some tools are available today, and many new tools are coming out already XML enabled. It's not important that accounts payable professionals understand the actual XML. It is important, however, that they are ready for dynamic collaboration and partnering on a global scale.

175

XML and the Internet

You knew this was coming. XML is described as being Web-centric, meaning that it is Web orientated. It uses the same protocol (HTTP) for sending content from one system to another. Realize, however, that XML will not replace HTML.

Thus, those who want to start using it do not have to invest in any new expensive hardware. They also do not have to upgrade network technologies. These two issues can be an obstacle to the implementation of any new system. The fact that they are not factors makes XML an easier sell. The costs are generally limited to the costs related to the development of software, programmers' salaries, and XML editors.

The other costs are related to education of the staff. These relate to items such as the purchase of books, attendance at conferences, and other training venues.

Current Use

Certain regulatory agencies are beginning to accept reporting in XML format. This will not affect the accounts payable function in the short term. Additionally, certain software users are incorporating XML in some of their products, including Microsoft (Office 2000 and Windows 2000), Oracle, IBM, and Sun Microsystems.

This list is by no means all-inclusive. The number of vendors including this functionality in their products continues to grow, and by the time this is published, many others will include it in their offerings.

Future of XML

XML will do for financial reporting and data sharing what the personnel computer did for office automation. It will change the way business is

done and information is exchanged. The question is how fast this revolution will take. Many experts predict that this change will happen quickly. There was a time, in the not too distant past, when the Internet and e-mail were foreign concepts. Today, most businesses depend heavily on these two resources.

XML will have the same impact. Like the Internet, it will probably not be necessary for accounts payable to understand all the intricate workings of the process, as long as they know how to use it. It is likely that most accounts payable associates will not need to know all the details of XML programming, just as most do not really understand how e-mail works, but know how to send and receive messages.

Summary

XML is here to stay and will make a big impact on the business community. Although it is not necessary to become an XML expert, it will become necessary to understand how to use it and what its documents mean. The more accounts payable associates learn about this technology, the better equipped they will be to become part of the accounts payable departments of the twenty-first century.

CHAPTER 15

Procurement Cards and Their Impact on the Accounts Payable Function

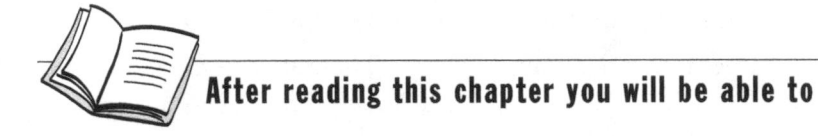

After reading this chapter you will be able to

- Understand the mechanics of using procurement cards (p-cards)
- Identify potential problem spots and adapt solutions for your organization
- Understand the different levels of data available
- Increase the use of p-cards in your organization, where appropriate
- Recognize the benefits of using p-cards

Procurement cards, better known as p-cards, are similar to charge cards and operate very much like the credit card you have in your wallet. When used correctly, they are one of the best tools for reducing the number of small-dollar invoices being processed in the accounts payable department. Many experts estimate that it costs approximately $150 to process a purchase order. This is an awful lot of money to spend to buy a $25 widget. To many it seemed like there had to be a better, more efficient, less expensive way.

How P-cards Work

Once a company determines that it wants to use p-cards, it gets bids from several issuing banks and selects a card issuer. This is the financial

institution that will issue the cards. Based on purchasing history, individuals within the company who regularly purchase items will be given a card. Usually, they must sign an agreement with their employer, which spells out their responsibilities for the card. These agreements usually contain a statement that says the employee understands and agrees that if he or she misuses the card they will be immediately terminated. Has this ever happened? Yes. Has it happened often? No.

Each month the company receives a statement from the card issuer with the charges for all the company cards. These statements are broken down by cardholder. The company then has as much as 30 days to pay the bill. It is expected that the statement will be reconciled in this time period. If it is not reconciled, the company is still expected to pay its bill in a timely manner.

There are various methods for verifying charges. Most companies send the statement to the employees. Some ask the employee to review the statement and verify the charges. Sometimes the employee will be asked to code the items for the general ledger. Most companies expect the employees to hold onto the signed receipts they receive when they make the purchase. A few require that the receipts be submitted to accounts payable. Some companies have a department representative reconcile each department's charges. This is especially true when more than one person within the department uses the same card (though this is rare).

Benefits of P-Cards

Most accounts payable professionals, if they sort the invoices they pay on behalf of their companies, will find that the *80/20 rule* applies to accounts payable: 80 percent of the invoice volume accounts for only 20 percent of the dollars spent—and that's if things are going well. In

some companies the numbers are more like 90/10. Obviously, using a PO, receiving an invoice, checking the invoice, processing it, cutting a check, and then getting that check signed is not an efficient way to handle small-dollar invoices. Bills for subscriptions, stationary goods, and the myriad of other small-dollar items that companies must purchase do not deserve the same intensive handling that a $100,000 or $1 million invoice deserves.

This was the thinking behind p-cards. Thus, companies began using credit cards to handle their small-dollar purchases. These cards are typically issued by the big three—American Express, MasterCard, and Visa.

Get Rusty Haines, an integrated business process manager for Alliant Energy, talking about p-cards and he'll tell you all the benefits. He was recently asked to identify the biggest benefits. Haines said, "It is very hard to state what was the 'biggest' benefit. There were three areas that created hard dollar savings.

"First was the reduction in the number of invoices A/P processed. The number of low dollar purchases being made using the p-card reduced the A/P invoice volume by 50 percent.

"Second, was the ability to negotiate better prices with vendors. Until the p-card, we never had the data required to negotiate more aggressive pricing with fewer vendors.

"Third, card companies pay rebates for using their card products. Although these vary dramatically, the rebate paid is revenue that usually far exceeds discounts offered for prompt payment of invoices.

"The most important benefit was the cultural change brought about by using p-cards. Without the 'cultural shift' to using p-cards, the eventual implementation of long-term Internet based e-commerce solutions would never have been possible. The use of p-cards became the 'baby steps' to development and deployment of a corporate wide e-procurement solution. "

Companies that have adopted their use have often radically reduced the number of invoices and checks cut in their accounts payable departments—but not without some headaches.

Obtaining Adequate Data

While p-cards are wonderful for reducing volume, they are not so great when it comes to the appropriate accounting. Think about your credit card bill. It tells you how much you spend at which vendor on what day. But that is it. It does not tell you what you bought. Thus, you may not know if you purchased a shirt for yourself or as a gift for someone else. And the bill certainly doesn't indicate that if the shirt was a gift, who it was for and what the occasion was.

Unfortunately, most companies require this level of information for accounting purposes. And most card issuers cannot provide it. Even if the card issuer can provide the information, the vendor may not have the capability of inputting the necessary information. Thus, many issuers who indicate that they can provide Level 2 and 3 data (more on this later) can only do so for a portion of your suppliers.

Many companies have adapted to this issue. They either do not care or they make some gross assumptions based on the party charging the products. If someone in maintenance at a local plant purchases a small-dollar item at a local hardware store, there's a good chance that this is for repairs.

Making Payments

The payment issue was not originally anticipated when companies began using p-cards. Many large purchasers pressured their smaller suppliers into taking the cards. Additionally, some suppliers who signed up to take the cards did not adequately think the process through and did not integrate the program into their existing processes. The result is that

a small number of vendors will send an invoice for a product that has already been paid for with a p-card. Given the lack of data provided by most credit card companies, these duplicate payments are exceedingly hard to uncover unless the purchasing individual catches the error. After all, there's no way someone in accounts payable will be able to decipher the line items on a credit card bill.

This assumes, of course, that the merchant is honest and is not trying to dupe an unsuspecting customer into paying for something twice—and a number of them are unscrupulous and will do this. This is another reason to make sure you know who you are doing business with.

Most recently, a number of accounts payable professionals have reported receiving invoices marked "paid for by credit card" somewhere on the invoice. This statement is not necessarily in the most visible location on the invoice. These companies cannot (or will not) alter their billing system to suppress the printing and/or mailing of invoices. Whatever the reason, it usually ends up falling on the shoulders of the accounts payable associate to catch these *already been paid* invoices. Don't rely on the purchaser—many an invoice marked "paid for by credit card" has arrived in the accounts payable department with an authorizing signature and a note to "Please Pay."

The discussion of these problems is not meant to deter a company from using p-cards. They are an excellent tool, especially since most employees are trying to get more done with fewer staffing resources. However, those using them should be aware of the problems that may be encountered.

The Data

Much has been written about the amount of data available on p-cards. The card issuer will generally provide what is referred to as Level 1 (the most available), Level 2, or Level 3 (the most desirable) data. The

National Association of P-card Professionals (www.napcp.org) offers the following definitions for these levels. NAPCP is a relatively new group, and its formation reflects the importance of this function in corporate America and backs up the claim that p-cards are not a passing fad.

Level 1 Data: Basic Credit Card Information

Level 1 data are similar to the information you would find on your personal credit card statement. This information includes:

- Date
- Supplier
- Dollar amount

Level 2 Data: Customer-Defined Transaction Data

Transactions that include *Level 2* data include Level 1 data plus

- Sales tax
- Variable data field

Suppliers who are Level 2 capable have the ability to pass sales tax information as well as a unique transaction data field (typically limited to 16 characters) through the purchasing card system. Some issuers pass this data to the cardholder statement. Level 2 data can be extremely helpful to the cardholder in reconciling charges, especially in the case of repetitive charges. Examples of Level 2 variable data include

- An order number
- An employee name (in the case of temporary service provider)
- A sample number (in the case of providers of laboratory testing service)

Level 3 Data: Line-Item Detail

Transactions that include *Level 3* data include Level 1 and 2 data plus

- Item product code

- Item description

- Item quantity

- Item unit of measure

- Item price

- Item tax

Control Features

Most companies limit the amount that any one employee can charge in a particular time frame. After all, if they didn't it would be like giving an employee access to the company's bank account—a very big temptation. Some of the ways companies control p-card usage while simultaneously encouraging employees to use it wherever possible include the following:

- *Limit the dollar amount of each transaction*—Some companies set this limit as low as $50 or $100.

- *Limit the dollar amount that each employee can spend in a given month*—A repair person might be limited to no more than $1,000 per month while the plant supervisor might have a limit that is ten times that amount. Limits can be initially set low and then raised as needed.

- *Use standard industrial code (SIC) blocks*—For example, some companies block furriers and other luxury good stores. The problem with this issue is that sometimes companies are in more than one line of business, yet they are limited to one SIC code. There have been instances where employees have been blocked from making legitimate purchases.

- *Insist that the department manager review and sign off on all monthly statements.*

- *Limit the number of employees who are given the card, but don't be too restrictive*—Remember, you want the card to be used.

Warning: You Will Get Complaints

Not everyone in other departments is going to be thrilled about p-cards. For starters, any time you change an existing routine, people will complain. Uses of p-cards is a big change, so initially, you should expect some resistance. However, once people get up the learning curve and are comfortable with the cards, they will be enthusiastic about them and spread the word to other doubting Thomases in the organization.

Some people will complain that the reconciliation work really belongs in accounts payable and they have to do extra work because of the p-card. They are correct; they will have to do something they didn't have to do in the past. However, they won't have to fill out purchase orders any more, either. Most importantly, the reconciliation work cannot be done in accounts payable. The knowledge base isn't there—it is with the employee who made the purchase and is therefore the only one who can do the reconciliation.

As you can see, not all companies use p-cards. However, the larger the company, the more likely it is to use p-cards. Some who are not currently using them are simply not doing so because they have not been able to devote the necessary resources to the project. Realizing the benefits of a p-card program, they intend to look into it in the near

TIPS & TECHNIQUES

Getting Support for P-Cards

The most successful p-card initiatives are those that have strong senior management support. Without that, the program will probably wither on the vine. The only way to make people use the card is to show them the benefits and then make sure they understand that management wants them to use the card. With a strong champion, the program will be a success.

IN THE REAL WORLD

A P–Card Success Story

Setting up, monitoring, and evaluating a p-card program can be like exploring new waters for the accounts payable professionals who have never ventured down this road before. Speaking at a conference for accounts payable professionals, Allergan Inc.'s Anita Breitzman provided a roadmap for the uninitiated. She walked the audience through the necessary steps to set up, evaluate, and manage a p-card program.

Establishing a Program

While most accounts payable professionals have a good idea about what they wish to achieve through a p-card program, more than a few do not. Breitzman recommends that the first step in establishing a p-card program is simply defining the goals and benefits expected from the program. Then, set measurable objectives. Without taking these two steps, it will be impossible to say whether the program is a success.

Senior management support is crucial to getting the rest of the company behind the program. Without it, the p-card program opponents will hinder the implementation every step of the way. Interestingly enough, other accounts payable professionals report that the individuals who most opposed the p-card programs in their companies ultimately became its biggest supporters after participating in the program for just a short time. The trick is to get involvement of all parties. Senior management support will ensure that others participate.

Once the goals have been set and quantified and management support is in place, a provider will have to be chosen. Ask hard questions of potential p-card providers. Network to find other accounts payable professionals who have card programs. Ask for recommendations and also find out the horror stories. Breitzman also recommends asking what your company will have to do to get started. Often times, she says, the providers will say that they will help you,

but when push comes to shove, the company must do more work than it initially anticipated. Make sure to find out exactly what will be expected of the company and then of the accounts payable staff—it could be substantial.

Like any other accounts payable process, p-cards need written approved policies and procedures. Without them, the accounts payable manager responsible for the program will have huge headaches. Since the program is new, the accounts payable professional has a golden opportunity to "do it right." Not being hampered by existing procedures or established bad habits on the part of card users, accounts payable professionals are in the unique position to get the program off on the right foot.

Always start with a pilot program. No matter how much planning goes into the project and how good the accounts payable staff is, there will be some rough spots in the beginning. This is not a time to be fair, says Breitzman. Pilot participants should be selected from those who support the program, not its detractors. There will be time to convert the skeptics later. You do not need them around should the pilot hit some bumps in the road.

Once the pilot program has run for a while and the are bumps worked out, roll out the program to the rest of the company.

Evaluating the Program

In the implementation stage, measurable objectives were set. After a reasonable amount of time, begin to quantify the results. Audit the information and get feedback from the p-card users. Breitzman suggests the following questions:

- What was learned?
- What was accomplished?
- What additional issues need to be addressed?

Follow-up on the additional issues is recommended. Begin a regular benchmarking program and revise it as needed. Finally, she says

that ongoing communication with the cardholders is crucial. This is
the only way problems can be identified and corrected before they
derail the p-card program.

Managing the Program

One of the great features of p-cards is that they allow the company
to set controls for each employee as needed. To get started, establish card controls for each employee or group of employees as company policy dictates.

When interviewing potential card providers, the issues of sales and
use tax and 1099 reporting should be addressed. The capabilities
of the card provider in these arenas (and they are not all the same)
need to be integrated into the accounts payable operations.

Work with the appropriate parties in accounting and IT to establish
whatever general ledger interface is desired. Different companies
do it in different ways, depending on the corporate preference and
the capabilities of the accounting software used.

Establish a periodic reporting mechanism to keep management
apprised of the success of the program and to provide others in the
company with needed information.

Similarly, Breitzman recommends setting up an audit program to
see if p-cards are being used as they should be and in all instances
where they are supposed to be. Some accounts payable professionals have reported setting up a p-card program and then those
who objected to the program simply did not use the cards when
issued. Actions such as this can doom an otherwise good program.
Senior management support is key to enforcing usage in situations
such as this. One company forces p-card use by taking the rather
severe step of refusing to pay for items not charged to p-cards when
applicable. This policy, of course, is an extreme; your company
might not be willing to go this far.

Growing the Program

The first place to look to grow the program is from existing card users. They often can see additional uses for the cards. Going to user group meetings is another good idea. By meeting with others using the same card program, accounts payable professionals will not only find unique solutions to their p-card problems but will also discover innovative ways others are using the cards.

P-Card Program Set-Up Roadmap

Use the following list to ensure that you cover all the p-card bases:

- Establish a program.
    1. Define goals and benefits.
    2. Set measurable objectives.
    3. Get senior management support.
    4. Select p-card provider.
    5. Establish policies and procedures.
    6. Begin pilot program.
    7. Roll out the program.
- Evaluate the program.
    1. Measure how objectives are being met.
    2. Audit the results and user feedback.
    3. Benchmark results and revise where needed.
    4. Communicate with cardholders.
- Manage the program.
    1. Set card controls.
    2. Sales and use tax.
    3. 1099 reporting.
    4. G/L interface.
    5. Set up reporting mechanism.
    6. Establish audit routine.
    7. Look for expansion ideas.

IN THE REAL WORLD

Who's Using P-Cards

Not all companies use p-cards. Some are concerned about their employees misusing the card and others are satisfied with the status quo. The latest statistics from the *2001 IOMA Managing Accounts Payable Benchmarking Survey* can be seen in Exhibit 15.1.

future—or so they say. There's an old saying about the road to hell being paved with good intentions. It appears that p-cards are on that road for many.

IOMA has asked this question in its last few benchmarking surveys, and the numbers haven't changed much. About one-third are using p-cards and about 20 percent plan to do so in the next few years—they just never seem to get the issue high enough on their "to do" list. Given the recent advances in differing payment mechanisms over the Internet, the feeling among some p-card experts is that usage by companies has tapered off. Those who are going to use them are already doing so and those who are not will not add a program, except in rare instances.

EXHIBIT 15.1

Corporate Usage of P-Cards

By Company Size	Currently use	Planning to	Do not plan
Up to 99	13.2%	13.2%	73.7%
100–249	20.2%	10.1%	67.9%
250–499	15.7%	26.5%	56.9%
500–999	26.9%	27.6%	45.5%
1000–4999	44.8%	22.7%	32.0%
5000 & up	61.7%	17.3%	21.1%
Total	35.3%	20.8%	43.9%

The growth in p-card usage will come from existing users who see the benefit and push for additional use within their company. There are a lot of those companies out there, so p-card usage within companies that have a program will grow.

Other P-Card Trends

Companies that push large volumes through their p-card programs have gone to their issuers and negotiated rebates based on volume. This is something that most issuers do not like to talk about—and, in fact, many contracts forbid those who receive these rebates from discussing them publicly. How much does a company have to buy before it can negotiate a rebate? Several years ago the number was $500,000 per month, but competition may have lowered that figure.

By the way, card issuers are not going to *offer* a rebate, in most cases. You will have to ask for it. Depending on the size of the company, the

TIPS & TECHNIQUES

Getting Employees to Use the P-Card

A few accounts payable professionals have found that they had to play hardball in order to get employees to use the p-card when making a purchase. Some have refused to process the invoice and issue a check for items that should have been purchased with a p-card. They simply send the invoice back to the person who made the purchase with instructions to pay the invoice using the p-card. Most employees don't have to get more than one or two invoices back before they get the message. There is one caveat to those trying this approach. Make sure management will back you up. If not, try a more subtle technique. There is nothing worse for an accounts payable associate than to tell someone no and then have that person go over your head and win.

rebate can be an attractive feature. Some companies, in an attempt to qualify for a larger rebate, have combined their T & E cards, freight cards and p-cards into what is referred to as a one-card program.

Summary

P-cards are a wonderful tool to use to reduce the number of small dollar invoices coming into the accounts payable department for processing. Using them and issuing one monthly check for hundreds of low-dollar purchases just makes good sense. Study the advice given in this chapter and see if you can find ways to get more of your company's invoices eliminated by having the purchase made with a p-card, rather than the traditional purchase order, invoice, check route. Your purchasers will be happy and the accounts payable department will be able to devote its limited resources to more meaningful work.

CHAPTER 16

Fraud: Vendor, Employee, and Check

After reading this chapter you will be able to

- Identify the most common types of fraud
- Recommend policies and procedures to guard the company against fraud
- Insist on the use of positive pay and know the reasons why
- Uncover fraud in your own organization, should it exist

B asically, there are three types of fraud that accounts payable associates may encounter: check fraud, vendor fraud, and employee fraud. This chapter takes a look at fraud and ways that accounts payable can help protect the company from fraud.

Check Fraud

One of the biggest growth industries in the United States, check fraud is estimated at approximately $10 billion annually. It includes

- Altering an authorized check
- Forging the maker's signature
- Forging the payee's endorsement
- Creating unauthorized check stock

195

- Drawing a draft on an account but not delivering the goods or checks
- Check kiting

A few years ago, banks usually ate the losses that accrued because of the fraudulent use of their customers' checks. No more. It has simply gotten too costly for banks to cover these losses. Why has check fraud grown so much? There are several reasons:

1. *It's easy*—Anyone with an inexpensive computer, a scanner, a color printer, and a little bit (and here the emphasis is on the word *little*) of knowledge can make a good copy of a check— good enough so that most banks will cash it. What's more, with the current technology not only can a crook make a good copy, the crook can also alter it so that instead of being payable for, let's say $100, it can be made payable for $1,000 or $10,000.

2. *The risk of getting caught is low*—Most police work is focused on violent criminals and those that commit crimes with dangerous weapons, rather than on people who commit fraud.

3. *Even if apprehended, the odds of actually serving prison time are quite low*—With the overcrowding of prisons, most people, including many reading this book, would prefer to see violent criminals behind bars instead of those who commit nice white-collar crimes that don't really hurt anyone. This last statement, unfortunately, is a misperception. White-collar crime hurts everyone—the harm is just not as visible as the damage done with a knife or a gun.

So, if you were a criminal, would you hold up a bank with a gun to gain a few hundred dollars and intensive police scrutiny, or sit in the

safety of your home with some fancy, low-cost equipment and print up bogus checks with little chance of police attention?

It doesn't take a rocket scientist to figure out why check fraud has increased.

Why Banks Are Rarely Liable

The Uniform Commercial Code (UCC) has been changed to address the check fraud issue. No longer can corporations ignore their responsibilities in this area and expect their banks to cover for them. The code now has a concept of *comparative culpability*. Check issuers must now exercise *reasonable care* in their handling of checks or they will assume culpability for the check fraud.

What Companies Can Do to Limit
Their Chances of Having Checks Copied

Let's be clear about one thing. Although you can never completely eliminate the risk of check fraud, there are many things a company can

IN THE REAL WORLD

A Positve Pay Ultimatum

Companies that do not want to be liable for losses should use positive pay. Although it is not yet a requirement, we can see the time in the not-too-distant future when companies not using the service will be deemed to be not exercising *reasonable care*. Some banks have gone out of their way to make sure they offer positive pay to all customers and require written notice of their customers' decisions to use or not use positive pay. These banks will have the necessary documentation to prove they offered the product but the customer declined to use it—if the use of positive pay becomes an issue in a check fraud case.

do to minimize the chances of having a crook focus on its checks. After all, if you make it too difficult, the crook will simply move on to another target—there are so many of them out there.

If preprinted check stock is used, the company can take these precautions:

- Keep it under lock and key.
- Limit access to the area where the check stock is stored.
- Keep a log of the checks used.
- Have someone with no access to the check stock perform a routine to determine the number of checks used.
- Perform surprise audits on the check stock by either the internal or external auditors.
- Authorized check signers should not have access to the area where the check stock is kept. This is for their protection, as well.
- Never, ever use a rubber stamp to sign checks. This practice completely negates a bank's liability and makes the company 100 percent liable, as rubber stamps are not considered using *reasonable care*. After all, who knows who stamped the check.

If a check signing machine is used, the company should take these precautions:

- The signing machine should be stored in a secure location where access is limited to a few authorized individuals.
- The signer should be kept separate from the check stock.
- The signature plate should be removed and placed in a safe or under lock and key—again separate from the check stock.
- Adequate controls should be put in place to monitor the number of times the signer has been used. Most have some sort of a counter on them.

Most importantly, use common sense. Don't think, "Oh, it's okay, Joe is a trusted employee, he's been here for ages." As you'll read a little

further on, most employee fraud is committed by the Joes of the world, those long-time trusted employees, who at least at this point are predominantly male—although as women gain momentum in the workplace, this stereotype is sure to change.

Check Stock

Reasonable care extends to the check stock, as well. Companies that go out and purchase the cheapest check stock available may be surprised to learn that they may not be adequately protecting themselves. Checks should have some, of the security features listed in Chapter 3 (page 40).

Some experts recommend against including statements on checks such as "not valid for checks over a certain dollar limit." Why? The experts reason that these statements do more to help the crook than the teller. The crook noting a notice about a $500 limit will simply write the check for $499. This is not to say that such limits should not be set on accounts—just don't notify the crooks by putting the notice on the checks.

Positive Pay

Without a doubt, the best defense a company has against check fraud is positive pay. Companies that use *positive pay* send their banks a check issuance file every time they have a check run. This tape, which can be sent electronically, contains information about the check number and dollar amount for each account. Before a check is honored it is matched against the file. If it is not on the list or has already cleared (and thus no longer remains on the file), the check is bounced.

Each bank has its own variations on how this aspect is handled. Some have a deadline that allows the company to tell the bank to honor the check—as mistakes do happen. Others simply direct their bank to bounce the check if it is not on the list. This is the plain-vanilla version

of positive pay. You will note that there is no attempt to verify the identify of the payee. That is the responsibility of the bank of first presentment.

There are several variations to the original positive pay:

- *Reverse positive pay*—In this case the bank sends the company a listing of all the checks presented each day, typically only check number and dollar amount. The company has a deadline, again usually around 2 p.m., to call the bank and tell it not to honor a certain check.

- *Teller positive pay*—This product requires timely input, processing, and updating online. As you can probably guess from the name, it puts the latest information at the fingertips of the teller in the bank who is being given checks to cash.

- *Payee name verification*—This product is not currently available, but will be shortly. It requires the input of additional data on the daily file and permits verification of the payee's name in addition to the dollar amount. This is a big improvement on an already great product. Bank of America may have its version ready before the end of the year, and other banks will follow. Of course, it will require additional work on the part of the issuing company along with some system changes.

Those companies not using positive pay are urged to do so. Not using it, especially after the bank has recommended it, could make a company liable for check losses. Accounts payable professionals using positive pay should consider payee name verification positive pay when it becomes available.

Some companies refuse to use positive pay because they fear the system modifications will cost too much. This does not have to be the case. There is an inexpensive product on the market, developed by IPS of Boston, that allows a company to convert its data for positive pay. It can be purchased through some banks, including Bank of America, or downloaded from the Internet (www.positivepay.com).

Identifying Fraudulent Checks

The sooner a fraudulent check is identified, the more likely a company is to recover its funds. Here are two tricks to quickly identify fraudulent checks:

1 When the checks are received back from the bank, quickly spread them out and compare the color. A forger may have gotten the color close, but the odds are quite good that it won't be a perfect match.

2 Check for perforations on the check if you are using the type of check that should have perforations—either from being ripped from the checkbook or detached from the stub. Crooks often neglect this feature when forging a check.

Vendor Fraud

In its very worst form, vendor fraud can be intentional on the part of existing vendors in collusion with your employees. In its mildest form it can be petty-ante scams for small-dollar amounts discussed further on in this chapter.

The first line of defense is the master vendor file. Good controls and practices regarding the master vendor file will eliminate certain types of fraud. For example, an employee, John Doe, who sets himself up as the John Doe Company will not be able to set up an account in the master vendor file for this new company and submit invoices if the proper controls are in place. Most fraudsters, however, are not this obvious. Here are other ways to protect the company.

1. Cross–check each vendor's address, phone number, and Zip code against those of the company's employees.

2. Check invoice number sequences of each vendor. Suspicious patterns should be investigated immediately.

3. Payments made without purchase orders or receiving documents should be scrutinized closely.

4. Most legitimate vendors can be found listed in standard business directories. Check out new vendors.

Phantom Vendors

Many fly-by-night companies exist for no reason other than to try and collect your firm's hard-earned money without providing any real service. Some of them do this by delivering low-quality goods, such as toner for copy machines, that no one ordered. These guys are slick. They will find out what type of printer or copy machine is used at your firm and then deliver shoddy goods for these machines. How do they find out what type of printers and copiers are used at your company? They simply call up and ask. If you get a call asking about the serial number for your copier, ask for the caller's phone number so you can get back to them. Watch how quickly they will hang up.

Once they have this information, the goods are shipped and an invoice is sent. The price on the invoice is very high. The goods arrive, and since no one knows who ordered them, they either sit in the mailroom or eventually get used. Meanwhile, accounts payable often pays the invoice eventually. These fraudulent vendors are also quite aggressive about calling and demanding payment for their product. Since the dollar amount involved is usually not great, the invoices are eventually paid, despite the fact that no one from the company ordered the product. And, what do you think these companies do once they find out how easy it is to dupe your company? Yes, another order is likely to appear, either for the same product or for another under a different company name.

Other Scams

The toner scam described above is just one of many. There are other variations:

- *The Yellow Pages ad scam*—If your company places an advertisement in the Yellow Pages, don't be surprised to receive another invoice for an ad looking just like the real one—only from a rival publication, where no order was placed.

- *The newspaper ad*—This scam works in a similar manner to the Yellow Pages scam. The target is usually companies that have placed a help-wanted ad. An invoice with a tear sheet will show up in accounts payable for the help-wanted advertisement. Only it will not be from the original newspaper where the advertisement was placed. The tear sheet will look exactly like the original ad.

- *The $2.99 scam*—This is a relatively new one. A check will appear at a company and usually find its way into the treasury or accounts receivable department. Since the check is usually for a relatively small-dollar amount, say $2.99, it gets deposited and put into miscellaneous income to be researched at a later date when someone has time. The tiny print on the back, usually in a light gray font, says that the depositor agrees to pay approximately $30 per month forever. Then, the monthly invoices start appearing, and many get paid. Since many companies don't have the resources to investigate invoices this small, they are paid each month until someone catches on.

These are just a few of the types of vendor fraud. The alert accounts payable associate will catch on and prevent further losses to the company.

Employee Fraud

No one likes to address this issue, but employee fraud is an issue—one that is typically swept under the table, as few companies like to admit that they were taken by one of their own. What's worse, since employee

fraud is rarely prosecuted, companies can't or won't taint the employee with a bad reference. Some employees who are involved in a fraud stop after one encounter. But many others, undeterred by a bad reference, repeat the crime at their next place of employment.

Segregation of Duties

Most auditors will continually harp about the proper segregation of duties, and with good reason. Many frauds are possible because of a lack of segregation of duties and checks and balances. If a person is permitted to authorize a payment and then the check is given to this individual to deliver, the risk is great. The check can be mailed. Most auditors will insist that checks never be returned to the requestor for delivery.

Similarly, certain functions, such as maintaining the master vendor file, check signing, payment authorizers and so on should be limited only to those who must have that ability. Never should someone have the authority to update the master vendor file, authorize a payment, and then sign a check.

IN THE REAL WORLD

Who Is Most Likely to Commit Fraud?

As already indicated, the "typical" fraudster is usually a trusted male employee in his mid-forties. He is usually good at what he does —his job, that is. Most companies choose not to prosecute the fraud. This reluctance is tied to the fact that executives do not want to let their investors, customers, or board of directors know about the lack of controls that allowed the fraud to take place. The employee is let go with no black marks on his record. In the best of situations, the executives then close the loopholes that made the fraud possible.

Common sense will tell you what other functions should be segregated. If in doubt, discuss the matter with your auditors. They will provide adequate advise in this area.

Vacations

Banks insist that all their employees take two weeks' consecutive vacations. Why? They believe that any employee fraud will unravel in that time period. And on more than one occasion, they have been proved correct. Most companies do not have the luxury of making the same demand on their employees, because they do not give enough vacation time to demand it all be taken at once. Still, an employee in critical areas who never takes a vacation is not a good idea. The company may be getting more than it bargained for from such an employee. (*Note:* Just because someone does not take vacation does not mean that fraud is involved, but it could be a signal.)

Everyone should have a backup and be away from the office for some period of time. It's healthy. Perhaps, in the United States, at least one week of consecutive days off might be a good idea.

Summary

Fraud is a growing problem. By being aware not only that it exists but also of some of the signs, accounts payable associates will be best positioned to identify situations that are not quite what they appear to be.

CHAPTER 17

How Companies Are Using Technology in Accounts Payable

After reading this chapter you will be able to

- Understand imaging and how it is being used in accounts payable

- Have some knowledge of encryption and digital signatures and how it will be used with e-mail

- Appreciate how Interactive Voice Response systems can be used in accounts payable

This chapter takes an in-depth look at how three new technologies are being used at some leading-edge companies to improve the accounts payable process. The individuals portrayed do not possess high-tech computer skills, although obviously they are knowledgeable about the technologies they use, but, rather, are inquisitive accounts payable folks who have taken the time and gone out of their way to figure out how to use some of the newest technologies to improve their departmental operations.

Imaging

Accounts payable departments in most companies are inundated with paper. *Imaging* (the scanning of documents for workflow and/or storage) takes a giant step to alleviating that problem. As discussed elsewhere in

this book, many accounts payable departments receive invoices, make a copy of them, and then send the original (or the copy, depending on the corporate philosophy) out for signature. Some of these invoices can be pages long. Every company uses its own invoice form, so the papers are all different sizes, different colors, and, frankly, printed with different-quality printers. Some are quite easy to read but others are almost illegible.

Assuming everything goes smoothly, the invoices (along with all the backup material and sometimes a copy of the check) are then filed after the payment has been made. Storage can take up a lot of space, even at a mid-size company. You can imagine the storage space needed at a large company. Now some might ask why all this paper has to be saved —after all, the payment has been made. For starters, most auditors insist that backup material be saved for at least seven years for tax reasons.

However, as anyone who has worked in accounts payable for even a short period of time will tell you, it is frequently necessary to refer to the paperwork for at least a few months after the payment date. Thus, anything that can be done to ease the workflow of invoices and to save storage space is welcomed by most accounts payable departments. Imaging addresses both those issues. The case study in "In the Real World" on page 209 demonstrates how imaging solved a number of problems for one large utility. The case study was presented by the company's accounts payable manager at several conferences. He was gracious enough to address some of the problems he encountered, as well.

Encryption and Digital Signatures

Although the Internet is great for easily sharing information, many executives are concerned about the security of the information both being received and being sent over the Internet. Remember, sending information over the Internet can be likened to sending a post card— anyone can read what it says. Needless to say, this does not make many

IN THE REAL WORLD

PPL Electric Offers Lessons on Setting Up an A/P Imaging Solution

Do any of your accounts payable processors leave difficult invoices for someone else to process? Do they wait until five o'clock to slide problem invoices past their supervisors? Are you sick of piles of paper and rows of filing cabinets? Well, if the answer to any or all of these questions is yes, imaging and workflow may be for you.

Brian Krom, corporate disbursements manager, shared his experiences with implementing an imaging and workflow solution at PPL Electric Utilities Corporation. First, however, is a description of why PPL wanted to move in this direction.

Why Imaging and Workflow

Krom enumerated seven reasons for moving to imaging and workflow:

1. *The increased process efficiencies and reduced cycle times.* This was accomplished by decreasing paper hand-offs, decreasing or eliminating bottlenecks, eliminating manual date stamping, reducing the delays in routing "trouble" invoices, and saving on labor costs.

2. *Work was better distributed through FIFO (first in, first out) processing.* Invoices were prioritized within or between queues and flexibility and control was added over individual image filters.

3. *Monitoring, tracking, and reporting of the vouchering (workflow) and backlogs improved.* This was achieved through real-time count of processed and pending invoices by operator type, scan date, and so on.

4. *Document retention, retrieval, and archiving was improved.*

5. *Customer service improved.*

6 *Fraud control improved.*

7 *Less storage space was needed.*

Imaging makes document handling much easier. For example, Krom can now print, fax, or e-mail images directly from within the system. He says that multiple copies of documents are no longer kept, nor are there lost, mis-files, or "out" vouchers. The need to copy and mail paper documents is eliminated, as is re-filing.

Krom warns that much of the labor savings throughout the process can be offset by the needed labor costs for invoice sorting, prepping, and scanning. He also said that sometimes those real-time reports of pending invoices could be quite depressing.

Imaging and workflow eliminates paper saving and keeping microfilm/fiche. However, some accounts payable professionals must observe certain rules to meet governmental requirements. Krom summarizes the SEC and IRS rules, but cautions that additional regulations may apply. He points out that it is not required to convert to imaging as your source document, but if you do, you must follow the regulations.

Storage Space Issue

Space saving is usually an issue whenever the imaging topic comes up. Krom demonstrated just how much space PPL saves. He says that the accounts payable department fills up 82 filing cabinets each year. Each cabinet takes up 8 square feet of floor space. This includes 2 feet to open the drawers. That's approximately 650 square feet of space each year. Trying to find something in one of these cabinets is another challenge.

The 5.25-inch optical platters used by the PPL accounts payable department hold 2.6 gigabytes of images. Seventeen are used for each year's information. Next year, Krom plans to upgrade to platters that can hold twice as much information.

Implementation

To begin with, PPL developed a business case. "Tentative" management approval was gained and a vendor was selected that satisfied accounts payable's requirements—as they understood them at the time.

PPL tried to understand the software functionality and tested and experimented with it. PPL spoke with other users and even insisted on talking to the technical staff, in addition to the salespeople. Krom urges others to do the same. He also recommends speaking with other customers of the software vendor.

PPL then mapped out the current process. This mapping process was more difficult and took longer than expected, but PPL learned a lot from the process. With the current information under its belt, PPL designed and mapped the new process.

Gaps in the process were identified and the company had to decide whether to change the process or customize the system. Hardware requirements were determined and acquired. These included workstations, server size, scanners, and jukeboxes, along with decisions about how much horsepower and what settings and configurations would be used. The software was installed, tested, de-bugged, and re-tested. Customizations were implemented. Then Krom says, PPL tested and tested and tested—and it should have tested more!

The company wisely decided to pilot with a small number of invoices, using one of its smaller affiliate companies first. PPL continued debugging and adjusting the process and software based on feedback from the pilot. It went into full production on January 10, 2000.

Lessons Learned

Krom says it was more difficult to adjust to imaging than he had expected. PPL experienced much resistance from its staff. However, most of these staffers came around fast after using the new system.

The project was more involved and intrusive than assumed, and what was supposed to be a turnkey solution did not turn out to be so. The start date was delayed from the original planned date of October 1999. Such delays are not ideal; however, this project came in remarkably close to deadline.

Possible Downside

These systems are expensive. The imaging and workflow system at PPL cost just under $100,000. This includes software, modules, hardware training, and installation. The annual maintenance fee is $6,500. For a company like PPL with huge volume (300,000 transactions per year), this is not a significant cost, although those with smaller volumes might look for a lower-priced system.

More of an issue is resistance received to the new project. The imaging and workflow resulted in several significant changes in the accounts payable department, and not everyone on the staff was happy about these revisions.

Scanning is a skill that needs getting used to. If your company deals with many different shaped and colored invoices, be prepared *not* to receive an exact match.

Final Thoughts

More time and effort was needed upfront for document preparation and sorting. Krom had to add a person to handle the increased workload.

PPL, like many other companies, experienced an invoice-processing backlog during the implementation of the imaging program. Krom concludes that even with all this, "we have already begun to realize many of the benefits and expect that to continue. It was an interesting road but worth the effort."

computer experts comfortable. This section examines the security issue and shows how one company successfully addressed this concern. One of the companies that has made great strides in using the Internet and incorporating stare-of-the-art security is Chevron. The solution to the security problem lies in encryption and digital signatures. A/P professionals need to understand that these new technologies are coming to accounts payable—quickly.

At several recent conferences, Chevron's manager of accounts payable reengineering, James M. Burstedt, and Ed Ames, a Chevron analyst for electronic commerce and a cofounder of the Unclaimed Property Holders Association, explained these approaches, and how they are reflected by Chevron's corporate policy. Ames and Burstedt are always looking to push the envelope when it comes to using new technology to safeguard Chevron's assets. In fact, they like to say that they don't want to be leading edge, they want to be on the bleeding edge.

Corporate Policy

The policy states,

> Information and the systems supporting it are key company assets, requiring prudent and proactive protection by information owners and users alike. It is the policy of the company to secure these assets from external and internal threats through a combination of technology, practices, processes and monitoring, based on risk and the value of the assets. The goal is to minimize the potential for damage either purposeful or accidental, to the company's computer and communications systems, company data and information.

This policy allows Chevron to focus its resources to protect its most important asset—its information. Like other companies, Chevron needs to protect itself from hackers, pranksters, dishonest insiders, competitors, and information terrorists. It is concerned about viruses, interception,

prying eyes, alteration or loss of data, communication blocks, and system disruptions. However, the biggest concern is unauthorized access.

Origins of the Problem and Its Solutions

Burstedt and Ames pointed out that security breaches can arise: an intruder masquerading as an employee; eavesdropping; data being changed en route; e-mail addresses being changed en route; or cracked passwords and IDs. The speakers also identified the defenses that stop unauthorized access to computer information transferred over the Internet. These include authentication (digital signature-private key/hash), encryption, digital certificates (ID validation/non repudiation), firewalls, and strong passwords.

The consequences of not having these defenses can be severe. Financial loss, damage to the company's reputation, loss of business, legal actions, and the loss of strategic information are only a few of the possible results.

When an employee has a laptop stolen, the biggest loss is not the cost of the laptop, but the strategic information stored on the hard drive. Thus, Chevron relies on what it calls *secured messaging*.

Secured Messaging

Chevron defines secured messaging as the use of encryption and digital signatures. Before defining what a *digital signature* is, let us focus on what it is not. It is *not* a digitized signature—the manual signature by an individual on an electronic device such as those used by certain department stores for charge card purchases. Burstedt and Ames provided the following definitions:

- *Digital signature*—Unique to the person and using a private key, digital signatures can be verified as belonging specifically and used solely by that person. It is linked to data, so any change to the data will invalidate the signature. It is also nonreputable,

which means that a person can prove they sent a communication and conversely, cannot deny that they sent it. It is the equivalent in the paper world to getting a document notarized.

- *Encryption*—This is the ability to transform electronic information into an unreadable format that can only be converted back to its original readable state by specific individuals previously authorized to do so.

- *Encryption engines*—Also known as encryption algorithms, are now powerful enough to generate truly random keys, taking this responsibility out of the hands of people. It also allows for session keys that can be used once or multiple times and then discarded.

Back to Math Class

Upon reading the word *algorithm* below, some accounts payable professionals may vaguely remember high school math class. An algorithm is a detailed sequence of calculations performed in a specific number of steps to achieve a desired outcome.

A *hash algorithm* is a function that reduces a message to a mathematical expression and is called a one-way hash because the expression cannot be reversed. For example, if every letter of the alphabet were assigned a number (a = 1, b = 2, etc.) any name could be reduced to a single digit.

J	U	L	I	U	S		C	A	E	S	A	R
10	21	12	9	21	19		3	1	5	19	1	18

The sum for Julius = 92   The sum for Caesar = 47

9 + 2 = 11   4 + 7 = 11

11 + 11 = 22

2 + 2 = 4

215

The speakers choose Julius Caesar because he was one of the earliest users of encryption. (See the previous example for a full explanation.)

Altering any original message or file including a change in the spelling of a word, eliminating apostrophes, or changing a comma to a period will result in a different hash.

Public Key Infrastructure

Messages are encrypted and decrypted using public and private keys. Expect to hear much more about *public key infrastructure* (PKI) in the upcoming months as commerce continues to move to the Internet. Burstedt and Ames also offered a clear explanation of how these keys are used.

> Two sets of electronic keys are used to encrypt and decrypt documents. Public keys can be shared while private keys are known only to their specific owner. An encrypted document is created using the sender's private key and the receiver's public key. The receiver decrypts the document using the sender's public key and the receiver's private key. The public key is the certificate authority. Separate pairs of keys can be used to encrypt or digitally sign to strengthen security.

> Whatever is locked by a private key can only be unlocked by the corresponding public key and vice versa. Encrypting and sending with the sender's private key and the receiver's public key can therefore only be decrypted with the receiver's private key and the sender's public key. Use the private key to create the digital signature/hash.

Readers should be aware that there is currently a huge debate going on over setting standards for the PKI. It does not look like it will be settled soon, as a number of entities have a vested interest in becoming the standard setter. These concepts may be new to many readers but it is imperative that anyone who works for a company that uses the Internet

Case Study: Chevron

Are you sure that every check and wire request that you receive is valid? Are you concerned that perhaps some of those requisitions for large-dollar payments from overseas may not be from legitimate sources? Do you want to verify that the money you send out goes where it is supposed to go? Does using the Internet for data transmission make you uncomfortable? Well, the accounts payable folks at Chevron also had these concerns, but they were especially concerned about the requests for payments coming in from overseas. Although the project started with accounts payable, the hope was that it would be broad enough to eventually encompass other applications in all departments.

Project Scope

Chevron had three main objectives for the technology solution it devised: (1) *employ* commercialized software to support encryption needs throughout the company; (2) *install* software that would initially be used to encrypt e-mail and documents for storage and distribution; and (3) *develop* an application for the payment request process using encryption and digital signatures. Chevron thought that it was important to use encryption in order to:

- Protect data from unauthorized access

- Transport confidential data across the Internet

- Have digital signatures for the authorization of transactions such as payment requests

- Ensure that the person who sent the encrypted note is the author, and also to provide confirmation of receipt

- Prevent exposure of confidential data when laptops are lost or stolen

- Select an industry leader as a software provider to increase the chances of interoperability

Although many people within Chevron already use encryption with e-mail, it was the goal of this project to include those submitting payment requests and the international sales staff in that group.

Accounts Payable Business Drivers

At Chevron, A/P started the project with a pilot. Although both ERS (evaluated receipt settlement) and EDI are used extensively, the accounts payable department still receives 11,604 manual payment requests annually. Of those transactions:

- 35 percent were under $1,000

- 10 percent were between $1,000 and $5,000

- 55 percent were for amounts over $5,000, and these represented 99 percent of the dollars

Certain financial transactions were being authenticated with manual keys, but the company did not think that the manual process sufficiently protected the company against potential theft. Chevron also felt that confidential data was not adequately protected. Finally, the company's Information Protection Compliance Policy required higher levels of protection, like encryption.

Pilot Application

The participants in the pilot had very definite ideas about what they wanted. However, what they wanted and what was available were not quite the same. The pilot program had a number of objectives, many of which were technical and set the groundwork so the program could be expanded after the accounts payable portion had been successfully implemented. The accounts payable specific goals included

- Creating an automated payment request form incorporating digital signatures

- Marketing the electronic form to company personnel

- Linking the payment request form to encryption (digital signatures and validation)

- Address the legal implications of digital signatures and HR issues for inappropriate use

Developing an Electronic Form

The accounts payable department now had the opportunity to reengineer its existing practices through the development of an automated payment request form. Specifically, A/P

- Replaced all existing payment request forms
- Made blank forms available through the company intranet, eliminating the printing and storing of forms issue
- Included all pertinent fields for both domestic and international payments
- Included a pop-up window with help information for each field
- Employed encryption software for digital signature functionality
- Required multiple digital signatures for preparation and various approvals
- Prevented unauthorized changes due to the digital signature lock-down feature
- Allowed for the verification of each digital signature against the certificate authority file
- Included instructions for completion of the form and processing steps

Passwords

The advice that Burstedt and Ames gave regarding the use of passwords is applicable to everyone, not just those implementing a high-tech system. Chevron advocated the use of robust passwords, or those that include both upper- and lower-case letters and alpha and nonalpha characters. In addition, sharing passwords was forbidden.

Pilot Survey and Results

To make sure the company was on the right track and to uncover any unforeseen problems, the team at Chevron conducted a pilot survey. Specifically, they asked about the following systems and procedures:

- Enrollment form and process
- Downloading and configuring of encryption software
- Downloading and configuring of electronic form software
- General instructions
- Ease of using encryption and electronic forms
- Technical support
- Results and recommendations

They were pleased to find that user satisfaction was very high. However, they discovered that users wanted a hard copy of the documentation rather than being pointed to the Internet for instructions. They were also able to identify who should be using encryption based on customer feedback.

Burstedt and Ames acknowledged that use of technology allowed them to reengineer the accounts payable processes. They see the accounts payable function evolving into one that is more analytical. They have shown what the future of accounts payable can be for those who grab the technology ball and run.

understands these concepts. Remember, there was a time not too long ago, when the whole idea of the Internet seemed alien.

Interactive Voice Response

Interactive voice response (IVR) units are used in a variety of businesses. Most people do not connect them with accounts payable. These are the telephone units that answer a phone and then instruct the caller

through a variety of responses to accomplish a goal. You may have used them to find out the time a movie was playing, place an order for a prescription or find a phone number. A number of companies have purchased these systems to allow their vendors and salespeople to check on

IVR Frees A/P from Annoying "Where's My Money" Calls

Accounts payable groups being inundated with phone calls regarding payment status will find interactive voice response (IVR) systems are a big help. This was especially true at Hoffman-LaRoche, Inc. where the accounts payable staff had two groups of difficult people—suppliers and their own sales force—demanding to know where their payments were. Nancy Sampson shares her experiences of IVRs, showing not only the benefits but also what should be expected of IVRs if a company installs one.

Definition

What is an IVR? Interactive voice response systems (IVR) allow people to interact with computers through their telephones. In the Hoffman-LaRoche example, a caller is able to obtain information pertaining to the expected payment date of certain invoices by entering a series of numbers in response to prerecorded questions.

Background

In 1995, Hoffman-LaRoche, Inc. installed its first interactive voice response unit in the accounts payable department. This was a boon to staff productivity. Suppliers could determine when their payments would be made, and so could the sales staff. This is particularly important at a pharmaceutical company such as Hoffman-LaRoche because it provides many honorariums to doctors and hospitals. When salespeople called on one of these people, they wanted to tell the customer when they would receive their honorarium money.

In 1999, the company installed SAP; the existing IVR system was not compatible with SAP and was disconnected. Recognizing that this would put a strain on the accounts payable department, the system was replaced by a person to answer questions formerly addressed by the system. This seemed like a reasonable solution. Unfortunately, the vendors and salespeople started calling individual processors, disrupting the workflow of the entire department. So an SAP-compatible IVR system was quickly purchased.

Overall Objectives

Like many other companies, Hoffman-LaRoche wanted to improve productivity in its accounts payable department. It wanted to

- Use technology to reduce costs
- Reduce non–value-added work
- Maximize the use of employee time
- Increase the level of customer service
- Provide 24/7 service availability

System Selection

The company reviewed three systems using three criteria to justify the ultimate selection: (1) cost, (2) efficiency, and (3) compatibility with SAP.

The system selected was SAP-certified and had one other big advantage: It had already been installed in the human resources department. Thus, there were cost savings due to the sharing of hardware and piggybacking on already-installed software. Finally, the accounts payable department was able to leverage other in-house resources.

The systems evaluated were Edify Electronic Workforce, Syntellect, and CCS.

System Requirements

Sampson demanded certain features from the new system:

- It must be simple to use.
- It had to have the ability to transfer to a customer service rep.

- It must allow letter to be input with three key strokes.
- It had to be expandable beyond the eight lines currently in use.
- Reports must be available to measure productivity.

She was adamant that the ability to transfer to a live person be part of the system, but that this feature not be available at the beginning of the call. The reports measured who was hanging up, what questions the suppliers were asking, and the length of time the calls were taking.

What the System Does for Suppliers

A few National Association of Procurement Professionals (NAPP) conference attendees expressed concern about security issues. Sampson assured the group that unless the persons requesting the information regarding payment had the necessary input information, they would not be able to access the data stored on the IVR system. Specifically, suppliers are able to query the system by entering any of the following:

- Purchase order and invoice number
- Invoice number and invoice amount
- Vendor number and invoice number
- Vendor number and invoice amount
- Check number

Only those who are entitled to receive information have the necessary numbers to access the system.

What the System Does for Employees

The company's sales reps use IVR to inquire about promotional expense reimbursements and the aforementioned honorariums. These reimbursements go directly to the sales reps or to third parties for expenses relating to sales promotions.Once the system was up and running, it was discovered that employees were using IVR to inquire about their T & Es and payroll. These calls are routed to a T & E

the payment status of their invoices. This can drastically reduce the
"when am I getting my money" phone calls that inundate some
accounts payable departments.

Summary

As you can see from the "In the Real World" case studies, technology
is rapidly changing accounts payable. Innovative solutions are possible
using virtually any type of technology. The future will be amazing—
and, we can almost guarantee, accounts payable will be very different
five years from now.

CHAPTER 18

High-Level Accounts Payable Concepts

After reading this chapter you will be able to

- Evaluate alternatives to the three-way match
- Fairly evaluate benchmarking issues
- Assess 1099 requirement
- Understand the sales and use tax issues
- Make intelligent decisions regarding escheat issues

The three-way match makes a lot of sense for big transactions. When a company pays a high-dollar amount, it should make sure that it got what it ordered and not a partial shipment, the product arrived in good shape and it was of the quality ordered. However, when the invoice amount is small (and the definition of *small* varies from company to company), the amount of effort that goes into verifying that everything is exactly as ordered can exceed the value of the product ordered. Does it make sense for someone in accounts payable to spend 15 minutes verifying everything on a $25 invoice? Yet, that is exactly what many companies do. This chapter addresses this issue, as well as some of the issues that come up on a less-frequent basis.

Handling the Small Stuff

There are several ways a company can prevent its verification processes from getting out of hand. Some companies use one or more of the following techniques:

1. *Assumed receipt*—As its title indicates, goods are assumed to have been received when an invoice shows up in accounts payable if the invoice is less than some agreed upon dollar amount. For some companies the level is $50, for others $500. We know of one company that uses a limit of $5,000. When the invoice is received, accounts payable schedules it for payment according to terms, say in 30 days, and then sends an e-mail to the person who ordered the product indicating that

   • the invoice has been received, and

   • it will be paid if accounts payable is not notified not to pay within *x* number of days.

   If accounts payable does not hear from the approved within the given time frame, the invoice is paid.

2. *Negative assurance*—Also for obvious reasons, some people call the approach described above as negative assurance. If the accounts payable department does not receive a negative reply from the purchaser, it pays the invoice, assured by the lack of response that the invoice is good, hence, negative assurance.

3. *Evaluated receipt settlement (ERS)*—This was first championed by the automotive industry. In fact, if you do business with one of the big automakers (or work for one of them) you are probably quite familiar with the approach. The theory behind ERS makes a lot of sense. Many in accounts payable feel that most of the payment discrepancies result from errors on the invoice. If the purchase order is filled out completely and both sides agree to the information

and the receiving dock thoroughly checks out all products received and matches the goods against the packing slip, why do you need an invoice? The answer is, of course, that if the two functions described are working properly, an invoice is not needed.

After all, the vendor knows what it shipped, the price, and the terms—as does the customer. If the customer simply pays on the due date, everything should be fine and less paper will be generated. In theory this is correct, although reality is not quite so smooth. However, if you want to do business in the automotive industry you'd better be able to do ERS. Also, a small but growing number of other companies are starting to use this innovative process.

Benchmarking

Benchmarking is the process by which a company measures its performance against the performance of a group of similar companies. Perhaps you can already see some of the problems. The best are usually referred to as *world class* or *best in class*. The process is filled with problems, yet most management teams at this point are insisting on some sort of numerical measurement, such as the number of invoices processed by each full-time employee, cost per invoice, staff size, or salary data.

The problem is that the accounts payable process is not uniform from company to company. Even those in the same industry might have different practices. For example, one company might have its checks signed mechanically as part of the check printing process. Another company might allow an assistant controller to sign all checks under, say, $500,000. A third company might require two signatures on all checks.

Differences such as these will account for a big swing in the cost to process an invoice. When you consider all the different steps, its easy to see why benchmarking presents such a problem.

227

IN THE REAL WORLD

ERS Issues

Here is a list of some of the problems that may be encountered should ERS be adopted:

- Many companies process payments by invoice number. Without an invoice number, accounts payable is back to dealing with invoices without invoice numbers, which can sometimes be problematic (see Chapter 5). Some substitute the PO number for the invoice number or develop other mechanisms to deal with the issue. Also, vendors typically apply cash using the invoice number so there can be problems on the other side as well.

- Some vendors, who do not use ERS for the majority of their transactions, cannot suppress the printing and mailing of invoices. Thus, the accounts payable department may receive an invoice (and pay it!) for an order that has been scheduled for payment using ERS.

- If the PO is not filled out completely, as sometimes happens, or the receiving dock does not do a thorough job, payments can be made incorrectly or for an excess amount.

- Shipping charges are difficult to handle. Many ERS experts recommend handling shipping charges separately.

- Other miscellaneous fees can cause problems and should be handled apart from the ERS process.

- If there are too many rejects or disputes, ERS will cause more problems than it alleviates.

- When ERS is first introduced, it is a new concept requiring new policies and procedures. Whenever change is instituted, some employees will resist making the implementation a little more difficult than it has to be. However, when the employees see the value and realize that ERS is there to stay, they usually get on board.

The other big issue in benchmarking accounts payable is the simple definition of what is an invoice. Clearly it will take longer to process an invoice that has 100 lines on it than it will take to process the invoice with one line on it—at least it *should* require more time and scrutiny. So counting the number of invoices per full-time employee is not always meaningful. Some prefer to measure number of lines processed.

Having said all this, accounts payable associates should realize that most management teams insist on some sort of benchmarking. And, it does have value. When an accounts payable department benchmarks its activity and uncovers that it is extremely uncompetitive, it should review its processes. Sometimes there is a problem with the benchmarking process itself, but at other times it reveals inefficient practices and a need to overhaul existing procedures. Thus, benchmarking can be a very useful tool. Exhibit 18.1 provides statistics on what companies are benchmarking.

IN THE REAL WORLD

Looking through Benchmarking Numbers

Common sense should also be used when evaluating benchmarking results. One department manager was surprised to see that the worker he thought the most productive actually had the lowest benchmarking results. How could that be? Were his perceptions incorrect? After some investigation, he discovered that the worker with the lowest benchmarking results was handling the most difficult invoices. The rest of the staff was skipping over the problem invoices. Which person do you think most companies would prefer to have on staff—the individual who can process a high number of easy invoices or the associate who is willing to take the problematic invoices and resolve the discrepancies?

EXHIBIT 18.1

Who Benchmarks?

Employee Range

Up to 99	7.7%
100–249	8.0%
250–499	13.6%
500–999	20.4%
1000–4999	30.6%
5000 & up	44.8%
Grand Total	24.0%

Industry

Agricultural/Mining	11.1%
Financial Services	24.1%
Manufacturing	24.1%
Other	23.0%
Retail Trade	36.6%
Services (Business, Legal, Eng.)	10.6%
Transportation/Communications/Utilities	41.1%
Wholesale Trade	12.0%
Grand Total	24.0%

Throughout this book, benchmarking parts of the *2001 IOMA Managing Accounts Payable Benchmarking Survey* have been included. They can be used to measure performance and see where improvements can be made.

Post-Audit Recovery Firms

In other parts of this book (see Chapter 5), there has been mention of recovery firms. Currently, there are anywhere from 30 to 50, or perhaps even more, of these firms that recover duplicate payments and other erroneous payments made by companies everywhere. Many of the post-

audit firms are small and regional. Some specialize in only a few industries, while others are willing to take on any client. The fact that the number of these firms continues to grow is a testament to the duplicate payment problem—despite the fact that many companies insist they never make a duplicate payment.

Some accounts payable associates are reluctant to recommend a post-audit firm because their management will then accuse them of making the duplicate payments that the firm recovers. Despite the fact that the accounts payable associate typically only makes payments after receiving proper authorizations from others, this is, unfortunately, a realistic concern. A good audit firm will identify the weaknesses in existing procedures, which should provide the necessary ammunition to refute the accusation and also alleviate that concern—unless there *is* a weakness in accounts payable.

Exhibit 18.2 provides the percentages for companies admitting to using an outside audit firm at some point in the last three years in the *IOMA Benchmarking Survey.*

Form 1099

1099s are those annoying forms that must be given to independent contractors once a year, usually in January, so the contractors may complete their income tax returns. The information is also provided to the IRS so it may monitor the tax payments made by the independent contractors. It is one of those functions that is handled in about three-quarters of the accounts payable departments, with the remainder usually handled in payroll.

Identifying individuals who should get the forms and then collecting all the necessary information is all that's required. Sounds easy enough, but it rarely is. Here's why:

EXHIBIT 18.2

Companies Using an Outside Audit Firm

By Company Size

Up to 99	13.2%
100–249	24.5%
250–499	26.7%
500–999	21.8%
1000–4999	40.2%
5000 & up	51.5%
All	33.1%

By Industry

Manufacturing	34.9%
Financial Services	25.6%
Transportation/Communications/Utilities	38.7%
Government	21.1%
Wholesale Trade	34.6%
Retail Trade	41.9%
Health Care	35.5%
Education	44.0%
Services (Business, Legal, Eng.)	25.7%
Other	28.1%

Source: *IOMA Benchmarking Survey.*

- Many companies do not start the process of preparing 1099s until the end of the year—or worse, until January. By this time, information is scattered and hard to collect.

- If a contractor received a payment and did not provide a tax identification number at the time, the contractor is unlikely to provide it at year-end. After all, if you can't report the income to the IRS, the IRS will have no record of tax due on the income.

- You might not be able to find the individual to get the required information or to send the form to.
- There are so many other tasks to be done at year-end, it is hard to devote the necessary time to this project.

Therefore, to minimize the year-end 1099 nightmare, many accounts payable departments insist on receiving the W-9 information before they release the first payment to the contractor. This does not make them popular with either the contractor or the purchasing department, but it ensures that they have the needed information when they have to prepare 1099s.

This is one area where accounts payable associates should stand firm and perhaps even argue with management if they try and push for the payment without the W-9. After all, why won't the contractor supply the required information?

The IRS has strict guidelines to use to determine who is an employee and who is an independent contractor. Its publication, *Worker Classification Training Manual, Employee or Independent Contractor,* helps determine the status. Those who will handle 1099s should get this publication.

Sales and Use Tax

Sales and Use Tax (SUT) is another area typically handled in accounts payable that requires specialized knowledge. The rules governing this vary from locality to locality. Here's a simple example of how complicated this can be. I live in Nassau County on Long Island, New York. I work in New York City.

- If I buy an article of clothing in New York City, there is no sales tax, if the cost is less than $110. If it is higher, the tax is 8.25 percent.
- If I buy the same item from a store in the same chain in Nassau County, the sales tax is 4.5 percent.

- If I drive about 25 miles in the other direction into Suffolk County, and again purchase the same item, the tax is nothing, again if the cost is less than $110.

Each year there are anywhere from 750 to 1000 changes in the sales and use tax regulations in different areas of the country. These changes can vary, as just demonstrated, from county to county.

Sales tax is a tax on the retail sale of tangible personal property and is only paid on retail sales and certain services. *Use tax* is charged by some, but not all, states for the privilege of holding or controlling property brought in from out of state that is not intended for resale. The rules pertaining to use tax vary from state to state and are quite complicated. It is imperative that someone in the company (and the function usually ends up in accounts payable) be knowledgeable about this topic and establish good policies and procedures to ensure the company is in compliance in all states.

It should come as no surprise to readers to learn that politicians are desperate for funds and would love to find a way to increase revenue without increasing taxes on the individuals who elect them. So, what better way to increase revenue than to get it from those big rich companies doing business in the state? Sales and use tax audits are on the rise, as are the fines that accompany them when a company is not in compliance. What's even worse is the fact that many states share information. If you are not in compliance in one state, the odds are you are negligent in the next. Many companies report that they barely get through one audit when an auditor for another state shows up.

Escheat

The first time most people hear about unclaimed-property laws as they apply to corporate America, they are astounded. Although there is some familiarity with banks and insurance companies turning inactive accounts

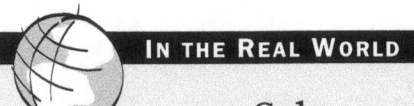

IN THE REAL WORLD

Sales and Use Tax Compliance

We asked Diane Yetter, president of the Sales Tax Institute (www.salestaxinstitute.com) and a sales and use tax expert, about the number of companies in complete compliance with all SUT requirements. Given the complexity of the issue, you won't be surprised at her comments.

Yetter says, "I believe that most companies—large and small—are not in compliance with sales and use tax laws to some extent. Those that don't have an active sales tax accountant are more likely to be more out of compliance. Being out of compliance can mean many things—the company might not be registered in all the jurisdictions where it is required to be so, it could owe tax on items purchased when the vendor didn't collect the sales tax, it might not have all its customers' exemption certificates to document nontaxable sales, it might have collected sales tax in states where it isn't registered, or it could have overpaid sales tax on items which qualify for an exemption.

"The reason for this is that sales tax laws are different for every state and can be very complex for companies that don't have a dedicated sales tax specialist. Additionally, sales tax isn't just one person's responsibility. People from all areas within a company have to cooperate to make sure all the sales and use tax obligations are taken care of. This includes purchasing, accounts payable, sales order, customer service, credit, accounts receivable, operations, accounting, and tax. No one person or department can handle all the sales tax responsibilities because sales and use tax touches every sale and purchase transaction."

If a company thinks it is not in compliance, it should take these steps:

① Evaluate where it conducts business and how it conducts business. Yetter says the company should ask itself these

questions. "Does it have traveling salespeople, does it use independent contractors, does it have resident sales or service-people in outlying states, what is its corporate structure with related companies, where is it registered to collect sales and use tax, are exemption certificates timely obtained from exempt customers, is use tax paid on taxable items when sales tax isn't charged by the supplier?" The answers to these questions will help the company identify where to focus its attention.

2. Work with a business or tax advisor to contact the states under a voluntary disclosure agreement to handle exposure problems, such as being registered or collecting taxes in the wrong jurisdiction.

3. Contact customers to obtain missing exemption certificates. If the company owes use tax, it could file amended use tax returns.

4. File for a refund of overpaid sales tax on purchases. Yetter says these functions can be handled by internal staff, or the company can contact a sales tax specialist.

over to the state, few realize that companies are also supposed to turn uncashed checks over to the state. Many companies simply carry the amounts on their books forever or write off any amounts outstanding to miscellaneous income after six months or a year.

Both of these approaches are incorrect—even though some accountants instruct their clients to follow the second approach.

The timing requirements vary from state-to-state, but in all cases after some time frame and attempt on the part of the check writer to find the payee, the amounts of money associated with each check are

supposed to be turned over to the states. The rules for determining which state should receive the funds to are also complicated. Those companies that do not comply put themselves in a position of being fined, and fined heavily. The comments about sales and use tax audit apply here as well. States see escheat (as the process is called) as an untapped source of revenue and some of their auditors have been aggressively pursuing it.

Limiting Annual Unclaimed Property Liability for Vendor Checks

We asked two escheat (unclaimed property) experts to comment on what could be done to limit a company's liability. Here's what Karen Anderson and Robert C. Murray, vice presidents with Unclaimed Property Recovery & Reporting, Inc. (www.uprrinc.com), had to say:

> The key to limiting unclaimed property liability for vendor checks is to perform a timely review of what may be reportable in future years. Most companies transfer reportable items into a liability account within one to two years of check issuance. Checks remain in the liability account to be claimed by an owner until they qualify for statutory reporting. The length of time a check may be held is called dormancy. States are generally categorized as three, five, or seven years dormancy states.
>
> Implementing procedures to review checks when they are posted to the liability account increases the probability that accounting errors (duplicate payment, wrong vendor, unrecorded credit memos, etc.) will be identified. Accounting errors are not unclaimed property. Also, a monthly or even quarterly review of such checks could identify systemic or control problems.
>
> After reviewing internal records, early contact with the payees also reduces unclaimed property exposure. Sending an inquiry letter to the payee after researching your records will cause payees

to either cash the check, to request that the check be reissued, or to tell you that the check is not owed to them!

[Futhermore], implementing an electronic payment system (where there are no outstanding checks) can significantly reduce unclaimed property liability for vendor checks. Adopting these procedures will require some effort but in the long run, they will avoid costs and save reporting time. Similar procedures can be adopted, as appropriate, for payroll checks, customer credits, and other property types that exist in your business.

Future of Escheat

Periodically, there is talk that business customers will not have to escheat balances due trade creditors. The belief, at least among those in the business community, is that balances between trade creditors and debtors should not be escheated as they, in all likelihood, represent a duplicate payment or some other type of excess payment. Similarly, this group also maintains that for the same reason, credit balances should not have to be turned over to the state as current requirements demand.

There has been some talk about exempting trade creditors and debtors from the escheat laws, but to date that has not happened and we are skeptical that it will—not because we don't think that the reasoning is correct, but because states will be reluctant to give up this source of income. Thus, it is probably a good idea to make sure your company complies with all state escheat regulations.

Petty Cash

Let me start off by saying that petty cash is not really a high-level topic. However, this is the best place to put it given the layout of this book. Responsibility for petty cash is not always in accounts payable—sometimes treasury gets stuck with it. And *stuck* is the right word. If the

company insists on having a petty cash box and insists on placing it under the accounts payable umbrella, they should limit those with access and the hours when funds can be requested. In addition, they should require thorough authorizations for disbursements, encourage other forms of payment, (i.e. through T & E), and reconcile frequently.

Summary

These are just a few of the high-level task handled in accounts payable. Clearly, those who want to have a career in accounts payable must have a broad base of knowledge covering a wide variety of topics.

CHAPTER 19

Managing Your First Accounts Payable Department

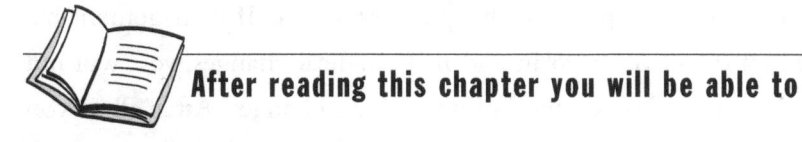

After reading this chapter you will be able to

- Know what to expect when you get your first management position
- Improve the department's reputation within the company
- Motivate the staff
- Hire the right people

Eventually, most of the associates reading this book will be given the opportunity to take the next step to manage their own accounts payable department. In many cases, the first promotion will be to the supervisor title working under the supervision of a manager. You will be responsible for hiring, training, motivating, and devising the most effective policies and procedures for the accounts payable staff. It is a big responsibility.

Your First Day as a Manager: What to Expect

The good news when it comes to hiring is that you probably won't have to do it immediately. The bad news is that you will likely inherit a staff. This means you will be taking on problems created by others and may also have to supervise some of your former peers. Initially, there may be some resentment, especially if some of your new subordinates

felt that they should have been given the spot. Also, they will not be accustomed to taking direction from you.

So tread lightly. You may be tempted to immediately go in and change things around to suit your own style. Immediate action may be seen as disruptive, so unless you have strict instructions from management, wait a bit and observe the team in action. You may see matters differently from your new perch as leader.

There is one exception to this piece of advice. If management has given you a directive to go in and make radical changes, you will not have the luxury of observing before making changes. After all, if you don't follow your boss's directions, you may be out of a job.

Departmental Reputation

This is a difficult issue to address. Be forewarned: In most companies it will take time. In a good number of companies, the accounts payable department has a lousy reputation. It's not because the department does a poor job, it's because it is such an easy scapegoat. It is just too easy to blame accounts payable for everything that goes wrong along the way. When a vendor doesn't get paid on time, it is much easier for the purchasing manager to blame it on accounts payable than to admit that he sat on the invoice for six weeks before approving it. Do all purchasing managers do this? Absolutely not! But, more than a few do. And the purchasing manager isn't the only culprit of this type of behavior.

Similarly, others within the company are also quick to point a finger at accounts payable. Executives who are not reimbursed for their T&E expenses in time to pay their American Express bill will not remember that they turned in their expense reports late. Most will prefer to blame it on accounts payable. The list is endless.

Turning the other cheek and ignoring the problem is not a good idea, for several reasons:

Improving the Department's Image

It is possible to change the company's perception of the accounts payable department. It simply takes time and persistence—and continually doing a good job. Here are some things you can do to make the company see the accounts payable department in a better light.

1 Educate the rest of the company. Once everyone understands what the accounts payable time frames are, compliance will improve.

2 Correct bad behavior. By constantly reinforcing the correct way of doing things, you will eventually improve compliance. You may also be labeled a nag, but so be it. You will be a nag who gets things done. You were hired to get a job done, not win a popularity contest.

3 Approach anyone who makes a derogatory remark about accounts payable or its staff. Ask for details and research the matter. If someone has made untrue statements, get back to the person with the truth—along with anyone else who may have heard the remark. If the comment is true, rectify the situation and let the individual know that whatever happened will not happen again.

4 Toot your own horn and that of your staff. No one else is going to heap praise on the accounts payable department, so it will be left to you to pick up that slack as well. This is hard for many people to do, but it is important. Write memos, praise the staff to management, and wherever possible, put the department's best foot forward.

5 Develop an in-house accounts payable newsletter. This can be as simple as one page (front and back). In it communicate new

policies and procedures, updated phone and e-mail addresses as well as positive news about the staff. Also, use it to correct common mistakes. Not only will it be your communication with the rest of the company, it shows the department off in a professional light.

6 Attend conferences and bring back new ideas. If possible, send the staff as well. As they feel better about themselves professionally, they will instill this positive feeling and outlook in their job.

7 Update outdated policies and procedures and share the changes with the rest of the company.

8 But before you do any of this, put your own house in order. Take a realistic view of the department and fix the problems.

- *If bad work habits are not corrected, they will continue.* The purchasing manager will never approve invoices for payments in a timely manner if not reminded of the consequences of his actions.

- *The accounts payable department isn't the only one tainted by these remarks.* The reputation of everyone who works in the department is also trashed. When one of the hard-working accounts payable associates applies for a position in another department, most are rejected outright because it is believed that they are poor workers, when just the opposite is usually the case.

- *It will be difficult to recruit others within the company to join the department if it is believed to be an ineffective department.* We know of one company that had to force an accountant to take the position of the department manager because no one within the company would post for the position.

- *It will be next to impossible to elevate people within the department, upgrade the jobs, or get the necessary money for training and conferences.* The company will deem it a poor investment to spend its money on the employees in accounts payable.

- *Your own upward mobility and salary increases will be limited if the reputation of the department is not improved.*

Motivation

One of the hardest tasks a manager faces is to motivate the staff. It is a big problem in corporate America and in many accounts payable department. There are some things you cannot change. If the company puts on a salary freeze, an accounts payable manager or supervisor is unlikely to be able to change that. However, there are accounts payable managers everywhere, working under tight circumstances, short staffed, who manage to have a happy, productive staff. The Tips & Techniques box lists some of the approaches they use to achieve this state.

IN THE REAL WORLD

How One Manager Found Out What Was Going on in His Department

One way to get a realistic view of your department is to pretend to be an outsider. One savvy accounts payable director called his own office pretending to be a vendor checking on a payment. He was astounded when his staff told him it was Friday afternoon and he should call back on Monday—especially since it was two hours before closing time. You may not have to use subterfuge such as this. Simply keep your eyes and ears open as you walk through the department.

TIPS & TECHNIQUES

Motivating the Staff

1 Have good work habits and a positive outlook yourself. The staff will pick up on your mood. Lead by example.

2 Set high but realistic standards.

3 Use praise abundantly and criticism meagerly and always in private. Never, ever, criticize an employee in public. Be careful how you praise remembering that it is possible to motivate one employee while demotivating the rest of the staff when one person is singled out for applause.

4 Share credit for a successful project. When a new procedure, technology, or strategy is implemented, don't take all the credit for yourself. Make sure that everyone who worked on the project is included in the praise. Sending a thank-you note to all participants with a carbon copy to management will work.

5 Set up each employee to succeed. Assign work according to ability, but do this carefully. No one likes to get the lion's share of the work but only an average amount of credit for successfully achieving an extraordinary goal.

6 Reward your top performers accordingly. Giving everyone the same raise is not a good idea.

7 Get the staff business cards. Most companies contract with a printing company, so the cost associated is minimal.

8 Get the staff the equipment it needs to do the best job possible. Is the accounts payable department always at the bottom of the new technology list? Does it only get computers already used in other departments when others get new machines? Negotiate with management to move accounts payable up on the technology list.

9 Be honest with the staff. When there is bad news, such as upcoming layoffs, be upfront with them. Better that they hear

TIPS & TECHNIQUES CONTINUED

the news from you than they hear it through the grapevine, where you know it will be exaggerated.

⑩ If possible, assign the more tedious tasks to temporary workers reserving the "fun" projects for the full time staff.

⑪ Don't assign all the "fun" projects to the same person; share the wealth.

⑫ Don't, under any circumstances, show favoritism.

⑬ Ask the staff for suggestions and recommendations. They have great ideas. If you really want to make a positive impact, get the company to spring for a pizza lunch where their ideas can be discussed.

The list is just the beginning. There are many other things you can do to motivate the staff. Perhaps the best piece of advice is to put yourself in their shoes and consider how you would like to be treated.

Hiring the Right People

Hiring is a tricky proposition. Not only do you have to get the best person for the position, but it is also a good idea to make sure that the new hire will fit in with the rest of the staff. Here are a few tips to get you on the right track.

1. *Write a job description.* List the must-have skills and the skills and attributes you would like to have, but are willing to either train for or live without.

2. *Set a realistic salary target.* This should be in line with the salaries in the industry and region. By realistically setting grade levels for the position, you will be well situated to get management to agree to a competitive salary. Set the compensation too low and you will not be able to attract qualified candidates.

3. *Post the position internally, if required.*

4. *Talk to your peers at other companies for recommendations of suitable potential candidates.* Be wary of your peers recommending someone from their own staff. Are they simply trying to unload one of their own problems?

5. *List the position with the appropriate employment agencies.* Your human resources area may handle this function. Work with them to make sure they understand your requirements. A bad hire is not an easy problem to rectify.

6. *Make a list of the questions you would like the potential candidates to answer.* If possible, couch them in this context: "How would you solve this problem or address this situation?"

7. *Conduct your interviews.* Do as little talking and as much listening as possible.

8. *When you've narrowed down your choice to the final three candidates, invite them back to meet the staff and your boss.* Let several people on the staff talk to the potential new hire without you.

9. *Get feedback from all parties.* Remember, the new hire will be part of a team so carefully listen to what your staff has to say. If you hire someone they are adamantly opposed to, it will be a de-motivating experience for them. Also, they will be reluctant to speak honestly in the future.

10. *Check references, check references, check references.* Some people interview exceedingly well—but that is where their skill set ends. This also means that if someone is a little nervous or doesn't interview well, that person should not be immediately crossed off your list.

11. *When you are satisfied, make an offer.* Expect your new hire to give notice of at least two weeks. If the employee is willing to walk out on a current employer, what do you think he or she will do, should the person decide to leave your employment?

12. *On the new employee's first day, make sure that the work space is ready.* Introduce the employee to the staff and proceed.

Hiring Issues with Existing Staff

Some accounts payable managers encounter a problem with their existing staff when a new employee is hired. If the new hire is better educated or the existing staff is undercompensated, resentment is likely to arise when the existing staff realizes that the new hire is being paid more than they are. The existing staff might not leave: however, their productivity and morale probably will decline.

Now, you can instruct the staff not to discuss compensation, but don't expect this directive to be followed. People talk about salaries regardless of what management says. So, expect the existing staff to know what you intend to pay the new hire. And, if the salary is higher than what they are earning, expect problems.

Some managers use the information they collect before making an offer to a new hire to get the existing staff raises. By having the jobs evaluated and the grade levels raised, you have taken the first step toward increasing staff salaries. Be aware, however, that this is not an easy task. In many cases, human resources will not be your ally in this endeavor. Still, you need to address this if you do not want to have morale and attitude problems with the existing staff.

You will need to work with your boss and human resources on getting grade levels changed. Expect resistance—if you are successful, the company will have to spend more for its accounts payable department.

If you are not successful, keep at it and look for other ways to compensate the staff (perhaps additional time off, tickets to a play, or any other creative perk you can develop).

Summary

Running an accounts payable department is a challenge. You will probably make some mistakes—virtually all of which can be fixed. If your staff sees that you have their best interests at heart and are doing your best on their behalf, half the battle will be won.

CHAPTER 20

Accounts Payable in the Twenty-First Century

After reading this chapter you will be able to

- Understand the revolutionary changes in the purchasing world that will impact the accounts payable functions
- Evaluate some of the new payment mechanisms
- Identify the new skills that will be needed to be an accounts payable survivor
- Plan your accounts payable future

As discussed earlier, the interaction between purchasing and accounts payable is critical. If the purchasing function changes, and it is, the accounts payable processes will have to change as well. Harris Bank's vice president, Hamish Forrest, follows the e-commerce world closely. His views on the revolution that is taking place begin in this chapter.

E-Marketplaces

An *e-marketplace* is an online location where companies gather to buy and sell goods and services from one another, says Forrest. Industry-specific e-marketplaces are sometimes referred to as *exchanges*. The medium of e-marketplaces is the Internet. These exchanges are rapidly changing the way business will be conducted in the next 10 years.

Probably the best-known exchange is Covisint, for the automotive industry. It describes itself this way (www.covisint.com):

> Covisint, LLC is a global, independent e-business exchange providing the automotive industry with leading collaborative product development, procurement and supply chain tools that give its customers the ability to reduce costs and bring efficiencies to their business operations.

> Developed by DaimlerChrysler, Ford, General Motors, Nissan, Renault, Commerce One and Oracle. Covisint is currently located in Southfield, Michigan. The organization has also established temporary offices in Stuttgart and Tokyo.

Other exchanges include

- For the paper industry: www.paperfiber.com/exchange/
- For the steel industry: www.gsx.com/home_page.html
- For the coal industry: www.thinkenergy.com/a/em1010.html
- For the aerospace industry: www.exostar.com

It should be noted that most exchanges, at least at this point, are not nearly as developed as the one put together by the automotive industry.

Types of e-Marketplaces

In addition to being for industry or for all participants, e-marketplaces can be categorized by additional groupings:

- Open marketplaces, which are usually for MRO (maintenance, repair, and operations) or indirect goods
- Closed or private marketplaces, which are typically part of a select industry and usually for direct goods
- Horizontal or vertical, and these can be open or closed
- Auction and reverse auction

The market leader, at least at this point, for auction-type exchanges is FreeMarkets (www.freemarkets.com). Reverse (or downward) auctions have the ability to drive costs down in a huge way.

Recently, Emerson Electric faced the challenge of consolidation millions of dollars of printed circuit board purchases across 14 global divisions. The company used FreeMarkets. It purchased goods that historically would have cost it $36.1 million. It had 43 ISO 9000–certified suppliers. The downward auction for these goods resulted in 755 bids being placed. The company introduced several new, qualified suppliers, and consolidating its supply base from 58 to 9—and saved $10 million in the process.

Why Does Accounts Payable Care?

For starters, with the kind of savings just mentioned, corporate America is bound to take notice and flock to these sites. Forrest offers the following answer to the "Why care?" question. He says that because an e-marketplace is one of the ways in which companies are changing the way they do business with their trading partners, everyone will be affected. Ultimately, he warns, the payment mechanism will change.

E-marketplaces provide a better return for companies than new business. Why? It is simply because the entire process improvement savings go right to the bottom line. Companies realize savings that can be attributable to both better pricing and process improvements, with better pricing accounting for only 20 percent of the savings.

E-marketplaces help control maverick purchasing, provide new sales channels and industry information. They also help automate the payment process, ultimately replacing checks with ACH payments.

More than one exchange has fallen apart because no one focused on the payment piece until it was too late. Finally, companies are focusing on the long-ignored payment function. Despite the Internet, 80 percent of all business-to-business (B2B) payments are currently being made by check. However, companies are trying to squeeze all possible

cost savings out of the procure-to-pay cycle and are now focusing on the payment process. One of the innovative ways they are doing this is through the use of payment engines.

Payment engines are electronic triggers for payment. They initiate the optimal payment vehicle based on rules you input. A simple example might be that an electronic shipping notice would trigger a payment 30 days after the date on the shipping notice. Forrest lists a few:

- financialsettlementmatrix.com

- clareon.net

- surepay.com

With their expertise in the payment process, Forrest says that it is only natural that banks be involved in the payment process in a trusted third party role.

Electronic Invoicing and Automation of Accounts Payables

One of the big changes coming to corporate America is electronic invoicing. Of course, this will mean that accounts payable will need to change its procedures. Tim Knewitz, a division business manager from Sandia National Laboratories, was the driving force behind the electronic invoicing task force, so we asked him about the impact that electronic invoicing will have on accounts payable in the next five years:

> Electronic invoicing should have the largest impact on the accounts payable industry over the next five years. Many companies have just begun the process of investigating XML-based electronic solutions. The next two to three years will be spent investigating alternative solutions, followed by an increasing amount of companies implementing an electronic standard. Utilization of this standard will accelerate the pace of electronic invoicing throughout industry.

The impact to accounts payable organizations will be traumatic. Organizations that currently process paper invoices may see as much as a 90 percent reduction in effort. Reductions will occur in invoice preparation, invoice processing, and customer service interactions. The impact will not be limited to accounts payable organizations:

- Accounts receivable (AR) organizations will require less effort to send invoices and receive payments.

- Information systems groups will need to support the implementation and maintenance of the electronic solution for both AR and A/P organizations.

- Mail services will also see a decrease in interactions with A/P organizations.

Electronic Invoicing

One of the most interesting Internet developments in the last few years is the electronic invoicing alternatives now available. Three are described by their innovators:

1. Internet invoicing enables Accounts Payable departments to automate the delivery, routing, approval and status review of electronic invoices, both PO and non-PO, from all of their vendors/suppliers. Application service provider (ASP)-hosted solutions maintain the hardware and software necessary to provide this service. Internet invoicing can be implemented very quickly, and incoming invoice files are formatted to the accounts payable system. Invoices are routed for approval and dispute resolution, and a clear document trail is created.

Internet invoice delivery provides accounts payable departments the ability to receive invoices electronically from virtually any vendor/supplier and to receive the invoices in whatever format

the A/P system requires. With just an Internet browser, vendors can send invoices to their various customers. Vendors can also check the status of their invoices online using the Internet service without having to contact their customers directly.

Internet invoice routing works in conjunction with delivery by providing accounts payable departments the ability to route, code, and approve invoices using business rules that are configured online to meet today's and tomorrow's business process needs. Because Internet invoice routing can be accessed remotely, approvers in numerous locations can view and approve the same invoice at the same time without ever leaving their office or handling any paper. (Ken Virgin, CEO, iPayables (www.ipayables.com))

2. Full-service electronic invoice presentment and payment (EIPP) solutions are designed specifically to meet the needs of corporate billers and payers. Consolidator solutions present one supplier's invoices to many payers, and consolidate electronic invoices from many suppliers for a single payer. The service works with billers to electronically present their invoices and permit customer processing and payment from a single, easy to use Internet interface. In addition, the service work with payers to electronically enable their supplier invoices so that payers receive the benefits of paperless invoice receipt and management, purchasing collaboration/ routing, online dispute resolution, and electronic payment. A consolidator service should be bank-neutral, enabling billers and payers to select their preferred banking partner and credit card provider to process electronic payments. The service is typically provided from an open, extensible Internet platform to allow billers and payers to integrate the solution with their existing legacy and workflow systems.

Benefits of a consolidated EIPP service include improved cash management, reduced processing expenses and better communication and collaboration within organizations and between trading partners. Consolidator services appeal to both billers and payers and provide an answer to the current adoption problems with biller direct or payer direct portals hosted on their own Web sites. (Cindy Yamamoto, Product Manager, BillingZone, LLC (www.billingzone.com))

3. Web-based transaction and workflow applications that enable large buying organizations to automate the delivery, management, approval, and routing of invoices from suppliers and employees. These solutions includes key features such as streamlined dispute resolution using an online dialog manager and easy Internet access to invoice history and general payables information from a central data source. They provide:

- Electronic delivery of invoices into your financial system
- Vendor access to all relevant purchase order, invoice, and payment history information
- A non-EDI, XML, standards-based electronic process
- Electronic matching of invoices, purchase orders, shipping documents, and payments
- Electronic routing of invoices for review, approval, and exception handling
- Centralized invoice-management system using the model of an A/P manager's "console," thereby allowing a variety of options for viewing, sorting, and processing of data
- Direct-dialog capabilities between A/P managers, vendors, and employees for problem reporting and dispute resolution

Benefits:

- Exercising vendor discounts
- Increased productivity while maintaining headcount
- Improved workflow efficiencies (in inside & outside A/P)
- Elimination of low volume tasks
- Strengthening vendor–customer relationship
- Scalable solution supporting company growth
- Increased availability of management information
- Minimal IT support–browser access

(Bruce Hanavan, CEO, president, Direct Commerce (www.directcommerce.com))

The Future of Accounts Payable

Clearly, those who succeed in accounts payable will be those who identify where the profession is going and then acquire the skills needed to meet those requirement. In five years, I expect that the following will be true:

- Everyone will use the Internet, not only for e-mail but to receive information from vendors.
- Accounts payable departments will be smaller, better educated and hopefully, better paid.
- Accounts payable will be part of purchasing in about 25 percent of companies.
- Broader-based knowledge and skills will be mandatory.

Needed skills will include

- Up-to-date accounts payable knowledge
- Internet fluency along with the ability to use XML

- Constantly updated accounting, treasury, purchasing, and technology abilities
- Good management and networking skills
- Understanding of international payment systems

Additional requirements will include the following:

- New entrants will need a college degree. Those with a two-year degree should be encouraged to get a four-year degree—it's what the market demands.
- An MBA won't hurt those who want to advance and those who wish to expand their horizons outside of accounts payable.
- The ability to solve problems in an innovative manner will go a long way.

Thomas F. Nichols is a consultant with Process Management Improvement. He formerly ran AT&T's accounts payable department. Nichols is a visionary who frequently lectures on accounts payable topics. Here's what he thinks the future holds:

There have been more feature and functionality changes in accounts payable in the last five years than in the previous ten years. I anticipate that this rapid change will accelerate at a faster pace over the next five years.

In the late 1990s many experts were forecasting the coming of the "paperless office." Needless to say, we are still inundated with paper. I believe in the next five years we will virtually accomplish the goal of eliminating paper invoices with ongoing technological innovations.

The Internet and intranets will fundamentally change the accounts payable function, where emphasis will shift to analysis of invoice data with much of the traditional invoice-processing steps eliminated. In addition to the traditional skills required, I

feel that four critical skills will be required for accounts payable professionals in the future:

- *Adaptability*—The accounts payable professional will need to have a positive attitude toward change and the ability to identify and suggest new ideas to get the job done creatively.

- *Interpersonal*—The accounts payable function will shift from an individual focus to a team approach in the future. These teams will need individuals who understand and work within the culture of the group, recognize and support diversity, and can plan and make decisions with others and support the recommendations.

- *Analytical*—With new emphasis on invoice data analysis, the accounts payable professional will need the ability to acquire, organize, interpret, and evaluate information and communicate results rapidly to the customers. The analysis of data should be viewed by the customer as adding value to the process, whether qualitative or quantitative in nature.

- *International skills*—As the world becomes a global community, accounts payable professionals will be required to effectively deal in the international community. Knowledge of international payment systems will be crucial. The ability to speak a second language will be a definite plus.

Summary

It's going to be a whole new world out there. Are you ready?

Additional Resources

1. Books

Schaeffer, Mary. *Accounts Payable: A Guide to Running an Efficient Department* (New York: John Wiley & Sons, 1998).

2. Newsletters (see www.ioma.com)

IOMA's Report on Managing Accounts Payable

IOMA's Report on Managing T & E

BNA—SUT

IOMA's Report on Managing Credit Receivables and Collections

IOMA's Payroll Managers Report

3. Internet

A/P discussion group (www.ioma.com/discussion)

Search engines (e.g., www.google.com)

A/P articles on the Web (e.g., www.ioma.com/)

4. Conferences

IOMA/IMI Managing Accounts Payable—held at two locations in the fall, usually Chicago and San Francisco, and two in the spring, usually New York and a southern California city. Each has many different speakers.

IOMA/IMI Advanced Accounts Payable Institute—held each June at various locations. This event has many different speakers.

Padgett-Thompson—one- and two-day seminars given throughout the year at many locations. One instructor usually teaches the entire session.

National Seminar Group—one- and two-day seminars given throughout the year at numerous locations. One person usually teaches the entire session.

Sales and Use Tax Institute—several seminars are held each year. The sessions all address sales and use tax.

American Payroll Association—In addition to its annual conference, the APA offers numerous one- and two-day sessions around the country.

Recap's Accounts Payable conference—held in the Ft. Lauderdale area each March. Features numerous speakers over two days.

IQPC periodically offers conferences with about a dozen speakers focusing on topics related to accounts payable and T & E.

IAPP holds an annual conference in the late spring/early summer, usually in Orlando. Numerous speakers.

5. Professional Organizations

AICPA

American Payroll Association

Association for Financial Professionals

Bookkeepers Association

Institute of Management Accountants

International Accounts Payable Professionals

6. Benchmarking Information

IOMA—two surveys, 900 + participants

IAPP—not done recently, 50 participants

Gunn Partners

Hackett Group

7. Other Useful Resources

IOMA's Managing Accounts Payable Yearbooks

IOMA's Accounts Payable Buyers Guide

Index